NECROTE...

"*Necrotech* bleeds with raw & unapologetic badassery. Riko is the cyberpunk heroine I've been waiting for, struggling with the truth that the tech we embrace to solve our problems just creates new ones, and no one has a chipset to fix humanity's bugs. K C Alexander dials up the attitude, anguish, and adrenaline in this explosive debut, and I'm looking forward to Riko's next run."
  Kevin Hearne, *bestselling author of* The Iron Druid Chronicles

"*Necrotech* is a tight, violent thrill ride in a fascinating cyberpunk world with one of the most interesting women protagonists I've read in a long time."
  Stephen Blackmoore, *acclaimed author of* Dead Things

"Sci-fi that's slick, sharp and snarky – K C Alexander doesn't 'write' so much as she fires words into your cerebral cortex with an electromagnetic railgun."
  Chuck Wendig, *bestselling author of* Star Wars: Aftermath *and* Invasive

"*Necrotech* is a high-octane cyberpunk thrill ride that starts at full throttle and never slows down. Riko is an amazing, diverse, ass-kicking character that will leave readers wanting more."
  Tim Moore, *Strange Horizons*

"Vulgar, vicious, and very very good! Alexander pulls no punches in this intense debut."
  Jason M Hough, *bestselling author of* Zero World

"Scalding and brutal as a radiation shower, punishing as a street fight, and as sharp as a blade to the jugular, *Necrotech* and its badass heroine, Riko, will grab your heart in a diamond steel fist and squeeze it to a pulp."
  Li...

K C ALEXANDER

NECROTECH

ANGRY
ROBOT

ANGRY ROBOT
An imprint of Watkins Media Ltd

Lace Market House,
54-56 High Pavement,
Nottingham,
NG1 1HW
UK

angryrobotbooks.com
twitter.com/angryrobotbooks
Fuck you

An Angry Robot paperback original 2016
1

A catalogue record for this book is available from the British Library.

ISBN 978 0 85766 623 9
EBook ISBN 978 0 85766 625 3

Set in Meridien and Stomper by Epub Services.
Printed and bound in the UK by 4edge Limited.

This one's for me.

I plunged into brutal consciousness.

The light searing through the thin barrier of my eyelids did its best to fry my already scrambled brains, leaving me groaning as I threw an arm over my aching eye sockets. My tongue stuck to the roof of my mouth, glued by a gummy layer of what felt like mange. Given the taste, something furry had crawled inside my mouth and spawned a litter.

That would explain the three-legged tango my guts were attempting, and possibly the incessant drone flattening all the wrinkles in my brain. Whatever chemical slank I'd gotten into last night, it wrecked me. Hard.

Keeping my eyes squeezed shut, I managed to work up enough foul-tasting saliva to rasp a groan. "Who do I have to fuck to turn that light off?" My voice, ruined by the mother of all hangovers, graveled.

I didn't get an answer.

"Nanji?" Nothing.

I tried again, too hoarse to inject it with my usual impatient demand. "Lucky?"

Still nothing.

I cracked an eye from under my arm. Shafts of light branded my retinas. My vision went supernova despite the shade, and what was left of my brain dried into a crusted scab. Groaning,

I squeezed my eyes shut again and desperately tried not to throw up all over myself.

Not my finest hangover. Not my first, either. I had a habit of waking up in places I couldn't remember blacking out in. Some called it one of my better traits – usually because it involved at least two of us fucked up and naked.

The problem here was that I wasn't supposed to be doing that anymore. I'd promised my girlfriend I'd tone it down, at least when she wasn't with me. What little I could glean here made it clear Nanji was definitely *not* with me.

Goosebumps rippled up the skin of my calves. I shuddered, which only drew my attention to the feel of my bare ass plastered against equally bare metal—both made colder by the frigid temperature of the room.

I'd gotten the fucked up and naked parts down okay, but where? The air smelled way too clean for a hostel. I couldn't pin the scent. It wasn't perfume or even that so-called refreshing crap the average air scrubber spat out to mask the usual nasal mugging. I'd never gotten olfactory analyzers installed, so while I knew mercs who could list off every molecule in a fifty-meter radius, I couldn't make it past *clean*.

That alone was enough to tell me I wasn't anywhere near my squat. Nothing short of an industrial air filter would make *that* ratfest smell good. I wasn't even sure what *good* smelled like. Not this.

This smelled like nothing. Sanitized, sterile.

Breathing took effort; it tasted like I was licking something's fecal afterbirth with every swallow. The dull bass beat pounding in my skull was either my chipset shorting out or the aftereffects of whatever I ate, drank, smoked, shot or snorted last night at the self-congratulatory *hey, we screwed the pooch and didn't die* revel. Hell if I could remember what I'd ingested, how much and with who. Knowing me, it could be anything, anyone, anywhere.

All I remembered was the club. Lights, skin. Sweat. I was

fresh off Lucky's chopshop miracle table, celebrating the life I almost wasted on a job gone bad, and then...

Nothing. I'd blacked out.

All the pins and needles streaking through my body made sure I knew how pissed *they* were, at least. Crashing on bare metal hadn't done me any favors. It was freezing beneath my ass, slick, and creepy as necro-balls to wake up on.

I shifted my arm aside.

The overhead light boiled. Yeah, still sucked. Swearing, I rolled to my left, raising my right hand to shield my sensitive eyes as the afterburn of six circular bulbs popped like sparklers in my vision. The sharp clank of metal on metal spiked through my mental diatribe as my left arm screeched across the surface of the table, almost pitching me right off it.

I hunched, shivering, a blur of bleached hair sliding over one eye as I struggled to suck in air. The table didn't even shake. Bolted, maybe.

The pressure sensors on my cybernetic limb sent all the right impulses to my brain, which told me that the chipset installed in the base of my skull wasn't completely fried. Relief. Quickly buried when the rest of my brain caught up and decided *by the way, today's gonna be a shit day for that arm you don't have*.

I hissed out what air I managed to inhale as pins and needles gave way to a crashing surge of white hot pain. It rolled up through the reinforced enhancements woven into my left biceps, streaked into my shoulder so high and tight I seized until I could crest it.

That I remembered.

It hurt like a son of a bitch. Not the sharp burn from a shank, or even that teeth-gritting shock of a broken bone. This went deeper than bone; an ache that settles so far under the surface, there isn't a biological name for it. How do you classify something only your soul misses?

Cybernetic limbs don't hurt, not within the synthetic

parts. They don't process pain or pleasure, like or dislike. They process facts. In the corner of my left eye, a series of values flickered rapidly, fainter than usual. They told me the temperature of the table under my hand, its surface tension – and other miscellaneous information I didn't understand and mostly ignored – calculated a variance and estimated that I propped my synthetic elbow on aluminum.

There was no setting for *today, I will feel like shit*. That was all me and my fleshbag brain, which hadn't yet figured out how to let go of the limb I'd already lost.

Probably a good sign. It meant I was still human enough to know what I was missing. If I were approaching my tech threshold, that point where the human body wasn't advanced enough hardware for the tech it housed, phantom pains and overcompensating muscle would be the least of my problems. I could count myself lucky on that score.

I cradled my arm with my other hand – a useless gesture that only served to remind me that a plated hunk of nanofactory diamond steel wasn't supposed to be hurting as bad as it did – and tried to think through the slurry my brain had become.

Unknown location. Definitely not my bed. Probably not the kinked-out pleasure palace of a seriously freaktastic fuckup, either – which only sort of worked out for me, but I'd deal with that part later. My girlfriend would understand. Maybe.

If she ever talked to me again.

The room boasted white panels for walls, the kind of seamed decorative choice you'd get from a mental institution but with none of the padding. The circular lamp over the table was fuckingly bright. The tile underneath the table was the cleanest I'd ever seen in my life, and the slab I perched on looked too much like an autopsy table for me to be comfortable staying on it.

The only color in the room was mine. Against the pristine cleanliness of my environment, my tattooed body stood out like an artistic temper tantrum. A quick pat revealed that the three sets of piercings I kept were gone. The stud in my left nipple was usually protected by body armor, and although I'd been kicked square between the legs once or twice, it didn't hurt the hood ornament any, so I'd kept them. An awkward grope at my ears mirrored the loss – no plugs in my open earlobes.

Medical reasons? This place *looked* like an operating room, without any of the usual equipment. That didn't fit the puzzle. Lucky made it a condition to detach everything that could be removed prior to any operations. The stuff messed with his system. Maybe it messed with whatever joint I'd been dropped in?

Obviously, I wasn't in my mentor's hands. Wasn't in a familiar place, either. Didn't remember getting here.

Didn't have my gear.

And my head felt like it'd been stuffed full of white noise and jammed on crooked.

Fucking A.

No time to panic. I'd spent too long living in a world that didn't give two shits and a used condom whether I lived or died, I wasn't going to freak now. The sweat on my skin was just standard operating procedure – my body, boosted by overworked nano agents, was trying to bleed out whatever junk I'd shoved in it earlier. Adrenaline and nerves tangled with my hangover and left me shaking.

My skin itched. I needed answers. Maybe a goddamn drink.

But most of all, I fucking needed *out*. Especially when the white lights in the ceiling flashed abruptly red.

I forced my body to move, to slide off the table and force my knees to hold my ass up when my feet hit the floor. My muscles screamed with the effort, joints popping like they'd locked into place while I slept. I blew my cheekbone-length hair out of my face and promptly regretted it.

Oxygen efficiency fail.

The blood drained from my head, left a mass of pins and

needles in its wake. The red-lit room flipped sideways on me. My stomach surged violently towards my sinuses.

I caught myself on the end of the slab, hunched hard enough that the corner gouged into my sternum, and retched.

Nothing came out. Damn if it didn't keep trying. Sweat congealed on my forehead, across my shoulders as I gagged and heaved, choking on everything that wasn't there. The dried-out husk of my guts wrung out everything they could, but I didn't have anything left inside me to puke. Whatever I'd eaten last, it'd been long enough that it didn't exist anymore.

The floor was cold under my feet, the edge of the table colder. I forced myself to open my eyes, squinted through the red glare and had to wait until the floor and ceiling swapped back to where they were supposed to be.

This was bad. My nanos were already struggling to catch up. I needed food to replenish the energy the little fuckers consumed to fix me. If I waited too long, nanoshock would put my shit on lockdown faster than any threat of security. Double fucking luck.

A clipboard hung from a narrow hook bolted into the edge of the slab, its transparent screen blank. Bleary, shaking, I grabbed the device, which woke it up and lit the screen to an opaque glow. My name greeted me in plain pixels.

Risa Cole.

My real. Cunting. Name. No one but Lucky should have known me and that name went together.

I blinked crusty eyelashes, clearing enough of my scummy sleep to peer at some basic physical facts. My height, 177.8cm. My weight and physique, in healthy ranges, edging more towards muscle than ideal feminine physique. I wouldn't win any bikini contests, unless it was for a Miss Universal Ass-Kicker. My body fat percentage was down. Too far down. I'd need to lay off the iso blends for a while.

Brown eyes – *hazel, assholes* – brown hair bleached out, no identifying scars and a shit ton of listed ink. A chart of haphazard racial markers didn't mean dick to me. Most I ever knew about my genetic makeup was that I didn't come out white enough for my anglo reserve mother.

Underneath it, a bulleted list catalogued my tech. Cybernetic arm (functional) with netware tools (disengaged) and extra ammo slot upgrades (empty); ocular interface with linked lateral display (active); accompanying chipset (modified basic).

Great. These assholes had disconnected my netware, which meant I'd get dick-all done if I needed to access anti-sec measures. Given the looks of this mess, I'd be running into security issues fast.

My role on the street was more of a splatter specialist than anything else; a killing jackofalltrades. Anything more technical than drilling the bandwidth is turf that belongs to linkers and projectors, and I was happy to let them have it. If I can't punch it? I don't want to mess with it.

This mindset has its limitations. Like when my netware fails. Fuck me.

I scrolled to the final line in the chart.

System failure: 14:37.

What the tits?

I checked again. Scrolled back up, but saw no date. Sloppy. I must've been too jacked up to make it through the night. My hangover could attest to that.

Was I in a hospital? Did I do something stupid at the club that landed me clinically dead for a while?

Not the first time I'd flatlined. You get used to that on a chopshop table, but I was usually on Lucky's and he hadn't let me down yet.

The lights overhead gleamed in uniform lines, painting the room in shades of blood and sickly pink – the off and on and off and on again damaged my calm. Definitely not a familiar place. And too quiet for any ER *my* criminal ass'd be accepted in. "Zen it, Riko," I rasped, forcing the words past the tightness in my jaw. The old mantra barely helped. Zen was the last thing I was.

What would my team linker tell me?

First, he'd ream me a new one for fucking around on his sister. I wasn't sure if that was true – wasn't convinced it wasn't – so I mentally glossed that part.

Linkers are masters of the signal, ground-floor operations with all the overhead intel to lead a team of mercs on the missions we take on. Without my linker's bird's-eye view, I was running on pure luck and wild guesses. Even if I had more info here, I didn't process data the way Indigo did. Laying down massive amounts of hurt was my specialty. Keeping me pointed in the right direction was his.

I was on my own.

There was no other data in the file to help me out. It didn't list my nano agents, either. Not surprising. Nanos are so commonplace that only people without are worth mentioning. If you're conceived in the city, you have nanos. The first thing they do is carve a SIN – a Security Identification Number – into the fetal brain, and that's that. Marked for life on a registry; a born sinner.

Babies conceived outside the city – if they manage to survive the seventy percent mortality rate – only end up with nanos if a parent is carrying. Even then, they won't do much against the unshielded electromagnetic radiation. A self-correcting issue.

If you're *me*, born nice and legal, you get those nanos reprogrammed and the SIN burned out. Not so nice and totally *not* legal.

So how did they get my old name? DNA database? Unlikely. They'd have to know exactly where I came from. Nobody in my sphere knew that. Not even my street doc. Without a SIN to go by, they had nowhere to start.

Except they'd gotten it from *somewhere*.

Popping out on-grid, even in a genetically cultivated anglo

zoo, meant my mother had my DNA registered with the community when I was still a baby. No way around that – short of a skilled projector and a price I couldn't afford – but if these fuckheads had access to that fiercely guarded database, then I was definitely dealing with the corporate sector.

That gave me an obvious next step: move from this room. Find a weapon somewhere.

Kill with impunity.

As a plan, it lacked detail. I was exhausted, running on empty and nursing the worst hangover I'd ever had. I was in no shape to take on anything, but fuck it. I'd be nothing but a victim if I stayed here, and I didn't *do* victim.

I took a deep breath. Pain lanced through my skull. "Fuck," I hissed between my teeth. "Taintlicking mother of a…" I dug the heel of my hands into my eye sockets, grinding out the grit so hard that sparklers flared behind my eyelids.

White walls. White floor. Blood splatter as pain lanced through my forehead.

"*Fuck!*" The best I could manage as a jarring cacophony of images collided, denying me answers. I did *not* have time to bleed.

I forced my eyes open, pushed myself upright against the table's edge. The colors inside my head – incessant white, a bloody arc of red – congealed in front of me. Security lighting, pristine tile painted by red bulbs. I was battling the kind of fatigue that turned the brain into a cheap shock show, but I'd done this before. A runner learns how to channel fear and adrenaline into something useful.

Street rule number one, the first thing Lucky had taught me: survive, and everything else could be dealt with later.

My legs were stiff, my knees uncooperative. It took way too much effort to make it halfway across the twenty-foot room. As I got close, the smudge of gray at the far end turned into the outline of a door. My optimism raised a notch when I didn't see any obvious signs of reinforced security. The door opened of its own accord, leaving me blinking into a darker corridor lit by the rhythmic wax and wane of alarm red. Shadows swallowed the end of the hall on either side.

So they'd fucked up their whatever operation, stuck me on a table and waltzed out without locking the damn door, huh? Shitlords. I'd show them what it'd cost to mess with me.

Hopefully, I'd manage to do something more than dry-heave on them.

The white noise in my head crackled, accompanied by a wave of nausea as my guts turned that intestinal tango into a thrashdance. I'd already tried puking. It didn't help. Moving on.

The hall was quiet, save for the aggravating throb ringing my skull and the slap of my bare feet on what felt like smooth metal flooring. I had to stop and lean against the wall more than I wanted, and I didn't see any signs of life along the way.

That didn't exactly herald victory. A place like this should have had *something* – security, technicians, something other than my battered meat staggering through the dark.

Anger simmered, but underneath, my nerves frayed.

I passed other doors. Two opened as I triggered sensors, but they remained dark inside. Finally, as I reached the end of the strip, red lights reflected off precisely aligned letters spelled out on the wall in front of me.

B L O C K – C.

Block. Like cell block?

All personnel to be armed beyond this point.

Oh, great.

Footsteps pounded down the hall behind me. I spun, muscles tensing. A bad move. My stomach sloshed, then seized. I locked my jaw when my throat expanded in preparation for vomit I didn't have, fresh sweat spreading like a stain across my chest and shoulders.

"Get to the uplink lab," snapped out a voice that echoed from the sporadic black. "All units, disconnect from main generators! Backup sources gamma-four. *Do not connect to main sources.*"

I shoved myself into the only corner available, my heart slamming as two, then four, then six men in black BDUs passed at a dead run. The lights glanced off visors and heavy-duty assault rifles held at the ready. Sauger 877s, bearing 5.56mm caseless rounds. Some serious firepower. Those are crunchers, spitting out half a thousand rounds in seconds. It chews through a magazine at an ungodly rate, but anything not outfitted with heavily reinforced dermaplating wouldn't make it past the first burst.

I wasn't dermaplated. No real fortification. Hell, I wasn't outfitted with a lot of the illegally available upgrades. I'd made the conscious choice to keep my tech streamlined to the necessary – and a few nominally risky cosmetics – out of sheer self-preservation.

The men filed past in triple-time, boots thumping the floor. The double doors pulled wide, then closed again behind them. Their footsteps vanished into the new corridor.

Whatever was going down at the uplink lab, it was big enough to need six men geared to the teeth with killing power.

I didn't have to wait long before the seventh sec monkey, the talker, made his entry. He hit the ground hard with every step, a full-on sprint that emphasized what looked like borderline panic to me. Grim, bloody panic. "Pull everyone off the street if you have to," he barked, his eyes wild beneath his raised visor. Like his buddies, he wore body armor and black fatigues, but didn't carry a Sauger. Coordinator, I'd guess. The corp version of a linker but with more bureaucracy up the ass. "Code six, do you morons hear me? *Code six*. This is not a fucking drill, get those goddamned sweepers down here!"

I held my breath as he darted past me. The door in front of him slid open again, hummed a note that grated a disconcerting counterpoint to the beating inside my skull.

Unlike his pals, he didn't roll through. He hesitated.

His head cocked.

Motherfucker.

2

I was already in midair when he turned. I launched off the wall, my tech arm pulled back for a textbook swing. It should have been the cleanest left hook in the world, aimed for that soft spot on his jaw that usually lands a man out cold – or at least spewing up his guts from the vertigo.

Instead, he jerked back over the threshold and caught my metal fist in his cheekbone when I overcompensated. The jarring miss rocked fingers of jagged regret through my brain. His skin split, bone cracked. Blood burst from his lip and nose in a crimson spurt made vivid by the lighting.

He didn't try to go for the weapon holstered at his hip. No time. Smart man.

He shifted to the side, swallowing the pain like the competent security agent he seemed to be, but I was already spinning on the ball of one foot. My momentum was good.

The lucky bastard got an eyeful of my snatch before the top of my foot connected with his helmet. Pain spiked through my bones; I didn't pause. I'd spent years conditioning my body.

I bet it hurt him more.

The visor cracked, the joint giving way to drop the disconnected faceplate to the ground, and his twitching body slammed into the wall. He got no chance to figure out his shit. As he slid to the ground, his eyes wide and more than a little crosseyed, I rode him all the way down, my fingers in his collar, knocking his helmeted head repeatedly into the wall to keep him off-balance.

I would've given good cred to know what was going through his brain. With a lapful of naked merc and the adrenaline of whatever crisis was going down, he had to be one giant flesh bucket of confusion.

I pinned him in place with my knees, slipped his gun from the nylon holster at his side as he struggled to force his limbs to coordinate. One hand grabbed my breast, but I'm pretty sure it wasn't on purpose. A knee drove up hard against my ass in an effort to buck me off. He grunted as I pulled my synthetic forearm up in an arc, colliding with the wrist of his grabby hand and forcing him to let go.

That caught my piercing. I flinched. "Hey, shit for brains," I panted, jamming the pistol against his forehead. A Phelps & Somers Manticore. A decent paramilitary piece, usually carried by serious corp security. Not great for pointblank range, mostly because of the mess, but if you let a runner like me close radius, you're already dead.

I opted for a shot at answers. "Where am I? What is this place?"

He froze, his eyes widening on either side of the barrel. One dilated, just as three separate optic panels winked open underneath his lash line – a thin flash of silver. He'd just taken my picture. *Shit.* I couldn't let him upload it.

"Stupid," I snarled, and pulled the trigger.

The guard's head exploded like a beer can left in the sun too long. Blood splattered across my face and chest, fanned out in a messy, pink-stained circle behind him. It was hellishly warm.

At the same time, something jerked loose in my head. A full-blown, ear-piercing echo that sent me staggering to my feet, gun-hand pressed to my ear. "Fuck!" I snarled. Only half of it penetrated the shrieking resonance rattling my skull.

I needed out of here. *Now*. Whatever else was going on, I wouldn't make it with strained reserves and shorting tech.

Stripping the dead guy of his clothing took longer than I wanted, but I needed the gear. I dressed fast. The cargos bagged, and the top half of a long-sleeve black skinsuit was much less tight than it should be. Both would provide fuck-all protection against bullets. It was temperature-modulation gear, comfort zone equipment, not armor. Problem was, his actual body armor was bulky as hell and his boots were too big for me to run in. I had to leave them.

But hey, I had his Manticore and a belt to keep the pants up. The rest was frosting.

I left him half naked and slumped over in a pool of his own blood, beyond any help his nanos could have given. Even if he'd gotten them upgraded, that much ruined brain matter was a one-way ticket to vegetable dreamland.

The smiley face boxers were a nice touch, though.

I had to pause long enough to roll up the stolen pants, which was awkward since I kept trying to throw up every time I bent over. I couldn't get a full breath. My ears buzzed, cutting through my mental faculties like a fifth of vodka with none of the fun. I'd picked up the angry wasps version of tintinnabulation.

Was this the worst situation I'd ever been in or just the weirdest? I couldn't decide.

I get around.

Once I got out of this nightmare, I'd retrace my steps. Figure out what the hell had gone down. Until then, it was all I could do to put one bare foot in front of the other. The gun weighed down my meat hand, my dominant hand, and I left it pointing at the floor. It took too much energy to keep it at the ready. Not ideal, but it was all I could work with. My world narrowed down to one step at a freaking time.

The corridor I followed wasn't as busy as the last.

Everything seemed eerily still. Shadows leapt and flickered under the flashing red lights, but that was all. I passed large dark windows, black and empty. I didn't know what they looked in on, but the whole thing had a sinister horror vibe that I didn't like.

When a frantic flutter of anxiety nudged at the fringes of my awareness, it shot icy fingers through my battlefield calm, merged with a bone-deep case of the shakes. That was seriously bad. It meant my nanos were exhausting their stores of energy, tapping so far into mine that I was running on fumes.

I blinked away traces of black clustering in my field of vision and tried not to notice. Freaking out would only force my nanos to work harder. Anxiety already made for nervous hands, strained calm. I was one bad call away from losing the shit I needed a handle on. If I didn't find the exit soon, my nanos would cannibalize me in the effort to fix me. If I hit nanoshock down here, I could kiss my tattooed ass goodbye.

It takes a hell of a lot to push a body this far.

Tech corruption is what happens when you get uncomfortably close to your tech threshold. Hitting corruption isn't necessarily terminal, but if you push farther and clock in to your threshold, it means you're dead *and* stupid.

Newly integrated tech can present corruption symptoms, but doesn't always. Nanoshock does. I'd pushed myself so far that the nano agents in my body were duplicating faster than they were dying off. That detritus overwhelms the system, clogs the machine, which boosts the risk of corruption beyond safe levels.

Not a deal breaker, if you catch it early.

Corruption is like the tech version of a fever. A trip to the local chopshop, recalibrate and recharge, and everything's fine.

Let it go too long, implant with more than your body can assimilate, or get rolled too hard for your nanos to deal, and that fever hits fatal. The tech corrupts the only processor available to it – the brain. Within a few hours, even minutes if it's aggressive enough, the human body converts entirely, becomes nothing more than walking hardware for the tech that wears it. We call this ambulatory wreck a *necrotech* – an obscene fusion of necrotic flesh and working tech with a viral need to kill.

Not that the risk stops people like me from getting implanted. It doesn't even stop people stupider than me from putting more in than they need. Augmentation is supposed to be highly restricted, but the corporations hand tech out to their own meat without the same regulations the rest of the world has to plow through. They started this arms race, upped the stakes until illegal chopshops started cropping up all over the city. More tech, more risk. More risk, more reward.

More reward, the more tech is needed to jack it, defend it, lock it, or kill it.

It's all part of the charm of running off-grid.

The universal rule is that street docs keep a failsafe armed at all times, which involves frying any potential conversion to a crisp long before it finishes cannibalizing itself. Anything less is necro roulette.

Outside a chopshop, smart runners carry energy boosts to recharge our nanos when we push them too hard. Whatever had landed me here had cost me everything I'd carried.

Like I needed more of a reason to haul ass.

Sweat poured off my skin in rivulets. I couldn't decide if I was hot or cold; all I could do was ignore the way it dripped down my shirt. I rounded a corner, sagged against it for a shuddering moment as the strip did a sudden dive in front of me. I cleared my throat, dried to a husk, and ran my cold metal hand over my face in a bid to stay focused. It only sort of helped.

A pale swath of blue light flickered from one of the wide windows on the left, and I forced myself upright. Change in light was good. It meant a change of scenery. Maybe even a way out.

Loping along as best I could, I managed to reach the closest edge of the viewing window before falling heavily against it. It thudded under my metal arm, but didn't give. Double-paned, heat-tempered. The unsteady lateral display in my eye told me I'd be shit out of luck if I needed to get through it. Not even a Sauger 877, fully emptied, would pierce that glass.

Which meant that the blue flames behind it wouldn't melt it, either. It was warm, but it wasn't fragile.

"What the shit." Not a question this time. It tasted more like surrender, and that wasn't okay. "*Move.*" My breath condensed on the tempered glass, only to vanish a second later.

My legs buckled instead. My forehead hit the glass and smeared. A flash of white and red tore through my vision.

My own voice ricocheted from somewhere far away, like a dream I didn't remember.

Just great. Nowhere near an exit and I was cracking.

I gasped for air, struggled to keep upright. Behind the tempered glass, the lab lay in shambles. Tables had been overturned, wires sparking – which probably set the fire along the far left edge. A pipe had burst somewhere beyond it, the vapor from inside it causing the flame to go blue. White powder drifted inside like snow, some kind of fire retardant that kept the flames at bay, but whatever fed it wasn't letting it die.

I forced myself to focus past the glass. Four bodies bled out where they'd dropped. The red lights turned blood to black smears, painted flesh in shades of blue and pink and sickly combinations in between. Computers flickered, a series of bolted screens filled with white and blue feedback. An open set of doors at the far end led into a room too dark to see into.

Whatever had gone down here, it happened fast and without warning. At least one corpse had fallen in a way that told me she'd managed to stand before whatever it was took her out. Now she was so much wispy hair over a crushed, viscous mess, dotted with dingy gray snowflakes.

White spots appeared in front of my face.

I stared at them in blank confusion. Too much oxygen? Or not enough.

Three more spots appeared, and tiny chips of dust exploded in a blue-tinged puff.

A figure darted past the open doorway in the back. Still mired in the eerie, muffled noise plugging my ears, it took me too long to figure out the orange bursts inside came from gunfire.

The glass caught stray bullets in front of my face.

I jerked back, swearing. I'd found the uplink lab. At least, I thought I did. If not, this shit was spreading, which was even more of a reason to forget everything else but *get the fuck out*.

I made it two awkward steps down the hall before something crackled through my shriveled brain. I staggered, pain snapping like a white sheet over my eyes, and caught myself on the window.

Thud! My body against the glass.

Thud, thud!

A shape slammed against the other side of the tempered pane. The last of my adrenaline, sapped down to bone and gristle, spiked. I whirled, Manticore pointed on pure reflex. My shoulder strained, palm sweaty with nerves and effort, but my grip was sure as I aimed the killing end of my stolen gun between two terrified blue eyes.

Familiar blue eyes.

"Holy fuck." My fingers went numb. The gun fell from my clammy grip, clattering inches from my bare toes. "Nanji." I barely managed to get her name out – it sounded fucking wrong echoing in this stark hall.

She mouthed something I couldn't hear, her cheeks bloody and tear-streaked as she palmed the glass between us. I closed the distance, pain forgotten, the swarming ache in my head shoved aside. Shock drove me, sheer confusion and an anger so raw it burned in my gut.

"Baby, hold on!" I shouted it, knowing that the glass was soundproof, but I didn't care. Didn't care that she'd never liked it when I called her baby. Too anonymous, she'd said. It was one of those things I never remembered. People were "baby" when I fucked them, and that name stuck.

She hammered on the glass, mouth moving, words I couldn't hear streaming from her as she battered at the barrier. Her olive skin had gone sickly yellow around the edges, her lush mouth stretched thin with fear. She was shorter than me, had always been curvy where I liked it, but blood plastered her tied white tunic and baggy pants to curves that looked thinner than I remembered. Her ink-black hair, thick and always braided back in a long tail I enjoyed stroking, had been shaved down to a fine fuzz.

A cut over one eyebrow dripped into her eye, oozing black sludge that collected white flakes from the fire-retardant drift. She slammed the glass over and over, until the skin of her left palm darkened and split. Plasma diluted by a dirty tinge smeared.

I flinched. "*Stop.*" My hands hit the glass where hers struck. "Baby, stop. Stay there!"

She shook her head. She couldn't hear me, either.

Her fingers flattened against the barrier. I opened mine over them.

So close.

Too far. The glass between us all but throbbed from the heat. The lab on the other side had to be sweltering.

She mouthed something else I couldn't read, something with her brother's name in it – Indigo. "Where?" I demanded. "Is he here?"

She shook her head again, this time pointedly. He wasn't. Relief swamped me.

The room behind her disgorged three men in the same black uniform I was almost wearing. I hit the glass over her head. "Look out!"

Her eyes widened. The whites tinged gray, another sign of nanos at the breaking point. Maybe like mine. I couldn't tell. The black spots popping in my vision looked too much like the black sludge at her eyebrow.

She spun around, arms wide as if she'd shield the glass I stood behind. As if she were tall enough, strong enough.

Whole enough.

She wasn't.

Ice splashed into my stomach, froze fury and fear into a wad of nausea so thick I couldn't breathe around it.

Metal shaped her spine, thrust from her smooth flesh like alien vertebrae, precisely machined. Tubes and wires looped from joint to joint, then screwed into her skull in an immaculately clean shell cupping the base of her head. Jacks dotted the plates, drilled into each side like some kind of nightmarish hook-up. The flesh around the implant was perfect, seamed into the metal like it had always been there.

It hadn't. Yesterday, Nanji had been one of the few SINless on our team who'd sported nothing more technical than nanos and a chipset capacity for photographic memory. Her back had been smooth, unmarred but for the lotus tattoo between her shoulder blades, twin to her brother's.

That ink was gone now, swallowed by the kind of cybernetics that earned a runner a bullet on the street. Her shoulders hunched like the weight was too much for her to carry. The wiring along her back rippled, reflecting back blue sparks in the shattered light.

Never. She would *never* get this kind of tech. It was all wrong, too obscene.

Too inhuman.

Horror froze me to that spot. Locked me down into a whirlpool of confusion, anger, chaos. What the hell kind of universe did I wake up in?

Nanji looked back at me, saw my face. Saw my revulsion.

I couldn't hide it.

Her mouth twisted. Sealed against a tremor. She didn't break down, she was too strong for that. She sucked in a ragged breath as tears pooled in her eyes – black like her blood. Her nanos had passed mine, launched beyond the point of overcompensation. Dead units leaked out of her body wherever they could. Ears. Nose. Eyes.

And she knew it. We both did. This was our world – our risk.

She wasn't the only saint to lose her shit to tech corruption.

But she was the only one I cared about who'd done it in front of me. I needed to get her to a street doc, and *fast*.

"Nanji," I said, knowing it wouldn't help. Knowing the sec-goons behind her wouldn't let her go.

All I could do was watch as she fisted one hand and punched the glass. It dusted to a layer of shattered white, but didn't break. Red and black smeared where her knuckles had cracked, backlit by the lab lights and blue flame. The black sludge in her eyes leaked over, mixed with the blood and sweat already caked on her cheeks.

My girlfriend was already corrupted. And I could do jack shit about it.

The three men behind her fanned out, weapons trained. A good strategy – one I would have employed if it were me and my team. If Nanji charged one, the other two could take her down before she reached her target.

But that was just tactics. *She* was my team. *They* were the well-trained enemy, and if they were prepared for something like *this*, then that meant they were in on whatever the shit this was. It was their fault. Theirs, and the spunk-sucking corporate tool that funded them.

I would murder every last one.

One of the faceless tools gestured, and Nanji jerked like

he'd said something that mattered. I punched the glass Nanji had already weakened, snarled when only one faceplate turned in my direction. "Don't you fucking touch her." Rage crackled. "Nanji!"

Her whole body shuddered. Something I'd never seen before flickered to life behind her stare, roiling under her skin like something alive pushed against the shell of her body. Her blue-black eyes flicked to the side.

Pain sliced through my head – a struggling, writhing pressure centered somewhere near my chipset and echoed in the bruised palms my nanos were too far gone to mend.

Her lips moved, easy to read this time.

Get out.

"No!"

Her mouth curved up. She had that habit, smiling even when she was sad. She touched her lips with two shaking fingers, pressed those fingers to the powdered glass. *I'm sorry.*

My jaw clenched.

The men behind her signaled.

I pounded the glass with fists, forearms. White dusted off the surface, but it held. I didn't have the strength that spinal replacement had given her. "Where's the door?"

Her eyes closed, black lashes so thick, she'd never needed makeup to darken them. Now caked with blood and the sludged remains of her nanos. Her hands rose, two fingers tilting to my right, dipping twice.

Two down.

When her eyes opened again, the irises were almost entirely black. She sucked in a breath; maybe she'd meant to say something, but they didn't let her.

The 877s aren't subtle weapons. Orange and white flared from the muzzle as three Saugers spat out a spray of bullets so fast, so chaotic, that the glass vibrated under the strain of catching them all. The panel went shock white, like a sudden frost too thick to see through. All I saw of Nanji before the screen went blank was the way she dropped to the ground, dug her bare toes into the floor and scuttled for cover.

I'd never seen her move like that, like her joints weren't limited by the same restrictions mine were. Her fingers spread too wide, nearly a full circle of contact with the floor. Alien. Predatory.

The truth, harsh and terrifying, took my breath away.

She'd waited too long. *They*'d waited too long, or maybe this was some kind of fuckedup corruption study. Whatever it was, they'd succeeded in one thing – Nanji wasn't just corrupted. She was going full necro.

Even if I hauled ass, even if I managed to get to the door in time, the only thing I'd be able to do for her was put a bullet in her head.

I was too fucking late for anything else.

But somebody had to. Somebody she trusted.

Fuck.

With the soundless echo of bullets throbbing and thrashing inside my skull, I slammed my synthetic hand against the window and took off. She'd indicated two doors down. I barreled for it, nearly bloodied my nose on the door when it didn't open. I hammered on it. I kicked it. I backpedaled, and missed the actual second door she'd indicated twice before I thumped a fist against my hammering heart and forced myself to *stop* and *fucking look*.

The door was all but invisible, a seam two feet from a plain black square.

I slapped it, swearing as if the vicious words could slow down time. Slow down bullets. My vision turned into a narrow tunnel of focus.

Save her. Could I?

No. Lucky had ingrained that in me from day one – don't tempt corruption, don't fuck with the converted. Necros didn't care. They killed.

By herself, Nanji wasn't likely to be much of a match, but

the tech they'd wired into her spine was a whole different story. They could have put anything in it, and based on the way she'd moved, they'd done something with her whole nervous system. It could have been medical testing, could have been some kind of illegal meat lab trading in human subjects, but it didn't matter. Even mobility tech wired into a body's base nervous system – spine, brain, whatever – can go off the reservation.

A body that moves because of technical help can be pushed beyond human limits when the brain powering it no longer cares about human thresholds. Tech doesn't feel pain, remember? Nanji probably had the strength to tear a body limb from limb.

I had to get to her. I had to be the one to put her down.

A compulsion, maybe. A need to see things through.

A way to cover my ass when I looked her brother in the eye.

I sprinted through the door when it was wide enough, clipping my shoulder, and found myself in a four-by-four square that reeked of stale piss and sour sweat. The door closed behind me, locked me in – or out.

By the time I grasped Nanji's deceit, it was too late. The elevator jerked upwards, and the reeking shaft absorbed my ragged, furious scream. I pounded on the now faceless wall. Hammered it until my metal fist dented the interior, but it wouldn't open. Wouldn't give.

The car eased to a stop. Behind me, a second set of doors parted, spilling me into a fetid, filthy alley. The hot night air rolled into the cramped space. It filled my nose and lungs, shocked my system for the last time.

The narrowed tunnel my vision had become went utterly black. The lateral display guttered once, twice, neon green values rippling before turning muted gray and flashing a stern *000*.

I collapsed into a pile of rotting refuse.

3

The unsteady *click-click-click* of the overhead fan filled the dingy interrogation cell. No pattern. No rhythm. Just unending amounts of irritation undercut by the derisive stare of the cop watching me.

We'd been playing this game for the past hour.

Jamming my thumb into my own eye would be more fun. Not that I could. My hands were manacled to a nanofactory steel ring embedded in the table in front of me. If I tried hard enough, I could budge the whole thing *maybe* an inch. As it was now, I could only brace my forearms on the surface and pretend like I wasn't ready to keel over on the spot.

I'd woken up in a police transport with my hands and feet immobilized in rotocuffs. They must have jammed some kind of emergency recharge between my teeth; cops and medics keep shit like that on hand for nanoshock cases. Wouldn't be enough to get me through much more than a few hours – less, if I kept getting into fights – but I'd take it.

Cops are government men, at least on paper, but bought and paid for by the corps that run the city. They keep the peace where they can, watch what they can't change, and occasionally come up with a serious case of something contagious when they're paid off to. They're underfunded compared to private security and overworked everywhere else, but they don't dick around when it comes to SINless. Especially ones running on the verge of corruption.

The jerkoffs had cut my sleeve away to fasten a bolt directly to the surface of my synthetic arm. It shorted the circuitry, turned the limb useless – and cost me a perfectly good skinsuit, on top of everything else.

It could have been worse. Back in the day, they planted the circuit bolt right on top of the chipsets at the base of the skull. The frequency it emitted shorted the whole thing, which also happened to trigger systemic failure of any life support. Countless perps with illegal tech had died in custody, a hazard of the lifestyle, but when a suspect with an advanced credit line and connections up the corporate ass had flatlined, the cops wised up.

After being sued into the cunting ground, naturally.

Now, they planted the bolt directly on any exposed tech. Lucky me. I got off with a forty-pound paperweight dragging on my shoulder, a two hundred-pound table attached to my wrists, and a three hundred and sixty-pound beefjock in city blue breathing down my neck.

I was exhausted, starving, filthy, and so far into nano meltdown I wasn't sure I'd ever crawl out again. I'd apparently been found wandering around, out of my goddamn mind, somewhere in the Third Junction. Not my usual haunt. The place was mostly tenements, lowball gangs and slum lords.

Not to say I didn't operate in those circles. Just not in that particular area.

No matter how hard the beefjock grilled me, I had no answers – none I'd give him, anyway. Nanji's black-sludge tears carved bloody furrows through my patience.

Was she dead by now? Probably. I hated that I hadn't been there when it happened. Hated the thought of those security fucks in black filling my girlfriend full of enough lead to drop her, tech and all. I hated the lingering guilt sucking on my conscience, and sitting here in this hotbox interrogation room replaying it over and over was pissing me off.

I couldn't remember what got us in that hellhole. And the only man who might have a clue was the same man who'd be completely justified in putting a bullet in me for the trouble.

This little side trip to coplandia? Frosting on my fucking day.

Officer Fagan, he of the perfect tan and spectacularly shiny badge, didn't care. As if he had all the time in the world, he leaned back in his chair – it creaked alarmingly beneath his bulk – and twirled a tablet stylus through his meaty fingers. A wedding ring glinted on his left hand. Most people didn't bother with them. Old fashioned guy, this one. "Let's give this another shot," he said, with a hell of a lot more patience than I had. "Tell me what you were doing prior to arrest."

Aside from taking a dirt nap? "Floss my balls," I said to the ceiling.

The harsh lights glared down at me, judgmental as hell. I got it, all right? This was my fault for ending up in police custody. The worst of it was that I hadn't even done anything to end up here – no police shootouts, no high-speed chases, no corporate fuckery. I may actually be the first runner in history to wind up in a cop shop because street uniforms had found me in the trash.

That was some bullshit I'd have to play down before it made the rounds across the network. It also meant that even if I had the juice to try and contact anyone on my roster for help out of here, I couldn't. Any saint who led a uniform to another runner would be so much paste by the time it was over.

"Come on, little girl." The officer's thick lips tipped up – too much a sneer to be a smile. "Just tell me what I want to know and I'll get you something to eat."

Tempting as it was, no. I didn't play with cops. Well, usually. "Should I use smaller words, Officer Fagging?"

The loose flesh at his jowls tightened. "It's Fagan."

"'Course it is. Hey, what gay parlor has a tanning bed big

enough for your fat ass?"

A vein popped out in his forehead. He very carefully smoothed back his hair.

Like I'd let that go. "You an all-over-shine boy or do they make cock socks in your size?"

He grunted. "You think you're so cute."

"Nope." Nobody in their right mind would ever slap that label on me. I was too mean for cute, too edgy for pretty. I wore clothes that showcased my build, sleek and lean. Cute girls got more leniency than I did.

And less fucking.

He didn't seem to care for my honesty. "Last chance to get this straight."

"We both know that's beyond us," I said, lifting my eyebrows suggestively. "Does your wife know you like dick?"

His left eyelid twitched.

I sniffed, then rubbed my nose along my shoulder. "Seriously, it smells like dick in here."

His hand came down on the table so hard, the sound echoed like a gong. I jumped, the cuffs locking me in place snapping taut, but no give. He leaned over the table. "Enough of your games," he growled. "Cough up your network, or I'll make sure you never see daylight again."

My legs tensed. My stomach cramped so hard, it was all I could do to remain upright – I didn't dare show him how badly I was hurting. No way I could kick this table into his gut. Much as I hated it, I needed *him* to come at *me*. It was the only shot I had.

They'd left my feet unlocked, which was stupid. If he got close enough, I'd get a crack at his weapons – and the personal recharges all cops kept in their tool belts for long days. One of those would do me until I could get somewhere I could crash. I needed sleep before I did anything else. Nutrients. Then I'd begin the hunt for whatever it was that put me and my girlfriend down in that nightmare lab.

It wasn't lost on me that I'd spent the past four hours trying to get out of shit I didn't remember getting myself into. Weird lab, police station – what next? I didn't dare ask, even as a joke. The universe was such a bitch.

So I smiled. I wasn't exactly a friendly smile type. Generally, my expressions slanted towards mean or hungry. This one didn't reach my eyes. It showed all of my teeth. It telegraphed things I'd bet Officer Fagan, with his clean uniform and softening gut and do-right haircut, had only ever seen on his torture porn subscriptions. I injected every ounce of violence, every inch of desperation, every kill I'd ever made into a smile that told him exactly how much of a psychotic mercenary he had on his hands.

I was definitely *not* cute.

That eyelid flickered like the wobbling fan overhead. Sweat beaded on his forehead, turning his red skin splotchy as the last fat-swaddled glimmer of professional pride buried in his psyche screamed at him to outstare the bitch.

"You know what we call beat cops?" The left side of my nose hiked, turning my smile into a soundless snarl. "Street meat. Guess why."

He jerked back from the table. Caught himself and gave me a long, deliberate sigh. It didn't fool me. I'd wiggled under his roasted skin and jammed my fingers into a place he didn't like to think he had. He straightened, sucked his gut up into his chest. Like I needed a reason to know how much bigger he was than me.

Hard to miss. His straining uniform shirt, short-sleeved in deference to the blistering heat outside and the struggling fans in this cramped interrogation room, fought to hold his bulk.

I also knew that I was on thin, very fragile ice.

As a SINless, I'm something between a bogeyman and a chlamydial sneeze to anyone working the standard life. One part threat, one part figment, seven parts *avoid at all costs*.

Everybody knows we exist, but we're the Other in their world. Your jobbers, your bums, your corp shills, your kids dripping snot and howling for attention; these are the everyday residents of the city. Sinners, every one of them, nailed to the corporations that supply them with an endless supply of gimmes. Their SINs are wired into the bandwidth, complete with visual set-ups much different than mine. While you can find apps for just about everything – if it isn't jammed into your brainmatter via carrier – every connection serves up two main courses of bullshit: bloatware and spyware.

One keeps you busy by throwing an endless supply of entertainment, lifehacks, and waste-of-time games challenging you to achieve best score, highest rank, achievement after achievement. Victories come with all kinds of rewards, from points spent at the local crankbar, VR time, maybe an uplink orgasm with three times the kick and none of the formalities. Anything to dull the pain of living, the pressure of working, the need to feed on something better than what they sell their bodies and minds and souls for.

All noise, no signal.

Which means they get your everyday worries: where to eat, who to bang, how to get the latest shine from whatever shopping vid they obsess over. Who has what, how to get it, work, work, work, play, play, play. Fester, fester, fester. Blinded by the bandwidth that feeds them, leashed by the SIN that promises protections and delivers fuck-all, the people just... exist. Unaware – willfully ignorant – of the fact that every achievement logs another entry in the corporate databases that track them all.

Enough creds will get rid of most of the bloat, but never lose the framework it's all built on. There are tiers, VIP and fuckingly expensive packages, but that's all top percentage shit. I've never been close enough to smell the ballsweat of a corporate shark wo could afford that kind of privacy, much less ever seen it.

Meanwhile, those of us without SINs take it one-hundred percent off the radar, which pisses off just about everyone who traffics in SIN tech. Our HUDs are streamlined to spec, lacking in all the bloat most chipset networks are frontloaded with, and completely off the registries. I don't even keep track of the days. Who cares? I'm not that hooked up on where I have to be; I have a linker for that.

SINless don't have to be any more dangerous than your average social failure shooting up a busy street, but it pays to be smarter. Losers and idiots die fast, so those of us that survive the entry process end up with a network of like-minded illegal mercs with talents for murder, mayhem, theft, espionage, and whatever else makes the corporate douchefactories piss their pants.

Which is my point. And Fagging's.

As a working runner, I'm worth my weight in credits. Or at least this cop's weight in cleared paperwork. Not quite worth a medal, but definitely a promotion. Big bad Officer Fagan, taking down his very own merc. If he could sweeten the pot with my contacts, he'd skate right from street meat to a desk.

I bet he'd swing his copper-toned dick around for years.

I never did much care for authority. Part of the reason I left home. It made me lippy. More, it made me forget that I was running on empty, which wasn't doing me any favors. "So let's get real here," I told him, drumming my only functional hand on the table. "I die in this box, you haul in a corpse. We both know your bosses want me alive."

A bit of a stretch, but I was banking on the fact Fagan didn't know that. Alive meant information, after all. Possible datadump from my chipset, possible informant. Dead means a runner's chipset goes nova and eats its data. Fuck you, forensic coroners.

"You can stroke your civic cock all day long," I added, waggling my eyebrows. "Maybe I die while you take your money shot. Maybe my nanos push me over the edge and then you got a fucking necro in your station." He blanched at that. Smart man. Time was on my side here. Sort of. I mean, *I* cared if I died, but he didn't know that.

Most everyday wage slaves figure SINless are one step away from batshit insane anyway, which is more or less true, but we still favor survival over reckless suicide. Whatever else the corps like to say about us, we ain't in it for the kicks.

Just for the kicks, anyway.

Perspiration rolled down his jaw. He wiped it away with a hand. The hair on his knuckles was thick and wiry. Darker than I expected.

A sausage-link finger jabbed at the air between us. "You talk, but you don't exist, do you, little girl?" Well, damn. Officer Gorilla-Hands found his courage. "There's nothing stopping me from jamming a recharge down your throat to keep you stable and hauling you off. You could..." He tried for a snap, but his sweaty digits wouldn't cooperate. "You could disappear, and who'd come looking? Your illegal pals? Bullshit. You're the dumb cunt that got caught by *street meat*."

All obviously true, which was why I needed him to come at me.

"Okay, Officer Fagan." I narrowed my eyes at him. "I got a question."

He frowned. "What?"

Oh, man. It's like he was asking for it. "How often do you scope out the other guys' junk in the locker room?"

He held my gaze, drawing on that good ol' boy macho crap that I bet he practiced on the wife and kids. "Shut up."

"Ever nail a perp in lockup just 'cause he couldn't say no?"

The sweat at his jaw dripped to his shirt.

"I bet if you ask nice, your wife'll peg you tonight."

His throat moved, flesh rippling under his too-tight collar. "Shut *up*, bitch."

I didn't care if I'd hit a nerve of truth or one his machismo couldn't handle. It was all the same in the end. I tilted my head. "Tell me, Fagging," I said, dropping my voice to a conspiratorial octave. "You touch your kids with the same hand you stroke off with?"

That did it. He surged to his feet, chair creaking, bellowing like an enraged bull. I braced, but I wasn't prepared for him to slam both fists into the table in front of me. The damn thing scooted three inches, spiderwebbed the cement under its metal legs with a sharp crack of sound, and rammed hard into my ribs. My chair slid back. I grunted, adrenaline pouring into synapses already fried to a crisp.

The beefjock was strong. Way stronger than I'd given him credit for.

Stronger, I bet, than anyone expected him to be.

Motherfucker. I'd misjudged the guy.

My smile strained. "Juicer," I wheezed, sucking in air through ribs that felt like they'd been jackhammered.

His eyes blazed, telegraphing more psychotic rage than I figured he'd normally have in him.

I was wrong. Way wrong. He wasn't *just* street meat. I should have noticed the signs sooner – maybe would have, if I weren't so strung out already. Wide shoulders, thick gut, the kind of heft Lucky would call soft muscle. Testosterone and rage and sideline expertise. His skin was tan, yeah, but now that I'd actually *looked*, it didn't look like the kind of color picked up from a tanning bed.

Fagan's features were all the usual mixes, the standard plethora of genetic grabbag this city bred like cockroaches, but this build, the tone to his skin, and the spittle peppering the desk made me consider black-market gene therapy instead – Maori, maybe, or Samoan; something that culturally favored bulk over lean muscle.

A serious problem.

Gene therapy is capitalistic science – legit in every way except the side effects. Some consumerist test panel took the best parts of a culture they didn't understand, shoved it into a pill and assumed everything would work like expected. Only it didn't. Science can isolate the genes, but genes don't end at skin and bone.

Right around the time the cultural fringe died out as a pure strain, psychologists stopped talking about genetic memory. Critics called it *the dying breath of an extinct race.* By the time scientists distilled entire cultures down into strands of DNA, there wasn't anybody around to remember the concept. Until the shit went viral in people too impressionable to handle it.

It was a lot like the brief and bloody fad for "real" pet wolves. They cultivated the raw genetic base into dogs, then farmed them out for major pay to bored fuckheads with more creds than common sense. Who then got a shitload of surprise when originally tame animals turned feral and savaged their owners.

Most pure strains went the way of the wolves ages ago. Only thing keeping native civilizations alive is the gene therapy that doesn't understand them and some seriously ignorant idolatry from naïve fetishists.

A man like Officer Fagan here probably wanted muscle and a warrior makeup to lord over his small-time beat, and ended up with enough additional testosterone and misplaced cultural fury to kill his brain cells. Not that science cared. Racial memory wasn't the kind of thing the corporations wanted to waste time disproving. In the spirit of entrepreneurialism, they ignored the evidence, marked the gene pills as all-natural and set it loose.

Fagan didn't strike me as the homeopathic type, but here we were. All for what? Some extra meat and bragging rights?

Fuck that. His armchair athleticism wasn't equipped to handle the instinct of a warrior culture murdered by the civilization that sold them, and I'd bet my life that his nanos would overcompensate for the surge of killing fury. That meant if he got angry enough, I'd be paste on the wall of this dingy interrogation room. He'd rip my arms off before I got the cuffs free.

So much for my bright idea.

I blew out a hard breath, my vision narrowing down into that black tunnel I knew was a bad sign. I didn't have it in me to fight a juicer, not while I was shackled to a table in the middle of a fucking police station and spiraling back into meltdown.

He gripped the edge of the table so hard, I swear to fuck the thing groaned.

As if on cue, the room's single door thumped once, and the knob rattled. Officer Fagan's head cocked, his blazing blue eyes slanting abruptly to the side as if weighing his odds.

At least he still had the brains of a low-rent cop.

"Aw," I murmured, a farce of a drawl in my wheeze. "So much for playing grabass in the hotbox, Fagging."

One day, I'll learn how to shut up.

His fist came up, a narrow distance but with enough weight to rock my head back on my shoulders. Pain exploded behind my nose, gouged into my brain. The chair scooted back, tilted on two legs while stars whirled through my skull, only to yank back into sharp alignment as the shackles around my wrists snapped taut. All four legs slammed back to the floor. I blinked rapidly through streaming eyes.

"That's *enough*, Carl!"

The voice snapped through the narrow room, jerking Officer Fagan's shoulders into rigid opposition. I almost laughed, but my throat was full of blood and I couldn't force the air through my swollen, leaking nose.

"I'll handle this," my unwitting savior said, his tone hard as the table I was bleeding on. "You go relieve Docking."

In my watery vision, I watched Fagan roll his wide shoulders. His eyelid had stopped flickering, at least. "It was an accident," he began, only to stumble into an awkward silence as the man with shaggy blonde hair and a hobo's grasp of shaving habits raised a hand.

"Just go," he suggested. It wasn't kind, but I didn't see any verbal bloodletting, either.

Then again, I was seeing two of each of them at the moment. I shook my head slowly, working my jaw, checking for dislocation or worse. The coppery tang in my mouth and throat was bad enough.

The door clicked close, and Detective Gregory Keith took an audible, too-long breath.

Smegging cockhole. This was not my hour. Not my day.

Not my life.

"Hey," I said thickly, my head tilted up to keep the worst of the drainage from my shirt. It wasn't helping. "Don't sigh like this is my fault."

"Riko, I swear to God." I grinned, which made him – hardboiled detective that he was – cringe at the blood covering my teeth. "Didn't I tell you to keep your nose out of trouble?"

He had. I guess he'd meant it literally.

Greg and I had hooked up once, about seven months ago. He'd been fresh on a promotion and looking to celebrate, I'd been high on a successful run and full of my own ego. He was nice enough, a religious man who believed in the Judeo-Christian God and who'd managed to grow up with an optimistic view of the world. I had expected the job to wear both thin.

There were lines at his green eyes that hadn't been as deep seven months ago.

I didn't like being in a position to know that. Ideally, we'd never have crossed paths again. What was going on in my life? Did somebody wake up and decide to just ruin my shit today?

He popped a trigger from a unit hanging from his belt, and the magnetic grip around my wrists eased. I shook off the manacles with one hand, peeled the other off my nonfunctioning arm.

"You want to tell me what happened?" he asked, pulling a worn bandana from his back pocket. "Use this, tilt your head forward, not back. Jesus, why aren't your nanos pitching in?"

"I'm running a little dry." Of nanos, patience, juice. He could take his pick. I jammed the cloth against my streaming nose with my good hand, wincing as the cartilage shot another fistful of pain up my sinuses. "You swear a lot, detective. Come with the promotion?" For Greg, using his Lord's name in vain was as bad as the filthiest epithets I could think of. And I could think of some nasty ones.

It was fun to say it while he was balls deep in me, just to watch his face flush and his eyes light up, but that was about it.

Yeah. Religion wasn't my thing, either. It probably tied into the whole authority issue. I didn't like when fleshbags told me what to do, much less some figment of a fleshbag's authoritarian wet dream.

"Eh." The grunt wasn't an answer, but it seemed the only one I'd get. He surveyed me, concern and frustration shaping his features. "What the hell happened here?"

Good question. Where did I start?

Oh, how about *fuck off* and on to *you fucking fuckhead*.

Nope. Wasn't processing too well.

I glowered at him.

Despite his profession, Greg wasn't otherwise unattractive. His features were narrow and his current rough 'do made him look like a beach bum masquerading as a cop. His denim jeans were worn, the green button-down left open to his collar bones, which also revealed a skinsuit underneath. Just in case. The stuff was durable, which is why I'd taken the one I was bleeding on now. His badge hung around his neck on a chain, but unlike Fagan's, it showed some wear.

I'd never considered anything more than a fling with the guy, and fortunately Greg had known better than to pursue. I don't think I was his type, anyway. He needed a sweet girl with stars in her eyes, the perfect cop wife who'd wait at home with the kids while Daddy was out nabbing bad guys.

I *was* the bad guy. And bad guys don't talk to cops. I mean, between fucking them for laughs.

He grimaced. "Why did he hit you?"

I had to clear my throat before I opened my mouth. "An accident." A total lie, the same one Fagan had delivered, but that was the point. I wouldn't be made into a victim, and I sure as hell wouldn't leave a complaint. It's not like I had any legal recourse here. I didn't exist. And if I did, my ass would be put in detention. Fast.

Besides, I was SINless. Off the grid meant off the grid, not filing charges. What was I, some kind of pussy?

His eyes narrowed. He was sharper, too. Yeah, definitely lost some of that shine in the intervening months. "Why are you even here?" he asked, leaning against the table. I would have answered, probably another lie, but I wasn't thinking very well, and he lifted the same authoritative hand he'd given to Fagan when he realized it. "Never mind. You won't tell me anyway."

"Yeah." I got to my feet, wincing with the effort when my dead arm swung uselessly at my side.

His gaze pinned on the torn hem of the skinsuit and the hunk of dark gray diamond steel hanging from it. The lines around his mouth deepened.

He'd lost some stardust. I'd lost an arm. Same thing. I presented my back. "Do me a solid?"

"Uh... Yeah." He circled around the crooked table, his nostrils flaring like a spooked horse. "That's, uh. That's new."

"You aren't kidding."

He worked the bolt gingerly. I glanced over my shoulder, impatience riding me as deep as the tunnel of exhaustion waiting to suck me in.

Whatever I meant to say, it didn't matter. His mouth was thinned to nearly nothing, his elbows splayed like he'd grown wings. He only touched the bolt with the tips of his fingers. Just enough to get it off me.

I almost snorted out the fragile beginnings of the blood clot. Greg had seen me naked, spent more than a few hours mapping out my body. He may have even thought fondly of me, when he bothered to think of me at all.

Detective Keith, on the other hand, didn't trust integrated tech.

No, that wasn't quite right.

He despised it.

He looked up, meeting my gaze over the ruined blue bandana he'd given me. "Let me guess," I said mildly. "Purist?"

The smile he gave me was wan. It was answer enough.

Purists don't believe in tech. If they could scrape out the nanos, they would, but the city's pollutant level is so bad, everyone needs them to survive. Besides, I'd never met a purist *pure* enough to mind the help the nanos give – minor regenerative capabilities, disease control. The right programming could ease fertility, reducing the harsh conditions that often lead to difficult or defective conception.

It's a hard world, and purists are only a very small part of the hypocritical lot. Most happen to coincide with the fundamentalist religious or political sects, though. Surprise.

I'd known he was religious. Hadn't known about the purism. Until a corporate strike gone bad had cost me my arm, I'd never sported anything more overt than vid ink, so not like I had the chance to learn.

As soon as the bolt came off, a jolt of something uncomfortable rippled down my left arm. If metal could have pins and needles, this did. I shrugged hard. The reinforced muscles comprising the shoulder girdle contracted sharply, but I didn't bother trying to use it until the system ran through its check. It'd have to reboot.

At least the numbers in my lateral display were finally displaying more than zeroes.

"Great." I sighed, refraining from rubbing at my aching muscles. If I did, I had no doubt Greg would comment. It'd been a rough day, and it wasn't over. I needed to get the hell out before he got up in my junk. I didn't think I had the patience. Or the mental functions.

No weakness allowed.

Wariness, not carefully hidden enough disgust, touched his pretty green eyes when he looked at me. At my arm. It pissed me off almost as bad as everything else on my plate, and I had a full smegging plate.

Maybe he noticed. His expression went blank. "Can you walk?"

Barely. I forced my spine straight. "I'll be fine. Just show me the back way out."

"Riko." His hand on my arm – my right one – only stopped me because, shit, I was tired. Too tired to wrestle with a cop. "Where are your shoes?"

As one, we both looked down at my bare, dirty feet, toes spattered with blood and blackened by I don't even know what else. I'd have to disinfect. The nanos dismantle most diseases, but there is a lot of gross stuff out there. For all I knew, I'd tracked in mutated syphilis.

Maybe he'd catch it.

This time, I couldn't quite keep the laugh between my teeth. It trickled out, a hysterical edge undercutting it.

Greg's features closed down. "That's it. You're on your last legs. Hang on, let me–"

"Detective." I raised my synthetic arm, relieved when it obeyed me, and very gently pushed his hand away from mine. His gaze fell again to the smooth, matte plates worked to mimic the shape of a human hand. It wasn't really grotesque, but it was obviously *not* flesh.

I watched his Adam's apple bob as he fought revulsion.

Yeah. Douchedick. "If you want to help, just call me a cab."

"If you wait, I can take you–"

"A cab," I snapped, and shoved the tangled mess of my hair from my face. "And make sure your genetic meatsuit over there destroys this report."

Greg fished a three-inch flexible screen from his back pocket. He studied it carefully as he punched in the order for my cab, giving him time to pull his shit together. "Yeah." He hummed it. "No."

Seriously, my brain wasn't working. It took me a full two seconds to process a two-letter word. "Wait." I frowned at him. "Seriously?"

The fan clicked overhead as the detective finished his order. Almost sixty seconds of nerve-rattling silence as I stared at his face, rapidly sifting through my options. What the shit was he doing?

But when he looked up, his eyes glinted – amusement, maybe. A bit of smug triumph. "I think I'll keep it." He tipped his head to the door. "Come on, I'll walk you out the back."

He left before I could manage to form up any protest, but waited outside to navigate me away from the main halls and into side corridors less populated. "Be serious," I told his back.

"I am." He stopped by a vending machine, slapped his badge against the sensor and dialed up a protein boost. "Here, for the ride." He pushed it into my meat hand. "Not as much juice as a recharge, but it should get you to wherever you call home."

Gratitude didn't mix well with severe amounts of *what the fuck*. "What are you doing, Greg?"

"Taking care of you," he replied flatly. But his mouth hiked up in the same smug line. "And maybe holding onto a bit of leverage."

"What leverage?" I scoffed. I dug a nail under the seal of the drink, but didn't pop it yet. My bare feet left black smudges in our wake – I hoped they'd make him clean it with his face. Assmunch. "You've got nothing."

"Then why do you care?"

Because he didn't actually have nothing and we both knew it. I gritted my teeth.

The report wouldn't just be Fagan's. It'd be a mix of this station's and the street meat that picked me up. It'd have a surface scan of my tech, thanks to the laws that allowed cops to carry the sensors corps outlawed across the city. It had more data on me – including my goddamn DNA – than any other piece of information I'd let fall into civic hands in recent memory.

DNA that was still in at least one database, if not two.

The assclown was hoping to blackmail me.

He opened the last door in the hall, and the sun streamed through in blinding fury. A wave of heat nearly knocked me off my feet. I staggered, shoulder colliding with the frame, but Greg didn't try to help – that meant he'd have to grab my synthetic arm. Not going to happen.

I paused, catching my breath and what was left of my energy. "What's it going to take to get that file from you?"

He squinted into the daylight. The sun caught in his eyes, turned them to cheaphack jade. "Don't know yet."

"Seriously?" I gripped the doorframe, hauled my ass fully upright and leveled the kind of look on him most wouldn't walk away from. "Don't fuck with me, Greg."

To his credit, he flinched, but he didn't run. Instead, he reached out, snagged the drink from me, and cracked the seal. "You look like hell," he replied. He passed it back, patting my flesh hand with sanctimonious care. "Talk to you soon, Riko."

There weren't enough curse words in the world. Not that I had the energy to spit them at him. Even the damn drink felt too heavy.

"Eat a dick, Greg," was what I managed, and hauled my ass out of the cop shop before something else went wrong.

He didn't try to wish me well. Probably best. I'd gone seven months without seeing him; I'd barely even thought of him. I took lovers the way I replicated clothing – I went for the mood, the fit, the color, the aesthetics. Whatever pleased me at the time.

Greg hadn't been any different.

But now things had changed. Of all the stations in the city, I got my stupid ass dragged into that one? And thanks to that, now he had info on me that I needed back – and destroyed.

For what?

A favor, probably. Or maybe he'd use it to try and get in my pants again, though that seemed pretty unlikely what with the purism and all. That helo had long since flown.

Favors. I hated owing a cop. They don't get cred the way runners get it. They understand the concept – everyone in the city runs on credits. People carry their data in their SIN and link it up to various modes of payment processing, each protected by six kinds of corporate sec encryption. But mercs run on more than just credits. We run on cred – reputation, the way people talk about us, how tough we are, how much backing.

Good cred earns good jobs, which earns good credits. Bad cred is like being the shitboy in a scatplay whorehouse.

And I'd been the stupid one who'd gotten herself rolled into coplandia. That'd be hell on both cred and credits, unless I fixed everything about the past twenty-four hours.

Where the hell to start?

So maybe I had some energy left after all. "Fucking fuck fuckity *fucking* fuck," I hissed as I slung myself into the back of a one-seater cab waiting by the curb.

"I'm sorry," replied a polite mechanized voice. "That is not an accepted destination. Please verbalize or input your destination."

"Fuck you, too," I growled, but punched in an address that wasn't mine.

The ride took ten minutes in heavy traffic. I downed the drink on the way.

It would have taken less time to walk, but I was only riding the thing out of sight of the station. If I'd had my usual gear,

I could have overridden the computer, faked out the meter, and ridden the whole thing home, but oh, no. Some jerkoff had disconnected my netware, made sure I couldn't hack into anything.

Greg had pre-fed the meter a credit account, so when he looked, he'd know I stiffed his offer. That was okay, too. I was so damned exhausted, I wasn't sure how I'd make it to my borrowed squat, but I'd freeze in Greg's Judeo-Christian hell before I led the police – or a certain smeghead detective – right to my front door.

I had no doubt I'd hear from him sooner or later anyway. Just add one more problem to a growing list of them.

When I staggered out of the cab, the stagnant heat did its damnedest to flatten me into a melted puddle on the pavement. That mechanized voice wished me a very nice day. I flipped it off as I took a step toward the sidewalk. In reply, it bombarded the space in front of my eyes with a barrage of blurred ads, including one reminding me to dial in for my next cab service.

I almost kissed the curb.

Augmented reality. The adspace exists in the bandwidth, which means anyone keyed in – love the SIN, love the security – doesn't get to strain out the noise. Most of these poor chums get used to walking around in a riot of color, motion, sound. Almost all of them have some array of apps to make it fucking bearable.

My chipset was tailored with a filter that did its best to keep up with the rotating bandwidth frequencies, but the junk was second-gen at best and needed at least one advertisement assault per district before it could key in. Given the mess I waded through now, I bet the assclowns in that lab I'd left behind had turned that off, too.

Scraping together every ounce of energy I had left, I tuned out the noise, ignored the ads around me, and began the long slog home.

Hot and tired as I was, those of us who survive in this city are the lucky ones. Although baked to a crusted scab already, anything outside the radiation shields has it a hell of a lot worse. That's what happens when the ozone burns off and the sun turns into a singleminded death ray intent on absolute conflagration.

Or, anyway, a slow, agonizing decline into melanoma-infested attrition.

Nanos can take care of the cancer agents, but only to a point. The sun and all the atmospheric gases killed off what couldn't take the heat, and so most of humanity gathered under shields like this one. There aren't many. Much of the continental midwest had gone down in a methane slag, bumping our climate future from *fucked real soon* to *apocafucked right fucking now.* Over time, the big cities on what was left of the coasts had merged into giant, verminous hives of people. Like locusts, only we didn't leave once we'd eaten everything in sight. We built on top of the bones and stuck around for shits and giggles.

More shit than giggle.

What the heat didn't suck out of me, this city would. The air reeked of oil-slicked pavement, burning fuel, garbage, and a vile blend of perfume, piss, and sweat. I wasn't standing in corporate territory, so there were no air scrubbers, no chemical washes to counteract the stench. The buildings towering on either side of the bumper-to-bumper street lacked polish, gloss or even a semblance of class.

Some districts are nothing more than tenements stacked like crooked dominoes, the roots sinking deep into the depths of a metropolis so big, even I didn't know all of it. Some of these neighborhoods are practically a city in themselves, with their own gangs and politics. There were heights I'd never been to and depths so dangerous you'd need a full squad and a shit ton of munitions just to cross them without casualties.

By night, this district would turn into a kaleidoscope of

neon, flashing screens, ad space and bait – jail bait, hooker bait, junkie bait, murder bait. The streets never empty. The daylight scavengers tag out with the nocturnal life and it's business as usual. Everything gets harder at night. Louder.

Friendlier, in a way that only those of us who live it understand, and rough as an ass-fuck with a rusted pipe. An acquired taste.

But that's city life. That's what happens when humans live on top of each other like rats on the bones of a stripped carcass. Everywhere I looked, people *existed*. Barely cognizant of anything more than whatever pathetic desire fueled their ambulatory shuffle, barely aware of the cesspit they forged through. Like a fucked-up clock with some seriously jacked-up gears, this city and its sinners ticked along. Waiting to live.

Waiting to die.

You get used to it.

I walked by early shift hookers working their wares in electric nylon, and a couple of haggling suits already sporting wood for a little relief they didn't have to use points on. I'd heard somewhere that you could always spot lawyers by the drugs in their pockets – ruined their sightlines. That little bit of wisdom had never steered me wrong; and always the hell away from lawyers. Scummy little bloodsuckers, even the quiet ones.

I passed a group of local toughs sprawled out front of a café that promised cold drinks, guaranteeing no toxic water or money back to surviving clientele. They'd stripped off most of their usual *I'm so badass* vinyl in deference to the heat, sporting enhanced muscles, chrome accessories that did jack-all but look cool, and throwback pompadours they thought made them seem dangerous. Chromers and their type can be found anywhere. They seem to attract each other, like douchewagons to a mirror. They're harmless, usually. Posers, usually too busy admiring themselves in their vid apps.

I walked by more hobos than I knew profanities for. I hate

career hobos. I knew for a fact at least forty-five percent of the beggars on this street lived better than I did.

Something about my demeanor must have warned them off from their usual hard sells. Probably the dried blood smeared all over my face. I was sporting two enormous black eyes over my swollen nose. Pretty rough shape.

I trudged over baking sidewalk that finally managed to thaw the ice in my bones, keeping my head down and my eyes open. Seeing through the augmented ads took practice, but like most of the signal to noise coming through the bandwidth, I'd learned to filter.

As I plodded through the sticky heat, I came up with a plan.

It wasn't a very calculated plan. It started with sleep, as much as I could handle. Then I'd try and get in touch with my team. I knew there were answers out there – this kind of shit didn't happen in a vacuum. Whether I had help or not, I'd start kicking down doors, looking for the answers *someone* out there had to have. I wasn't crazy. I hadn't gone off the deep end, and just because my nanos were committing suicide one by miniscule one, didn't mean I'd fried my brain.

I didn't hallucinate anything. I'd woken up in hell and watched my girlfriend go necro. I didn't know if I'd abandoned anyone else below, and the amount of information I *didn't* have was going to make explaining fucking impossible.

Would Indigo believe me?

Hell, I wouldn't. But I'm kind of a suspicious bitch.

As the sun beat down on my head and shoulders, warming my tech arm, I struggled to hold on to the details I'd seen in that lab. The whole thing felt like a nightmare, like something that happened in a dream after a bad night's colordust snorted off a hired asscrack.

As I walked, forcing one foot in front of the other, I made myself go over the things I'd learned. The things I'd seen. The digital file, the security forces, the variety of darkened rooms.

The sound of bullets pattering the shatterproof glass.

I forced myself to go over Nanji's last words, over and over until the echo of my seething rage overwhelmed the clamor of the pedestrian rats sweating all around me; incessant drones eager to get nowhere.

Honestly speaking, there were any number of ways I'd fucked this mess up, and my own systems were on that list.

I flashed back to all the signs of corruption I'd learned to look for. Irrational behavior was one, but I wasn't sure current events counted. The black tint to my eyes and blood had looked pretty bad, but since I'd downed the boost, my nanos had settled enough that I figured I'd eased back from nanoshock. This was a good sign – maybe. But I should still check it out.

My arm was working okay, give or take the stuff I needed to turn on, and I didn't exactly feel the need to squish anything for kicks. I wasn't sure how corruption was supposed to feel, but Lucky said it worked like a virus. A technological fever. I figured I'd know.

Small victory, but fuck it, I needed one. It gave me the leeway I needed to put off seeing my mentor. Explaining what I didn't have a handle on felt like an overwhelming task.

It took me forty-five minutes to drag my sorry ass all the way home. The place was a towering shack, squeezed in with a block of them, stacked like crates threatening to crack. It had been fenced in by the ramshackle offerings of tenement hoarders determined to protect what was theirs by any means necessary. Rusted iron, fragments of car frames jacked from who knows where, old bed frames, rotten couches. Probably the remains of trespassers.

I let myself in through the back entry, took the stairs until I was ready to give up and roll my aching body right back down them in desperate need of oblivion. The place was dank, dingy, rocked like a scream queen group and a chilldive technician were having some kind of soundwave orgy, but it was safe.

Enough. Safe enough.

You take what you can get.

I slammed open the door, muttered the passcode that let me bypass the temporary security I'd set up – a portable voicelock capsule stuck to the wall, rigged to drop toxic shells if my voice didn't register within four seconds of entry.

No bodies greeted my bleary survey, so I must be leaving an impression with the locals. The first two jackwagons who'd tried to break in, I'd tossed out front with the rest of the "treasures" the neighbors collected. Either they'd been nabbed by carnivorous dogs or regained enough mobility to get the hell out.

Kicking the door closed rearmed the security, and I made my way down the narrow hall, up the short set of creaking stairs, and into the single bedroom.

I didn't even bother to disinfect myself. A million credits weren't bribery enough to care. I collapsed face first onto my cot – liberated from said neighbors and liberally doused with sanitizer – and closed my eyes.

I'd have a lot to do when I woke up. I had to try to get a hold of the contacts in my roster I hoped would help, try to figure out the price I'd have to pay for it. Try to explain to Nanji's brother exactly what happened. Whether he did or didn't believe me, I'd need to find a team, steal a file from and generously pay back a certain nosy cop, get my tech system scrubbed and turned back on, put my girlfriend to rest – and for all that, it'd take a crowbar to peel me off this bed.

I'd do everything later. All I wanted, all I desperately needed, was uninterrupted sleep.

4

Like any piece of hardware, the body is a functional machine. Ages ago, scientists figured out that the brain was just a kind of fleshy processor shooting out electrical impulses to the rest of the system. From there, it was only matter of time before corporations turned theory to reality and started shilling.

Software upgrades came after the obvious hardware upgrades. A cheerleader cramming for her college exams could pop some intelligence enhancers while a single dad in the 'burbs – that is, any one of a dozen neighborhoods not currently featured on the crime feeds at any given time – could score a packet of no-sleep without too much trouble.

Then hardware transitioned from necessity to a competition. Need an edge? No problem, replace your hands, your legs, your heart. Medical innovation gave way to military, and from military to aesthetic.

It seemed an obvious step, moving from video calling to data jacking, and from data jacking to projected uploading. The signal wavered and the noise got louder, and that's the way the soulless consumerist spunkchuckers of the world like it.

And, hey, if the price to pay is an occasional, quietly eradicated rash of corruption among the middle-class sheep, well, the cost of doing business and all.

But projected uploading is also why I could take a call in a state of deep sleep, converse with someone else and remember it clearly. Even better, I didn't have to miss some seriously needed rest.

Although my meatspace body remained flattened out in my tiny cot, my brain responded to the haptic tap at the base of my skull. I was too damn tired to respond consciously, so the call protocols kicked in and I found my projected body in a white projected room. A plain table waited in the middle of it, the usual centerpiece of a baseline projection interface, and so did an endearingly boyish detective seated at it.

Less usual. Less expected.

Less welcome.

The place was stark. It looked more like a cleaned-up, colorless version of the police station interrogation room than a place to have a casual conversation, but that's the augmented reality business for you. You can pay to make your cyberspace a little more ritzy, include all kinds of little apps, but why bother? In about three seconds, all that empty space is flooded with ads.

Unless you pay for that, too.

The bright-eyed man at the table, with his hair cut and his three-day beard shaved, leaned forward in anticipation. "Riko, I'm glad–"

I held up my hand. "Wait a sec."

Greg's voice died off.

We didn't have to wait long. With two confirmed connections, color vomited across the server. Hot pink and green, red and blue, purples, oranges, screaming text and neon vids. Jarring on the best of days, and downright vertigo-inducing on a day like mine.

Wincing, I crossed the small space and slid into a seat. Like its matching table, it was plain. Cold, simple metal with no distinguishing features. The kind of thing easily projected. "I'm not going to ask how you got my freq." They'd scanned it off my chipset when I was at the station. I'd need to scrub the markers and reprogram my frequency sooner rather than later. "Talk fast. I am not in the mood for shit."

He had the grace to look sheepish, which his fresh-out-of-school persona telegraphed exceedingly well. The creases by his eyes, the lines I'd seen carved into his mouth at the station, were gone. His hair was a little bit brighter – not much, just enough – and his jaw a smidge harder.

The vain bastard. He'd cosmetically enhanced his uplink appeal.

"Sorry to bother you, but I couldn't let it go." His smile, when he turned it on me, carried the programming equivalent of boyish charm. As if an *aw, shucks, ma'am, t'weren't nothin'* could be distilled into visual magnetism.

My lips quirked. Not a smile.

Unlike him, I didn't enhance my persona. The only thing I made sure of was that I was dressed and clean – because let's face it, nobody likes meeting people with blood, sweat, or the haze of burned-off slank smeared all over them. I kept my persona up to date, which meant my bleached hair was long at the top and hanging down the left side of my face, shorn to a buzz at the sides. My roots came in dark brown, courtesy of the genetic fuckup my mother hadn't paid for. At least my eyes had come out hers – a dark hazel that went moss green or swampy brown depending on the light. Even my tattoos made it onto the projected copy.

And so did my synthetic arm. Which Greg was very studiously avoiding.

I leaned against the table, folding my arms on top of it, flesh over diamond steel. It pushed the shiny red tanktop my persona wore against my breasts, and *that* good old Greg noticed. I couldn't claim much by way of stacking, too much muscle to be top-heavy, but it hadn't stopped me yet. "Let me guess." I dropped my naturally contralto tones an octave or two. Practically a purr. "Courtesy call?"

Damn, but his face lit up. You'd think I'd offered him a handjob under the table.

"Something like that." He grinned, unabashedly flirtatious in a way that was part refreshing, and mostly funny.

Cops and SINless don't mingle. I wasn't the only saint to flirt with that line, but I'd never pictured good old Greg buying in. I wondered if he was having some work troubles, or maybe he wanted to flex some muscle without all the regs tying him down. It was obvious that I was something new and interesting, and the file he held over my head made him feel like he had more leverage than he'd ever get again.

Given our history, brief as it was, I had a sneaking suspicion that my new arm turned me into forbidden territory. A way to stick it to the Purist Man.

Maybe he wanted me to call on his God while he stuck it to *me* again.

Too bad. Once was fun, twice was a rental.

"Cute, but no." I shook my head, leaning back in my chair – away from him so obviously that he'd have to be stupid to miss the memo. "You're having a rough year, right? Miles of red tape, clocked in and out like a civic official but given none of the perks. Overtime at half the going rate?"

A faint wince around the eyes. "Salary, mostly."

Poor bastard. "Too good to take a kickback?"

His mouth tightened.

I bit back a sigh. Wasn't *my* fault he had principles. "So you want something from me. That's why you kept my file." I crossed my legs under the table. "Leverage, I get. But you better play these next few seconds smart, 'cause you won't get a second chance at this."

He frowned.

When he didn't immediately answer, I perched my chin in the palm of my metal hand and waited him out.

Did I glitch him? It was always a risk. The bandwidth held steady enough for short calls, but got crazy twitchy around high time. When the system clocked the average consciousness of over twenty-six billion users at any given moment, the bandwidth – already straining under the payload of thousands of feeds, hundreds of thousands of terabytes of data – suffered.

And that's just in this city alone.

Most sinners get a basic package for their upload needs, and it comes with shit stabilizers. You learn to ration this app for that, tweak that signal for this drag, but like everything else, those who pay more – to broadcast and to receive – get better signal.

I wasn't a paying customer, and Greg couldn't afford it. Not on a cop's credline. We coped. Or, like me, we cheated. Well, would have cheated if all my shit was working and I felt like risking enhancing the feed for this.

It wasn't, and I didn't. I was too tired for this. Too wired.

Finally, he breathed out a long sigh. It twitched twice and his avatar flickered, but the connection held. "Okay, fine, I knew you'd crash out. You were in pretty rough shape. I thought the best thing to do was wait a few hours and then initiate a call."

Because I'd be guaranteed to pick it up, assuming I survived the nano burnout. I pulled a face. "I don't have time to fuck around with you."

"You're sleeping," he pointed out.

Yeah, like I needed the reminder. He was right, of course. If I wasn't here, I'd still be sound asleep. No loss of time.

Just of patience.

My girlfriend had gone necro right in front of me, and I was stuck playing footsie with a cop. *Again.*

He winced when I didn't so much as blink at him. "I wanted to say sorry." He rubbed the back of his neck with a hand that wasn't as callused as the ones he'd used to open my protein boost.

Vain, vain, vain.

"And to tell you that Fagan's been assigned to desk duty, pending investigation." His mouth pursed, eyebrows drawing together. "I pulled his report, so you don't need to worry."

"You keeping it safe personally?"

"Yeah." His tone would have made me laugh, all confused cop and eager to please, but I didn't have it in me. Moron. He should have left it on the system.

Bone-deep tired scrapped for space beside resentment. "Apology accepted," I replied, slapping both hands on the table and standing.

He raised his hand. "Riko, wait, I–"

"No."

He looked taken aback. "You don't want to hear what I have to say?"

"Sue me." I ran my hand through my hair, but it wasn't quite same as if I would have done it in the real world. It felt different; smoother, finer. I knew it was hair beneath my fingers, managed to tuck it behind my ear so it wouldn't fall over an eye, but it wasn't quite right.

A body paid for perfection. Corporation credo. If I wanted better sensory data, I could fork over the creds. Not worth.

"But I–"

Ugh. "You're a government official, detective." I stressed the title. He scowled. "I'm a saint. I'm not interested in whatever you've got. Either throw me something you need, one-and-done, or dick out."

Since he didn't bat an eyelash at the street euphemism for SINless, I assumed he'd already heard it. Would have been surprised if not. A good detective kept his ear open. "I'm not asking you to marry me," he said, his jaw tightening.

That didn't even warrant a response. Very carefully, I scooted the chair under the table. You don't want to break things in a projected room. The maintenance systems get real spiky about it. "Leave a message at the Mecca when you need that favor."

His perfect hands clenched on the tabletop. His gaze dropped to them, that deliberate charm cracking some. "What if I said I'd give you the file in exchange for this?"

"Is it one thing?" I asked. "Or a string of them?"

He didn't have to answer. I read it in his face.

I would have smacked the back of his head – mostly to irritate him – but you can't do that in a projection room. Most basic servers, which I had, aren't designed to mimic reality. I could touch my hair and feel the strands because I knew without a doubt what my hair was. I had my whole life of knowing. I couldn't touch Greg because I didn't know if his hair was smooth today or laden with product, if his jacket was synthetic or real. If it was cold or warm, rough or soft. I didn't know what *he* thought of his jacket, or how he felt his own hair. Without smoother integration, I could overload the system and fry my communication receptors. Or his.

While the possibility of shorting *him* had some merit, the damage it'd do to my chipset could blow the whole thing. Not worth a little peace and quiet.

"I could help you," he insisted. "Listen, all I'm asking is to be a name on your roster."

Oh, for fuck's sake. He didn't even know what he was offering. Putting your name on a merc's roster is basically asking to get your shit shot up on a semi-regular basis. Sure, the cred – both the reputation and the monetary kind – might be good, but it's a one-way street to hell.

I pinched the bridge of my nose between my flesh fingers. "I don't have time for this, Greg."

"Not even for–"

"If you try to bribe me with that report again, I swear to your God I'll break your jaw in six places." My threat cut him off with so much flat denial that he closed his mouth, eyes narrowing. "Look, that thing is important, and you know that. But you and I both know this is a one-off deal. I do something for you, you give me the data. Because if you don't," I added, leaning down to flatten both hands on the plain table, "you know that your cred takes a hit where you can't afford it. And mine" – I flashed that hard little smile I knew bothered him – "goes up when I hunt your ass down for it."

Cops hover closer to sinner than saint. That doesn't make them immune to the concept of street cred. A badge without a certain amount of reputation finds his job boring as balls. A badge who hopes to wield his cred for kicks suddenly finds his ass the subject of everyone else's betting pools.

Maybe that was why he came here hoping I'd take him on. Maybe he was bored. Or in over his head with something else already and hoping to use *my* cred as his shield.

I'd rather suck on a bullet.

"Tell me why," he said.

I gave him half of what I figured. The irritating half. "Aside from the fact that you're pretty much textbook blue and I don't think you can lie for shit," I said flatly, "I don't need a toothless badge to babysit. I'm busy." Also, I was busy on the kind of thing that would make a man like Greg scream like a little kid, but I didn't want to tell him that. One, it sounded like I was protecting him. Which I sort of was, and I didn't care to explain it. Two, he'd ask questions.

He'd have to. He was still a cop. If I so much as hinted that I'd glimpsed a necro conversion, there'd be a serious problem.

His shoulders slumped.

My cue to go. I tried to feel bad for him, I really did, but I honestly could give a bag of dicks. I was racked out cold back in my squat, sleeping what I figured was the sleep of the dead, but even occupying myself with this projected call didn't erase every detail of Nanji's face. Of her corruption.

I should have... done something. Anything.

Not that I could. The only thing that kept me from corrupting on the heels of nanoshock was the recharge the cops had shoved in me.

She'd gotten bullets.

Greg felt laughably surreal, a weird cherry on a diarrhea day. I didn't know what he'd hoped to accomplish here. A shaky offer of contract work seemed like an unstable plan, even for the lure of that file – which he'd basically just taken the teeth out of by keeping it off the system. If he was personally hanging onto it, that meant a good linker could relieve him of it for less than the cost of a police system incursion.

But I was saving his ass. From me, as well as anything else being on my roster would set him up for. "When you need a favor – one," I added firmly, lifting one finger, "you leave a message with Shiva at the Mecca. I'll get it done. You give me the file and erase all copies and we're square. That's how this works."

"You are stone cold."

"Don't ever forget that," I shot back. The look I leveled at him wasn't sympathetic this time. "Don't fuck around anymore."

I headed for my exit without waiting for a reply. It was easy to spot, the only patch of white in a wall that looked like a collective of graffiti artists threw up on it. Pasha's Den of the Exotic – exactly the cheap contract sex service it sounded like – fought for territory with the Rat Café and every possible rendition of corporate propaganda you could ever want.

They used to put ads on the disconnection doors, but too many complaints of confused users getting stuck in projection earned them a lawsuit they couldn't buy off. Although most of us don't need to use the door to activate our protocols, a lot of older gen users prefer the comfort.

As for me, I just liked leaving on a, well, bang.

My hand was on the panel when Greg's voice cut the silence. "I have a kid, Riko."

I hesitated. I shouldn't have.

"She's three years old."

Fuck.

I turned. A three year-old kid confessed to a recent fling? Smooth. "Married?"

He nodded. "Yeah."

Surprise, surprise. Guess he'd had that sweet little wife all along. Only instead of waiting at home while her cop husband nabbed the bad guys, she waited while he fucked them. Heh.

"So?" I asked, raising my eyebrows.

Greg ran both hands through his hair, finally meeting my eyes from across the neon-spattered floor. "She wants a divorce."

How was this my problem?

I really couldn't handle complicated people. "That sucks."

He frowned at me. Obviously, that wasn't the response he'd wanted.

I snorted a laugh that caused him to draw back as if he'd been slapped. "What do you want me to say? Is it supposed to make me feel guilty that I was complicit in your extramarital affairs? It doesn't." Not even a little bit. Greg was an adult, he could handle his own decisions, and I'd handle mine. "You'll be fine," I assured him. "You're a cop. You probably know a good lawyer."

Something hard and desperate banked in his green eyes, something that could have been anger, but looked more like envy to my tired brain. It twisted his upgraded mask into something ugly, undoing all that cred he put into the work. "I need better income."

"So?" I asked again.

"So I can't get a second job, Riko. A cop doesn't get to put his badge away for another shift."

Ah. *Now* it made sense. It wasn't about me; it was about the income contracting out to a merc could give him. I was probably the only runner he was on good terms with. Damn it. "No," I said again. "Hell, no."

"I love her, you know."

Maybe. Maybe his grasp on that subject sucked, too. "I'm glad," I said evenly. "What's her name?"

"Sandra."

I didn't notice anything different on his face. Hearts didn't sprout up around his head, hosannas didn't play behind his voice. No sparkles. Nothing that could tell me if he loved this woman or was spinning me some kind of song.

Honestly, I didn't care. "Then patch it up with Sandra," I told him. "Work out your financial issues together and leave me out of it."

"You're the only one I've ever cheated on her with, Riko. Doesn't that mean something?"

My fingers cracked against the panel.

"Yes," I answered, very slowly. As if I was talking to a child. "It means that you're a purist *and* an asshole." Not always mutually inclusive. "And that I liked you better before. Actually, scratch that." I gave up on the door entirely. "I liked you better when we weren't talking. Chunk off, Detective Keith."

"Riko, wait—"

Triple *hell no*, with a dash of *eat a dick* for flavor. I gave up the drama of the door and dropped the projection.

I slept for almost thirteen hours, and I was still nursing a grudge when I woke up.

Groggy as hell, I forced my eyes open around a seam of scum and grit. As soon as light touched my optics, the numbers in my arm's informational display faded into view. Green, simple, brutalized into the minimalist programming I preferred. Back to normal.

Groaning, I rolled over and shrugged my left shoulder, testing gingerly for hurt. Fortunately for me, today my meatsack brain didn't feel like being a dick. Awesome. I wasn't in the mood.

Normally, I'd check the shit that mattered. Palm up my readout – which was tied in with my disconnected netware, so fuck *them*, very much – and check messages. I couldn't engage that display until I had Lucky recalibrate my chipset and turn my netware back on. All I had going for me was the structural data coming from my arm's feed and basic chipset functions.

Not helpful, unless I was desperate to know exactly what my rescued mattress was made of.

I'd catch up on whatever I'd missed the past few days later. Right now, I had a mission. One that didn't involve worrying about the time or the weather. I could guess both: time for a drink, and hot as hell.

I rolled off the cot, feeling a thousand times better and still about thirty percent into *fucked*. Dragging myself to the small shower, I shed my filthy clothes and dropped them a pile. I'd shred them later.

I wasn't disorganized by nature, but I wasn't a neat freak, either. I just didn't own all that much stuff. Especially now that my everyday arsenal had gone the way of the memories prior to waking up in that hellhole.

I missed my guns.

I took a shower in the crappy standup, which took longer than I liked my showers to be. Given the chance of water poisoning at any given part of the city on any given day, the safest disinfectant comes in the form of highly regulated and intense bursts of ionized radiation. People who make a decent living tend to have a nice radiation unit with speed settings. People who make enough to floss their asscracks with credsticks usually boast several units and a supply line into a private water purification process.

In this rundown shack, the radiation wasn't so much a *burst* as a queef.

I stood there for ten minutes, naked and sweating, as the radiation took care of anything I'd picked up in the lab or on my adventurous trek through the city. I could have simply sprayed myself down with a can of sanitizer, but I liked radiation better. It's always thorough, dry, and doesn't leave you smelling like you'd rolled in alcohol and deodorant.

Shocking what a civilization with cancer-ending nanos and a complete lack of moral ethics could come up with.

My shower was slow, true, but at least the place had one. The city took radiation sanitation seriously. It kept some of the nastier infections from spreading among the cramped populace.

The downside to standing here was all the time it gave me to fume over Greg's miserable failure of a reach-out. Married, cheated on her, and trying to hit me up for payday over it.

I mean, even if we got on like slankers and whores, he was police, not corporate. The boys in blue rank lower, pull shit duty, and have about as much security clearance as I did. Less, really. I knew people who could skate along clearance lines for the right price. Police get a gob full of red tape for the trouble.

Besides, helping me would probably cost him his job. I'd deny it if anyone called me soft, but now that I knew he had that little kid of his to feed, I was even less inclined to bring him on. He smelled like bait, and my line of work wasn't easy credit.

Even if we spent it like it was.

I pulled my clothes on – the second of three sets I stashed, and none worth more than the time it took to dial them up from a cheap printer. Replacing the nanosteel jewelry I'd lost was just as easy. I'd get better shit later.

The light rod hanging from the ceiling painted the room in soft gold, providing me enough illumination to get dressed by. It turned on automatically at night, then spent the day recharging from the ambient daylight. Good tool. I always made it a habit to have one in any place I squatted in.

I opted for universal black pants, built a lot like the BDUs I'd stolen but better fitting. They bagged around my legs, loose enough to let me run without cinching, riddled with cargo pockets, and hung low enough on my hipbones that the light tattoo on my lower back was easy to see. Given my intended location, I would have gone for a sexier vibe, but I didn't want to waste my red vinyl. Just in case tonight's plan went cock-side-up and blood flew.

An electric yellow wraparound halter bared my arms, which meant nothing to get in my way. Dancing. Fighting. Breaking limbs. I was multipurpose like that. It folded around my nape, wrapped around my ribs. The front tapered to a point over my waistband, covering my navel and baring my back. If it got shredded, I'd call it street chic and wear it anyway.

The design showed off my ink. Since my genes had never been pure enough for my uptight mother anyway, I'd taken my authority issues a step further and burned the genetically formulated white right out of myself using as many colors as I could get away with. My right arm and shoulder sported an esoteric map that started with a retro Dia de los Muertos skull and graduated to toxic flowers and abstract designs. I'd had all the bare spots between shaded, outlined, textured by whatever the street artists had wanted to draw.

More vivid color stained my left ribs, my hip, all the way down my left thigh. My left shoulder had once been home to a lotus that matched Nanji's and Indigo's – most of us on the regular team sported at least one – but that had gone up in smoke with the rest of my arm.

A thought turned the vid-ink up to a thin gleam. Luminescent lights dotted the designs in complex patterns.

The pants could conceal more than a handful of weapons, but tonight, I only slid a single knife into my thick-soled, matte silver boots. The sheath fit right into the cuff, ideal for just this occasion. If I was lucky, I wouldn't need it.

I didn't put a whole lot of stock in luck, which explained the serrated interceptor blade. I was going in as close to naked as I could get while clothed. I didn't like the feeling. My instincts screamed that I needed more – more weapons, more heat, more fury.

I didn't know what was going on, but somebody was going to die for it. Brutally. Since I couldn't achieve that without Indigo and the team, I had no choice but to check my shit and focus on the next step.

Nanji deserved better. Across the board, she deserved better. I'd make sure the jackhole behind it all knew her name when he died. Preferably with my fist in his chest.

I ran my hands through my hair, wrinkled my nose at the state of my borrowed crash pad. A layer of grime had settled over everything, like a dust storm had wandered by and I'd left the windows cracked. Totally not healthy. Was it this bad last I checked?

When was the last time I even cleaned?

At least now I could tell myself that dead girls didn't have to clean.

Ah, *shit*. That reminded me, far too late. I should have brought that damned tablet out with me. Aside from the obvious problem – you know, that part where I wasn't actually dead – it could have served as proof when I hit people up for answers.

Then again, if I'd done that, Fagan would have gotten his fat fingers on it. I doubt he would have recognized the value of the information.

Chunking cops.

By reflex, I grabbed for my harness out of habit and remembered that it wasn't hanging on the edge of the window sill anymore. Fuck. It killed me that I'd lost my gear to that shithole I'd woken up in. I loved that harness. It was designed to carry almost any weapon I needed through its ingeniously constructed straps, and I'd broken it in perfectly over the past four years. It, along with all the weapons I'd been carrying when I vanished into that lab, would be mourned.

Assholes. That would cost them, too. Just as soon as I got the help I needed.

Some SINless runners work alone, banding into teams only when a job requires it, staying together long enough to get the job done and get paid. The problem with that life is the longevity. A good take split four ways suddenly becomes better split three, even better two, and best for one.

If you want a long – well, *longer* – life in this business, you find a group of people you trust and you make them trust you. You run together, take on jobs everybody understands, and split the take fairly. I'd found that in Nanjali and Indigo Koupra.

One old man may have taken my cocky swagger and turned it into a lethal machine – no pun intended, since the same old man had outfitted my arm – but Nanji and Digo had made sure I survived the effort. We watched each others' backs. Got in, got out, got paid. We'd gotten good at it, built up a hell of a team. Cred came fast and easy. Well, easier than going alone, anyway.

Indigo had always been the brains of the operation. He was a dervish with a computer and knew more people than I'd met in my whole life – a qualified linker no matter what side of the divide. You know that person who always seemed to have a guy? A clothes guy, a getaway guy, a tickets guy.

Digo was that person. He had a guy for damn near everything.

Unlike the rest of us, he'd always kept an eye on the team's bottom line. Nanji'd gone with gut, which explained why we'd bonded, but numbers were Digo's love affair. Numbers and information, and Nanjali.

We didn't always gel about the latter.

If anybody knew what was going on, what happened to me and Nanji and how to get to her, it would be Digo. And I knew the club to locate him. Calling him would have been easier, but at the same time, I didn't trust him not to fry my chipset with a temper tantrum – not that it wouldn't be well within his rights to do it.

If it were me, I'd do worse. Even knowing what I knew. Facing Digo in meatspace meant I had a shot at kicking his ass if he came at me.

I seriously hoped he'd hear me out first.

I didn't bother with makeup. My eyebrows were as brown as my roots, my lashes dark enough that compared to my bleached platinum hair, it looked like I made an effort. Besides, makeup smears, unless you have the program to keep it in check, and I didn't. Surprise. More tech I didn't have.

I took a quick glance at myself in the cracked bathroom mirror, turned to make sure the neon pink arrow at the base of my spine shone brightly, and nodded to my reflection. The nanos, fueled by the protein boost I'd inhaled earlier and some much-needed sleep, had finally repaired the damage to my face. The blood was cleaned, swelling vanished, headache gone, and my nose looked no worse for wear.

I was obviously a thug. There was no hiding it. I'd never make a best-dressed list and I wasn't anyone's idea of arm candy, but I looked fierce, lethal, and wired to blow.

I had this. As much as it was going to suck to look Indigo in the eye and tell him I'd watched his sister die, I was pretty sure he'd be all for finding out *why*.

The why would lead to the rest of the whys rattling around in my head – why we'd been down there, why I couldn't remember anything.

That data was worth killing for. Hopefully Digo would see the value in that. It was all I had to give.

I hoped it was enough.

5

The Mecca had a distinctly fetishized Eastern Indian vibe to it, which explained why the Koupras had adopted the place as our unofficial turf. It took up residence in the rack – the district midway between corp gloss and street shine, filled with a metric asston of other clubs. Just one in a long list of too loud, too bright, too full, low-cost, merc-friendly joints. A lotus flower outlined in startlingly bright neon was its only sign, and the clientele usually came out of SINless ranks.

We tend to blow creds like we have the stuff to swallow.

The Mecca was a dance floor, a fully stocked bar, an *over*stocked drug cartel, a brothel, a meeting place, and job forum. It was run by a woman who called herself Shiva – like some old god – and there was a lot of rumor about her original state of being.

Transwoman, fashion savvy man in drag, ass-kicking cis female, it didn't matter to me. I didn't ask. She was gorgeous, soft-spoken to anyone who wasn't *really* listening; mostly Kongtown with some bottom-shelf mix of ethnic markers too muddled to place at a glance. And she had a single rule: unless creds changed accounts *first*, nobody fucked with what was hers.

The woman's dick was bigger than mine in the only ways I cared about – she owned the turf, and had saved our asses more times and in more ways than I cared to admit. For a fee, naturally.

Otherwise, the Mecca was a haven for those of us without a Security Identification Number and the go-to for some of the best highs this side of the Fourteenth Divide.

As I pushed inside the foyer doors, neon popped and flared across the darkened entry. Music slammed into me like a velvet fist, a savage beat that thrust into my chest and twisted. The sticky, cloying heat of the city turned into the slick, hungry swell of writhing bodies, slamming everything they had – flesh and bone, need and naked rage – on the dance floor.

The bouncer inside gave me a cursory once-over, but didn't bother with a full scan. That was Shiva's policy. Anything that damaged her business, she pulled out of skin and favors. It's our own risk to take.

I grinned at the beefy black man perched on a stool that looked ready to splinter underneath his bulk. Unlike Fagan, Jad was all muscle, all the time, and didn't mind flexing it when he needed to. I wouldn't say he was all natural, but he didn't showcase any metal and I'd seen him deadlifting three times his own body weight. That left any number of enhancements that wouldn't ping anything short of a gene-sniffer.

"Hey, baby," he greeted, his slow, sultry bass booming over the music's beat. "Long time no see. Thought you'd gone and left me for good."

I grinned, waving that away like the worthless air it was. The streaks of light accenting my ink left thin trails in the dark. "Hasn't been that long."

A large, thickly groomed eyebrow climbed up his pronounced brow, almost lost but for the neon barrage around us. "You finally here to give me a piece of that action?"

He wasn't talking about *me*. While I was pretty sure Jad liked women fine, I only knew of one thing that made his palms sweat and his eyes light like the inside of a nuclear reactor.

Munitions.

Specifically, my Mantis Industries Valiant 14, one of only fifty ever manufactured and a gift from the man who'd saved my life when I was young and stupid and a cocky little shit. Where Lucky had gotten it, he'd never said.

Although Mantis's reputation wasn't built on arms, the Valiant 14 was a joint experiment between it and rival company TaberTek. It outclassed, outperformed, outravaged everything else on the market, but to hear Jad tell it, true love was never meant to be. Before the Valiant could hit mass production, the corporate world rumbled, the big money maw split wide, and TaberTek crumbled like so much dust.

I didn't have the heart to tell him that my favorite firearm was missing. Thinking about the attached heat baffle specially built for deadly 12mm rounds and included laser sight would only make me tear up. Like my harness, I'd make them pay for its loss.

My smile faded to a grimace. "Man, you are hard on a girl's ego."

He laughed, his even white teeth brilliantly stark against his dark as a sinner's wet dream skin. "Like you need me on that ass, fine as it is." He said it the way men breathed; like he didn't even think about it. Jad was a sweetheart.

I'd also seen him tear a merc's head off with his bare hands. So there was that.

"No Valiant, then. You carrying tonight?"

I shook my head, and when he raised his eyebrows, added, "An interceptor in my boot."

"Not your usual."

"Aw, Jad." I blew him a kiss. "You worried about little old me?"

He rolled his broad shoulders. "Yeah, yeah. Go on, girl." He jerked a thick, square thumb to the beaded curtain behind him. "Digo's in there somewhere, been here hours already."

Exactly what I wanted to know.

A knot formed in my guts. I bumped my knuckles against Jad's and pushed through the swinging curtain. It clattered, the sound all but lost under the frenetic pace of the trancelike beat.

Whatever else I'd missed, the Mecca wasn't hurting for love. The floor was packed, a writhing, rhythmic sea of skin and neon and metal; just as I remembered it last. Sweat gleamed where the lights skimmed over the crowd, eyes and light tattoos and bits of tech left hanging out reflecting it back in a myriad of colors. The smell – spicy, sweaty, thick with a thousand different base notes and a top shade of lust – slammed into me.

Something kicked in my chest. As if that velvet fist uncurled, it thumped back against the cage of my ribs and begged to be let free.

All that skin. All those naked limbs.

All that hunger.

I flattened my bare hand against my breastbone, teeth clenched as I staggered for a nearby pillar.

The place was full of them, heavy decorative columns twined with reflective fabric designed to catch the light and bend it into diamond glints. I leaned against the support, resting my head back, my throat bared as I swallowed a jagged knot of something lodged there.

What the hell? Maybe my nanos hadn't entirely recharged yet. An emergency recharge and one protein shake wouldn't cut it.

It took me a few, but as soon as I could breathe without feeling like I was going to choke on something, I flagged down a serving girl – a pretty redhead with wide hips and a cute rack. Shiva was obviously on another sari kick. This girl wore enough fake silk to smother a mummy, most of it trailing from the swatches covering her breasts and crotch, and her light tattoos mimicked electric green mehndi designs. She looked like something straight out of a pervy Indian fantasy.

Pretty much what people like me paid for.

She flashed me a smile, cute as hell. "What can I get you?"

"A recharge," I shouted over the beat, "and Indigo."

"The drink or the man?"

I'd forgotten the bartenders had named a cocktail after him. Sharp on the tongue, hard on the wallet, and mana on the brain cells. My mouth twisted into a wry grin. "The man."

She pointed past the dance floor, where one of seven ornate arches carved into the fake stone façade, and vanished back into the crowd. Lapis lazuli and mother-of-pearl – or what was supposed to look like it – glinted over the arch, while sheer fabric hung underneath in a semblance of privacy.

Not the usual room. We may have been among Shiva's favorites, but some clients paid more.

I didn't trust my energy reserves on the dance floor yet, so I circled it. The lights flashed and popped, strobed counter to the frenzied beat turning the dark feverish. If I were feeling better, if I had less important things to figure out, I would have been in the middle of all that.

I love dancing. The more aggressive, the better. Thrashing isn't a hobby for the faint of heart, and tonight's crowd wasn't in a drawing blood sort of mood, but the barely contained aggression leaking from the sultry backbeat wouldn't be denied for long. As I passed a couple of girls, one popped a fluorescent purple square into her mouth, licking it off her finger with relish.

Mood enhancers, or maybe uninhibitors. Something to take the anxieties of the day and turn them into something sweeter, usually with a side-effect of temporary loss of all common sense. Memories, too, if you're unlucky.

Good times.

I passed them both, took the opportunity to flash her friend a smile – a willowy girl whose love affair with a razor had turned her hair into a blocky fall of rainbow colors. She grinned back, one stranger to another in the dark, and licked her thumb.

Yeah. I liked the Mecca.

Feeling inordinately better, I sidled around a knot of half-naked guys. One sported a synthetic brace over his forearm, a bridge model. It glowed like a galaxy of neon stars. Another turned his head, showcasing a chrome curve drilled into his brow bone. It framed the plucked arch of an eyebrow.

Fashion slaves. Slumming it, probably. The Mecca was too far down the rack to be any rich kids' first stop.

I didn't see Tashi until she was on me. She was almost seven inches shorter than I was, but it wasn't her build that allowed her to ghost through most places like a cat. Something about the way she walked, the way she bled through a crowd, usually meant she didn't register on somebody's radar until too late.

My smile brightened. "Hey–" I also didn't see the interceptor, serrated twin to my own, until it flashed inches from my throat. "Fuck!" I slammed my stiffened palm against the hilt, smashing her fingers against it and spinning out from her reach at the same time. "What the shit, Tash?" The music drowned me out.

The lights skated over her head, flickering over the white tattoos etched into her hairless brown scalp. Her eyes were flat and dark, the titanium bar framing the underside of her lower lip winking as she set her jaw. The knife switched hands, nearly faster than I could track.

I had height and ordinarily would have claimed reach, but she had a way of moving that made professional dancers look like kids at their first party. Eerily fast, with superior agility boosters and a skinweave designed for flexibility and durability, she was wicked fast with knives and murder on the thrash floor.

A hell of a dance partner. Just *hell* as an opponent.

I bent my knees into a nervous crouch, sweaty hand splayed at my side as I watched her eyes. Not the knife. That hypnotic blur would land me dead. "What the fuck are you doing?"

She'd never been much of a talker.

Like a serpent, she struck out with the knife in her left hand. I caught her arm between mine and my right side, felt my wraparound tear, and wrenched hard. Her shoulder popped upwards, bones sharply defined. I didn't hear it, but I knew the sensation of a dislocated shoulder.

She didn't make a noise, even as lines of pain bracketed her mouth. Unnerving woman. Always had been.

I cracked her in the face with my metal fist – bone crunched. I winced in remembered sympathy. As the patrons moved around us, I stuck my foot behind her ankles and pushed hard. Caught between my foot and my grip on her arm, she hit the ground on her back, blood gleaming like synth rubies in the streaming lights, and didn't move.

Shit. I checked her pulse.

Okay, so I'd only knocked her out. That was good. I did not want to open this subject with Tashi's death. Not when I was already reporting another.

I stepped over her, leaving her to sleep it off away from the dance floor. My teeth clenched so hard, I heard them grit over the brainmelting throb of the Mecca's music. Running a hand over my side confirmed my suspicion. Sure enough, my shirt was torn. I stuck my finger in the hole she'd carved in the wrapped end, measuring by feel how close she'd come to skewering my ribs.

Too close. And for what?

I pushed through the dancers this time, making a straight line for the lapis arch.

Moving through a floor of writhing, gyrating, usually drugged-out dancers is an art form. It requires grace, a certain understanding of the ebb and flow, and fast reflexes. I was good at it, I'd spent a lot of time out here. Earn enough bruises and you wouldn't even feel the occasional elbow in your ribs or knee in your thigh.

A hand slid over my naked back, another caught my arm. I disengaged easily, didn't smile back when a man with shock-blue hair hanging over one eye tried to catch my attention. Didn't even notice when an electric orange boot lodged between mine.

I went down like an amateur.

Eye level on the Mecca dance floor is intimidating enough, but hitting the ground is the fastest ticket to getting your teeth kicked out. Many was the bruised and battered body the staff had carried out at the end of a rowdy night. Some were even alive.

This wasn't the rowdiest crowd I'd ever seen, but down on the floor, trapped beneath a seething mob of sweat and adrenaline, it was unintentional war.

I rolled immediately, collided into more legs than strictly should occupy one space, and struggled to my knees. The ground was gummy – spilled drinks and worse. It crackled, a sticky film clinging to my skin as I pushed myself into a semblance of balance. Elbows slammed into my head, more than one dancer stepped on my calf, kicked my legs and knees by sheer accident or lack of attention. I felt something in my ankle give, hissed and shot my metal elbow back.

The weight on my leg lifted.

An orange blur in my peripheral warned me a nanosecond before the sweaty, careless dancers disgorged a combatant. I dropped, felt the air shift over my head, rolled again. A heavy boot slammed into the ground where my head had been, this one wider, more square than fleshbag feet ever got.

Goddammit. Boone and his wide foundation replacement feet.

Which meant the orange belonged to Fidelity.

Fuck, fuck, *fuck*. Why was my chunking team trying to wreck my junk tonight?

"Lay off!" I shouted, already knowing it was useless. They couldn't hear me over the chaos, and the music didn't care. I tried to get to my feet, but something sharp and mercifully organic slammed into my temple, knocking me for six as a thick hand twisted in my hair. Boone rang my bell with a dense fist, popping my ear and turning my vision inside out.

Vertigo kicked in, my lip curled into a snarl, and I turned into the weight of his grip. Curving both arms, I shoved my fists hard into Boone's solar plexus. I heard his groan, felt the impact turn his body into a curved snap of pain, and the fingers in my hair loosened.

I ripped free, ducked on instinct. Just in time to watch an orange leg sail over my head and collide with Boone's already hurting chest.

The look on Fidelity's sharp-featured face was priceless. Idiot. I'd taught him that move.

Boone toppled into the crowd; short screams punctuated the crash. He was a large man, heavier than his frame suggested thanks to the tech that turned him into a human battering ram. The fact he hadn't corrupted was one of those things nobody could figure out, but there it was.

I stepped into a lunge, seized Fidelity's planted ankle with my tech hand, and yanked. My lateral display told me he was wearing full vinyl again – his favorite fashion go-to.

He hit the ground, swallowed by the aggressive crowd before the shock cleared from his reddened face.

That was three.

Sweat drenched me, anger turned my adrenaline high into a murderous beat. I shoved through the horde, caught someone's flailing elbow in my metal grip and twisted. She spun around, stumbled into the arms of a knot of dancers. Swearing, laughing; limbs flailed behind me.

By the time I made it across the pit, I was snarling with the effort.

Valentine waited outside the arch, his muscled arms folded

over his bare chest like some kind of mythical genie. He fit right into Shiva's theme tonight. His hair was ice white and cut short; a black goatee framed his mouth. His bronzed skin was completely free of scars or tattoos.

That was four. Just fucking great.

Unlike the others, Valentine had been around the block longer then I had. He was handsome as sin because he'd paid good cred to be that way, but no amount of retooling would undo years of hard slaughter work. Something about him – his poise or the set of his jaw, something in the eyes – betrayed him for the killer he was.

Valentine was a munitions specialist, all about weapons where Boone was about survivability in the frontlines, but the lack of weaponry on him now didn't make me feel better. No shirt, the sculpted beauty of his chest open to all comers, and black pants similar to mine completed the effect. All he needed were some gold bracers and an earring, and he'd be somebody else's wet dream.

Me, I wasn't biting. He was as lethal with his bare fists as Tashi with her blades, and four times as experienced.

Valentine and I had never gone round for round, respecting each other from a safe distance. I found him too artificially perfect to appeal to my libido and too dangerous to mess with otherwise, and I don't know what he thought of me.

He watched me as I forged a path through the club, a muscle ticking in his left pectoral as if he was flexing one hand, over and over.

I didn't bother with niceties. By the time he realized my intent, it was too late. Too close to give him any more time to prep and too far to grab, I lunged into a sprint, lowered my head, and rammed my shoulder so hard into his ribs I felt something pop. Him, me, I didn't know. Adrenaline turned it all into fuel.

Valentine tried to grab for me, but he'd never seen me go for brute force – it wasn't my usual standby against immovable objects like him. With my arms wrapped around his trunk, he staggered, my weight bearing him backwards. I howled with the effort, pain working its way into my collar bone, down my flesh arm, as we fell into the curtains, tore them off the rod, and collided into Indigo's table.

Glass rattled. Shattered. A man cursed.

My fleshy surfboard rode the wave of impact for me, but damn, it still hurt. Fabric slithered off the table, skimmed over my back, Val's side, and coiled gently on the floor.

He groaned beneath my metal palm as I planted it on his face, using it to prop my aching body up.

"What," I snarled, jerking my pale hair from my eyes, "the *fuck*, Digo."

My answer was the unmistakable pump of a Sauger Quad 54 primed for firing. I looked down the barrel of a blocky, dinged-up shotgun and couldn't help myself.

I laughed.

6

Indigo Koupra looked enough like his sister that seeing him tore open the bloody wound of guilt I'd been trying not to suck on since I woke up in that station. Like hers, his skin was olive, his hair mostly black where he hadn't streaked it dark blue, and he kept it long in a thick braid. He had more edges than Nanji did, taller and more defined. His eyes were lined with the same thick black ridge of envy-inducing lashes, but his gaze gleamed a much darker blue.

He also had a tendency to look at me like I'd grown a second head, unlike his sister.

Fidelity once asked why I'd chosen Nanji over Indigo's exotic, masculine appeal. It came down to three things: she already had a crush on me, they weren't into sharing, and he liked to think I was crazy.

Well, and fourth point, I had a weakness for curvy ladies. Nanji wasn't into rigidly defined athleticism.

Not for herself, anyway. She was hella into me.

Indigo stared at me now, his full lips twisted into a grimace torn between anger and wary disbelief. "You are one crazy bitch, you know that?"

Beneath me, Valentine hadn't moved, his eyes closed. I knew he was alive, I could feel his heartbeat beneath my forearm, but he'd recognized the sound of the shotgun and knew as well as I did what it meant.

There was nothing precise about that spray.

My laughter dried up. "I'm going to get up," I told Digo. "We're going to chat. While we do, Val is going to go buy drinks for the others."

"Stay right there."

"Come on, boss," Valentine grunted beneath me. "Her knee's in my gonads."

"You shut up," I said mildly. "You don't get a vote."

Indigo stared at me a moment longer. I don't know what he read in my face – I was going for stone cold – but he jerked his chin in a nod. "Slowly."

My weight shifted, knee easing the pressure off Val's junk. His breath worked out on a sterling note of relief. His hands closed on my hips – warm, callused and rough – and he practically benchpressed me onto my feet.

Okay. Inappropriately timed as that pulse in my snatch was, I could appreciate a strong man with a sure grip.

Never mind that I had too many other issues topping off my plate. I didn't need to add this one. Besides, in my experience, the strong ones usually ran too extreme: too scared to let a woman call the shots, or one-trick dicks full of their own vanity.

Too much work. I'd appreciate from a healthy distance.

He set me down, fingers squeezing my hips once, and let me go. Pain radiated up my ankle, but not as much as I'd expected. The nanos were already working on my minor injuries. I'd need the damn energy recharge I ordered, but at least they were working.

Val didn't stick around. Giving me a nod – a glint of humor in his otherwise steady hazel eyes – he got the hell out of the way.

That left me and Indigo, staring at each other over a shotgun and the ruins of a whole lot of drinks.

The team must have all been here, having a good time,

drinking, when somebody called in word I'd arrived. Who? The redhead?

No reason; I didn't know her.

But everyone here knew *me*. I was a regular, like Indigo and our team. Any one of them could have sent word. My fingers tightened into fists.

"What are you going to do now?" I asked, eying the shotgun. "You only get one shot, and that piece of shit's too front-heavy to aim."

"You're like a foot away," Digo retorted. "I don't have to aim."

Good point. I lashed out an arm, popped him in the throat with my extended fingers. The shotgun jerked, he staggered back against the table. Glass rattled, bottles tipped.

But he didn't shoot me.

His eyes widened – fear, maybe, surprise for sure. I snagged the gun from his loosened grip, flipped it around and jammed it so hard against his chest, I knew it'd bruise before his nanos could hit it. He hacked and choked, one hand at his neck, the other braced against the table behind him.

"Let's try this again," I said, tight and barely level between clenched teeth. The metal was smooth, cold, faintly damp from Indigo's sweat. "What the shit, man?"

"Nice," he croaked.

"You started this."

His gaze flicked to my right. As sweetly telegraphed as it was, I didn't expect a cold metal barrel to press into my skull over my ear.

"Please do not make me charge for cleanup."

Shiva's dulcet tones were already in a throaty range guaranteed to muddle anyone's sense of gender identification. On a threat, her voice turned to pure velvet.

Smug triumph replaced Indigo's fear. For that reason alone, I wanted to shoot him. It bit deeply, raked diamond steel talons into my brain and *squeezed*.

I wanted blood. I wanted his eyes, shocked and wide, I wanted blood on his teeth and a lung on the floor.

All I had to do was squeeze this little bit of metal.

I could feel the trigger move, even hear the faint give.

The gun nocked against my skull dug in. "Riko, darling, you know how much I enjoy you..." The mild words faded. The meaning did not.

She would shoot me, and Indigo, and anyone else who messed with her business. She'd never even lose a wink of sleep.

Not one of my finer moments. I was a merc, sure, but I wasn't into murder for kicks. Regardless of how pissed I was right now, this wasn't helping anything.

I choked it all back. Hauled my anger, vicious and hurting, back into a dark metal closet and slammed the door. There'd be time for that later. There'd have to be, or else the vicious rage would eat me alive, but not right now.

With a theatrical sigh, I pulled the gun out of Indigo's ribs. He fell back into the curved booth, rubbed the spot. "Get her out of here," he snarled.

The metal at my head eased away. A long-fingered hand with shimmering golden nail polish reached around me to relieve me of the shotgun.

I let Shiva have it. Better her than Indigo.

"No," she said, patting me on the shoulder. "You kids have things to work out. I will send refreshment, on the house." In the corner of my vision, I saw long purple hair, golden silk with more fabric than she allowed her girls to wear. I couldn't see her expression, but her voice frosted. "Don't ever again, Koupra."

I don't think she meant about the guns. It only confirmed what I suspected – one of Shiva's had sold me out, pitting their loyalty to Shiva against helping out a Koupra.

Dumb. Fucking. Tool.

Indigo paled, hands clenching on the table's surface.

I helped myself to a seat as Shiva departed in a swish of fabric. Staff was already fixing the curtains, which would give us some privacy, but I didn't wait for them to clear off. I pushed aside a sea of half-empty glasses. "You want me to ask you again?" was my opening gambit, and his jaw tightened.

"You have a fuckton of nerve, coming back here."

"Where else am I supposed to go?" Rotating my right shoulder sent sparklers of pain through it. "Fuck. At least tell me why Tash tried to fillet me." I mean, I knew why I would have tried in her place – but I didn't think *he* knew what I knew.

If he did, I'd have a whole new barrage of questions to ask.

He usually sulked like a kid. I was used to his temper, but the black rage underscoring his champion glower caught me by surprise.

Anger didn't do it justice. It was rage and hurt and grief and something hot enough, brutal enough to melt a man's conscience. Whatever damage I was fighting, he knew his own demons and he saw them when he looked at me.

I'd never felt so close to him as I did in that moment.

And I never wanted to beat his head against the table so much.

I very carefully flattened my hands against the sticky surface, palm down. No threat, see? No weapons. Just me, unarmed and harmless. Shiva's orders. "Indigo, I have a lot to tell you."

"I'll bet," he spat.

I frowned. "But you're going to have to give me something to go on here. Last time we spoke, everything was fine. What changed?"

"What changed?" Digo's voice rose an octave. "What *changed*, Riko, is that you betrayed me. You betrayed Nanji!"

The accusation was a slap in the face. My fingertips dug into the wood – fake blend, nanofactoried to decent specifications, probably replaced every week for damage. The numbers scrolling past my lateral display assured me it was more than heavy enough to break over Indigo's skull.

He knew. How much? My jaw ached as I repeated, "Betrayed Nanji. What are you talking about?"

"I mean you *vanished*, Riko. One moment here, leading my sister around on your leash, and then you killed her." Indigo's tech wasn't visible to the eye. It gave him hyperfocused perception and mental agility, and, like his sister's, it catalogued everything he saw. Being around the Koupra siblings was like being flanked by cameras. They saw it *all*.

For that reason, I knew he clocked my confusion. I didn't try to hide it. "I... killed her?" That was a stretch, even for me.

"Quit repeating me," he spat back. Hatred sizzled across the table, carried on a spray of saliva and reeking of alcohol. "You talked her into that upgrade, *you* caused her conversion."

The world fell out from under me. My stomach knotted. "Upgrade." The metal reams replacing her spine, the nerve tech, the conversion. "I talked her into that?"

"Fuck!" He seized a glass and hurled it, spilling topaz yellow liquid in a long, luminous stream.

I threw my metal arm in front of my face. The projectile shattered against the diamond steel, sprinkling me with fragments and droplets of yellow.

I didn't fight back.

In my mind's eye, I watched Nanji's trembling lips mouth an apology. Her near-black eyes. The spinal replacement.

I'd done that?

I couldn't remember. Why would I do that?

Indigo opened and closed his fists between us, as if he could squeeze out his fury. His loathing. "The only thing that kept me from losing my shit," he said from between clenched teeth, "was the fact you vanished. Dead, for all I cared. I was working on it, Riko. Nobody could find you, so I'd made my fucking peace. Now, here you are."

Gingerly, I shook off the glass fragments. "Nice." When he

took a sharp breath, my fist slammed into the table between us. Glassware jumped. His retort, whatever fucking last thread he intended to snap, arrested. "I didn't vanish, you smegging cock. I was *missing*. I didn't just walk off into last night's sunset – and oh, yeah," I added bitterly, "thanks for giving up on me so fast."

"Not fast enough."

Oh, fuck him. "Then how's this for fast?" I shot back. "Give me two minutes to explain. If you still think I'm at fault, I'll walk right out of here and never look back."

"The hell you will," he countered. Not the easy, good-natured taunt I remembered, or even the annoyed sulk of the put-upon older brother. This was menace, cold and edged.

He'd changed. I wasn't sure it was for the better. Of the three of us, I'd always been the stone cold merc. The role didn't suit him.

But it seemed a lot had changed in a couple of days. More than I expected.

"Two minutes," I repeated thinly.

"You have them."

I started talking. It took longer than two minutes. The redhead waitress dropped off a glass brimming over with pink and gold liquid, my weirdly green energy boost, and a tall blue chute for Indigo. He didn't touch his. I shot back the somewhat salty recharge, toyed with the Cellular Sunset that Shiva must have ordered for me, and told him everything I'd seen in that hellhole I'd woken up in. The guys with guns, the cold lab room – even about Nanji, locked behind that tempered glass.

When I told him about his sister's conversion, his hands whitened to yellowed knots on the table. I could read the mistrust in his face, the confusion that had to stem from what I told him versus what he thought he knew, but he didn't say anything.

When it came down to our own, Digo's policy had never

been negotiable: if it flips its shit, kill it. Nanji's behavior fit right in that definition.

But I couldn't shake the memory of Nanji's last words. It was *her*, her eyes and her sad smile. She'd been fighting the corruption with everything she had.

Now here I was, basically telling Digo that he'd given up on her before she'd actually died. That *sucked*. That sucked harder than anything else I'd gone through, but how bad did it suck compared to his point of view of *me*?

All in all, I was so screwed.

I didn't mention the cops. I couldn't afford the scrutiny. When I was done talking, I drank every last drop of the Cellular Sunset and waited for him to call me on my shit.

He was silent for a long time, letting the frenetic thrashjam in the background fill the quiet. He stared into his glass. Rotated it idly between two long fingers. His hawkish nose seemed more pronounced in his face, his cheekbones sharper. In fact, now that I took the opportunity to study him, he seemed thinner underneath his dark blue neoprene. Always lean, he couldn't afford to drop weight. His arms, ropy with muscle, looked tighter, less filled out and more sinewy.

Fuck, he was starting to remind me of me, except that I think I could still out-brutalize him in a fight. That was my job.

I chewed on my questions as the alcohol hit my system like the sunset it was named after.

Finally, he looked up. Flat, level blue. "You're telling me you were down in some secret lab for two months."

I snorted, brushing that aside like the bullshit it was. "No. Couple days at the most."

The skin around his eyes tightened. "Then where were you until then?"

"I don't follow."

"Fuck you, Riko, it's not astrophysics. It's July. *You* went missing in May, the same day I last saw Nanji."

Something cold gripped my chest. "May?"

"The eighteenth." Just after my birthday.

A birthday I didn't remember having.

The date. I needed to check the date, but that wasn't processed through the software that managed my arm. A projection call would log dates, but users don't see that data without the interface. An ad, somewhere, might list a release date for something, but I'd long since learned to tune that shit out.

Fuck. "Prove it," I whispered.

Wordlessly, Indigo flicked open a hand. A projection screen lit to brilliant red. With a few swipes of his fingers, the screen flipped so I could see it right way around.

A calendar.

July.

Months, not days.

I stared into the dregs of my drink, frenetically searching it for answers it didn't have. I wanted to order another, desperately, but given what little I was working on, I didn't trust my nanos not to take it and run. Shiva's drinks weren't nano fuel, they were nano psychedelics. One Cellular Sunset was probably enough for this conversation.

May. I was missing since May, he'd said. But I knew that wasn't possible. I couldn't remember May. It wasn't even supposed to *be* May. I gripped the glass so hard, red numbers pooled into the feed in my eye, warning me I was a second away from structural failure.

I eased up, but it didn't help the pressure in my skull. My throat.

"Riko?"

I shook my head, hard. "Yeah, sorry. I, uh..." What the hell was I supposed to say? That despite *his* memories of me in May, *I* couldn't remember anything for longer?

I was on dangerous ground here. The run I thought happened only the night before I woke up in that lab had gone down in April. I remembered it clearly. It was already hot as balls, and we were smack in the middle of a hit on MetaCore property. We'd gotten the requisitioned dataspike, ransacked the place so it looked like an everyday break-in, and were well on the way out when the whole place had gone up like Kongtown New Year.

They'd dragged me into Lucky's street clinic with a piece of rebar in my gut and a bottle of whiskey clutched in my good hand. It seemed like a dream.

I couldn't even be sure it wasn't.

That didn't explain why I couldn't remember anything after the night I got off Lucky's table. We'd gone dancing, a party that started here at the Mecca and roamed the rack. Then... What? Apparently, I'd wandered around for over a month. Then vanished, and woke up in the lab.

Months, gone.

Shit. If I confessed to that, I may as well rip out my own spine and offer it on a smegging platter. An operation on a chopshop's table followed by extended amnesia sounded too damn close to corruption to risk Digo's *better safe than sorry* mentality.

I needed time.

Given the circumstances, I'd trade time for a team and get at the truth the old-fashioned way. "I know how to find answers," I added grimly.

"Shit." Indigo groaned the word into his hands, rubbing them over his haggard face. "Look. I'm not saying I believe you, but let's pretend what you're telling me is true." Asshole. "According to that tablet you should have taken with you" – I winced – "that makes *you* clinically dead."

"I am *not* dead," I snarled.

"Obviously." A sour edge, there. He rested his elbows on the table and stared me down with more aggression than I was used to from him.

It made a little more sense now. I thought he'd ditched me after days.

Turned out he'd had months to suck on this one.

"What do you possibly expect me to do about this?"

It wasn't exactly an arms-wide welcome back, but I pushed for gold anyway. "I want a team, Digo. I want the best of your lot."

"Hell, no."

I glared at him. "Don't give me that shit. I know you've got them. I want a heavy and two splatter specialists. I want you linking, a 'jector you trust, and–"

"*Riko.*" Indigo's eyes flashed in narrowed impatience. "Slow your roll. You're talking about some seriously deep shit. Corporate prisons? Labs? Stasis? First thing *you* need is a headscan."

And there it was. The thinly veiled accusation I knew would be coming.

It didn't sting any less. Even though I knew how close I'd skated to nanoshock, it pissed me off.

I stood, bracing my weight on my flattened hands. The table creaked. "I am," I said, so quietly I think the music must have drowned it, "*not* crazy."

Perceptive as he was, he heard me anyway. "Says you."

I didn't need a scanner to weigh in on that one. He wasn't running any less hot for his veneer of calm. "Digo, you know me," I pressed.

"Yeah." He leaned back in the booth, folded his arms over his narrow chest. The blue neoprene didn't crease. "Once. That cab has jumped the curb."

I resisted the urge to slap the table; it wasn't getting me anywhere. "For Nanji, Indigo. At least help me figure out what the shit put your sister and me in that vault."

"You mean my *dead* sister? The one that was already supposed to *be* dead by the time you crawled out of whatever hole you came from?" The sharp fury in his eyes wasn't gone. I'd only managed to sheathe it in glass. I push too hard, I'd shatter it and lose him again.

I took a deep breath, but I couldn't force myself to sit down. If I sat, I'd crack. If I cracked, either I'd cry or bleed something. I couldn't remember the last time I cried.

I didn't do emotions well.

"Look," he said, watching my hands curl and uncurl over the edge of the table. "*If* what you're saying is true – and trust me, Riko, that is a big, fat flaming *if* – you got my sister into some deep shit. I want those answers, but you need scanning first."

He wasn't wrong. Hell, I'd have said the same in his shoes. Just smegging *awesome*.

"Lucky's still on the edge of Kongtown. Go get cleared." He held up his hand again, as if to forestall anything I wanted to say. "When you're all cleared for action, there's this guy. He's legit," he added before I asked. "He's got resources I don't. See what he says."

"Outside help?"

"Just do it. If he gives the okay, then *maybe* you'll get a team."

Something smelled off. Frankly, everything smelled off since I collapsed in that alley. I frowned at him. "What's wrong with your own fixers?"

Digo leveled me a look that begged to know if I was serious. "Name one that won't think you're fucking with them."

"Taylor Jax."

"He's not a fixer, and you know he'll only fuck you in the end."

Good point, obvious innuendo notwithstanding – been there, done that.

I wasn't in the mood to fine tune the deal. "Fine. I'll meet this guy."

Even though he'd made it part of the bargain, Digo looked surprised. I guess I couldn't blame him. Before now, I'd have asked all kinds of questions.

It's not like I had options.

"Arrange the meeting." I kept my voice as even as I could make it. My shoulders straightened, not even a hint of pain. Nanos functional, just like I liked them. "Have him meet me at Plato's Key. Nice and public." When he frowned, I pushed. "Tonight, Digo. Now. An hour. Whatever. And *then* I'll see Lucky, okay?"

"Why?"

"Because everything's fresh," I snapped, covering the knot in my gut with temper. "Because the whole shitting place was on fire, Digo, and if they – whoever the fuck *they* are – get there first–"

"Wherever the fuck *there* is," he cut in with pointed sarcasm.

I leaned on the table. Bright, sunshiny yellow fabric did nothing to take the edge off my twisted smile. "My point," I said, very slowly and very clearly, "is that they have all the advantage. The least I can do is ride their asses on time."

Indigo leaned back, and maybe it was partially because my reach could clear that table. Maybe he just gave up. Whatever it was, he didn't argue, he just nodded and raised his drink in my direction. "One hour. I'll see if he's free." He gulped half the blue shimmer in his glass, looked into it for a moment, then glanced up. "Just rein in the cyberbitch persona, okay? You don't want piss this guy off."

"It's the Key," I replied dryly. I let the crack about my persona go. That was all natural, and he knew it. "Public, filled with bouncers, and ask Fido over there about my dance floor moves."

He didn't smile. "I think this one will have moves you don't see coming."

"What do we have on him?" I asked, intrigued by Digo's caution. "Sinner? Saint? Corporate bulldog?"

"Surprisingly little. But he's discreet and he knows his shit." Which was enough to make most problems go away, in Digo's book.

I shook the fabric of my yellow shirt. Glass shards glittered as they fell to the carpet at my feet. Charming. "This guy have a name?"

"Reed. Malik Reed." He drained the rest of his drink. "You'll know him when you see him."

"Great." I turned, the middle of my shoulder blades itching as I made my exit. I knew he'd have a clear shot at my back from where he sat, and Shiva hadn't patted either of us down for weapons.

I'd never thought of Digo as a threat before. It burned all the way down.

"Riko."

I tensed, paused in the door. "What?"

His voice remained tight. Angry. "I really think you should see Lucky first."

"*After* I see Reed."

His curse fragmented on a frustrated sound. "Whatever. Don't say I never gave you anything."

Not one of the things I'd ever say about Indigo Koupra.

At least, not until now.

7

It'd take the better part of an hour to get to the other end of the rack, where Plato's Key claimed turf riddled by chromers and fashion slaves. The district was busy, packed with all the night life activists, the scum-suckers, the nocturnal denizens who didn't want to – or couldn't – step outside in the light of day.

I passed prostitutes who weren't shy about shaking their bare breasts or ass-crack shorts at anybody who looked like they were carrying – credits or drugs, it was all the same. A hairless, dark-skinned man smiled up at a large sallow man whose face showed nothing but rapture. As I walked by, a glint of neon light picked out the metal tubing extending from the paler areola of his left nipple, vanishing into the john's pants. Didn't get much more black market than that. Buy him for an hour, and he'd do all kinds of things with the tubular attachments he'd probably stashed all over his body.

Tech fetishists got off on that kind of stuff. The spreading stain at his crotch said the guy he'd marked was an easy payday, and his hands rifled the john's pockets like it was no big.

It probably wasn't.

He wasn't the only john gagging for it, either. Not a meter away, a thick-thighed whore with a wealth of bright blue dreads flapped her bared asscheeks at a dark-eyed teenager sporting some serious flopsweat. He'd bite. They get that bad, they're already in it – just not *in it*, if you get the idea.

All the pros have menus. Load 'em up easy. A quick search is all it takes.

The city at night comes alive in ways that the daytime can't touch. A heavyset man strapped into purple satin tapped his pal on the ass – a boy wearing a black suit, his face painted up like an homage to the skull on my shoulder. The voice that came out of his delicate boy lips was bass deep, and laughing. Another couple sauntered arm in arm, both sporting the same facial tattoos and wicked purple mohawks. Twins or into the kink, I couldn't tell. You could buy a face.

I saw boys, girls, both, and neither. Genetically modified people who wanted to live the life of an exotic; ethnic people who wanted to maintain their own cultural purity no matter the cost; old, young, filthy, chromed. Black, yellow, red, white, and every color in between poured into a giant melting pot and smeared liberally with propaganda and opportunity. Everybody out for something. Credits. A high. A hit. A favor. A good time. A hard time. Blood. Profit.

Always profit.

The heat eased off some by night, but the air sparkled under the canopy of brilliantly colored luminescence. Signs, ads, flashing girls and blinking warnings. Sex offered, tempted, bought and sold; looking up netted a galaxy of pornographic stars.

Eat here, go there, pay for this. Airborne viruses could drop a genetically solvent human in days, but a little bit more programming, and nanos could take care of *everything*. Stuck with a venereal disease and don't want the lady to know? There's tech for that.

Slipped in between the official ads were the ones that flickered on the edge of awareness. If my chipset had been working right, I could have keyed in to those, seen the kind of ads oriented towards those of us with certain needs not wholly legal. Tech, cyber implementation, projection upgrades, software and all kinds of inbetween.

I *had* to get my filters fixed. The augmented adspace was easy enough to ignore, but the constant effort was killing my brain cells.

A woman wrapped in the ruins of a long brown trenchcoat stumbled into my arm, the board over her shoulders wet in one corner and reeking of urine. Bright orange paint, congealed into filthy rivulets, proclaimed her wisdom.

The end is cumming!

I think she meant coming, but don't quote me. People are fucking weird.

I turned a corner, keeping my stride long, my pace unhurried. Any woman walking alone and with a purpose was a prime target for assclowns who loved nothing better than to get in her way, and I didn't have the patience to bust some skulls tonight. I glanced at the empty wall beside me, flinched when an ad exploded into existence.

Are you safe? it asked me, thick white letters, blocky and uniform. *Is your SIN registered with us?*

Oh, hell. Propaganda avenue. Just great.

Keep yourself safe with this one easy reminder…

Jaw clenching, I resisted the urge to swat at the space and pushed my way through the pedestrians.

Beside me, the letters kept pace along the wall, turned blood red.

Necrotech conversion is real. You will murder your families. Brutalize your loved ones.

Probably the truest thing the corporate propagandists ever wrote.

Don't take the chance, it suggested. *Removing your SIN will cause irreparable brain damage and increases risk of conversion by 87%.*

Bullshit. That was pure indoctrination. The Security

Information Number was nothing more than a leash, a way to keep track of everyone, for any reason. It was the first thing I'd removed. The surgery had some risks, sure – mostly that burning out the SIN would kill the nanos programmed to it, but that wasn't impossible to get around.

A good chopshop knew how to handle it.

The bad ones? Well, they usually killed their patients on the table. End of threat.

I turned my back on the glaring text, which now proclaimed a nice, healthy white reassurance. *Love the security provided. We are here for you. Anytime. Anywhere.*

I didn't recognize the logo offhand, but it didn't matter. All the big companies had ads like this. They got paid by the clocked consciousness, which I'd just contributed to by looking at the damn thing.

First thing I'd have Lucky do was scrub my nanos and reboot my chipset. *Then* I'd have him install new filters. Fuckheads.

Plato's Key was a lot like the Mecca, except it catered more towards visual aesthetics and a shit ton of creds than it did towards SINless looking for a job. I'd gone once or twice, usually for a lark, but it wasn't my scene by choice. Filled with posers, hustlers, and slick cons in slicker suits, it was one step away from a corporate bar and still trying to pretend like it belonged to the street. Rich kids and chrome, mostly. You could tell the difference by the level of shiny plating, glittering lights, and cosmetic enhancements the kids sported. Like it was a game.

Still, it was highly public, well out of range of my usual stomping grounds. It would be filled to the brim with fashion slaves wearing vinyl and sporting light tattoos they could turn off later to hide from mom, which, all things considered, meant they'd be twitchier about casual violence.

The entrance was glass – tempered, because windows didn't survive without tempering in this district – but the surface played home to so many ads and commercials, I couldn't tell one apart from the other.

The doors slid open for me, depositing me in air that was so much cooler and fresher-smelling. There was a dreadlocked bear of a man in black, typical bouncer uniform, who didn't so much study me as raise both shaggy eyebrows and glower at me over the thick, crooked ridge of his nose. "Weapons?"

I grinned, arms at my side. "Just this ass."

He didn't look impressed. My tech arm got a long, hard scrutiny, but he wouldn't find anything interesting there. I still needed to get the netware system reconnected, and my ammo slot was still empty. Not like I had any guns to put any ammo in, anyway.

Mimicking Jad, he jerked a thumb at the door behind him. It was sleek, paneled like wood, and lacked all the pretty accessories Shiva slapped all over the Mecca. "Go on in."

"Cover?"

He snorted, which I took to translate meant I was attractive enough to forego the cover. I didn't take it personally – it was standard policy at places like this, especially when attendance was down. I hadn't seen a line, which told me they were looking for skin to fill the seats. The exotic girls got in for free. It made the guys with creds want to come play. Some things never change.

The door opened automatically, letting me enter without breaking my stride. Another smooth touch. The soul-deep beat of music not nearly as aggressive as the Mecca's washed over me, carried on electric graffiti.

Several mirrored balls spun over the dance floor, sending multihued sparkles over the interior. Lights streamed from the high ceiling, sliding through the dark in rhythmic match to the music thudding against my skin; pop-culture lyrics, twisted into what this place probably thought was hardcore. No thrashing here. I expected to see a lot of perfect skin, carefully chosen tattoos, suits and red lips and drinks with umbrellas.

I saw nothing but an empty club.

"Shit." I stepped back immediately.

Too fucking late.

The door closed behind me. My back hit the panel, jarring me into a hard grunt. It did not open again.

"What the shit." I snarled. My elbow collided with the barrier, a sharp crack of metal on paneled metal, but I didn't turn my back on the exposed space in front of me.

Tall round tables filled the space beside the dance floor, surrounded by skinny chairs padded with silver vinyl. There were two floors, with balconies overhead looking down into what I assumed was a gyrating mass of middle-class humanity on an average night. The lights flashed and shimmered, the music fell into a dub drop, and exploded back into a woman's remixed alto.

On the other side of the dance floor, a recessed dip in the floor gave way to an arranged pattern of padded couches, armchairs, smaller tables and drink pads. The bar filled up the far wall, floor-to-ceiling shelving backlit to let the bottles inside glow with unearthly colors. The small bots programmed to acquire the bottles ordered were silent and still, perched on the bar and powered down.

A streak of blue light passed over the seating area, merged with orange and briefly outlined a black silhouette. Athletic shoulders. Gray suit. Dark head, featureless in shadow. The lights skated away and left him in shadow again, but for the pale blue luminescence of a projected screen in front of him.

Well, fuck me.

Empty, the place was already eerie. With a single man perched in an armchair, it was downright surreal.

And I was rapidly approaching pissed. Trying to zen this one would net me dick-all.

I stepped away from the exit, eyes narrowed against the light assault, and scanned the immediate area for other ways out. I didn't see any signs, but that didn't mean much.

I was a third of the way across the empty dance floor when a whisper of movement flickered in my peripheral. I refrained from turning my head, but I saw him. A man in black fatigues. The helmet was full-coverage, black faceplate patterned with a faint grid of a heads-up display, and his chest was shaped by the bulk of light armor.

The body armor was similar to the goons in that prison, but most security forces tended to look alike when they weren't sporting corporation branding.

Another silhouette to my right shifted into view. Same gear. Same general build.

The music rolled over the floor, a visceral hum that only punctuated my mounting irritation. I was in the middle of the dance floor when two more stepped into view, one in front and one – I checked, already knowing what I'd see – yeah, one behind. One was trimmer but not by match. Maybe a woman. Maybe not.

Maybe it didn't shitting matter.

I deliberately relaxed my shoulders, my hands loose at my sides. A trap, then.

I was going to *kill* Indigo.

"All right," I told them, resigned. "Let's get this over with."

They came at me as a unit.

I squatted low as the first reached for me, hooked the back of his knee with my right hand and pulled. He countered by firming his weight on his right leg; I smashed his kneecap with my metal fist. It crunched. He screamed. I rolled out of the knot of hands and feet.

Pull, jab, down, all in one second.

One of them pulled his buddy up by an arm. He hobbled a bit, but I assumed his nanos were already working on it. I put my hands back by my sides again, deceptively loose.

Four black truncheons slid into four palms. A flicker of blue energy at each empty hand told me they'd activated shields.

Were they kidding me? This was practically riot gear.

I checked my left, but the suit hadn't moved. Engrossed in the glowing square perched above the table, he didn't spare me – or his goons – so much as a glance.

My choices weren't ideal. I could try and keep them at arm's length, stay far enough ahead that I could look for an exit, but there were four of them. Five, if the suit got involved. It'd be only a matter of time before they cornered me. I did *not* want to get stuck in a corner.

All I could do was fight.

My mouth tightened. Inside my skin, fury simmered into cool regard. Adrenaline flooded my system, feeding nanos and nerves with the same surge of raw energy.

I was good at this sort of stuff. I knew what to expect in a fight. I could cope with physical pain a hell of a lot better than I coped with emotional baggage.

This was what zenning it looked like to me.

I turned my gaze back to the four men. "Fine." I lifted my foot, unzipped the fake pocket and pulled out the serrated knife that was all I had. The hilt was cool and comforting in my hand, the matte blade swallowing the light as it popped over us. "Bring it."

They brought it.

I don't care what anyone out there tries to sell, the only thing that can even the odds of four-on-one is a full-body replacement – and unless a merc has Boone's unholy luck, that's a one-way ticket to necro-land.

I held my own for the longest thirty seconds of my life. It became rapidly clear that I wasn't a match for four lethally trained enforcers working as a unit. I bloodied my knife on one. Light armor isn't made to withstand a stabbing, and definitely not when I knew where the seams were.

I kicked another in the faceplate, cracking the plastic and shorting his display. Another earned a shattered elbow. His truncheon hand dropped useless to his side. If his scream caused his boss to look up from his stock tickers, I was too busy to see it.

Problem was, for every point I scored, there were three of them to score one each for their battered buddy.

I caught a truncheon in my side, cracking ribs. Wrenching at it did nothing – the sticks were designed to snap into place with the gauntlets, negating disarming attempts like mine. Another jammed into my kidneys. Pain roiled under my skin, turned my vision inside out and nearly dropped me to my knees. The only thing that would keep me from pissing blood later was the nanos, but not if these sec-level spunkguzzlers did as much damage as it looked like they intended.

I punched the visorless one in the face with my tech arm, calling it a draw for the blood streaming from my mouth and into one eye, and gave it a little extra thrust for kicks. He dropped.

I had no time to celebrate. A boot slammed into the back of my right knee, another smashed into the side of it. Ligaments wrenched, popped with sickening visceral agony, spilling me to the floor and jarring my teeth. My knife went skittering across the tile.

It was all I could do to fight the urge to curl around the excruciating pain in my ribs.

No time. I rolled, biting back a scream, avoided the hands reaching for me. I hit the edge, found the stairs leading to the pit by sheer accident, and flailed ass over elbows. There were only two steps.

My broken ribs and devastated knee found both of them.

The lights, the music, the world turned into a black, tunneled vacuum.

8

If I passed out here, I was dead.

It took effort, but I sucked in air through gritted teeth, forced myself to stay conscious. I just needed to wait out the damage, ride the pain.

Maybe seriously consider some pain dampeners; shove the risk.

I slung an arm over the rim of the padded table shoved into my back. I couldn't see out of one eye, and the floor was jerking back and forth, but I didn't need perfect vision to glare at the four silhouettes coming down the steps at me.

The pale glow behind me went dark. "That's enough."

All four stopped.

The suit didn't shout; he didn't have to. His voice wasn't as deep as Jad's, but it carried the kind of weight you can't program into tech. It was effortless, patient, and cool. A signal that cut through noise with pure authority.

I was going to rip his voice box out and make him eat it.

"Bring her."

My ass. I tried to get to my feet. My damaged knee buckled hard, twisting out from under me. Before I hit the ground, two sets of hands curled around my upper arms. Pulled me upright.

I bit my tongue hard enough to draw blood as torture

streaked through my broken ribs. It came out on a mangled, "*Fuck.*"

They half-carried, half-dragged me to a plastic arm chair across from the suited man, and set me gently into the padding. Two sets of hands clutched at my shoulders, holding me firmly in place.

"You must be Indigo's friend," my host said. His eyes met mine across the neon-drenched club, too dark to see the color of.

Pain banked. Rage burned in its place. "Go to hell."

He inclined his head. "Not my faith."

Thought he was a bag of laughs, huh? "Listen up, *Malik*." I drew his name out like poison, every muscle in my body taut with the effort not to launch myself at him. Or hunch into a miserable ball of pain. "You have exactly one minute. And the only reason I'm giving you that is I need the time to knit."

"Understood." Malik Reed did not smile. Or, at least, he didn't actually curve his lips and reveal his teeth. I wasn't even sure he could – he didn't seem the type. His top and lower lip were thick and full, but when matched with his high cheekbones and the sharp angles of his face, there was nothing soft about him. He wasn't commercially handsome, not by a long shot; his jaw was too square at the edges, chin too pronounced and nose too wide. All in all, probably the kind of bone structure a woman would die for, but he wouldn't score any points for charm.

Not that it mattered. The impression Malik Reed left was one of wealth, power, and the kind of prestige that comes with assloads of unshakable confidence.

And a seismic lot of fucks he didn't have to give.

He'd started this with blood. My fucks had exponentially increased, and not in the way I generally liked them.

In the club's light-speckled interior, Malik's gray suit looked crisp and perfectly tailored, creased at the pant legs and hemmed over shiny black shoes I bet cost too much.

The shirt underneath his fitted jacket was black, a mandarin collar buttoned neatly at the strong lines of his throat. All very corporate chic. The whole thing probably cost as much as my cut from a decent run.

I printed my clothing by machine. Malik Reed had his tailored by hand.

That meant backing. Probably corp-level, since private sector didn't usually come paired with sec-level forces. *That* meant I couldn't twist his cunting head off his spine. I'd have to play this one carefully. SINless versus corp exec one on one, and I'd own his ass.

SINless versus a corp exec and four enforcers?

I was meat.

I gripped the arms of my chair, uncomfortably aware of the hands curled over my shoulders, the mind-altering waves of pain radiating from knee to ribs to, oh, every bone in my body, and the taste of blood on my tongue. I narrowed my eye. The other one was already a bloody slit. "Get your spunkchuckers off me."

In this techno-strobe mess, I couldn't tell what color Malik's skin was. Dusky, anyway. Given the features, I'd guess a blend of anglo, African, and a handful of other landmarks from Native to Mexican. Muddled, like most of us beyond the restricted cultural reserves. His eyes were practically black in the shadows, his limbs long and movements precise as he gestured in two directions.

The hands at my shoulders let go. He didn't stop there, turning his head to glance somewhere to my left.

The lights played over the harsh, sculpted angle of his jaw, outlined his profile briefly, and slid back onto the dance floor somewhere to my right. "Now you have my full attention," he said, turning his gaze back to me as if he'd done me a favor.

My fingers fisted. "Great." I showed him my bloody teeth. "Just for the record, I am going to kill you."

"Why?"

The answer was so obvious, my brain hitched. *Why?* Because he'd stood by while his tapdancing assclowns beat me down like a stray dog. Because if he was corporate, that meant he knew people. Probably knew some of the same people that operated in my sphere. In my line of work, reputation was everything. It didn't matter how good I was, it'd all go to shit if he opened his girly lips and blabbed about the trap he'd set on me and the damage his team had caused.

I had more to prove than he did.

"Because," was what I managed, and this time, he did smile. Sort of.

The faint kick of humor at the corner of his mouth slammed a shard of something hot and hungry in my chest. Need, yes. Not the sexy kind. Not, anyway, *all* the sexy kind.

I recognized his magnetism, but I wanted to hurt him. I wanted to hurt the men I *knew* hovered just out of range.

I wanted to pull him out of his too-expensive suit and see if he still thought he was hot shit without it.

That thing I'd mentioned about his voice box? Forget making him eat it. I was going to shove it so far up his ass, he'd have to bark his orders upside down.

Red numbers spiked in my lateral display. The arm of the chair splintered, disintegrating under my grip like so much straw.

His gaze dropped to it, then back up to me like it didn't matter. "I appreciate the display. Are you finished?"

"Come a little closer, jackass."

Not even a twitch. "Let's not waste time. Your attempt to set up a meeting on your..." His gaze flitted to the empty club, disdain flaring his nostrils. "This isn't your territory, that much is obvious, but you obviously wanted to discuss business in a public venue."

"So, what?"

"Your terms didn't agree with me. No," he cautioned.

"Don't make that mistake."

Shit. I'd only shifted, testing my footing, but he'd seen.

"You claim to need a minute, but your right knee is going to require six and your ribs fifteen. You're hardly running at optimal."

He'd scanned me. More, he'd probably used that fight to get a total readout on my abilities. A sneaky way of doing it.

I ground my teeth so hard, the noise shaved the edge off the music thumping in the empty club around us. "Go fuck yourself."

"There is tech for that," he replied, "but you may be disappointed to learn I don't have it."

"Get it. Then go fuck yourself."

This time, Malik's smile revealed even white teeth and crinkled the corners of his dark eyes. It did nothing to soften his hard edges; nothing to ease the corporate stink surrounding him like a toxic cloud.

It made me feel a whole lot like prey, and I wasn't prey.

But my breath sucked out of my chest anyway.

There are people out there who have smiling down to an art form. Someone might say that a person can light up a room or make a bad day go away.

The club was still dark and strobing, and my bad day was still bottoming out at shitty, but this guy was wired for social programming in ways even a politician would envy. One smile, and I practically swallowed my tongue.

Pheromones? Even as it occurred to me, I trashed it. I wasn't close enough. Besides, it wasn't that kind of curve. No one in their right mind, drunk or sober, would call that slash sexy.

It reeked of power and ego and raw masculinity; maybe not unexpectedly, it made *me* think of blood. Lots and lots of blood. The kind that drew hungry predators.

I could shape my smile into a visceral promise of ruin, but I didn't like the razor-honed potential in his.

"I will take that under advisement," he told me, in a tone that said he wouldn't waste a brain cell bothering. He turned his right hand palm up, fingers flicking. "When you're done sulking, let me know."

That screen flicked on again, turning his features into a wash of pale blue light and demonic shadows. The projection probably came from his watch, or maybe a chip inserted somewhere in his palm. He left me scowling at him as he returned to whatever charts filled the space between us.

At least it let me get a closer look. The light revealed the shadow of a finely sculpted goatee framing his mouth. And, much to my surprise, freckles. A mass of them speckled over the bridge of his nose, his high cheekbones and scattered faintly over his forehead.

They did nothing to make him look naïve or innocent. Not even close.

"Your ego must be enormous," I said.

He didn't look away from the projection. "Yes. That's why I cleared the club."

"Didn't want to be seen slumming it in the Key?"

"Would you?" Absently cool, like he only spared half a thought for my distraction.

To my chagrin, a corner of my mouth twitched. My jaw clenched against it.

Two minutes.

"All right," I said, breaking the music-studded silence between us. "Tell me why Indigo suggested I meet you."

For a moment, I wasn't sure he'd respond. The spotlights glazed over his head, picked out his extremely short, coarse dark hair in a startlingly bright gleam of pink luminescence and glanced off my yellow top before skating away.

Finally, he curled his fingers under the projection. It collapsed, winking out entirely.

"Tell me why you wanted a meeting," he countered, "and I'll tell you what service I can provide."

"Service."

He only watched me. Like it or not, I had zero viable options. He'd already proven he had the upper hand, and no matter how angry I was over it, *he* didn't need *me*. I, however, probably needed him. At the very least, I needed something, and Indigo recommended him.

Don't say I never gave you anything.

Had he known? Had Indigo walked me into a trap?

That thought shot a white-hot ball of rage into my chest.

Then again, maybe Malik had taken Indigo's request to meet and made his own arrangements.

It was better for *everyone* that I bought that one. If I stopped to think about the fact that Digo had turned me over to this suit, I wasn't sure what I'd do. It was too big for the space my head was in – too fucking complicated.

As long as I figured Malik for the smug exec he seemed to be, I could play the game.

Suits always liked to think they had the upper hand on us runners. Lucky for him, I actually needed whatever it was Indigo claimed Malik had. I needed that help.

Not like I was getting it from anywhere else.

Did I dare tell him everything? Did Indigo already? I should have made sure first.

"Are you a fixer?" I asked.

"No."

At least he didn't dick around. Great. So much for that. "Then you can't help me."

"Don't be closeminded."

What the tits? Lessons in tolerance from a suit. Fuck me. "You think you can help? Fine. I need a team," I told him, as much a challenge as anything. "A real one, street-trained and savvy." He didn't even blink, eyes level beneath thick black eyebrows. I took that as encouragement to go on. "There's a corporate prison and they've got data I need."

"What firm?"

"I don't know." And because I didn't like the fact that he'd judge me for it, I added, "They stripped it of all branding. The security held Saugers and Manticores, and they didn't have badges."

"Both firearms easily acquired by any agency." He didn't frown. He didn't even nod encouragingly like a shrink on autopilot. He just watched me. Catalogued me.

Creepy.

"Tell me about the place." An order.

I let him have the luxury. Told him what little I knew. It took a hair under a minute. I left out everything that even smelled like necro, because, hell, for all I knew, he'd order the place razed when I found it.

Four minutes down.

The ache in my knee was easing. The guy knew his statistics.

"When you say corporate, you mean what?"

"Clean," I replied. "Stark, bare of all things with soul or even aesthetically pleasing, and, oh, yeah, riddled with assholes. You know the type."

Black eyes didn't waver. "I am the type."

Well, hey, at least he was honest with himself. "Then you see why I said corporate."

"No, I see sloppy assumptions based on dogmatic sentiment." His deep voice hardened. "I can't possibly give you what you need based on this."

My fists clenched. "What do you want, then?"

"It's not a question of want, it's a question of time and effort versus payoff. Right now, I see a wild story spun by a delinquent with no concept of the amount of assets required to carry you on your crusade."

My cheeks stung. Anger. Worse, embarrassment. "That's not–"

He held up a hand, his palm paler in the partial light. "I need evidence. More than your word."

"My word is good."

"Only as good as your reputation." His mouth quirked again, that tiny half curve that made me feel like I was twelve years old and seated across from an imposing teacher. My palms itched to wrap around his throat. "I don't know you from Jane Eyre, and what I've seen tonight doesn't impress me."

"Four on one," I gritted out. "Fuck you."

"Excuses." He leaned back in his chair, propping one leg up on the other knee, and studied me with calculated scrutiny.

I didn't fidget. Seven minutes had mended my knee, but breathing was like sucking hot air through a tube. I met his gaze with a glare of my own. "I can go anywhere else for this."

"Unlikely." Not so much as a twitch. "You would have already."

Fuuuuuuuuck. He was right, and we both knew it. "Fine," I snapped. "I'll get you your evidence. And then I damn well want my team."

"If it's worth the resources, you will have your team, and then some."

The barest concession, and probably the only one I'd get out of him. "I'll hold you to that." I rose, my knee pinging once as the joint popped into place, but he remained seated. Charming guy.

Instead, he slid two fingers into his inner jacket pocket and pulled out a thin black square. He held it out.

"What do I want that for?"

He didn't sigh. I'll give him that. I bet I got on his nerves, though. "It's a card. It holds the frequencies you can use to contact me."

"Frequen*cies*, huh?"

He didn't rise to my snide bait. "I'm a very busy man."

"So am I," I replied, and turned my back on his offering. "Indigo'll be in touch."

I tried to walk like I wasn't favoring my ribs, but I knew

I wasn't fooling him. He probably had every broken bone catalogued, right down to the second it'd take my nanos to seal the remodeling.

At the base of the recessed pit, I turned. "Who the fuck is Jane Eyre?"

The glow of his digital screen lit his face in ghoulish shades of blue and gray. He didn't look up. "Read a book," was his only dismissive-as-fuck answer.

Who the hell had the patience to slog through one?

Setting my jaw, I jumped up the two steps to prove I could, and didn't see any of his security detail as I crossed the dance floor. Maybe they bugged out.

Maybe they were tracking me to make sure I didn't turn around and make good on my threat. Hell, if security was my gig, I'd practically glue myself to my ass.

The lights pulsed in my eyes, slammed in time with the music I seriously was starting to despise.

No. I could have enjoyed the scuffle, but I wasn't stupid. The odds weren't in my favor, and I didn't want to get my ass handed to me a second time. Once was embarrassing.

Even if his team split, the man was an unknown. I hadn't seen any traces of tech, no signs of enhancers of any kind, but it didn't mean he was all flesh. And though it pissed me off to admit it, he was right. I wasn't exactly at optimum right now.

But I would be. Next time, I'd be at better than optimum.

With my heartbeat thudding in my reknitting ribs, and visions of ritual massacre dancing in my head, I left Malik Reed alone.

The bouncer, on the other hand, was fair game.

This asshole had known exactly what I'd been walking into – had probably been paid to keep everyone else out while the suit inside sicced his goons on me.

Eye for an eye, fuckface.

The door slid open – miraculously unlocked – and I didn't give him any time to pull his dreadlocked beard out of the slank he was snorting on the podium. Ribs protesting every move, I darted in before the door closed behind me, chopped out with my right hand and caught him under his Adam's apple as he raised his head.

He choked, caught somewhere between trying to stand and trying to protect his stash.

I grabbed his beard with one hand, palmed the back of his head with the other, and slammed him face first into the pile of golden dust. He shrieked as bone crunched.

The slank bloomed like a piss-stained cloud. I sucked it in on a hard breath, coughed it out when the taste burned my tongue. "What is with people today?" I demanded through my teeth. "Did you all wake up and decide to fuck me over?"

He flailed, snorting out gobbets of spit, blood and half-dissolved drug.

I slammed his head again. *Thud!* Another flare of yellow. I turned my face away. Then echoed his curse when one of his sledgehammer elbows caught me square in the busted ribs. Nerves detonated.

Briefly blinded, I missed the glint of light on steel. Didn't miss the sparks as he swung up a long curved blade with a hooked edge at the tip. Fortunately for me, he hit my tech arm. And his form was shit. He probably kept it back there for show.

I shoved him hard against his podium, heard the fake wood snap under his bulk, and seized the sword-holding wrist in my metal hand.

He froze. I squeezed.

His screech cracked on slank-induced gibberish.

"That's right," I purred, false sympathy oozing in every note. I could feel the burn outside my senses. That press of wicked heat testing my resolve.

I didn't have much. Just rage. Naked, hungry, *needy*. Not ideal ground to take slank on, if you valued your wellbeing. Or waking up in the morning.

Not that it mattered. I was beyond caring.

"Yell some more," I coaxed. "Come on. Let me hear it. You drew the short straw, didn't you? All alone. No one to come running now. Was the pay worth it?"

The boundaries of the scene sputtered black, edged with painful bloody red. My ribs had broken again. This guy had a swat like a cement hammer.

He grated out a guttural protest as I flexed my fingers. I could barely understand him. A shame. It meant he might not remember this tomorrow.

I wanted him to. I needed him to remember this. Screwing me over. Then paying for it. That's what passed for cred on this street. That's what losers needed to know.

Don't.

Fuck.

With.

Me.

My focus narrowed. The numbers in my lateral display turned red.

He screamed, jerking like a fat fish on a golden hook. What I could see of his thick neck above his shirt mottled red and purple where slank-streaked drool hadn't smeared it.

I leaned against his back, jerking his arm up, up, farther than a man of his muscle and build could handle. "You ever, *ever* mess with me again," I breathed into his ear, "and you will lose more than your shitting stash. What's my name?"

Sweat and fear rolled off him in waves. Underneath his blotchy skin, nanos were gathering, hustling to the damaged sites – snapping ligaments, crushed wrist. Only they'd be inhibited by the slank we'd both inhaled. Slower.

I could practically smell them amassing. Iron and meat.

My fingers closed another centimeter. Squeezed another fraction of an inch.

His whole body jerked. His babbling took on an inhuman squeal.

"What's my goddamn name?" I snarled.

I could visualize it. As if it played out right in front of me, I could see the tendons tearing. See the bones crack, splinter, and then erupt from the skin in a spray of gristle and bone.

I could squeeze until the veins broke and the blood pooled and he would scream and scream and never forget me.

What the *shit* was I doing?

I sucked in a breath that tasted like rancid sweat and jerked back, letting go of his bone-white, still-intact wrist. Agony rippled through my side.

He sobbed, lost in a drug-addled haze of pain and fear and a really, *really* bad high.

Had he been sober, I doubt I would have handled him so easy. Then again, had he been sober, he may have thought twice about messing with someone like me. Maybe.

The fact he hadn't – the fact everybody was taking me on like I was some kind of chumhead fresh off the SINburn – was starting to eat at me.

As my head threatened to split open, my guts churning, I staggered out the front door, slammed into an overwhelming wall of heat, light, sound and ads. Faces turned, neon popped. My eyes widened, senses going nova. The slank wasn't great. I'd have gotten better quality at Shiva's.

Totally fucked, I ran into someone, fell, was pushed into someone else. Flesh and metal and plastic and neoprene. It all blurred.

The city folded in on itself. My brain turned inside out.

9

The worst of the slank wore off in a back alley, drenched with humidity and reeking of urine. I huddled, hands fisted in my hair, as I breathed in and out. In and out. Good mechanical habit there. Air in. Air out.

I was intensely aware of the people wandering out of sight. I could hear them, smell them, taste them like a pulse on the back of my tongue. I could hear my own heartbeat, loud and too fast.

I wanted to rip it out of my chest and inhale its luscious, bloody fragrance.

Slank can fuck a body up. Whoever ran Plato's Key ran a damn sloppy ship. That would never have played out at the Mecca.

I needed to get somewhere safe. Somewhere out of reach and quiet enough that I could rest.

My nanos had already been strained after fighting Indigo's team – I couldn't bring myself to call them mine anymore – and the suit's goons just made it worse. I shouldn't have gone after that bouncer. I shouldn't have stretched it.

Why had I tried?

Because my goddamn cred would take a beating if word of today's idiocy got out.

Because I was too angry – no, what a lame word for it. I

was too *enraged* to let the bouncer who screwed me get off without payback.

My breath shuddered out.

Slowly, using my elbows against the alley wall, I scraped myself off the ground. Upright. I didn't fall. Good.

The stench of shit and rot assailed me. My senses reeled; my guts twisted, splashed back and forth. Swallowing hard, teeth gritted, I pushed away from the wall and staggered for the street.

I made it three feet from the alley mouth when my knees turned backwards, spilling me to the rough ground. The Cellular Sunset I'd swallowed down came back up in an acid tide of purple and brown, punctuated by the thicker remnants of the recharger. I heaved, choked on my own vomit and hacked it all out until my guts were empty and tears of effort streamed from my straining eyes.

Gasping, I wiped a shaky arm across my mouth and rolled away from the cooling pool.

This was not the way I'd hoped to spend the night.

Draping my metal arm over my eyes, I sniffed back iron-rich mucous, cleared my throat. I struggled to form my thoughts into a cohesive plan.

Slank had never screwed me up so badly. It had to be the combination of the Cellular Sunset, the straining nanos, and the stuff I'd inhaled.

Or it was something else. Something malfunctioning in my chipset? I'd be annoyed if I had to go back and tell Indigo he was right. But maybe, just maybe, he *was*. Maybe whatever the fuck was wrong with me was in my brain. Enough imbalances in the wiring, and permanent vertigo could set in. The odds of corruption increase with every fuckup in the system. A scan couldn't hurt.

And if I was corrupted – if I really was fucked by that lab – only one man would give me a shot before he, well, fucking shot me.

As my head hummed, snapping back on fried synapses of pain, frustration, anger and anxiety, I closed my eyes and activated the projection protocols. The haptic note shoved up against my brain smegging *hurt* when the bandwidth opened.

In the space of nanoseconds, I appeared in a plain white room. Same table, same chairs. Baseline stuff.

I didn't have to wait long.

"Riko, is that you?" My mentor's voice was cranky on the best of days, and downright inhospitable the rest. I'd factor this one somewhere near grumpy, with a side of annoyance.

Same old Lucky. He'd figured out that receptors in the projection calls correlated avatars with connections. The programmers had decided, early in testing, that everybody who could make the ideal persona would. Who wanted to be a nobody?

This meant that Lucky, a nobody, wouldn't trigger the ad blast. Win-win.

Illegal, but whatever.

I didn't know where to look, so I settled for straight ahead. "It's me."

"Screw this box," was his greeting. "Where are you?"

Yeah. Same old Lucky all the way.

"Alley near Plato's Key, I think," I said. The room flickered around me, and I managed a wan smile. "I might be losing consciousness, so–"

"Goddammit, girl," he grunted. Then silence.

Would he find me? I didn't know. I couldn't ask. Here and gone again, not a kind word in between. Lucky was harsh, but fair. And the best street doc I'd ever known.

He didn't owe me anything.

As the room turned to gray around me, I let go of the projection and came back to myself. Nose deep in street sweat, vomit inches away from my face reeking of acid and sugar.

Ribs aching. Head pounding. Limbs twitching.

I rolled onto my side. My ribs shifted.

I clenched my teeth over a shriek of startled agony and fell back, gasping.

Not healed yet. Not good. There was no reason why my nanos wouldn't be remodeling the bone, even while I puked my guts out.

My vision turned black, speckle by speckle. Nanos. Love them or hate them, all they want is to keep your bits operational. Even if they have to steal your own resources to do it.

Everything has a price.

This one insisted I lose my shit in a back alley of the rack. Just another day, right?

Fuck this.

10

"Damn it, girl." A sharp pain through my chest bowed my back, frissons of pins and needles slicing through my limbs to explode in a net of electrical shocks between my eyes. "Wake up!"

I was exhausted. I wanted to sleep. I groaned. "'S' a sec," I slurred.

"No." Another slam of currents that peeled the enamel off my back teeth. A scream lodged in my throat.

My eyelids flew open.

Tired brown eyes hazed into a struggling focus above me. Worn lines bit deep into a skeletally thin face, cheeks and bridge of his crooked nose spiderwebbed with broken capillaries. Lucky's predominantly Kongtown features didn't match the harsh gruffness of his street-worn way of speaking. Idiots always expected him to sound like some vidscreen Asian stereotype. Didn't matter which one. Any of them.

Lucky wasn't the type. Any type.

"One more," he said tersely, "*then* you sleep while I see to your chipset."

I tried to lift my hand, but it wouldn't obey me. Struggling only made it worse. I was trapped. Restrained. I sucked in a breath. "Lucky?"

"I'm right here." A thin, work-rough hand wrapped around

mine. "Zen it, this is going to suck." That was Lucky's version of comfort.

I licked my parched lips. "Get this working fast," I rasped. "I have to… I have..." My breath twisted in my chest.

"I said *zen it*." I heard metal clink, heard the hum of a charge building. A needle slid into my neck and burned. "You been taking shit care of yourself."

"Not dead yet," I croaked.

"You sure about that?" His silhouette faded into bleary dark. "This much heat will take some time. Bite down."

There was no bracing. The spark gathered, lit, and every limb, every digit, every cell seized. My head was strapped down, I wouldn't break my own neck, but whatever Lucky was doing, it stripped me of my own kinesis.

I think I screamed. Then it all went white.

11

I woke up hurting, prone under a familiar gray ceiling – shingles laid side by side, rippled and stained by time, welded together with thick lines. Daylight trickled in under high, slotted vents tucked in beneath the slope. The usual cacophony of the city wasn't all that far behind.

Lucky's living space. Used to be mine, too, back when I was fresh on the street and – as Lucky would call it – built to break. Young. Naïve. Made to get fucked, in whatever way this city wanted.

I got lucky. Literally, I guess.

The bed under me wasn't as hard as the cot I'd claimed at my place, but it was running a damn close second. It was clean, though, and didn't smell like a vat of sanitizer.

None of my hurt could be attributed to the bed. My arm ached like I'd taken a red-hot poker to it.

I lifted the limb, heard the fine rotors whir and shift into place. The daylight settled over my synthetic hand, picking out the faint seams where plates had been put together to mimic hand and finger mobility.

I'd never be great at fine detail work, but I could pick things up, tighten a fist, crook each finger. Lucky had even polished it up some. He couldn't abide grimy tech. Called it lazy.

My ribs weren't tender, my knee seemed fine as I lifted my

leg, bent it experimentally.

I sat up. Slid my bare feet to the floor.

The rest of me was in one piece. I felt calm. Healthy. Not hungry, which meant he'd plugged me into something while I slept. Needle marks would be long since regenerated, but I suspected he'd tubed me up.

Stretching didn't make my arm hurt less. Instead, my shoulder tightened. As the inset filaments linking the reinforced biceps to the arm unit shifted, I winced my way through a quick muscle warm-up and contemplated painkillers as I crested the ache.

If I wanted them, I'd have to break into Lucky's stash to do it. No, thank you. I'd only just been put back together.

I was wearing a pair of brown board shorts and a faded blue, bleach-stained tanktop, both left from the stash of extra clothes I kept in a corner of Lucky's closet. Sometimes, I came by to kill a few days with the old man. Other times, I needed the getaway. It hadn't happened all that much recently.

In any case, he must have cut my clothes off me, which annoyed me. I was rapidly losing my wardrobe. I made a mental note to grab something from his hacked printer.

Cradling my arm, as if taking the weight off my shoulder would help, I got to my feet, stepped out of the narrow alcove that served as his guest room, and leaned against the railing looking out over Lucky's chopshop.

It wasn't much in the way of creature comforts.

Some chopshops go for quantity. Stack them in, operate fast as you can, cauterize them back together. Some places count a seventy-five percent survival rate a win. Not Lucky. This place was a one-at-a-time joint, with a single metal operating table in the center flanked by an array of various equipment. Computer system hookups, cold storage at the far wall, garage doors across the way that were, far as I knew, welded shut. The operating table waited silently from within a plain metal circle, which would rise to meet its twin from the ceiling in case of conversion feedback.

I'd only seen it used once. Some jackhole fresh off the SINburn had swaggered in with a metric ass ton of creds and a jacked up sense of his own ego. What he'd wanted was suicide, but he thought he could take it.

The smell was godawful, the screams of the man inside ear-bleeding. I was... what, sixteen? Still fresh on the street. Still built to break. I still remembered Lucky's hands at my wrists, forcing me to witness the searing blue crackle, hear the agony of a man whose body couldn't support the tech he'd demanded.

"Never forget," my mentor demanded.

I never did. I also never knew if Lucky had done that on purpose despite suspecting how it would end. Just for my benefit.

Asking seemed harsh.

I padded down the bare metal steps. The grille dug into my soles, but didn't bother me. The bottoms of my feet were no longer the delicate soles of a middle-class girl.

Just off to my right, a kitchen offered a wide sink and a riveted shelving fixture made out of plastic crates. Coffee mugs gleamed from hooks beneath it. The aroma of Lucky's special brew lingered in here.

The place hadn't changed much. The floor was still stained with the legacy of decades of wear, but clean. A plant in a mason jar sucked up whatever light could flicker through the frosted window over the sink, and a battered green printing unit hunkered by the entry. On top of it, a hotplate shimmered blue energy beneath an aluminum pot.

I let go of my arm, wincing when it pulsed in protest, and reached for a mug. Like all the rest, it was lopsided and lacking in paint. Lucky made a lot of his own home décor. He wasn't exactly an artist, but he'd always preferred functionality over anything else.

I'd helped him with this one. One of my better memories, actually.

I found a big plastic syringe, one of those thick ones you could use to suck fluids out of a wound, and tucked it between my teeth to hold while I pulled the lid off the pot.

My fingers stilled over the handle, gaze falling to the curt note left on the printer beside the burner. The paper was rough and grainy, made of old pulp and shredded recyclables.

Recalibrated nanos. Don't push your chipset, you fried your netware. Recharge. Coffee. Get out. Don't be there when I get back.

No signature. There usually wasn't. Lucky's handwriting was distinctive to me only in that I'd gotten lots of notes over the years.

Get out, huh?

Worry crept in under all the pain twinging my nerves.

What did he find in me? What did he know?

A sick knot gathered in my stomach. Logic dictated that he hadn't fried me, and he didn't seem worried about my setup, so odds were good I wasn't corrupted. But if I wasn't corrupted, then I was running with something else jacked up in my head.

That smelled too much like *feelings* for me to be comfortable with. And maybe something less meatspace than busted tech. Something, I don't know, mental.

I didn't know anything about mental space.

Only one way to find out what the hell Lucky meant. And why. If nothing else, I could count on him to tell it to me straight – *if* I bothered to ask. He didn't do casual enlightenment.

I wrapped one hand around the mug, pulled the syringe from my jaw before it cramped, and activated my projection protocols.

At least this time, the pulse registering the connection didn't hurt. That felt like a victory. Sort of.

The all-too-familiar room squared up. I was vaguely aware

of Lucky's kitchen around me, the mug in my hands and the smell of coffee, but it dimmed to a dull murmur around me. My protocols gave the projection room priority seating.

This time, I waited longer. But because I was something of a shit, even on a good day, I did wait.

Sure enough, the door opened. Lucky's voice followed. "You forget how to read?"

Always charming, my mentor. I sat on the table, arms folded under my chest, and glared at nothing. Probably part of the reason he pulled this disappearing act, too. Can't glare at nobody. It made me look stupid. Which I felt acutely enough that my voice sharpened. "Why am I getting kicked out?"

"You kidding me?" He'd never win awards for tender, but his tone was flat enough this time to border offensive. "Riko, how long have you run these streets?"

That was obvious enough to both of us that I didn't answer directly. I didn't have to. "What are you saying?" I asked, but a knot formed under the sick gurgle in my stomach. "What do you know?"

"I know I didn't teach you to be a cunting idiot." The plain white room only seemed to emphasize the sharp edges of his accusation. "Your cred's in the shitter, girl. Six ways of screwed. Whatever you did is mired in crap, but you know as well as I do what that means."

The knot dissolved in bile. My throat dried.

Confirmation. The kind of confirmation from the only man I never wanted to confirm this kind of thing. My fingers bit into my arms. The metal of my synthetic arm was no more real in this room than Lucky was, but a rolling wave of pain surged into my shoulder anyway.

Asshole arm.

Flinching at that seemed a lot easier than flinching at my mentor's truths. "How bad?"

Lucky knew what I was asking. He didn't bother accentuating. "Bad enough I can't have you hanging around my shop till you fix your shit."

For a chopshop doc of his rep, being seen with someone whose cred had taken a massive hit would drag him down long before it pulled me back up. He'd already set his cred on the line for me once – only an idiot took in a girl right after SINburn.

He wouldn't do it again. No matter what I said.

I couldn't ask.

I slid off the table, lifting my chin. I didn't know where to look, so I didn't bother. Staring straight ahead, I said simply, "You got any details for me?"

"I ain't your keeper," Lucky snapped. "Fix your own shit. Don't come back until you do."

"So it's like that."

"Riko." There. A measure of resignation I hadn't been sure my mentor would feel. It went a little way to smooth the ache, but not by much. Especially when he followed up the name he'd given me with, "It's *always* like that."

True that.

I nodded once, a sharp acknowledgment, and dropped my arms to my pockets. Jamming my fingers inside the loose seam, I waited until I could be sure I was alone. All I really wanted to do was throw up.

I didn't. I didn't dare. Lucky may have been kicking my ass to the curb, but it wasn't exactly unexpected. I'd always known what I was supposed to do here. What his raising had cost.

My cred would affect his. Period.

What pissed me off – what made me feel like I was choking – was the fact that whatever had gone down in my missing memories, it had cost me all the reputation I'd worked so fucking hard to earn on these streets.

A runner without cred was running on borrowed time. How far had my fall already spread? Who else knew?

Lucky had contacts everywhere. For a doc, he rivaled a lot of fixers I knew when it came to chatter. If I felt like being optimistic, I could consider him the vanguard to the shit I'd be dealing with as soon as gossip hit the rest. Mercs loved their gossip.

So I'd have to fix it. And fast.

I didn't promise I would. Not to Lucky. We knew each other well enough to understand without saying it aloud. I'd earn my shit back, or he'd never see me again. The end.

I was ready to disconnect when Lucky spoke again. "Riko."

"What?" The word snapped, harder than I'd meant. My synth palm slammed against the table. It was almost a punch. I reined it in just in time.

My mentor's voice graveled. "Have some coffee."

It was as close to affection as he'd ever show.

For whatever it was worth.

I only had one question left. "My scan. Was it clean?"

"It was clean." Then, gruffly, "You need new filters, replace your netware entirely."

Which I wouldn't get from him. Yeah. Without a word, I disconnected, came back to myself in the familiar kitchen with the smell of that brew thick in my nose, and realized I'd crumpled the syringe in my nanofactory steel hand.

"Damn it," I hissed. The least of my feelings.

Lucky wasn't just my mentor, he was my doc. My heals on wheels and my general technician. Nobody knew my tech the way he did, and now, I'd have to find a new doc – one who hadn't heard about my apparent fall from grace – or I'd be in serious trouble next time I had a bad run.

It's always like that.

It wasn't personal. But fuck me, it felt like it.

Whatever I'd done, whatever had put me in that lab – hell, whatever had actually happened in there – it was costing me *everything*. Far beyond frying my tech, which could be replaced, I got caught up in something that destroyed the reputation I'd worked too hard to build. Tech could be bought with credits.

My street cred was bought with blood and sweat.

I closed my eyes, took a deep breath. The phantom pain, the knot in my gut, the taste of bile on my tongue, all of that came a serious second to the knowledge that I was rapidly running out of allies.

And options.

I needed to know what happened. I *needed* to know what kind of shit I'd gotten into, and whatever else would be waiting in the freaking void of my head. I'd gotten into something; that much was clear.

I needed resources. Malik Reed was the only resource I had, and he wanted more answers than I could give.

Digo could barely talk civil to me. And I still wasn't convinced he didn't set my ass up.

I wanted my team, but they didn't want me.

Now I knew why. It wasn't just about the fact I'd supposedly convinced Nanji to tech up – though fucked if I knew how. It was that and more. My cred. Digo's cred.

And he'd probably feel the hit from whatever I'd done to tank mine. Shit on shit.

"*Fuck,*" I said, drawing the word out on a ragged, frustrated snarl. I slammed the mug onto the stove and threw the twisted syringe into the waste receptacle behind it. I fetched another, muttering every foul word I knew to fill the silence.

Opening the lid shot a hot cloud of perfumed steam into the kitchen. I inhaled, and nostalgia flooded me with a bittersweet burn. The smell alone had me imagining that I could feel the ache in my arm ease. It was a lie. Nothing would make *this* go away but lots of alcohol, lots of painkillers, or time.

The first two would screw up my motor skills. The latter would take too long. Lucky wanted me out. I wasn't naive enough to assume this place wasn't set up for surveillance. He'd know to the minute when I left.

I wait too long, and he'd take care of it himself. It wasn't personal. Right? *Fuck me.*

Coffee first. It was the least he could do.

Despite the agony lancing through my tech arm, I managed to load the new syringe full of a brew so dark, it was nearly black.

Good old Lucky. Where he got the beans – rare as virgins and twice as expensive – was a mystery. How he roasted them was a secret. It smelled like something tropical, bitter, and sharp. Hit the taste buds like something peppery and strangely nutty. Looked like motor oil.

Tasted a little bit like motor oil, too.

I squirted the hot liquid into my mug, shook out the syringe and tossed it in the sink to wash after. Cradling the warming mug between my hands, I inhaled until my lungs were full of the familiar fragrance.

Another surge of nostalgia washed over me. For a moment, a freaking rare moment, I took the opportunity to simply indulge. Maybe it'd be the last time I did.

I didn't often get the chance to hang out in Lucky's kitchen like this. Even when I was younger, with more determination than sense, I didn't spend a lot of time just hanging around. He put me to work. First, cleaning around the place. Then, cleaning after his operations.

When I didn't show any inclination to throw up at the sight of blood, he had me help out during. Nothing too crazy, we figured out pretty quickly I didn't have the patience for delicate work. But I was good for holding and fetching, staunching, and was even passable with the cauterizer.

Lucky was a hard man to get close to. An easy man to disappoint.

When I wasn't working for him, he passed me around to a few of his acquaintances – nobody I'd have called friends then, but I liked to think of them now and again with a certain fondness. They trained me to protect myself first, then taught me how to fight on the street. I was given guns, lots of guns, until I was proficient with all of them.

No, I didn't get a whole lot of love from the man, but if I'd wanted love and safety, I picked the wrong profession. What I got from Lucky was a thousand times more important to me: he taught me how to survive.

Not just physically, but completely. How to *live*, how to make the best of everything. What it meant to have cred, *real* cred. The kind that earned you credits to spend, allies to fight with.

And what it meant to lose it.

Warmth slipped into the space behind me, a hard body hemmed my back. I stiffened, snapping back to my surroundings as muscled arms banded on either side of me. Broad hands gripped the edge of the sink, as dark as the coffee beans Lucky used, each tattooed on the back with a nearly indiscernible blue. An open circle on one. An eclipsed circle on the other. They'd glow full moon bright when the vid-ink activated.

"Creds for your thoughts," murmured a familiar, all-too-intimate voice in my ear.

Balls. "You can't afford me," I shot back. My body softened, but not by much. It didn't pay to go soft around this one. "Back up, Jax."

Masculine laughter dusted across my bare shoulder. The warm, strong line of a fit body against mine was always nice, but this one belonged to Taylor Jax, and I couldn't afford him, either. Besides, he still hadn't figured out that I hated it when he cramped my space.

"You say that with such disdain," he said, his tenor teasing in my ear. "What, no hug? No kiss? No welcome-home fuck against this sink?" He jerked on the steel basin, arms taut on either side of my waist. The sink didn't so much as tremble. "Seems sturdy enough."

The fact that he was even asking was clear enough signal that he was screwing with me. I turned in his arms, thrusting my steaming cup against his chest. He could either step back or wear the brew. And since he was sporting very little over the muscled breadth of his chest – a tanktop, like me, but red to contrast his dark, dark skin and worn denim over black combat boots – he chose to step back.

"Lucky isn't here," I told him flatly. "Come back later."

"You didn't accept my offer."

"Oh, you noticed."

He didn't flinch at my saccharine sarcasm; I didn't expect him to. Jax was one of those men who wasn't pretty. He wasn't handsome, not like Indigo's hawkish good looks or the expensively chiseled Valentine. He couldn't even claim striking, not like Malik Reed with his aura of power and slick suit. What he had – what I think he and I shared – was an intensity that translated across cultural restraints. That vibe, the one that says we're in it for the good time. Probably one of the reasons we'd hooked up, a few years back.

And for all that, I still wouldn't fuck him on the sink. Not that the idea didn't have a little bit of appeal. His skin was so dark that it practically swallowed light, and his eyes glowed in that black skin like emeralds set in front of a naked flame. Definitely eyecatching.

Being around Jax made a person feel like tomorrow wasn't worth worrying about. He was selfish, but he had a way of wrapping you up in it with him. A kind of shared egocentricity. Dangerous in one man, downright suicidal in two of us. I knew my limits. Well, *now*.

"Seriously," I groaned. "Why am I tripping over all my sexual misdeeds lately?"

"Easy." Jax grinned, nano-perfected smile stunningly bright. "There's a lot to trip over."

I scowled at him. "Like you can talk." As if hearing it from Greg wasn't enough.

"Hey, kitten, you know you're my favorite slut."

As if. We may have been great in bed, but we were shit in a relationship. We were too much alike in all the ways it sucked, which made for some fierce competition along the way and more than one stray on both sides of the fence. One great big abusive party.

Our split was the stuff of legends. His pride took the kind of beating a man like Jax couldn't let slide. Mine didn't. I didn't have the same emotional investment in the relationship – or, rather, in the appearance of the relationship. He needed a partner to fawn over him. I didn't.

Something else his pride couldn't handle.

Our relationship had always been hot and cold, before and after. I guess he was feeling balmy today.

Or he had a snake up his sleeve. If Lucky knew about my shit, there was no telling what Jax knew.

I'd have to play the next few minutes carefully.

"But," he continued lightly, "cute as you are in that baby blue, I'll have to pass."

Like I'd offered. The fact he called me cute said a lot about why we'd split.

He moved back, snagged another mug and helped himself to the pot, dipping the ceramic edge into the steaming brew. I almost rolled my eyes again. "I guess you can help yourself to the coffee," I said, too late and ignored anyway.

"Nobody can make it like Lucky does."

"Does he know you come in here?" I leaned against the sink, crossing my bare ankles, and sipped while Jax shot me a raised eyebrow. His hair, long and coarse and pulled into thick dreads, was pure black today. Last time I'd seen him, he'd gone pretty in pink.

Cosmetic tech. Jax could do anything he wanted with his hair, when he decided to unkink the filaments from something approximating natural. A neat party trick.

"I've got a standing invite," he assured me.

"Liar."

He grinned, neither confirming nor denying my level accusation. Sure as shit that Lucky knew, but I wondered just how far Jax liked to play with fire. "So, what was the prodigal daughter thinking while staring wistfully out into the middle distance?"

Jackass. I shrugged one shoulder – my good one. The other was a corded streak of pain I tried hard to suppress. "I was thinking about the time Lucky introduced me to the Kill Squad's first." A lie, but not that far from the truth. It was the first time I'd *really* understood what it meant to be street.

What Lucky meant about cred.

Jax's smile faded. "When?"

"About nine–" I caught myself, mouth twisting as I recalled my missed birthday. "Maybe ten years ago."

"Dancer? You met *Dancer*."

"That's her."

He whistled. "What for?"

"To get the street," I replied, also only partially the truth. I didn't know then what I'd been pressganged into. "I survived two days with them, then ran back here." Jax sipped from his mug, his eyebrows arched high like I was turning polka-dotted in front of his eyes. "She and a few of the Squad came to drag me back. Show me what happens to a member who wouldn't stick."

I spoke casually, my tone easy; it masked the terror I'd experienced then. Time had erased the nightmares. Nothing softened the lesson.

"Damn, Ree." He studied me, head to toe as if he could ferret out some clue in my nonchalant posture. "What'd Lucky do when they came for you?"

"Watch them take me over a crossword." My smile was wry. "He said, 'Ten across, ends with c. Unconscious.'"

"Cataleptic," Jax said, as casually over the rim of his mug as if he'd been talking about the hot weather. "Obviously."

The skin around my eye twitched. It was easy to forget how smart Jax really was.

Then again, I'd never expected Dancer to be so smart,

either. As I was begging Lucky to save me, the old lady had turned to him with a smile in her glass-hard eyes and answered him. *Cataleptic*. Just like that.

And cataleptic is what Lucky got.

In a gang like Dancer's, a member who tries to run finds themselves on the receiving end of a grisly train, all comers invited. Fists or fucks, blood and spunk; didn't matter what or who. That's what it meant to betray a family like that. Full, fucking retribution.

Maybe it was because Dancer had a different code, or maybe it was Lucky's influence, but I missed one of those trains. Instead, I was returned to Lucky's doorstep with broken bones, internal hemorrhaging and at least three concussions. Or whatever.

I never begged again. A week later, after Lucky had set my legs long enough for the nanos to heal the damage, I went back to the Kill Squad. I don't know why. Maybe to prove I could.

"What happened?"

I shrugged. "I rolled with the crew for a month. When I left for good, I put a bullet in Dancer's spine."

Jax snorted. "How come I didn't know about this?"

"Because we weren't much for life stories," I replied with a shake of my head. And while that had been the start of my own reputation, I'd done plenty more to overshadow it.

A street doc fixed the old bitch up fine. She was killed a year later on a run against a drug manufacturing plant she'd suspected had been dropped on her turf by a satellite of GinZeng Pharma.

"You are one scary cooch, you know that?"

I raised the mug in his direction. "And that's why girls don't like you, Jax. Your lingo is filthy." I tipped the brew into my mouth, savoring the taste as it scalded all the way down.

It was a little bit appalling how good that made me feel. Like nostalgia, but bitter and black. And painful.

Jax grinned at me. "I don't remember you having such a problem with my cunning lingo once upon a time."

I ignored that. Not that I didn't have something to say, but my arm hurt and my shoulder felt like hot screws twisted inch by inch into my flesh. Oh, yeah, and I had to get my ass out of here before Lucky decided I was officially infringing on his space.

And every moment spent with Taylor Jax was another layer of neurosis piled on paranoia.

He drained his mug in one long swallow. If it burned, he didn't seem to care.

The silence that descended was a little *too* companionable. Suspicion filled me. "So, what *really* brings you here?" I asked, crossing my arms under my breasts, mug held easily in one hand.

His grin only brightened. "Professional courtesy, if you will."

"I don't."

"Aw, Riko, don't be so prickly."

"Go fuck a rusted pipe."

His grin widened. "Maybe later. You really want to know?" When I only stared at him, refusing the obvious answer, he shrugged. "Word on the street was that you'd vanished."

"Yeah, so I'm told." I scowled at him. "Professional courtesy, huh?"

"A man's got to have a rival."

"You have a whole black book of them."

He didn't bother with humble. "I totally do, don't I?"

Jax was a projector. Where a linker holds a team together through feeds and filtered information, Jax walked the bandwidth like I did the street, and his tech proclaimed him loud and clear for what he was. The open jacks at the nape of his neck, the base of his skull, and the four inset along his spine allowed him to interface with the system in ways too dangerous for most of us to try. He had shit in his brain that would have fried a lesser man. It was also about seven different shades of illegal, and an automatic kill on sight for every law enforcement agency in the city. And some cagier runners.

Anybody could project, we all did it when we worked the bandwidth, but not anybody could do it like Jax did. He was in rare company. I only knew of four living 'jectors in this city, and two had gone off-grid in the past year. Rumor had it that conversion nailed at least one.

Society had moved beyond the barbaric jacks pretty quickly. Only the real freaks among us kept it alive. Jax worked his art with such unabashed joy, I'd long since clocked him in as more than a little bit insane.

I shot him a hard stare. "So, now you know. I'm alive. Thanks for checking in. Get out."

"Whoa, there." He held out his mug, sparkling green eyes overflowing with sincerity. Immediately suspect. "You know I'm just checking up on an old friend."

Bullshit.

I took the mug, dumped both of them in the sink and eyed him until he rocked back on his heels, thumbs tucking into his pockets. "And," he admitted without shame, "maybe see if I could do anything for you."

"Now I know you're full of it," I said. "What for?"

His smile tilted up to the ceiling. "'Cause."

"*Jax.*"

His smile vanished. "Okay, killer. Indigo's been going around the past month telling everyone you got his virginal little sister fried." His tone leveled. Not cool, not even remote. Just steady. Like he was reciting facts out of a book. There we go. Business mode. "Next thing I know, word on the wave is that you're back, minus one virginal little sister."

"She was hardly virginal."

I should have kept my goddamned mouth shut. "Yes," he said, with all the relish of a man with experience on the subject. "I know. In fact, she used to do this thing–"

"Shut it," I interjected, before I could be regaled with anything more.

So he'd gotten to Nanji before I did.

In the scheme of things, it didn't *really* matter, but the fact I'd put my lips where Jax's dick had been was only slightly more offensive than the fact I'd let him dick *me* over a few times, too. Literally and metaphorically.

Saints tended to become one great big incestuous fuckfest. *Ugh.*

Nanji had never said anything to me. Probably smart. Conversations that included me and Jax in the same breath never ended well. "Do me a favor and get to the damn point, would you?"

He shrugged his wiry shoulders. "It's all information, sugartits. You're into something big and bad, I can help. You want it or not?"

I refrained from knocking a few of those nice white teeth out for the name. It was only one in a long list.

Turning my back, I cranked the regulator until Lucky's illegal tank kicked in, and boiling hot water sluiced from the faucet. I let it cascade over the two mugs and syringe. A cloud of steam enveloped me.

"Aw. You're so domestic, Riko." I didn't have to see his face to know he was grinning again. "When are you going to settle down and have my beautiful black babies?"

I growled. "Ever been shoved face first into boiling water?"

"Not once."

"Want to?"

"God, you're sexy," was his response. I bared my teeth. "Last offer on the help."

And that was the pretty much the shittiest offer I'd ever been handed. Not because I'd been handed it, but because I didn't have much choice. My cred demanded I find answers. The loss of it made it a life or death situation. When a runner like me tanks on reputation, lesser mercs start gunning for her. Some out of a need to prove themselves against someone who'd once been untouchable, some because a merc doesn't get to be that badass without stepping on a few dicks along the way.

I'd rather avoid shootouts in the street. Especially when they're shooting at me, dicks or otherwise.

But if I accepted Jax's help, I'd all but confirm his suspicions. I may as well put a neon light on my ass claiming it as up for grabs.

Fuck me. Life was so much simpler when I could just kick a man in the teeth and be done with it.

"What's the cost?" I asked without turning.

His voice hadn't shifted from his claimed corner, so he was respecting boundaries this time. "A favor, to be named when I need it. No questions."

"That's a big damn cost." But I was definitely thinking about it. One favor. In exchange, I'd get Jax's resources on the bandwidth, which could turn up nothing or everything. Or something in between. I was flying blind already. And for all his attitude, he wasn't in the business of screwing around with facts. He knew what he knew, and when he said he'd help, he meant it.

The name Taylor Jax had more cred on it than almost anyone else I knew, save maybe Lucky's. I ran with an elite cunting crowd.

But this brought up a whole new concern. "Why help at all, Jax?"

"Let's just say I'm keeping an eye on my bank."

He didn't mean a financial institution. Of all the things projectors dealt with, financial worries wasn't one of them. When the system works on a digital level, 'jectors tend to be rolling in credits. And cred. Lucky, suicidal bastards.

I shot him a look over my shoulder, but his face told me nothing. "Are you prepping something big?"

"Not yet." His eyebrows rose and lowered, salacious inquiry. "But I can't have cops luring you over to the forces of good before I'm ready to make an offer myself."

There it was. I turned. My tech hand clanked on the sink, fingers curving over it. I didn't pinch the metal, but the act sent a throbbing pulse through my brain.

Damn, it hurt.

My shoulder twitched. "You better not be monitoring me." I stopped shy of a serious threat. Regardless of our history, neither of us had ever really crossed that line. I wasn't sure what would happen if we did. I could take him on in meatspace, but I'd lose on the bandwidth. Lose *hard*. If we ever became enemies for real, I'd get one chance – provided he was in front of me when the gloves came off.

These are the things a saint thinks about. Where to run, where the exits are, and how much time it'd take to reach them. What tech to risk and how best to maximize a killing edge. How to win a hypothetical fight with a buddy, because that buddy could sell you out tomorrow. I barely even noticed it anymore. Survival was king.

Jax's smile upped about a thousand watts. "Relax, kitten. I was actually stalking *him*."

That earned him a blank stare. "Detective Douchedick? Why?"

He shrugged easily, a fluid line of red on black. If the name caught him by surprise, he didn't show it. "Investments."

Easily translated. In short, Greg hadn't made any secret of his financial difficulties, and Jax – maybe other saints – had clued in. I wondered how many fixers had paid for that information already.

And how many had sold it.

Damn. Well, that was life on the street. I couldn't do much for the detective now. If he wanted creds so badly, I hoped he was smart enough to know the good jobs from the bad.

Unlike me, who knew the difference but currently lacked

the backing to get the good ones.

I sighed. "Stay off my freqs," I told him. "I'm just starting to like you again."

"Does that mean you're interested?"

I let go of the sink. "In your offer of help, yeah," I replied evenly. "But you can keep your babies to yourself, whatever color they are."

That smile flashed again. "I'll be in touch for that favor. How long are you staying here?"

"I'm leaving soon as I rep up some clothes."

"That explains it." Jax ran a hand over his dreads, pulling them over his shoulder the way a girl would to catch a man's attention. It wasn't quite the same with Jax. He just really liked his hair. I did, too, but I also recognized exactly what kind of leverage it gave me in a fight.

"What?" I asked, frowning.

"Lucky kicked you out."

I briefly thought about arguing, but then I realized his green eyes weren't looking at me. He'd seen the note.

Of course he'd seen it. Nosy bastard. "So?"

"Well, that's some shit right there." With his hair arranged, he ran both hands into his dreadlocks, scratching at his scalp. It lifted the hem of his tanktop, bared a flat, muscled expanse of belly. "Hate to say it, but there's a few flags flapping out there."

"'Course there are," I said wryly, then stilled. "Wait." I glared at him. "Did you just bargain with me when you *already* have info?"

"Sort of." He tilted his head, lazily studying me from half-lidded eyes. "More like a lead. And I'm willing to part with it. Call it an advance on what I'm thinking is an ongoing problem of epic proportions. In good faith."

Great. "Why?"

He hesitated. Then, with another one of those lazy shrugs, he replied, "People don't vanish, Riko. Even when they get themselves splattered, there's trace. Except then you went and actually *vanished*."

"So you tracked me."

His eyes banked, a trace of anger and more than a little intrigue as he studied me. "No, I tried. You went so far off-grid, it's like you stopped existing. Only thing I dug up is a little bit of info on a certain virginal little sister."

"Stop calling her that," I snapped, and turned my back on him to stab the screen on the hacked printer Lucky maintained. He'd know it when he came back, but regardless of everything else, he wouldn't begrudge me clothes.

"Indigo hired me to find her." Jax's voice carried the verbal equivalent of a shrug. He didn't care. "Then when the bit surfaced of one Nanjali Koupra going up in chopshop flames, he hired me to find *you*. Is it true you sold her out?"

That was the kind of news I couldn't gloss over. "Wait. Back up. *Indigo* hired *you*?" My surprise shifted into abject disbelief. My lip curled. "You're making that up." They hated each other. I'd never cared enough to know why, but the fact Jax had banged Digo's sister put some of that into clarity.

I hated feeling kinship with Jax. Ugh.

"Wish I was, sugartits." Shoving the mass of his dreadlocks back over his shoulder, he shot me a look that didn't leave any room for amusement – easy or otherwise. "So did you sell her out?"

"No." Maybe. I didn't fill in the blanks, but I didn't waste any breath explaining, either. Word got out fast when a 'jector got involved. "I didn't sell her out. I ended up in the same place she did, but they had me in some kind of stasis, I think, so I don't have any memories of the time. I woke up thinking I'd only missed a day."

"Yeah, bullshit." But that lash of determination wasn't aimed at me. I knew Jax well enough to get it. His pride was stinging. "You know I don't like unanswered questions."

Fair enough. In the scheme of things, it was better to have

Jax annoyed and on my side than annoyed and out to get me. "Fine," I said. "I can respect that. What do you have for me?"

"Fuck It Jim."

I blinked. Bukket Jehm was a fixer. A man who parceled out jobs for money, took on goods to sell on the market, and otherwise took care of the annoying details. He was a small man with a thin mustache, weasely enough to do the job but the least trustworthy among the established fixers. That's how he'd earned the moniker Fuck It Jim. It was easier to say *fuck it* than try.

Indigo didn't deal with him as a rule. Too much trouble.

"That guy's smeglevel," I said, skeptical. "Why him?"

"'Cause he's up to his little spunked-up nose in your shit, that's why."

Well, that made everything clearer. And so simple. "Okay." I nodded, like it was no big. "I'm going to go kill him now."

"Yeah, that might have flown *before* you started working with him."

I froze, my finger hovering over the button that would start the printer. My stare landed on Jax with one part surprise, two parts mocking amusement, and enough teeth to make him raise his hands in a gesture of goodwill. "Bullshit," I said clearly.

"Yeah, you can say that, but c'mon, Ree. We know. You and me?" His mouth curved in a humorless smile. "We *know*. And so do enough people who started wondering aloud what the fuck you were doing with a lowlife like Jim."

Which now explained part of the hit my cred took. If I was rumored to be working with Fuck It Jim, my reputation would slide like a greased chromer spiked naked down an oil slick.

Fucking A, if *Lucky* got associated with that sniveling little anus wart, he'd lose work. No wonder he was so eager to get me the hell out.

Goddamn son of a bitch fixer and his little ratty fingers got all over my business.

"Only thing I can't work out," Jax continued, watching me closely, "is what you were doing with him, but you won't tell me. So I'll figure it out."

If he did, if he beat me to it, I'd be so boned.

But I couldn't very well admit to running around the city out of my mind since April. Even Jax knew that wasn't cool. Lucky may have cleared me of corruption, but that didn't change the fact that somehow, a whole chunk of time was missing from my brain.

Which meant – what if I *was* working with Jim?

"Fine," I said, stabbing the button. The printer warmed up. "Why do you think Jim's the key?"

Jax's smile crinkled his gleaming eyes. "Because out of everyone you worked with, Riko, he's the only one *everyone* knows would screw you over."

I grimaced. "Fan-fucking-tastic."

"Hey. I'm just a guy bringing you all the good faith data you need." Jax kissed his fingers and flicked it my direction. "The rest is all you, pussy." He said it like an endearment. I growled under my breath as he turned. "Oh." He glanced back at me over his shoulder, which admittedly did nice things for the shape of the muscles there. "Can I offer some advice?"

"Can I stop you?"

His eyes twinkled in that good humor I knew was as much a front as his cosmetic appeal. "You don't have to kick the shit out of everyone in your hot pursuit. At least try to be cool."

I scoffed. "Please. I only do that for losers and chumheads. I don't *have* to curb stomp people just for answers."

"Yeah, sugartits. That's what I'm *saying*." Jax left the kitchen before I could argue.

I shouted at his back, "In good faith, my ass!"

"Give me time."

My recommendation of what he could do with his time followed him out of the chopshop. He was laughing when the door closed behind him.

Shit. Jax liked to think of me as one of his rivals, but he was weirdly protective of those rivals. If he'd come looking to help me, it meant there was something in it for him. As a 'jector, he was just as connected to the data wave as a fixer was, but he didn't farm out jobs. He just liked having information, even if he didn't know how it all came together.

That's what made 'jectors so damn dangerous, street side and in the corporate broadsheets. You never knew what they'd waded through, and what they'd hold against you later.

Well, that and their rate of tech corruption skyrocketed at an alarming rate compared to the rest of us.

So he led me to Jim, and I owed him a favor. Jax knew I'd keep it; hell, at this point, he might be the only one taking me on faith. I'd all but confirmed the mass amounts of shit I was in, and he still fed me this lead.

At a steep price, admittedly. I recognized a baited hook when I saw one, but it happened to be attached to a lifeline.

If my cred was so bad that Lucky was tossing me out? I'd have an uphill battle. Jax's favor, suck as it was, would help me earn it back. Hopefully.

I scrubbed at my face with my drying hand, groaning.

Fuck It Jim operated out of a ratbag motel thirty-seven minutes away by cab. Whatever he had, whatever data he knew that I didn't, it better be worth more than just my tanked cred – it damn well better be worth my life.

There was no telling what Jax would ask me to do later.

12

Fuck It Jim's place hovered right by squalor plaza and within spitting distance of suicide lane. Dank and dirty as a testicular fistula. The dingy motel didn't look all that different from the other buildings nestling against it – diseased fuck-buddies all crowding for the same soiled blanket, layers of drab color interrupted here and there by bold paint from street taggers with nothing better to put their mark on.

I didn't bother checking in with the front desk. Place like this, I was just as likely to meet the business end of a shotgun as a friendly word. I'd had about enough of getting shotguns shoved in my face for a few days.

The row of stained brown doors and curtained, semi-boarded windows smiled at me as I stared at the façade. By the blackened edges, the last seven on the left had all suffered fire damage, which made them only slightly less unlivable than the other thirty-six rooms like it. Bugs, vermin, stains you were better off not asking about, room service that was comprised of a daily hammering on the door, a fat man in a cheap suit screaming for rent...

Yeah, classy place, this.

Unless he'd changed his MO, Jim was behind door number 14 – the age he liked girls best, he'd said when I'd first had the pleasure of meeting him. Inside joke.

Ha, ha.

I'd changed out of the board shorts, swapping them for a pair of printed denim loose enough to take a boot to Jim's head. I didn't think I'd have to, but sometimes the man played hard to get.

I wasn't in the mood today.

Of course, if I did kick his teeth in without at least trying, I'd have to deal with Jax laughing down my neck.

Assholes. Every one.

I took the stairs two at a time, the whole broken down thing wobbling with every step. To my left, I caught movement in another unit's window – a flutter of a curtain, a glimpse of crooked teeth and shadowed eyes – but nobody came out to see me. I didn't expect it. This was a pay-by-the-hour kind of joint, where questions weren't asked because the answers might just get you killed, entrapped, or worse.

My fist against door number 14 echoed hollowly, every thud of flesh against the shabby paint sending jolts of echoed pain down my other arm. "Open up, Jim!"

Silence.

It didn't occur to me that the fixer wouldn't be in. The guy had a hate list about three miles long – he hated the world at large and everybody in it. It made him willing to sell information on anyone; a double-edged sword. People hated him, too, and I assumed it was only a matter of time before somebody wrung his scrawny neck.

I slammed my fist against the door so hard, the whole frame juddered. "If I break this down," I yelled, "you're going to have to explain it. You know they'll raise your rates."

Like most men of Fuck It Jim's persuasion, he was a stingy bastard.

I counted back from three. On one, a lock clicked.

The hinges creaked as the door cracked open an inch. Just enough to reveal one bloodshot silver eye. It widened. Then it flashed.

"Now I have to warn you that if you do anything with that snapshot," I continued, not unreasonably, "I will rip the storage chipset out of your shriveled little brain and make you eat it." My standard policy.

"Riko." My name on his lips wasn't welcoming. "What are you doing here?"

"First, delete that file," I replied, flattening my metal palm on the door and pushing until the chain holding it snapped taut. The impact of the tension sent tiny fingers of pain up my shoulder.

I didn't wince. Wincing would give the man ammunition, and I needed him unarmed in every sense.

So I gave him my best smile. Something lacking in teeth. "Second, I want what everyone wants from you."

The ocular replacement framed in jaundiced skin narrowed. "Do you want to kill me or do you want to give me creds?" He meant money. It didn't stop me from thinking I'd already given him too much cred and wanted desperately to take it out of his grimy skin.

I didn't say it aloud. "I need information," I said instead.

He brightened. "Creds, it is." The door closed, the chain clinked, and then Fuck It Jim opened the door wide, his smile thin and sharp and naked with greed. "C'mon in. Why didn't Indigo tell me you were coming?" He paused. "Or, uh, is this for another thing?"

"Nice to see you, too, Jim." I stepped inside.

Bukket Jehm wasn't an imposing figure. He was shorter than me, with swarthy skin painted yellow from some defect I didn't know and his eyes metallic silver in the iris. Ocular implants – straight-up replacements, probably. The whites of his eyes were *too* white, instead of yellow with whatever condition turned his skin sallow, and it gave his stare an eerily bright disposition. The fact that they were implants and *still* wormed by startling red told me whatever he was into, it wasn't good.

His stringy brown hair was kept too long, one of those braids that thinned until it was nothing but a wisp at the broken ends – crowned by the fact that he was balding at the top – and his hooked nose was usually running. Or plugged. Or bleeding, although somebody had usually punched him for that one.

Drug habit, I'd bet. A nasty one. Nanos weren't much good against drugs these days. As technology got better, so did the smart drug lords, the cookers, and the designers who made narcotics to counteract nano interference.

That's one of the things that made slank so popular. Easy to make, easy to cut, *and* easy to deal.

Swish was easier to make, but left a trail of burned-out corpses in its wake. Canker was about the same as rinsing your mouth with piss and bleach – the poor man's purgatory – and colordust was expensive to produce and harder to score outside corp and rich-world contacts. Strych hadn't seen a revival in years. That left only, oh, about a hundred other options.

Whatever Jim was spooning himself, I didn't recognize the signs.

He was dressed in his idea of luxury, though to me it looked like he'd gone bargain bin shopping in Kongtown. His garishly green silk pants and embroidered tunic looked as out of place in the cheap motel room as I'd look at a rich wedding.

But Jim, he liked flattery. So I gave him my best once-over and offered, "Nice pants."

He stroked a hand down the front of his tunic, leaving a sweaty smear in the silk. "Like it? Got a whole set in every color."

This didn't surprise me.

"How you been, Riko? Life treating you any better?" He waved at the only seating available – one of two beds – and took position on the closest.

There wasn't much else to pick from. The farthest corner from the door was cluttered with makeshift shelving, riddled with computer screens in various sizes and hunks of metal – wires exposed and linked together, dust gathering in between them. Makeshift hardware. A wave of palpable heat shimmered from the systems array, making the marginally cooler room seem stifling.

The curtains covering the windows were a weirdly streaked mustard color, thin enough to let the light through but too opaque to see more than silhouettes between the cheap threads. Scattered food cartons, most from places that delivered, peppered the floor near the nest of tech, which suggested Fuck It Jim wasn't much into fresh air or relaxation.

Or furniture.

If he thought I was going to get anywhere near a mattress with him, he was out of his mind.

I stood, feet braced, my arms folded under my breasts. I'd taken the time to put a cropped bra on underneath, so as his eyes flicked to my less than impressive chest, disappointment flashed across his features. Way better than greed. Only thing I wanted him lusting for was my credits.

"Better than what?" I asked pleasantly. I wasn't sure how much of anything he knew. He wasn't top shelf, but it never paid to underestimate a man with information at his fingertips.

"Well." He gestured at nothing. "Better than when I saw you last?"

Fuck. I didn't even know when that was. Last time *I* remembered dealing with Jim, I'd threatened to scalp him over a few hundred stray credits. "I'm alive and kicking," is what I said instead.

"I can see that." His thin nostrils flared. "No one knows you're here, right?"

"Sure, Jim." Again, I smiled. This one showed teeth.

Fuck It Jim lost a little bit of color in the face. "Uh..." He shifted a little. "Is this about that last transaction?"

Because I didn't know the first thing about sweet-talking a weasel, I didn't drop the smile. "Maybe."

He sprang to his feet, scuttling so fast the bed was between us before both of his feet even hit the floor. "Now, hang on," he stuttered, both hands held out. Pleading? Warding me away, anyway. Interesting. "You got your creds, fair and square."

My creds? Hell if I'd ever gotten fair pay from the guy.

But I tried for tact, first, because he was enough of a rat to spill the goods if it came down to his skin or mine. "I'm not here to argue that, Jim."

Probably not the way most people tried to commune with the guy. He stared. "You... aren't?"

"Nope, not even a little." I didn't move from my spot on the stained floor, didn't drop my arms.

I probably could have jumped on him, beaten him until his teeth fell out and demanded answers, but Jax's caution made my skin itch.

I didn't *have* to beat everyone up. I just found it easier.

And Fuck It Jim's little rodent face set off every instinct I had – he deserved a beating. I wasn't sure for what, but he'd know even if I didn't. It'd be fair somewhere.

Instead, I had to stand here, feeling stupid while I tried to be *nice*. "But you know how things go," I continued, wrinkling my nose. "Something goes sideways, and the bosses want all the details in a neat, orderly list."

Jim's chuckle cracked. "Heh. Yeah."

"So, you know. He sent me here to ask a few questions."

"He?" Jim's face closed down – far too late for poker.

Oops. I had no idea what the hell we were talking about. His response made me wonder how much he knew, and whether I'd fucked up with "he". Maybe I was reporting to a woman?

Jim shifted uncertainly. "You okay, Riko? You seem..." He hesitated. "Different."

"Nothing a little chat can't fix." I leveled him with my best patient stare. "Can we just be honest with each other?"

"Fuck, Riko." Jim stroked down his tunic again, and I noticed he'd left another damp smear. He was nervous. "You know I can't do honest."

"Yeah, you can." I rocked back on my heels. Nothing to see

here. Totally harmless. Right. "Be straight with me and I'll be straight with you. It's easy."

His eyes darted left. "If I do, I'll lose some serious cred."

Like I had in dealing with him? The rat owed me.

My smile didn't slip. "If you don't, you'll lose some serious blood."

"Heh." His laugh was weak, too thin, and he scooted a bit along the mattress. Another foot between him and me. "You get real scary real fast, you know that?"

I dropped my arms, ran a hand through my hair to push it from my face. "Hell, Jim. This isn't scary."

"No?" He asked like he didn't believe me. Like I was joking.

"No," I repeated seriously. And then I closed the distance. It happened so fast, I don't think he even marked the point where I'd shifted from idle to speed. My feet dug into the floor, his throat was in my left hand, and I had his short body off that bed and pinned to the wall behind it with my arm servos straining. The muscles in my shoulder girdle screamed.

I'd tried it Jax's way. I'd felt stupid doing it, and it didn't net me jack. Now I'd see about mine.

My teeth bared, and this time there was nothing smiley about it. "*This* is scary." He gurgled. "So here's how this is going to roll," I told him, only a little out of breath. "You're going to tell me everything I need to know, and then I will very nicely not squeeze your liver out through your nose. You get me?"

He struggled, gasping, choking around the vise grip at his throat, but his thin fingers couldn't force the metal digits around his neck to loosen. His face mottled under all that yellow, turned ugly green and purple.

Jim was light. Way too light. The heads-up numbers put him at a hundred and two pounds, and this close, I noted how far his clavicle protruded under the thin silk.

Sick. A whole lot sicker than I remembered him being.

His nostrils flared wildly, feet kicking, thudding against the wall, shaking it. I waited him out. He'd lose it before I did, no matter how badly my shoulder hurt for it.

His eyes bulged as he spat out curses that would have made a delicate woman blush. Instead, I grinned.

That did not go over well.

"Get away from me," he managed to choke out. "You crazy bitch!"

"I've been hearing that a lot lately." Bracing my knees, I shoved more thrust into my shoulder, forcing him higher against the wall. He squeaked. It was probably supposed to be a scream, but there wasn't a lot of room between my fingers and the narrow diameter of his windpipe. "Make this easy, Jim. You don't want to die here."

Despite my general dislike for the man, I found sympathy in my voice with that one. It was obvious whatever was eating at Bukket Jehm, it wasn't a guilty conscience.

"Tell me everything I need to know about our working relationship, and I'll let you go."

"Why?" he gasped.

"Because I can't remember," I said tightly, earning a bulging-eyed stare from the man whose throat moved beneath my diamond steel fingers.

Yeah, he was the one hanging by a fleshy straw, and *I* was the crazy one.

I snarled. "Now, Jim!"

"Agh...!"

I chose to believe that was an "all right". I let go, letting his frail weight drop to his feet, slump gracelessly to the floor. He hunched over, gasping, coughing, forcing blood back to his brain.

I hoped it helped. This wasn't my trump card. This was simple intimidation. If I had to start breaking fingers, I wasn't going to feel very good about my day.

Normally, a guilty conscience wasn't my problem, either, but things were a little off kilter since walking away from Nanji. I wasn't sure what exactly I felt there – guilt, fury, confusion – but if I killed Jim here, Jax would know. Facing his knowing mockery later would really scrape my nerves raw.

I crouched, balancing lightly on the balls of my feet, and pressed my fingers lightly together, elbows braced on my knees and close enough that if he so much as twitched, he'd be in reach. "So," I began slowly, "let's start with the reason you gave me a payout. What the hell did you get me into?"

"How can you not remember?" He stared at me like I'd grown a second head. I was getting a lot of that lately, too.

"Doesn't matter." I knew my stare made him nervous; he was perspiring through his collar, staining the silk under his pits. "What has Taylor Jax sniffing around your accounts?"

Of all the things I could have said, that probably wasn't my brightest idea. Apoplectic rage replaced the purple mottling on his face, his weasel-like features twisting into something ugly and vicious. "Jax," he spat, hoarse. "You tell that donkey-fucking spunk-bucket that he ca–"

I angled my fingers towards him. "Jim."

His lips pressed so hard together, they turned into a seam of white.

His eyes darted to the right.

"Spill it," I encouraged. "Last chance."

A muscle jumped in his thin face, just at the point where he was probably trying to grind his teeth into powder. "Fine," he snarled. "Fine! Just let me get up."

I rose, looking down on his shivering, curled figure with something I was pretty sure was pity. And revulsion. It felt strange, to feel both at the same time, but Bukket Jehm had a way of making you feel sorry for him even while you were pretty sure he'd sell your grandmother for a crate of something snortable.

I stepped back.

I hated that Jax had me second-guessing my usual methods. My forced goodwill turned into Jim's opportunity as he threw himself between the farthest bed and the wall, rolled under it faster than I could lunge. His skinny ass cleared the lip with room to spare. "Damn it, Jim!" I thumped the wall with my flesh fist. "Get out here."

"Make me!" The voice was high with victory.

Too early. It was a goddamned bed, not a fort.

And I was done talking. Setting my jaw, I bent, grasped the foot of the metal frame with my tech arm and tested the weight.

Too much, according to my lateral display. Way more than I'd have figured for a wire frame.

I heard shuffling, like rats clawing at walls, and then the unmistakable sound of something metal clanking against the frame I held. "Are you hiding under the bed?" I asked. "Seriously?"

"Fuck you," he wheezed, fear making his voice tremble. "You go back and tell them the deal's off!"

Deal? What deal? How the hell had I become the principal here? "You," I grunted as I tugged at the bed, "and I are going to talk, Jim. *Now.*" This bitch was nailed down. Of course it was. You give somebody a chance, they'll make off with anything that isn't. Explained the lack of decor.

I squared my stance, fingers tightening on the frame edge. Every muscle from my reinforced biceps to the hesitant ache under my scapula twanged a warning.

I ignored it.

Sucking in a hard breath, I yanked. Hard. Much harder than I thought I could have; much, *much* faster. The bed frame shrieked, the springs clanked in the old mattress, the floor groaned as the bolts tore out of their moorings. I cursed hard and long as every nerve in my nonexistent arm turned to molten lava and Fuck It Jim made the last mistake he'd ever make.

He pulled a gun on me.

The mattress was still in freefall, bed frame carving plaster furrows down the wall I'd thrown it against as I stepped in, kicked the gun out from his shaking hands. I don't remember making the decision. I simply reached down and seized his face in my metal hand. I slammed his head against the floor. Once.

He screamed.

Twice.

Three times, and the floor boards cracked.

He stopped screaming.

I didn't stop breaking. *Thud.*

Crack.

Again and again.

When his head fell apart in my fingers, turning to so much mush and bone at the stump of the very motionless body I still straddled, I stopped.

Plaster dust rained like filthy snow, more gray than white, gathering like a fungus in the ruined shards of the fixer's head.

Like a switch had been shut off, I couldn't move, couldn't look away.

Blood dripped from my metal hand. Seamed between the small plates. It smelled like iron and sweat and the noxious stench of voided bowels – shit and ammonia and raw, stinking fear.

My heart didn't slow. It hadn't even launched into the adrenaline-fueled race I was used to. It beat. Slowly. Surely.

The coldest kill I'd ever done.

Holy tits. Holy mother of freaking fucking *hell*. What was *wrong* with me?

I pushed off Jim's inert form, my gaze skating away from the carnage of his head. Blood everywhere. Pink mush, gray bits. Plaster turning brown and red. Strained meat and pooling plasma.

I'd killed him. And it'd been so easy.

I staggered, half-crawling backwards, until my back hit the

wall I'd pinned him against.

I'd killed before, obviously, but this was... different. It'd felt different. I hadn't been riding a wave of adrenaline or fear. I hadn't felt hatred or been paid or any of the usual reasons a person like me killed a man.

I'd simply... reacted.

And Fuck It Jim was dead.

Dead before I'd gotten the answers I so desperately needed. What the hell had gone through my brain? Why? I hadn't even thought about it, I'd just... *Squish*. No more Jim.

That wasn't like me.

My meat hand shook. My insides trembled violently – nerves. Serious nerves. Lucky had cleared me, but what if he'd missed something?

What if it wasn't something his scanners could see?

"Oh fuck," I gasped, bile welling up in my throat. Whatever had gone sideways, whatever it was, I knew enough that it was *wrong*. It wasn't me.

And I wouldn't get any answers from Jim now.

Something cold, sharp, and bitter curled into my chest. I shuddered, suddenly freezing where before I'd been warm. I sucked in a breath. My teeth chattered; I clenched my jaw.

It didn't help.

Shaking, I stared at the corpse, the ruined bloody stump pointing to the pile of raw mush I'd made of his face, and I couldn't manage to think in cohesive words.

Something was *so* wrong with me. But who the shit could I trust to help now?

The sunlight darkened behind the thin curtains, turning the congealing stains black. I blinked stupidly at the body. Glanced at the dimming daylight.

A muffled thump shook the complex.

Instinct threw me behind the other bed a nanosecond before the windows shattered inward.

13

The apocalypse rained down in Fuck It Jim's hotel room.

Glass sprayed a glittering volley of sharp edges and razor points. I felt it pepper my head, my bare shoulders like sand. The bed groaned beneath the impact, but held. The one I'd ripped from its moorings went flying, slammed into the far wall, juddering the whole room as I clapped my hands over my ears.

The high-pitched whine of a helo was as unmistakable as the impact of booted feet hitting the floor.

What the *shit*.

Now my heart spiked into overdrive. Adrenaline slid through my limbs, narrowing my focus away from Jim's corpse and to the voices barking out orders nearly incomprehensible in the chaos.

Surprise was my only weapon.

I reached under the bed, grabbed the bare springs and dragged myself underneath the frame. The metal edges scraped against my front, bunching my tank. Ouch.

On the bright side, if my tits were even a little bit bigger, I'd have gotten stuck. Eat that, Fuck It Jim.

Well, posthumously.

My feet vanished as a set of boots circled around the foot of the bed, moving quickly to the small door I figured led to the bathroom. "Clear!" I heard.

Sucker.

I reached out from under the bed – every kid's worst nightmare – and grabbed the second guy's ankles. Jerking sharply rammed his shins into the metal frame, providing me the leverage to pull myself out. I wrenched his ankles on the way past and sent him staggering for balance.

Rolling to my feet, I seized one of his windmilling arms, jerked hard and ducked under his elbow as his weapon came around – another Sauger 877, which was probably a coincidence, given Sauger's standing among paramilitary personnel.

That part where it could cut me in half was just frosting.

The gun in my dance partner's hand went wild, bullets spraying. It peppered the wall, tearing holes through the plaster.

The man shouted a warning to his companion as I kept hold of his elbow, and I spun behind him, my arm hooked in his until we were back to back. I was shorter than the guy – he couldn't clock me with his helmet and I wouldn't be target practice for his buddy.

As I used him as a shield, I craned my neck to mark the white logo splashed across the back of his all-black, heavily armored uniform.

An *M* and a *C*, interlocked together in a circle. Son of a bitch.

The letters were as familiar as the city's unique stench. MetaCore, Incorporated isn't just a company. It's a megacorporation that eats smaller firms for breakfast, lunch, *and* dinner – the kind of superconglomerate with fingers in everything from tech development, arms, and industry, to multibillion-dollar style and beauty firms. Sauger had been an independent firm before MetaCore had bought them, as had the makers of the TekSpek software that now held prime turf as the go-to for most weapon-to-HUD linkups. This was the kind of overarching umbrella group little companies died at the feet of.

Died, or sold out to.

Which meant way too big for a smalltime fixer like Bukket Jehm.

What had he gotten into?

Or was it me they were after? I flashed back to that botched MetaCore job that was my last real memory and couldn't shake the hunted feeling plucking at my survival instincts.

Was I being tracked? Followed? What for?

Fuck.

The other guy didn't fire at his buddy, which suggested he'd been trained not to shoot randomly. Great. More competent assholes. Just what I always wanted.

"What the *hell* is your problem?" I gritted out, straining as my reluctant companion struggled to pull me off balance. The most prominent disadvantage to full armor was the lack of flexibility.

The bonus was, oh, he'd be a bitch to kill.

Lights seared through the window, painting the scene in florid blue and white. The heat from the helo's backdraft burned out the air in the little apartment, and I heard shouting, barking orders, status updates, even while I danced with the one to keep him between me and his buddy.

My odds here sucked.

"Stand down," ordered the man I grappled. "You are ordered to comply with Civic Code–"

Oh, screw this.

I reached back with my free arm, hooked my metal fingers into his faceplate and jerked as hard as I could. His words halted as his head snapped back, which cracked the top of mine hard enough to send stars shooting through my vision. It hurt me more than it did him, but it wasn't his skull I was going for.

His elbow lashed back into my ribs, scored a direct hit that blew my breath out. I jammed my boot heel into the back of his knee, felt it catch on plated armor, but he jerked. When he staggered, I rammed my back into his, forcing him forward, right into his similarly outfitted pal.

I'd get one shot at this.

"Don't move!" shouted the second guy. Er, lady.

Whatever.

Still didn't work.

I palmed a smoke grenade off my dance partner's belt, then let him go at the same time I shoved my foot between his. He flailed into his friend, armor meeting armor in a clatter eaten by the sound of the helo's thrust outside the shattered window. The curtains flapped wildly, roiling up debris.

I spun around, launched a flatfooted kick into the guy's back to make sure he stayed tangled with his galpal, and didn't stop to watch them work out their balance. Darting across the room, I had a split second to decide which of Jim's units would provide me the answers I needed.

And possibly make me a continued target for MetaCore, but if I could get out, I could shake them.

"Get her!" yelled one of the faceless freaks.

Naturally.

Eenie, meenie, miney, *fuck it.*

I palmed a unit, a handheld tablet hooked up to a dock, ripped the device out of its frame and sprinted for the opened window.

Glass crunched under my feet. The men behind me must have sorted out their differences because the deafening whine of the helo blocking the light was suddenly torn wide by the report of bullet spray. My skin crawled beneath a sheen of sweat, my heart pounding as I waited to feel the horrific agony of flesh and bone brutalized by 5.56mm caseless rounds.

For once, luck was on my side.

Muscles straining, legs screaming, I bent, and as I launched myself into the air – rolling and hunching gracelessly around the tablet I held to my chest – I thumbed the trigger on the canister I'd stolen and dropped it in my wake.

A woman yelled out something I couldn't hear and the bullets ceased. Nobody saw the canister hit the floor until it exploded in a rapid burst of thick purple smoke. It belched out of the window I tore through, so fast I failed to see how close the helo really was until I felt the burn of its engines score my cheek, my bare arm, sear my shirt against the skin of my back.

I wrenched myself in mid-air and managed to tuck and roll into the most awkward dive of my extremely screwed up life.

I'd forgotten about the railing.

I skimmed off the top. My knee collided with the flimsy rail and bent it, which was enough to send me spiraling out over concrete. Landing one short story down drove the breath from my lungs, jarred my bones and my shoulder, and shot sparks where my metal arm scraped across pocked asphalt. I rolled, over and over, scrambling what was left of my brains, tearing away all sense of up and down.

When I finally stopped, laid out on my back and the world spinning, every inch of my body shrieked a string of curses I couldn't summon the breath to vocalize.

So. Much. Pain.

My fingers cramped around the edge of the tablet as I forced myself to sit up.

I smelled burning fuel, a sharply acrid tang that only undercut the oppressive reek of a city baking under the summer heat wave. People had started to gather, a blur of color and open-mouthed faces gathering behind a line somebody stupid had designated as "a safe distance". The hovering black machine hanging over what used to be the fixer's base of operations backpedaled on an upsurge of thrust I felt singeing the fine hairs on my skin. What was left of it, anyway.

Shit.

The torrent of purple smoke was more than enough to cover my tracks from the ground crew, but if that helo locked on me, I'd never outrun it.

I leapt to my feet, gritting my teeth against the waves of pain surging from ringing skull to aching heels, and took off – right for the crowd watching it all unfold like some kind of daytime soap feed.

Eyes widened. The bodies comprising the stupidest idiots in the area rippled.

"Corp raid!" I shouted. Probably the most effective call to arms this city would ever care about. Raids were a fact of life. On a good day, there wasn't a person existing in these streets who wasn't fucking around with something illegal, intentional or otherwise. The question was how much it would be worth to the corps to litigate it.

The motel looked like a military strike zone from the outside, which meant to anyone with any street sense at all that MetaCore wasn't playing patty cake. Raids like this, even spectators would end up dead. No one would care. The whole place could go up in smoke and it'd be just another footnote in the feeds.

But people love a good show.

What a bloody, abraded mess of screaming fleshbag couldn't accomplish, the helo's efforts to pull back and orient did. The spectators scattered. Like roaches under a light, thirty or so people darted for cover – cars idling in the street, alleys tucked between pay-by-the-hour shitholes like the one I'd left, whatever was handy.

The helo shuddered, swerving away from the smoking motel. A pack of people headed farther down the street, scared into a stampede as the helo's loudspeakers crackled behind us. "Cease and disperse," it droned. "Return to your homes. You are in violation of Code 311.875c. Repeat, cease and disperse."

Chunk that noise.

Smelling my own sweat and blood beneath the reeking assault of garbage, oil and fear, I ducked my head, hands tight around the stolen comp unit, and ran like I was one of the crowd.

As I'd hoped, the smoke covered my trail from the ground team. Without a definite lock, I was just a warm body among a bunch.

Honestly, MetaCore should have been better than that; except maybe, I figured as I sprinted into an alley barely big enough to run through, they'd been surprised by my presence in Jim's room. If they'd been there for Jim, and whatever he'd been digging into, then I was an unknown. A side project.

The last thing I wanted was giant MetaCore on my dick. As if my reputation wasn't shit enough. Once everyone else learned I had some kind of massive target on me, my cred would only be as good as the bounty a corporation would pay for it. MetaCore could afford just about anything.

I couldn't afford jack. But given the lack of pursuers in my wake, maybe that was one problem I didn't have to worry about.

My breath came in hard gasps as I slowed halfway down the narrow alley. It was little more than a runoff drain, filled with the debris thrown out the windows inset into walls overhead and left to rot. I stepped over decaying clothing, abandoned plastic containers, crates broken into jagged angles, and shattered glass.

I was sweltering. The sun baked my seared skin into a crusty mess, sweat stinging the rapidly healing gashes the pavement carved into me. My throat was a dried, raspy column of bottled-up obscenities, and I wheezed a few for emphasis as I finally stopped running and sank into a gasping, aching crouch.

"What," I panted, "the shit." *What* the *shit*. What had Jim been dealing in to bring Meta-fucking-Core to his doorstep? He wouldn't be the first fixer to wind up dead for dealing in the wrong information, but I never expected Jim to aim that high. MetaCore was serious baggage.

The memory of the sweaty stain his hands left on his own shirt flashed back through my rattled skull, and I swore again for emphasis.

No wonder he'd been so scared. I'd thought whatever it was he didn't want me to know had done that. Had he been afraid of a raid?

That cunt.

I sucked in a long, slow breath, let it out on a gust.

So much for answers.

Idly, I flipped the comp unit over in my hands. The screen was already on, jarred awake by my rough handling, though it didn't seem sure what to do with the remains of the dock still clinging to its connector. More than a few files had opened on the screen, probably from my stray fingers.

As I focused on breathing in and out, clearing the adrenaline-fueled rapid pulse from my chest, I eyed the info.

Names. Places. Dates. Bits of shorthand phrasing I suspected was Jim's way of reminding himself what meant what.

And a single document called *retirement plan*.

Aw. So the weasely little bastard had his own dreams of a happily ever after. That was kind of sweet, in a naïve and definitely too late kind of way. Not that it was my fault. I mean, sure, I'd killed him horribly, but he was probably dying anyway.

This business wasn't made for retirement.

Yeah. I'd pretend that somehow made what I did to him better.

Shifting my weight onto my heels, I flicked the folder open with a finger. Contract lingo filled the narrow screen.

I skimmed it. More names. More dates. More places.

And a shit ton of creds. Payouts, each listed with far too many zeroes to be right.

Only difference here was that I recognized the names on that list.

January. Indigo had brought her in on a run last year. Solid splatter specialist; I'd taught her a few tricks along the way. Young but hardcore.

Deck. A linker who'd worked on a co-op with Digo on a big score against a GinZeng operation.

Lingo. A fixer Indigo trusted enough to share a few intel lines with.

Fuck It Jim had been brokering deals to sell mercs. Somebody had been working with that weasel-faced fuckwit to *sell* SINless.

Among them?

Nanjali Koupra.

Sold to a chopshop in the Vid Zone.

The Vid Zone, exactly one ward north of the Third Junction – where the cops had picked me up.

How could you not remember? Jim's incredulity slammed into me like a bullet. If I was the principal, then it meant I was working for Indigo. Period. I wasn't stupid enough to work for anyone else when I had a good gravy train right here, and that meant Indigo knew.

He knew, and he'd fucking sold me out.

What relative calm I'd managed spiked into a red slash of rage.

The common denominator here was clear. I secured the tablet into the waistband of my pants and shoved everything else aside. Indigo had wanted info?

I'd jam proof of his greed so far down his throat, he'd die with the copper taste of revenge in his mouth.

14

Tracking down Indigo was as simple as putting in a call to the Mecca. They knew me enough to know if I was looking for Digo, it was important.

It was. Just not the way they thought.

He'd gone home with the redhead waitress. Laila.

She lived in an apartment complex within walking distance of the rack.

The place was a shithole, like most of the districts nearby, and as I pushed my way inside the boarded, shattered glass door of the complex, a huddled knot of filthy homeless grumbled profanities at me like I was the intruder.

Covered in dried blood and dirt as I was, they probably thought I was trying to horn in on their marginally cooler squat. I shot them a filthy gesture as I passed, ignoring the elevator – a deathtrap, was my guess – in favor of the creaking stairs somebody had tried to shore up with stolen street signs.

Classy.

Seven flights of stairs didn't take the wind out of my sails. Instead, it pushed my blood into a simmering, steady beat.

Laila's door was the third on the right.

I didn't knock. I drew back and leveled a kick near the seam that tore the tumblers right through the doorjamb, twisting the metal into uselessness. It slammed into the far wall, and all hell broke loose inside.

Laila was sultry in a sari, but she was cuter naked, her light tats turned off and her hair snarled from a night of some serious fucking. Her eyes were huge in her pillow-imprinted face as she screamed, rolling off the single narrow bed in the one-room apartment.

Indigo was definitely leaner than I remembered, but he was still more of a thinker than a front-liner. As a linker, he'd processed the intrusion before Laila hit the floor, and I'd give him credit for the fact that he leapt out of bed and came at me, but he lost massive points for the free-wheeling slap of his balls against his hairy thighs.

This? This is why a man shouldn't sleep naked. Especially when dabbling in shit that'd get his door kicked in.

Recognition filled his hungover features an instant before I hooked his swing with my flesh arm, sidestepped, and used his own momentum to toss him out into the hall. He stumbled over the threshold, slammed into the opposite wall and reeled.

A girl's voice shrieked behind me.

On instinct, I sidestepped a second time, stuck out one hand to catch her, and tangled Laila's bare ankles with a foot. She stubbed her toe on my boot, yelped, and instead of leaping on my back – *why* do people think that helps? – she found herself guided in a full circle and thrown onto the bed in the same stunt I'd worked on Digo. Her round ass rippled as she bounced across the surface.

The girl had a mattress that *bounced*. Serious jealousy.

"Riko, what the fuck!"

I turned, my teeth bared in a snarl ripped out on a harsh breath. "She leaves or she dies."

Indigo had grabbed a picture frame from the skewed table beside the door I'd ruined, holding it in front of his junk like it'd somehow stop me from throwing myself on all his manly glory.

Please.

Angry color filled his cheeks; I'd never seen his blue eyes so enraged. "You wouldn't dare."

I pointed my metal finger at her without looking away from him, aware that she had scooted back on the bed, clutching the sheets over her nakedness. Her eyes were so wide, they were nearly all white. "Laila, right?"

She didn't answer me with anything more than a low, strained whimper.

Blood-covered merc kicks your door in, I guess it'd be a shock. Good. "Get some pants on," I told her, my voice pitched for menace. "Go away. I'm going to do some seriously bad shit to your fuckbuddy, and you? You don't want to see this."

"Fucking twat," Indigo began, but Laila was already moving like the hounds of hell were on her pretty tail. Within thirty seconds, she'd grabbed whatever clothes came to hand and sprinted out of the apartment, trailing her sheet and sidling around Indigo like she'd catch on fire if she touched him.

He watched her go with helpless fury. When her footsteps vanished, he rounded on me. "You need get your shit checked out," he seethed, fingers white around the picture edge. "What the fuck is wrong with you this time?"

"Lucky says I'm fine," I replied. "You? You got more to explain than I do."

I could have just jumped on his ass and been done with it; Indigo's strength wasn't hand-to-hand. But as pissed as I was, as fucking *furious*, I hesitated.

I knew myself well enough to know that some part of me was seriously hoping Indigo would have a good explanation for the evidence I'd brought him. Some little, fragile corner of that girl come down from middle-class safety, who still thought things like friendship meant more than cred.

Yeah. I hadn't managed to brutalize her into silence yet. I was working on it.

"Get your smegging clothes on," I said, every word a ragged

edge. "I don't want to be talking to your junk."

The color in his face pinched almost white around his mouth. "You…" His voice trembled with it, he was so pissed. The muscles in his arms, his abs, even the muscled thighs framing the picture centered between them shook. "What… I don't even know what the fuck to say to you right now."

"Then let me help you," I shot back. I stalked to the bed, sex-rumpled and pillows astray, found the black pants he'd worn to the club the night before, threw them at him. He caught them easily with one hand. "Let's start with Fuck It Jim."

I watched contempt undercut the fury etching his sharp features. "Turn around."

I rolled my eyes at him, but presented at least my profile. It allowed him to half-turn, using his body to hide the dick I wasn't even remotely interested in, without forcing me to lose sight of him in general. "What about Jim?" he demanded, setting the picture frame down.

Smooth. Not so much as a flicker of guilt.

Was that how he'd done it? Did he seriously not care?

"First," I said, as evenly as I could manage, "he's dead."

I had excellent peripheral vision. Still not even a hitch as he drew the pants over his swarthy hips. "So what?" He turned back to face me again as he zipped up. "He's worthless."

My fists clenched. "Then why were you selling him mercs?"

Blue eyes narrowed.

"I know, Indigo," I snarled, reaching into my waistband to withdraw the tablet. I tossed this one gently, unwilling to lose evidence to his thick skull. "I know you've been selling information on *your* contacts to seven chopshops. Most recently, one in the Vid Zone. You've been making *bank*, and you've been using *me* to do it, you son of a bitch!"

Indigo processed information like I processed oxygen. He only needed to glance at the featured data, scroll through it once.

I watched the contours of his already sharp features settle into rock-hard planes.

Good. Now he was as pissed as I was, for the same reasons. *Explain that, asshole.*

"I didn't do this," he said, but he didn't toss the tablet back. I didn't expect him to. His grip turned his fingers sallow around the scuffed edge. "January dropped on a Mantis run, Deck was blown up in a raid on his swish shack. Nobody's heard from Lingo in months, but that's usual for him."

"Yeah?" I thrust my chin at the tablet. "That says they were handed over to a chopshop. Paid, Digo. Paid in full, with a cut to Jim. You know who else is on that list?" I didn't let him answer. "Your sister. You fucking sold out your own sister."

Indigo's mouth curled in a soundless snarl as he dropped his gaze to the information he clutched.

We stood there in Laila's cluttered apartment, silent and staring for what seemed like forever. I watched Indigo battle to work through the facts, and the first seeds of doubt unfurled in the middle of all my fury.

This was not the reaction of a man who'd been caught redhanded.

With my heartbeat pounding against the confines of my skull, my hands clenched at my sides. "Cut the act, Digo. There's your proof. Now tell me what the fuck you did to me. Memory crack? Did you have a 'jector *hack* me just so I'd be your goddamn errand boy?"

His gaze wrenched to mine. The corners of his mouth pinched. "I did not do this," he repeated, the intensity of it edged like a razor and tight enough to turn his voice into something brittle. Barely contained anger. "First, I *wouldn't* sell my sister, chunk your proof. Second, less importantly, the payouts listed here aren't nearly enough to cover the losses."

Well, that was just factual enough to confuse me. "What?"

"The *losses*, Riko. I run a goddamned business. Each one of them was worth more than the payout listed," he pointed out impatiently. "Given their skillsets and reliability, we would have made six times as much in a year just *working* with them."

"You're serious."

"Fuck you, what do you think I am? A charity?"

Not even a little.

Well... shit. That was a point I hadn't considered, and that bit of logic put a spike in my emotional rollercoaster. I opened my mouth, but caught myself before I asked the question that formed inside my head.

He glanced up at me, eyes flat. "What?"

If Indigo wasn't the principal, then that left one other candidate: me. Jim had suggested as much. If Indigo was telling the truth, then that evidence now pointed to me. I couldn't say it wasn't with any certainty, not while my memories were on the fritz.

And if he was lying, then how could I prove it when I couldn't even state my innocence with any real certainty?

Fuck me.

Fuck him.

Fuck this whole scumsucking business.

"Looks like Jim's playing a lot of angles," Indigo continued. He rotated the tablet between his hands. "But I swear, I didn't get a single payout for any of them. If this is true, if someone has been selling out my roster, then I damn well intend to find who."

I couldn't fault his instinct, but I don't think he got the whole picture. "We need more than that."

He raised the scuffed tablet. "This started six months ago. Do you know how many names are on this list?"

I frowned. "Hold up – when?"

"Six months, give or take." His teeth bared. "Six fucking months, and I didn't know what the hell was happening to my people."

Hallelujah, a ray of smegging sunshine. I *remembered* six

months ago. There was no way I was involved with this.

But that didn't explain the end of April and early May, when Digo said I'd been walking around.

I fisted my hands beside my forehead. "We need to check that chopshop, Digo. The one in the Vid Zone. That's where *all* the information will be."

"How do you know?"

I couldn't very well admit to getting picked up by the cops. My cred was already in the shitter – suspected dealings with the police would only make it worse. So I lied. Flat out. "When I escaped the place, I was beyond lost. None of my shit was working. But when I hitched out, I was in the Third Junction. That's walking distance from the Zone."

"Coincidence."

"Like hell."

I could practically hear his teeth click together from across the room.

"Malik Reed said to get him evidence," I pressed, dropping my hands to grip my thighs and pin him with a stare. "That tablet is evidence."

He waved the unit at me. "This is enough to turn just about anyone on *me*, Riko. Look at what *you* did after a cursory examination." A none-too-subtle nod to Laila's ruined door.

"Eat my dick," I shot back. "You sent me into a trap at Plato's."

His nostrils flared; that look he got when I'd just said something he found offensive. "The hell I did."

Oh, for fuck's sake. I didn't have the time or the patience to play the blame game anymore. He said, she said, they *all* had something to say, and right now, I was way too confused to sort it all out. "Look," I said sharply, once more surging to my feet with way more energy than I would have figured I'd had stored.

Digo took a barefoot step back.

My heart slammed again. I forced myself to stay still, hands fisted at my side.

Christ on a pipe, I wanted to hurt something.

His expression told me I wasn't hiding it.

"Look," I repeated, deliberately going for calm. "Taylor Jax sent me to Jim."

Digo wasn't enough of an actor to mask his surprise.

"Yeah," I said to his silent question. "It surprised me, too. You know what else surprised me?" When he only looked at me, that same wariness warning me I was sprouting another head right in front of his eyes, I bared my teeth. "That you hired him to go looking for me."

The black fan of his lashes narrowed. I expected him to deny it. He didn't bother. "I used what I could."

"Yeah, well." I rolled my shoulder uncomfortably. Not because it hurt – the ache had mellowed, finally – but because I didn't know what else to do. "Thanks, at least, for trying." His mouth tightened, and I shot him a faint, bitter smile. "Even if you only wanted to find me to kill me."

He didn't deny that, either. "Jax failed."

"And he knows it." A shaft of amusement split my anger into something mildly more tolerable. I took a deep breath. "Thanks for that, too. Humility burns Jax like holy water."

Indigo held my gaze for a quiet moment, his face unreadable. The tension in his shoulders eased a fraction. "Yeah, well." A repeat of my own discomfort. "You're welcome."

We stood awkwardly for a moment, caught in a tangled web of our uncertainties. Old friendships, new hatreds. So much doubt.

I didn't know how to address it – any of it. All I could do was try to find the information that would explain all of this – my memory gap, Nanji's conversion. I had to make this better the only way I knew how.

Clear my name, stock my cred, before anyone else came gunning for me.

Without cred, I was losing allies fast. That much was

clear. A lone runner? Especially one who'd chunked a few smegheads on the way up? Yeah, it was only a matter of time before I was so much meat.

"Anyway." I cleared my throat. "Turns out, whatever Jim was up to, it brought MetaCore on his ass. And mine." I gestured at the mess I presented. "So, I'm a little wired. Sorry. I'll pay for Laila's door."

"You're balls-out insane," he muttered, but at least he relaxed enough to start pacing. I watched him stride through the small room, stepping in and out of the curtain-dappled sunlight. He slapped the unit against his palm rhythmically as he did it.

For the first time in, oh, hell, a couple years, I really *looked* at Indigo's trim body. Under all that olive skin, I decided that he wore leaner muscle well once I got used to it. His back shifted tightly, rippling the bold colors of the lotus tattoo. With his bare feet and naked, hairless chest, he looked a hell of a lot more lethal than he used to.

No wonder Laila had taken him home.

I almost snorted a laugh, and as he turned to throw me an inquisitive, impatient glare, all that anger, that emotional undercurrent of rage, drained right out of me. With the sudden loss of adrenaline-fueled anger, all those muscles tightened to the breaking point around my synthetic arm. Pain unfurled like a flame.

I rubbed at the curve of my neck as that phantom arm ached from false fingertips to brain, lancing every nerve in between.

Digo glared at the tablet. Then back at me. "Right now," he said flatly, "you're on my shitlist in a big way." He held up the tablet. "This may be something, but you're still the one who fucking watched my sister die." He paused. "If you're even telling me the truth."

Ouch.

"I'm not sorry I hired Jax to find you," he said grimly, "but it's infuriating to think I paid him for counterfeit intel."

An angle I hadn't considered. That wouldn't be good for Jax's cred, either. At least Indigo acknowledged that there was something wrong with this whole situation. Whatever data Jax had managed to get, it was nothing more than a ruse. A way to ensure nobody went sniffing around after Nanji.

Jax got bad intel. Indigo was losing his roster and didn't even know. I'd... sold that roster, maybe? Fuck.

So why? Why give Nanjali Koupra a finite end on a chopshop table but leave Lingo with an unexplained disappearance? But January and Deck both had solid reports on their deaths, too.

Whoever did this counted on the fact someone like Indigo would check up on it.

Was it something that would even occur to me? I didn't think so. But then, sometimes I surprised myself with my random acts of intelligence.

I dug my thumb into my eye to ease the headache pounding behind it. "There's a source for all of this," I said, weary now. "That tablet tells me where to start. And now I have Reed's evidence. He can get me a team."

He frowned at the unit. Stopped pacing. Then, to my surprise, he tucked the tablet into his waistband. *Mine*. He may as well have pissed on it. "Then we're going to go question Reed," he said. Like it was already decided.

I blinked. "We?"

"The hell I'm letting you do another meeting in secret," he said, his jaw stone hard as he glared at me. "I'm going this time, and I'll be asking all the questions."

I stood. Fuck me sideways, I didn't have a choice. Very deliberately, I curled my hands into fists, ignoring the shot of pain through my shoulder. I'd have to spend every moment of this meeting balancing Malik Reed's douche factor with Indigo Koupra's raging trust issues. While hiding the fact that I *was* keeping something from them both.

I opened my mouth to argue, but he cut me off.

"You want to play with the big boys, Riko?" He jammed his feet into his boots, kicking at the programmed lacing until the material tightened up around his ankles. "Then you start figuring out when you're supposed to stroke your dick and when you're supposed to stow it." He shot a hard look at me, thrusting at his own face with a finger. "That's *my* specialty. Don't fucking forget you're just a splatter specialist off her goddamn rails."

I forced myself to hold still, to lock down the automatic need to drive a fist into his twisted face. A lump swelled thick and ugly in my throat.

He was right. Much as I hated it, I couldn't meet Reed without him, and I wasn't willing to kill him over a *maybe*. I needed Digo to set up the meeting.

I needed Reed to fund a run to that Vid Zone chopshop.

I needed to play the smegging game.

And I was so cunting tired of needing everyone else to do it.

"Fine," I gritted out. "Set up the meeting." He exhaled soundlessly, like he'd been holding his breath. Only to curl his lip when I couldn't stop myself from adding, "Asshole."

"Keep stroking it, Riko."

His inflection suggested I needed to shut up.

15

Indigo left a few credsticks for Laila. To replace the door, I think, without my help. I said nothing, but I did avail myself of her shower and printer while he made the call. Unlike mine, her radiation shower was fast enough to deal with. She had decent digs, for the shithole the building was, and at least she tried to make it comfortable.

"Let's go," was all he said when I stepped out to find him dressed and waiting.

I'd opted for black, because trite as it is to go for a badass vibe in black, it hid blood well and didn't stand out in the street. I actually preferred color, but this was me. Being practical.

Lucky would be so proud. Except for that part where I tanked my cred, assaulted and alienated one of the only friends I had left, and pinned a MetaCore target to my back.

My pants were close to the ones I lost to Lucky's table, though Laila's database didn't have my chosen make and model. I'd traded the ruined baby blue for a skintight sleeveless shirt that wouldn't bunch under the harness I intended to requisition soon. I'd even pulled out a pair of cheap wraparound sunglasses. I looked like the streetcore mercenary I was.

Indigo had replaced his own neoprene blue with black,

which made us look like a twin set, but whatever. If anyone had anything cute to say, I was itching for a fight.

He said nothing as I followed him out of Laila's apartment. He did mutter a string of profanities when the door refused to sit straight, and I very determinedly refrained from contributing to the non-conversation. I doubted anything I had to say would have helped.

He was still fuming as he backed his motorcycle out of the alley he'd stashed it in. I got to ride bitch. Lucky, lucky me.

There was no sense of easy camaraderie between us as we headed out past the rack and hit one of the boundary byways. I watched the scenery go by, focusing on the sharp, jagged streaks of pain the cycle juddered through my left side because it hurt less than the knowledge that I'd lost pretty much everything I'd made for myself in the past few years. My reputation, my team, my mentor.

My girlfriend. Even if she was one in a string of many.

Poor me. A real quality pity party on the back of Indigo's babied Wolfram K-700. Built for sleek menace, high visual appeal and road domination, the metallic blue and chromed motorcycle had been his longterm girlfriend of choice for as long as I'd known him. I loved the bike – had even considered replacing my less sleek Vix Jp with a similar model after a run had trashed the Vix a couple years back.

Maybe one day. Runners aren't great at saving. We risk our lives for thrills and pay, and spend that pay for more thrills. Without Indigo in my corner, I'd have to freelance. That meant it'd be a long ass time before I could afford it.

He threaded through traffic like the cars around us were other people's problem. For an hour, we rode straight through. No talking. No stopping. By the time we pulled up to what I assumed was our destination, we were ass-deep in corporate polish. The bike slowed, darting out of the steady flow of vehicles that had steadily turned cleaner, sleeker, classier with every block in.

He idled at the curb, next to a complex whose glassy front started at street level and climbed into the pristine blue sky. It was clearer here than the districts I haunted, less baked into a crust by the sun bloated and brilliant overhead. Tighter shields. Just enough to let the summer season in, not enough to turn loose the pollutants that infected every part of the city to some degree or another.

Fancy.

I leaned a little bit over, tapping his shoulder. "You're telling me Reed actually shacks up in C-Town?"

C-Town was what we called most of the corporate boroughs from the Fourteenth Divide on up. The "C" stood for Capital, but was often replaced by any number of epithets. Corporate, cred, chum, cunt. Insert your own at your leisure. It was full of suits, polished to a shine, and screamed corporate propaganda.

We were about seventeen blocks in, surrounded on all sides by soulless metal and glass. But way less ads flooding my filters. I clocked it in at three seconds before my chipset calibrated to the district and they all winked out. Much, much nicer than the standard fifteen.

Indigo spared me a shrug. "He's got a credline that goes deep. Don't tell me you didn't notice."

"Oh, I noticed." Once the blood had cleared from my eyes.

The bike tilted, all the warning I had, before he zipped back into traffic – earning three horns and a flash of LEDs – and circled around to a parking garage. The air abruptly turned cool, the light dimmed, and I breathed in gratefully as Indigo found and claimed a parking spot in the shadowed interior.

I hopped off first, stretching my aching arm. "How did you know about this?"

"It's my business." A short answer. Fair enough.

He flicked a screen with a finger and stepped back as a faint blue shimmer rolled over the machine. Security. The kind that would deliver a blackout jolt of juice to anyone who laid a finger on it. Standard street procedure. Only complete fuckwits risk touching a SINless vehicle without testing it first, and I didn't think it'd be a problem this time. He'd been nice and legal about parking.

Indigo strode for a bank of elevators at the far wall of the garage. He didn't have to hit a button. That wouldn't have been classy at all. Instead, sensors picked up on our presence and one of the doors slid right open with a merry little chime.

We stepped in, and I took the opportunity to smooth one hand over my tousled hair, untangling it with a quick run of my fingers.

Indigo punched in a code. When the doors closed, he made damn sure not to meet my gaze in the reflective walls.

I bit back a sigh, barely even noticed when the elevator car lifted, it was so smooth. No music. Just a panel counting up as we passed floor after floor. Super awkward elevator silence.

The elevator chimed again, announcing our arrival a hundred and fifty-nine stories up. Nice.

When the doors slid open, I expected a hall. Instead, we stepped out into a vast lobby that would have fit the entire row of my squatter tenement inside it and still have room for the junk they hoarded around the perimeter. Delicate music played over discreet speakers, while lush green plants provided an atmospheric touch to the professional digs.

I whistled.

A tall cream-colored desk took up the center, though there was no lettering or signage to tell me what the hell I'd been dragged into. A woman with sleekly knotted blonde hair looked up from the translucent projection screen her fingers hovered over, a welcome smile already in place. She was maybe my age, maybe a little younger, with nondescript features geared toward unremarkable anglo – modest genetic cultivation, I'd stake what was left of my cred on it – but good bone structure beneath reserved makeup. The perfect unobtrusive welcome. "Good afternoon," she said brightly.

Her brown eyes gleamed with unconcealed sincerity behind wide-framed glasses. "Do you have an appointment?"

Indigo nodded. "Made it about an hour ago."

"You must be Mr Koupra." The receptionist turned her expectant, unreasonably cheerful gaze to me. "And guest?"

"And guest," I agreed before Digo could open his mouth and say my name.

She waited a moment, head tilting. I didn't elaborate.

"Give it a rest," Digo muttered, low enough that I wasn't sure the receptionist heard. "Everything's a fucking competition with you."

I ignored him. If she did hear, the receptionist simply shrugged her shoulders beneath a blouse I was sure was real silk and said, "Mr Reed will see you both." She gestured with a manicured hand to our left.

Indigo strode off without another word.

"Thanks," I said as I followed.

"Of course."

The wide lobby didn't narrow. Instead, it kept going, with crystal clean windows on one side looking out over the wide expanse of the district – broken, naturally, by skyscrapers as tall as this one – and a paneled wall on the other. Pictures filled it, art that I didn't recognize but was sure was expensive. Probably originals of some kind, though I couldn't tell at a glance. Art snobs and rich assholes liked to claim a difference, but the great replications didn't look any different from one copy to the next.

I couldn't tell if this was a business or a home. It kind of reeked of both. The view was a guaranteed power play, but even I had to admit it was kind of pretty. As much as this soulsucking shithole of a city could be pretty, anyway. The golden haze coloring the sky between gaps in the glass skyline was interesting enough, if you didn't stop to consider that it was pollution hovering in the distant wards.

There were no signs, no logos. Nothing that told me

what corporation, if any, this guy worked for. Which made me think it wasn't much more than a place to meet people. Probably one of many setups he had in place. He seemed cagey enough.

The corridor ended at a set of double doors. Indigo pushed inside first, which made me glad I'd left my shades on as the modulated sunlight seared through the overhead skylights.

Malik Reed stood beside a heavy glass and metal desk, scrolling through data in a projection tablet about a thousand times more advanced than the junk Fuck It Jim had been cobbling together. He was dressed in another gray suit, this one lighter but obviously expensive. His pants were precisely creased, tailored neatly to his long legs and narrow waist, and accessorized with a thin black belt. This time, he wore a pale blue dress shirt, a tailored vest in the same color as his slacks, and a tie colored a cross between blue and gray. Black shoes to match the belt, less shiny than last time but no less exclusive. The only concession to the summer sun streaming through the window was the suit jacket hanging up on a coat rack to my right.

The overall affect wasn't one of casual welcome or easy comfort. Any other man I'd known would have rolled up the sleeves, or loosened the tie. This man stood in the middle of all this glass and sunshine and made it look like it was just another day in the office.

Hell, maybe it was.

He didn't look up as we entered, but he did gesture to the chairs arrayed in front of his desk as he turned away. "Have a seat."

Indigo sat, shoving his sunglasses up on his head.

I didn't. "Nice to see you, too," I drawled.

This time, Digo didn't bother vocalizing his impatience. He knew better. The receptionist was one thing, but Malik Reed was a player in the game. It *all* came down to cred, to swagger, and Digo needed to keep face as much as I needed to regain mine.

Whatever our host needed, I hadn't figured out yet.

His eyes were dark as motor oil as he seized the projected screen in one hand and tossed it to the side, gaze pinned on me. The screen vanished. "You look like a third-rate burglar."

I showed him my teeth. "Worried?"

"Not even a little," he replied, dismissing me easily as his gaze shifted to Indigo. "What can I do for you, Mr Koupra?"

Digo, for all his years on the street, couldn't match the other man's perfect air of control. He leaned forward, elbows on his knees, balled-up frenetic energy. "Riko's got intel for you. I have questions." He tilted his head at me. "Start with her."

Malik's eyes returned to me, coolly reproachful. "You should have taken the card."

"You should have paid that bouncer better," I returned. I tilted my head, arms folded under my breasts. "How is he, by the way? Did you promise medical?"

A black eyebrow lifted. "He'll live."

"Oh, good." My tone said I didn't give a shit.

Unlike the earblasting confines of Plato's Key, the music in the lobby didn't reach this room. The light didn't leave anything to the imagination, and I had no trouble discerning the complete lack of amusement in his features this time.

"Not even a sigh," I pointed out, pulling my mouth into an expression of affected dismay. "I must be losing my touch."

"You are also losing my attention."

Jackhole.

"Indigo." I glanced at him. "The data."

He withdrew the tablet from its place in his waistband. Maybe he was making a point, too, because I took way too much pleasure from the fact that it left a streak of black on the nice clean desk he threw it on. The clatter forced a faint tightening of Malik's shoulders.

Most wouldn't be able to tell, but I could sense Indigo's nerves. I couldn't blame him. Being on Malik Reed's turf was a great big fuckoff unknown.

I was too stubborn to play nice. "There's your evidence," I said. "Now get me my team."

A long-fingered hand lifted the device. A ring winked in the bright daylight. I didn't remember seeing it before, but I hadn't exactly been focused on his hands.

A wedding band, obviously, and in gold. Most couples who bothered with rings didn't usually pick gold. Titanium or platinum, or, if you were trendy, diamond steel with microchips that could contain all kinds of fun surprises. Honeymoon photos. Tracking bugs.

Aphrodisiacs.

Yeah, that was a thing.

"Did you run over it a few times before you brought it here?" he asked mildly, turning the screen rightside up with two fingers.

"You could say that." I could have mentioned MetaCore, but I figured I'd hold off on that one. I didn't know who the man worked for yet, and if he had ties to the conglomerate, I wanted what I could get from him before I blew that bird cage open.

I waited in silence, stooping to lean on the back of the other chair as he scrolled through the information. He, like me, did not sit; a fact I think made Indigo even more nervous.

I kind of hoped one of them would do something stupid. It was that kind of mood.

Instead, Malik glanced up. Not at me, but at Digo. "Are you aware of current events in the Vid Zone?"

The linker shook his head, his features tight. "Most of the information streaming out of the Vid Zone has been unofficially gagged."

"Not surprising," Malik said. "They gave up on pretense yesterday, strangled the feeds."

"Hey," I said sharply. "You want to share, or is this a boys only club?"

I expected Malik to answer. Instead, Indigo shrugged, folding his hands over his belly as he kicked his feet out in a long line. Yeah. Totally a boys' club. Jackwagons, the both of them. "Something closed communication in a four-block radius, smack in the Vid Zone."

As if it was nothing.

It wasn't *nothing*. "You mean," I asked slowly, my irritation unfolding like a slow tide, "the same Vid Zone that chopshop is listed in? The one you *know* is our only link? That one?"

He shot me a look no less irritated. "Yeah. That one."

"And you didn't tell me?"

"Riko," Indigo replied with a total lack of patience, "stow it." *Shut up and play the game.* In fewer words.

The fact I was too busy throwing a tantrum instead of paying attention to the details said a lot about my state of mind.

I'd never grilled Indigo for every last fact before. I didn't like knowing too much – I found it complicated. I couldn't be upset now that Digo hadn't fed me this data on a plate.

Except I was.

Which wasn't fucking fair, and that about summed up my entire existence at the moment.

I set my jaw.

"There's only three reasons a communications gag would happen," Digo pointed out when I didn't say anything.

"A power short," I said, aware of one. "Or rolling blackouts."

"Yeah, but that's not the case." Indigo squinted into the bright, airy office. "The second is an official gag order, which is a political move that would be heavily covered by the rest of the surrounding feeds and talked to death on every daytime newsline from here to Northside Commons. There's no civic unrest in that area to warrant it."

Malik was silent, letting Indigo carry the educational part of this show. He watched me with a cool intensity that made the fine hairs on the back of my neck lift in wary acknowledgment.

I was being judged. I did not like being judged.

I glowered at him. "What?"

"Take your sunglasses off."

The order felt like a verbal slap. My fingers clenched on the chair. "Why?"

"Because it's rude," he said, holding my gaze through the dark lenses as if he knew I was watching him. "Take them off."

"Oh, for—" I snatched the sunglasses off my head, throwing them on his desk in a fit of impatient temper. "What's the third reason to cut communications?"

Malik didn't seem impressed with his victory, small as it was. A muscle ticked over the sharp angle of his wide jaw. "Necrotech activity detected."

My irritation vanished under a pitched slam of cold comprehension.

An image of Nanji, tech sprouting from her back and her limbs splayed, filled my head. Slowly, I straightened from the back of the chair, absently cradled my arm as the motion pulled at muscles too hooked on pain to take it with grace. "You're shitting me. A blackout?"

Malik met my eyes with level intensity. "That's right. A blackout. Which means your so-called lead is dead in the center of a necro quarantine."

16

The computer-controlled windows darkened, filtering the sunlight enough that the map Malik called up on his computer shone stark green on the wide, wired glass behind him.

I circled the desk, studying the layout of the Vid Zone. "Each block is about six miles in diameter, right?"

"Correct."

A thick red border outlined a four-block radius, a sharp contrast to the shimmering green outlining the rest of the zone. What the map didn't show was the rat runs – the alleys and walkways that made for prime hunting ground top to bottom.

Not ideal. But not insurmountable.

Scary as hell, fucked six ways to sideways, but definitely not insurmountable.

Repeating it to myself didn't help. I was so not zenning it.

"According to this information," Malik said, tapping in a few commands to a handheld, "the site you want is here." A blue dot appeared almost in the exact center of the red square. "Middle of the quarantine."

"Easy," I said, shrugging. I lied. "Get me the right team and I'll be in and out."

His gaze was cool as it flicked to me. "Have you ever seen a necro blackout?" When I shook my head, the dark line of his lashes narrowed a fraction.

"Chunk off." I folded my arms. "Necros aren't my specialty."

Necros weren't anyone's specialty.

As aware of conversion as we all were, necro infestation was rare as hell. I'd only ever heard of three in my lifetime and each one was burned out before it spread farther than the faulty chopshop failsafe it came from.

Malik's hip angled against the desk, a casual perch that still somehow failed at nonchalant. He was too neat for it. Too smooth. "You seem very confident."

Indigo snorted.

I shot him a sidelong glare. "I know what I'm doing."

Malik seemed less than convinced. "How knowledgeable are you on the subject of conversion sciences?"

That was a fancy way of asking how much I knew about the process. Fucking educated people.

I eyed him, briefly considering calling him on the aggravatingly obvious command in the question. I didn't answer to him. Malik Reed seemed to have a bad habit of assuming everyone around him did.

Instead, I opted for professional courtesy. "No more or less than what's usually out there," I said, tipping my head. "If you're unlucky enough to hit your tech threshold, the tech infiltrates the human nervous system, scrapes out anything that isn't its own signal, and converts the brain. When it turns on autopilot, it does what it does best." Problem is, for a lot of SINless, what tech does best is kill.

That doesn't mean that Susie Housewife with her cosmetic enhancements can't convert. It's a lot rarer, and her brand of going apeshit is a lot less initially lethal than mine or Boone's would be. Tech is a tool. You can kill someone with a showerhead, given enough time and effort, but someone with a chainsaw would kill faster.

It's a numbers game. Most SINless are illegal because we choose to be. That kind of life comes with strings. Saints tend to be mercs, and runner tech tends to be deadly.

Just adds to the bad rap propagandists like to spew. Go SINless and convert. Whoo.

"If," I added, "the necrotech is wired into something, it spreads like a computer virus, overwhelming the systems it's wired into." This was one of the reasons projectors were shoot-on-sight. A 'jector that corrupts while jacked corrupts the system in seconds.

Fortunately, Nanji wasn't plugged in when I saw her last. Not for lack of them trying.

My hands fisted.

"Statistically," Malik said, inclining his head like I'd scored a point – fuck him – "necrotechs operate individually."

"Obviously. People are individual units."

Malik's eyes glinted. "Which clearly outlines the current question."

I glanced at Indigo.

He shrugged.

"What?" I asked, feeling baited.

He tapped at the window, toggling something I couldn't see.

A dozen red blips flashed into place, staggered across the quarantine zone.

I stared at it. "Hold up." I pointed at the map. "You're saying there's more than one necrotech in there?"

Malik answered with the same patient voice – hella impatient words. "Twelve known hits on the feeds before the signal was cut."

"What are they doing in there?"

One thick eyebrow arched. "I'll send you in with a census board and you can ask them."

"How's that fuck-yourself tech acquisition coming?" I replied with saccharine interest.

A corner of his full mouth twitched.

•••

Indigo shifted in his chair. "Given the, uh, reproduction going on in there," he said slowly, "how do we feel about the theory that necros are a few short hops away from legit AI?"

Whatever smile he didn't seem inclined to give in to, Malik's lip curled into sheer irritation. "That's a romanticized notion." He may as well have called bullshit for all the disgust his civilized opinion framed.

"Gee, Malik," I said. "You sound almost human."

"Trust me." His deep voice dropped into a low growl. "Compared to the economic and evolutionary destruction an AGI would cause, I'm a bargain."

I cupped my elbow with the other hand, an idle gesture that let me dig my thumb into the synthetic arm's elbow joint. It didn't help anything, but at least I'd managed to tamp the pain down to a low, chronic hum. "Now you sound bitter."

"Do I?" He looked at the map. "Tech operating on its own, and that's what you get."

As arguments went, I couldn't disagree. Everybody knew that some of the corps had seriously considered AI technology along the way. The government rhetoric was largely silent on the matter; that happened when all the conglomerates threatened to stop funneling creds towards a civic service that had long ago become little more than a pretense to keep the drones happy.

I had no doubt there were labs somewhere devoted to exploring the possibility, and some conspiracy theorists even whispered that necros were the result of early attempts to force the issue of artificial general intelligence. We'd never made it past ANI – artificial narrow intelligence. That was an intelligence so rigorously defined that computers never went any farther than what they were programmed to be good at.

We had programmed robots, self-maintaining nanos, tech that operated in tandem with the human body and with human needs, but no recursive self-improvement. AGI and its big brother ASI were, apparently, the nuclear option when it came to tech. If anybody was dabbling, nobody was dumb enough to hit the big red button. Yet.

I didn't bother with the conspiracy theories. I wasn't into what-ifs and far-reaching hypotheses. What I liked were goals right in front of me, and right now that big, thick red line and the necro obstacles behind it were in front of me.

"Purism aside," I began.

"I'm not a purist."

I grimaced at Malik. "Does it matter?"

"I'm a lot of things," he assured me, his gaze unreadable in the dark. Not that I expected light to help much. The man played his cards too close to the vest to figure him out. "You can call me any of them, but I'd prefer you didn't make them up."

"Balls, you're annoying."

One side of his mouth quirked. Finally. "I'll accept that."

"Damn right. Can we get back to the point?" I gestured at the window's glimmering map. "That chopshop is smack in the middle of a quarantine that you're telling me is dotted with necro activity. Are they all the same necro?"

"The frequencies were different in all logged cases."

I nodded, like it was no big deal.

It was a shitstorm of a big deal. "I need inside," I said. "The rest we can chunk as we go."

"Based on the information, it's obvious that Jim was dealing there," Indigo pointed out.

"Nanjali Koupra was sold off there," I said flatly, as if reminding him – reminding them both, and myself too – why it mattered. "I walked out from there."

"But your name is not on this list," Malik noted.

Figures he'd caught that. "So somebody's a sloppy record keeper."

He waited me out. Still. *Again.* I hated that he could.

I glared at him. "After I escaped, I hitched out of the Third Junction."

Malik didn't blink. "The Third Junction isn't the Vid Zone."

"It's south, genius. And I wasn't exactly in the best frame of mind when I escaped, so let's extrapolate from there, okay?"

"You're saying you walked without memory of it?"

"I'm saying I'm right," I shot back.

Malik didn't sigh. I expected him to, a lot like Indigo sighed when I locked down into stubborn, but he only studied my features.

I wasn't a diplomat for a reason. I'd go with him, or I'd go through him, but I was getting inside that shop.

Maybe he got it. He gave in with surprising ease. "Let's hope you're right." He reached over, a touch of a button somewhere on his desk, and the map faded, windows losing their tint. Sunlight streamed through the glass again, forcing me to flatten a hand visor-like over my eyes. "Standard operating procedure demands a burn team go in and raze a quarantine down to the last foundation. It takes roughly an hour to mobilize all the protocols. I can extend that time, but you need a team before the borrowed time runs out."

Which I knew. I knew because my team wouldn't work with me, and I didn't dare bring them in. One necro was bad. More was suicide, and I wasn't even pretending not to know that.

But I wasn't ready for the hollow feeling it left in my chest.

I knew that team. They knew me. We worked well together, had been on more successful runs than not. Hell, Boone and Tashi had been on that MetaCore run that landed me on Lucky's table.

Objectively speaking, I couldn't blame them. I'd vanished, taken Nanjali with me, and for all they'd known, she was dead and I was a traitor.

That's why I needed to do this.

"Then get me a team," I began, only to jerk in surprise as Indigo said, "I'll go."

"No," I said flatly. I didn't even look at him.

If I went, maybe I died. For real. Fine. I could live with that, in a manner of speaking. If he went and he died?

No. No way. Things were rough, but I wasn't going to be the cunt that dragged her best team into hell with no hope of actually making it.

"Don't even try it, Riko."

I turned to face him, arms tight around my ribs. "Shut up," I said, one cracking syllable away from boiling over. "I don't care where we are, I will break your fucking face if you think–"

"Yeah?" He shot to his feet. "Bring it on," he snarled. "What the hell else could you do to me? You're a smegging nutcase."

The fact I wanted to step back, recoil like he slapped me, infuriated me.

"You've *changed*," Indigo said grimly, "and we all know it."

My shoulders tightened. "I'm doing whatever it takes to get the information about your sister's death. It doesn't mean *you* have to go on a suicide run."

"My sister?" His laugh bit, not a trace of humor in Indigo's sharp-featured derision. "You mean your girlfriend? The girl you were supposed to love and protect, not escort *in* to that hellhole."

"Chum off, I never said I was marrying her!"

Indigo froze.

Oh, fuck me. Fuck fucking *fuck*.

With the words out, it didn't matter that I spat them on a tide of mounting frustration. It didn't matter that I'd only thrown them between us as a way to make him pause, to hurt him the way he was hurting me – tearing open the fragile scab of my guilt and jamming his fingers into the seeping wound.

They were out, and they reeked of truth.

His face pale, Indigo drew himself up, his hands fisted tightly by his side. "Thanks," he said, so evenly, so detached it was as if I was talking to a stranger. "At least you're finally honest about it."

"Digo–"

"No." He turned his back, his long braid swinging at his rigid shoulders. "Just admit for once that you're only here for your own selfish ends and stop hiding behind Nanji."

Silence fell, thick and angry between us. I struggled to find the words, any words – something to mend this rift.

Nothing came. I had nothing to give him but empty promises – the data, maybe. Whatever it said, I was betting everything on that intel.

And what if it burned me?

Indigo was right. I didn't really play well with others; not like the Koupras had. It wasn't about Nanji, and now I'd leave Digo up here in a heartbeat if it meant I could be rid of his baggage, too.

But I swear, it was only because I expected that baggage to be dead weight. And I didn't want to risk anymore dead anything.

I couldn't carry that.

"This is a suicide run," I began, voice low.

He cut me off. "As I said," Indigo said, tone cracked down to level, "I'm going. If that intel exists, I'll be the one securing it."

The whiplash was enough to give a girl vertigo. My heart kicked up in a sudden surge of adrenaline I couldn't lock down in time.

It irritated me.

I forced my face into tight lines. "You *really* don't trust me, do you?"

"Seriously?" He looked at me, and there was *nothing* friendly about it. His blue eyes practically spat venom at me. "What's the problem, Ree? You hoping to shake me so you can cover your shit up? Not happening."

I took one step in his direction.

Malik's hand flattened over my chest. It wasn't much by way of a wall, but the feel of it – warm and firm and steady when I felt like a freaking yo-yo – yanked me back into line better than any order. "You both sign on," he said with all of that so easy authority, "and I supply you a team."

My heart did a painful ricochet.

Too late, I realized he'd witnessed every word. Every bitter moment between Indigo and me. So this was vulnerability, huh?

It sucked. No wonder Lucky had always been a loner.

I turned slowly. More than a little numb. "A brand new team on a suicide run? They better be incredible."

"They're professionals." Malik's gaze held mine, but his expression hadn't changed. If he thought anything about our exchange – about me – I couldn't tell. The sun painted his eyes a strangely warmer shade of brown, turned his freckles to lighter golden flecks against his dusky skin. No sympathy there. Not even understanding. He could have been a robot, for all the emotion he showed me.

Now I felt unbalanced. Exposed.

"Great," Indigo said, clipped from behind me "One question. Why bring her?"

I jerked. "Shut your cocksu–"

"She's the only one who's been inside," Malik said, resonant conviction that sliced right through my streak of temper like it didn't matter. "We've got no blueprints of the interior and we're already flying in blind. Her boots on the ground take some of the risk out of the operation, which means I'm more likely to provide you the backing you need."

If he could feel the hammer of my heart against his palm, he didn't so much as look at me. I'd give him points for that one.

I was ready to punch someone. Just on principle.

"She could just as well increase the risk," Indigo said flatly.

I bit down on my retort so fast, I'm pretty sure the sound cracked through the room. It was kneejerk to fight back, but the fact was, he wasn't entirely wrong.

I was not in my best shape. I'd had blackouts. I killed Jim without even batting an eyelash.

But that wasn't corruption. Lucky had cleared me. And Digo didn't know about the rest.

He was just being... angry.

I hated this.

When I stepped away from Malik's hand, he still didn't bother looking at me.

"I'm bankrolling the both of you, a unit. Her inside knowledge, your expertise. If you want that team, you have your terms." Malik's stare leveled on Indigo. "Mr Koupra, I'm willing to offer you a sum three times your current rate for data extraction." He reached beside him to pull his expensive chair back from the glass desk. "Aside from your pet project, I want you to locate the source of the infection and download it to a mobile unit."

Well, that was unexpected. A side quest. How cute. "Isn't that impossible?" I asked.

"No." This from Indigo, surprising me. His jaw was still locked tight, his words forced through thinned lips, but he spoke like he knew his shit. As a linker, there were few I trusted more. Even now. "Necro conversion starts in a flesh-tech hybrid, but if it's going to spread, it has to infect a system just like any other computer virus. There's a point of entry."

I glanced at Malik, who waited in silence. His expression, on the grim side of patient, didn't shift. "Why doesn't it infect the bandwidth and take it all down?" I asked.

"Fucking A, Riko, don't jinx it," Indigo said sharply. He scrubbed at his face with both hands. "Whatever the reason, necrotech code spreads through physical connection. It's never hit the bandwidth, just burns out on wireless hubs. I don't know why."

"There are working theories on the subject," Malik offered in his deep, steady voice. If he was at all worried by the subject, I sure as shit couldn't tell.

"Reassuring." I folded my arms, eyeing Indigo cautiously. "*Can* you find the source?"

"It'll be in the data logs, if I can get in far enough back."

"And you're... willing?"

His gaze flicked to me. "I'm not willing," he said flatly. "I'm insisting. If you have to be there, fine, but I'll see this with my own eyes." Before I could do anything to the intel. He didn't have to say it for me to get it.

There was so much uncertainty, so much weird, that we didn't have anything else between us. Just hatred and suspicion.

That sucked so hard.

Indigo was all I had left. Whether he liked it or not, he was the only one who had even a grasp of how in-fucking-credible this whole mess was, and I needed him to stay alive with that knowledge.

He might hate me, he might blame me for Nanji's death, that was fine. Just as long as he helped me figure out everything on that file.

Now that he'd cut me loose, actually dumped my ass, I wanted him back. Selfish as that was.

But it could mean losing him for real. "Dead men don't spend creds," I said, voice low as I stared at Indigo. "Are you sure you want to do this?"

Digo stared down at the floor between his feet.

"Three times your going rate," Malik repeated. "On top of what it is owed for previous services."

Owed? For what?

"Fuck." Indigo rolled his shoulders. "Fine. I'll work with her."

Whatever just happened between them, I wasn't sure. I turned, jaw set, shoulders so tense, it turned my phantom ache into a bone-deep vibration. "Damn it, Digo, I am trying to save your life."

There was nothing remotely friendly in him as he gave me

his back. "Wrong time," he replied shortly, "wrong Koupra."

Motherfucker, that one hurt. Bad.

He left the room without another word.

Sucking in a breath, I whirled on Malik. "What just happened there?"

"Happened?"

I pointed at the door. "That. What you just did. What do you owe him for?"

He studied me with mild interest. "Do you think Mr Koupra wants your nose in his financial concerns?"

"Fuck what he wants." My jaw thrust out, mulish to his cool reserve. "Did he set me up our first meeting?"

He tipped his head faintly. An inquisitive line. "That question completely fails to credit me with any of my own agency."

"You're saying that was all you and your douchedigger crew?" Malik's eyes creased faintly at me, that hint of a smile playing around his mouth again, but he didn't give me full-on teeth. Or an answer. I slapped a hand on the desk. "Why are you willing to let him go along?"

"Because he wants to ensure that you're telling the truth," he answered mildly, "and I am willing to afford him the opportunity to soothe his conscience while equipping the team I'm sending down there with the best information available. That's your firsthand knowledge and Mr Koupra's coordinator – excuse me," he corrected pointedly, "his linker expertise. It's a guaranteed win for me."

"You're using him."

"I'm using all of you," he replied. Didn't even try to smile his way out of that one. "Make no mistake. I couldn't care less about your so-called cred or whatever emotional tug-of-war you're playing. I want the intel in that lab. I will use every asset I have to achieve what I want. You may consider doing the same."

"Digo's not an asset."

He shrugged. "On the contrary. He is an extremely valuable

asset. Have you thought about affording him that much respect, at least?"

I stared at him. "What, I should walk up to him and tell him how much of a stellar tool I think he is? He's my *friend*."

Was. *Was* my friend.

His mouth slanted, a corner twisted into humor that might have been rueful. Or just amused. "The way you treat your friends, I wonder how you sleep at night. Speaking of," he continued over my sharp inhale and bitten-off challenge, "I suggest you get some rest. There won't be time for sleep later." He reached into thin air over his desk and withdrew that pale screen between three pinched fingers, the projection flawless. He focused his attention on the data.

Dismissal. Damn him. My hands fisted at my side. "You think you're so cute."

"Like you, I suspect, *cute* is not a word I often hear." Before I could decide if I should be surprised or insulted, he looked up, a glint in his dark eyes. "Thank you." *Bag of dicks.* Those two words combined with that sure confidence, and I remembered exactly why he pushed all my buttons.

"That wasn't a compliment," I muttered.

"As you say." But I'd lost him again to the data on his projection. "Ms Ramsay will show you to your quarters."

Okay, so I could admit some admiration for the guy. He had implacability down to an art form. I shook my head. "Fine," I said, unwilling to let him have the last word. I folded my arms over my ribs, rocking back on my heels. "But only because I refuse to leave Indigo in your hands unsupervised."

Malik Reed was not the sort of gentleman to let a lady have the last word. "I think Mr Koupra would rather get paid. Even if he has to do it with you."

Such an asshole. Which worked, because I was no lady.

I shot him a raised finger as I left the sun-dappled office with its crystal clear skylights. If he noticed, he didn't make any sound.

I'd gotten what I wanted – a team, Reed's support. Even a linker I more or less trusted to know his shit. I would have felt better if Indigo stayed behind, but then, I didn't trust anyone else out in the field to see this through. It made my job harder.

Still, I was not going to let Digo take this on without me. No matter what.

If Malik wanted him to link it so bad, I'd be riding Digo's ass all the way to hell.

And then we'd both know what happened to me.

For better or for worse.

17

I wasn't a complicated girl. I liked things simple, to the point, and up front. I wasn't into angst, didn't much care for chrome, and rich kids swaggering into my turf were tedious as hell to deal with.

But they sure knew how to live.

I'd expected some kind of barracks. A bunk out of the way, someplace quiet to rack out until we were ready to go. The "quarters" turned out to be a full-on suite of rooms linked together by double-wide archways. Short on doors, heavy on windows, light on the color palette.

"Do you like it?"

The receptionist's first name was Hope. I'd learned it on the escort up another seventeen flights. Being trapped in an elevator didn't leave a whole lot of room to avoid the small talk.

On the plus side, she didn't seem to mind that I wasn't as chatty as she was.

"Mr Reed suggested this room personally," she continued, crossing the open expanse of bare flooring to nudge one of the handful of throw rugs into some kind of better positioning. The palette was all in gray, shades of charcoal and smoke and other words for it I didn't bother coming up with, but the accents were pastel. Lavender, pale blue.

"It's..." I scrounged for the right word. "Delicate."

Hope's polite smile compressed into a mischievous line. "You don't like it."

"It's just..." I spread my hands, as if I could encapsulate the whole room on one end, and me on the other. The contrast between the soft colors and my tough, ink-spattered edge was pointedly ludicrous. "It's..."

"Feminine? Soft?"

"Not even a little bit my style."

To my surprise, Hope laughed. "You'll get over it for a few hours." She turned, her curvy figure in its pristine black pencil skirt and belted blouse looking as perfectly at home as I did out of place. "The bedroom is through there," she said, gesturing to a far wall and a double-arch, also lacking in doors. "The bathroom is also there. There's a shower and a tub, so feel free to–"

"Hold it." I didn't move from my spot in front of the door, weirdly afraid that my boots would leave marks on the floor, but I did raise my voice.

Hope tilted her head. "Yes?"

I stared hard at her. "Tub? A real tub?"

Inquiry turned to deeper mischief in her smile. "Yes, ma'am. A tub. A real bathtub, with water and everything. It's even hot." She chuckled as she added, "And it's completely safe."

Holy shit. I mean, *holy shit.* I could count on one finger the amount of times I'd been in a hot water scrub, and that had been a brief luxury I'd paid dearly for. Even the decent places only had hot water for sinks and maybe a timed shower. A full on bathtub meant gallons upon gallons of water; pure, hot, *expensive*.

Hope studied me, her hands on her flared hips. She wore sheer stockings under her professional skirt, her blouse was buttoned to her neck, and her dark blonde hair didn't allow a single strand out of place. Even her glasses were plain frames, with none of the shine shopped around on the sales feeds. The overall effect was definitely a cultivated air of proficiency, too old for her youthful face.

"You are welcome to come in, you know," she said pointedly. One hand gestured at me, an efficient *come here* as if I were a stray dog needing a brisk order. "The place won't bite, and you're not under arrest or anything."

"Right." I didn't move. "Uh, look, Miss Ramsay–"

"Hope."

I shot her a raised eyebrow. "Is that professional?"

This time, I think her smile caught her off guard. Wide-lipped and full, it was also crooked – a touch wider at one corner than the other. "You *really* don't like it, do you?"

Sort of. "It's not the room. It's a nice room," I protested. But I offered both arms, forearms up, as if in evidence. "It's not my kind of room."

"You want me to order in some rebar and neon girders?"

I narrowed my eyes at her dry tone. "Would you?"

"If you worked for us."

Her level gaze was so mild over her smile that I couldn't tell if she was yanking my chain or was as earnest as an aneurysm. "Seriously?"

She didn't snort. I think she almost did, but she cleared her throat instead, shaking her head. The sunlight filtered through her bound hair, picking out glints of red here and there, tossing off a corona of gold. "You're an odd woman." She approached me, empty hands swinging idly by her sides.

I stared dumbly when she stopped half a foot away.

"Ah..." She gestured. "You're blocking the door."

I moved. "Sorry."

"Relax," she assured me gently. Easy for her to say. My shoulders felt like I'd banded them in cement, and the back of my neck hadn't stopped prickling since I'd walked out of Malik's office.

The door hissed open with a touch to a silver panel, and

Hope paused. "Take a bath or use the shower, whatever you need. Just use this panel if you get hungry." Her eyes sparkled through her simple frames. "We deliver."

I eyed the bright, airy hallway behind her. "Are you sure I'm not under some kind of house arrest?"

"Relax," she told me again. "Really. It's a word."

"So is 'trap'."

"So is 'paranoid'," she replied. "You can walk around all you want, but given your discomfort, Mr Reed figured you'd be better off taking it easy." Her smile returned, but her brisk tones didn't soften. "You'll have a full exam in one hour, so I'll make sure you're escorted to—"

I raised a hand. "Stop. Back up. Revise. I'll have a what?"

Hope tilted her head a fraction. The sunlight pooled in her glasses, hiding her eyes. "An exam. It's standard procedure before any excursion."

I backed up a step, putting distance between us and folding my arms. "No."

That surprised her. So much so that she adjusted the glasses that didn't need adjusting. "I'm sorry?"

"No exam. I'm here, I'll work with your boss, I'll work with his *professional* team, but screw his exam." If I sounded a little bitter, tough. The fact my ex-team had given up on me still smarted. Hope opened her mouth to argue, but I didn't care. "If he has a problem with it, *Mr Reed* can deal with it himself." Preferably by fucking himself with the implements I'd already suggested he acquire, but I figured I'd let that go unsaid.

She shook her head. "I'll deliver the message," was her reproachful acknowledgment. She said nothing else, stepped out of the threshold. The door slid shut, soundless and quick.

I glowered at the panel.

So I was being a *little* antagonistic. The reasons were more practical than I let on. A SINless has two things going for her: a lack of a Security Identification Number, and complete faith in her tech. If we are smart mercs, we choose our chopshops and street docs with care, and we never, ever let our bodies fall into the hands of people we don't trust.

Well, for medical reasons, anyway.

It's just good policy. Half our systems are strung together on individual metrics custom tailored to our chipsets, needs and patterns. The last thing I wanted to do was let Malik Reed's people fuck around with my setup any more than it already was. Annoying him was only part of the fun.

But it was more than that.

What if Malik's people found something? What if he tested my arm, or found some kind of brain anomaly, and used that to keep me off the team? Out of the loop?

If it were me, I'd do it to myself. Hell, if we were talking standard op, Indigo would yank me so fast, my head would spin.

No. It was better policy to keep myself *to* myself. I'd have to find a new doc sooner or later – or clear my cred so I could go back to Lucky – but I didn't need to risk that just yet.

I spun in a slow circle, rolling my tense shoulders as I took in the bright, spacious room with its sparse but neat furniture and inset arches. Columns. Honestly. Who put columns inside a living space?

I wrinkled my nose, finally stepping completely into the quarters I'd been allotted. If I checked behind me to make sure I wasn't leaving boot prints, at least I was alone to do it. Physically, anyway. I wasn't positive that these quarters weren't under surveillance, but since I had no plans to do anything to impede the run – and only minimal ideas to do something dirty in case I had a virtual babysitter – I let it go.

The space was quiet. Soundproofed, probably. The light streaming in through the wide windows was warm but not uncomfortable, and the place smelled clean in a way that seemed less intrusive than the overly sanitary fragrance of a hospital or that gutwrenching clinical disinfectant I now associated with a lab. I approached the curtainless windows, squinting against the light.

Pretty view, in a reflective kind of way. Miles of glass and metal, intersected by the byways linking taller buildings together in a crisscrossed grid of streets and overhangs. A spot of green here and there had to be some kind of deliberately cultivated garden in allotted alcoves, and below, cars and people streamed in a jumbled streak of black and occasional glint of color.

I pressed my left hand against the glass.

Durable. Hybrid material, bulletproof. Most of the numbers scrolling through my display meant nothing – one day, I'd sit down and work out all the various digits, but I only bothered to learn what I found immediately useful – but I knew enough to get the impression of shatterproof glass and hardcore security.

Must be nice, living in all this safety. Like fragile little birds, rolling in the creds. Probably even something of a good life, if it's the life you want, but who would? Anyone with a SIN is ripe for overwatch. The whole concept of freedom got trumped by the demand for security decades ago. It started with communication taps and bled into everyday existence from there. Maybe you aren't being watched *all* the time, but it always bothered me that no one seemed to mind it meant anyone could clock into your freqs simply by pulling up your SIN.

Granted, most couldn't read the SIN without illegal tech, but that stuff is only illegal for the people who can't afford it.

I guess if you like power with strings and a leash, being a sinner isn't so bad.

"Chunk it," I muttered, turning away. I'd take my freedoms, hard and dirty and bloody as it got.

I briefly contemplated calling Indigo, checking in with him – see if he got a sweet room like this one – but I discarded the idea. He was... not happy with me. Okay, understatement of the year. He was pissed, which only frustrated me. Not fair, I guess, but *come on*. I was trying to fix a mess I didn't know the whole scope of, and it was his sister.

My girlfriend.

I winced, rubbing my face.

I needed to stop calling her that. My words, sharp and angry, echoed in the silent room around me.

I never said I was marrying her.

And because I said it, because saying it had made my shoulders loosen some, I'd gone from feeling guilty and responsible to feeling guilty, responsible and a lot like the cunt I was.

I never did promise her anything but what I had at the time – my attention, mostly. But that didn't make it any less of a shitty thing to say.

If we found out that she was targeted with no help from me, would that absolve me of the guilt I carried for stringing her along? Would I be given the chance to make it right?

How much of an asshole was I that I didn't think it'd matter? It couldn't possibly be worse.

"Balls," I muttered. That was enough. I couldn't sink down into all this, not right now. Malik Reed had one thing right: a merc needed some time off before a run, or at least I did. And some downtime after. The what-ifs I said I didn't like? They tended to double in those hours before a team headed out.

Indigo had taught me to deal with the details in the days leading up, then take a day off before. It was a system that worked for me. For most of us. I could make the best of the time I had.

Even if I would have done it *with* the team before all this.

A pang in my chest forced me to shake myself before I went right back down that road I said I didn't want to go down.

There had to be something better to do.

Something I could do in some kind of effort to... I don't know, fix things.

When the idea hit me, I didn't even think twice about it. I closed my eyes, sat back on the couch, and uploaded a call through my projection frequencies.

The room was as it always was, and I didn't sit in the chair this time. I perched on the edge of the table, legs stretched out and ankles crossed. My arms folded over my shiny red tank-top as I waited for Greg's connection.

He didn't keep me waiting. His persona looked no less worse for wear as he strode into view – a strange mix of digital processing and physical movement that made it look like he blurred into existence. "Riko," he said in greeting. "This is unexpected."

But not entirely unwelcome, I gathered. I flipped him a crooked smile as the walls bled neon advertising and the white door closed behind him. "Are you busy?"

"Compared to what?"

"Point."

The detective didn't sit either, eschewing the metal table for the space in front of my outstretched legs. He hooked his fingers into his pockets, a patient stance that drew my eye to the lean shape of his shoulders beneath his brown coat. His badge glinted from a chain around his neck. It didn't surprise me that his persona still wore it.

I think most of Detective Gregory Keith's personality was wrapped up in that badge.

I wouldn't tell him this, but it had a lot to do with why I turned down his offer. Some people were born to be cops. They had the attitude, the ability, and the means to deal with the shit. Good or bad, easy or hard, they knew how to cope.

Problem was, I didn't know many – saint or corporate assclown – who gave a damn. And I wasn't sure Greg himself knew how valuable that perseverance was.

Unfortunately for him, current events trumped idealism. I had a purpose for him.

"So?" He cocked his head, returning my study with raised

eyebrows. His persona's chiseled features still made me want to laugh, but I could admit they delivered. He was cute. "I can't get a lock on your frequency. I take it this isn't a social call."

I grinned. "That's right, you can't." *Thank you, Lucky.* "I'm here to offer a white flag."

His eyes lit, reflecting back a snap of poison green as an ad flickered behind me. "Surrender?" he asked hopefully.

I raised my chin. "Truce, detective. Just a truce."

I half-expected that warm glow to bank. It didn't. His mouth curved up, and he leaned forward just enough to show his interest. "I'll take what I can get."

"Even when it comes with a tech limb?"

Okay, that was a low blow. It kind of didn't help my case – especially when his gaze flicked to my folded diamond steel arm and skated away. He shrugged, but didn't apologize.

Neither did I. "Let's keep this honest." I unfolded my arms, braced my hands on the edge of the table. "I'm not here to talk about you, your wife, or your after-hours inclinations. Word on the wave–" Damn, I was turning into Jax. "Word out there is that you're on the market."

His shoulders tightened. The vaguely sheepish cant to his smile faded to a grimace. "Why do I get the impression you're not talking about dating?"

"I'm not."

"Crap."

"Yeah, my thoughts, too." I tipped my head to the white door behind him. "You talk to anyone else out there?" He didn't have to say anything. I read the answer clear as day on his face. "You did," I guessed before he could try to deny it. "Of course you did."

"You turned me down."

True, but he was the idiot who'd gone blabbing. "Why do I get the impression you wandered down to the rack and started asking questions?"

The look he shot me was almost as good as a sigh. "You really think I'm stupid."

Yes. Well, sort of. I waved that away. "Let's try this again, detective. I think I could have work for you."

Greg dragged a hand over his adorably – and deliberately – mussed hair, but at least he didn't look like he was calculating the results on my libido. "Why the change of heart?"

"Honestly?" I raised one eyebrow at him. "I think you're going to get eaten alive if I don't make it clear you're mine."

"*Yours*?"

"In my black book, then," I returned impatiently. Even temporarily. As soon as he signed on with me, I could giftwrap him for Indigo.

That's right. I was delivering a cop to my linker.

It was a multipart plan, and as long as Indigo didn't lose his shit when I told him I had a pocket cop for him, it might work. As a sweet bonus, it would net Indigo Koupra a decent uniform in his network.

Sort of like delivering flowers after a fight, except I was the bad boyfriend in this equation and I wasn't sure Indigo was girly enough to accept it.

All I could do was try. "Look, pride's all well and good, but you're a sinner in blue messing around in sainted turf. The rules are different."

"Uh huh." He didn't look appeased. "So what you're telling me is that you don't think I can hack it."

Pretty much. Still, it didn't sound all that encouraging, did it? I straightened, easing to my feet with an exasperated sound. "Trust me, Greg. Once you start to get the lay of the land, you'll understand. Until then, take the smegging help."

"What's in it for you?"

I loved that question. It usually meant people were willing to deal – or at least closer to it. "Information, now and again. Sometimes, people. And the occasional freelance job."

Greg rocked back on his heels, surprise evident on his

artistically enhanced projection. "To kill?"

I shook my head. "Nah. You're a cop. Your strength is in that. Any saint worth her shit knows better than to blunt a tool using it for something it's not meant for."

He didn't like that. I could tell by the way his jaw tightened. "I am not a tool."

See? Malik was wrong.

"Look," I said, sighing with it, "you want in on this world? This is how it goes. You're a cop and a sinner, which makes you second to a corp fuckhead in a suit. You've got zero cred. You have to start somewhere."

"Is this how you started?"

It was how I was having to start again. My lip curled. "Not quite. I started as somebody's pet project." The fact I respected Lucky kept me from worrying on that bone longer than I had to. I was done here. Patience wasn't much of a strong point for me, and he'd tapped out what little I had left. "Think about it, Greg. And keep in mind what I told you."

"What, that I'm a *tool*?"

Oh, for fuck's sake. The fact his indignation mirrored the shit I'd flipped Malik for his assessment of Digo's *assets* made this even more ridiculous. "No, you idiot," I growled. "That you're marked. And I promise, most saints who have reasons to want a cop on the take are going to have a shit ton more tech than me, so consider growing a pair, okay?"

"I will if you'll tell me something."

I hesitated, turning enough that I could slant him an impatient nod without opening up any deeper discourse. "Make it fast."

His hands had come out of his pockets. Big hands, but I preferred them callused over this perfected persona. One pointed at my left arm. "Why did you get that?"

Always back to the arm, huh? I opted for honesty. "A run went sideways and it took my arm with it."

"Why not regrow it?" A valid question.

But a whole lot ignorant, too. My smile slashed into a bitter shade of pity. He was going to have to learn, and fast. "Rule number one, detective. Saints don't have insurance." I closed out of the projection before he unraveled what was left of my goodwill.

It wasn't his fault. The guy had basically painted himself red and slapped a sign on his ass declaring *fresh meat.* He'd figure it out. With or without my help, he'd learn. Dealing with SINless meant different rules.

He wasn't completely wrong about my arm, either. Medlabs *could* regrow amputated limbs, but the bio gel worked slowly and needed constant maintenance to get right. Nobody on the streets had that kind of funding or time. Much as I made fun of the civic departments, the one place they didn't skimp was injury coverage. If Greg ever got unlucky enough to lose a limb, they'd pay for as many months of intensive care as needed to get him back on the street without resorting to too much tech.

Sure, all kinds of police went bad all the time, but *nobody* wanted to risk tech corruption in a precinct full of cops.

Besides, the arm wasn't so bad, once you got used to it.

I took a deep breath.

My good deed for the day was done. If Detective Douchedick signed up – and now that he knew he had options, I expected him to – I'd have my very own bouquet of cop to give to Indigo. It was manipulative and probably a little creepy, but I was what I was.

Digo would come around.

Maybe.

I scrubbed at my face. Enough. Enough guilt. Enough dealing with other people's shit. I needed my mind off everything, and the siren call of hot water might do it. I pushed myself to my feet, stretching the kinks from my abused muscles. Nanos could fix a lot, but I'd bet all that hot, clean water would feel like Greg's Judeo-Christian heaven.

The bedroom offered a huge bed that looked comfortable

enough to sink into and windows that were tinted against outside voyeurs. Curtains covered the panels, sheer and gauzy, and while it was nice enough, it didn't rock my world.

The bathroom, on the other hand, pretty much ruined me for life.

"What the *tits*," I breathed as I stepped out of one pristine wonderland into another. The colors didn't change, replacing furniture with fixtures that sparkled in satin-finish silver and floor-to-ceiling windows with narrow panels interspersed with mirrors in between. The floor was a mosaic in the same pale gray, blue and lavender colors, and the walls echoed the smooth satin plating.

It was like a zen masterpiece in here. Dull, but calm.

Made all the better by the stand-up radiation shower inset into one corner, the wide bathtub beside it, and – oh, holy fucking balls of joy – a shower. An actual *shower*. A legit water-falls-from-pipes-of-heaven walk-in shower.

Maybe I would have gone for the bathtub, but that seemed too peaceful for my frenetic energy.

My boots hit the ground so fast, I heard the laces stretch. In seconds, I was naked, grinning like a kid in sugar heaven, and standing within the confines of gray metal and squeaky clean, frosted glass.

A monitor by the shower door flicked on as my feet hit the tiled floor, showcasing an array of sliders. "Welcome," said a gentle, mechanized voice. Mostly masculine, though in a range that put me in mind of Shiva's mystique. "Temperature?"

I was in paradise.

"Scalding," I told it.

"Temperature set to maximum heat for organic users," the voice told me politely. "Pressure?"

"Brutal."

"Pressure set to maximum therapeutic levels. Please enjoy."

A thrum went up through my feet. Within seconds, panels I hadn't noticed in the ceiling overhead slid wide, and water tore through the pipes. Hot, heavy rain scored over me, splattered to the tile, and I couldn't help myself.

I laughed. Holding my arms out like I'd fly away, I let the heavy, pounding spray wash over me, fill my mouth and eyes and ears, and I laughed until all the what-ifs faded.

Like I said, I liked things simple. A hot shower ranked up there as one of life's gifts a girl just didn't turn away.

Steam quickly turned the glass panels white. I shook my ass under that shower for I don't know how long, ignored the perfumed soap proffered by another panel inset into the wall, and stood beneath the spray until my fingertips wrinkled and the pads of my feet went white.

If I ever became so rich that I had creds to burn, I was installing a permanent, legit water filter in Lucky's place. That man needed to know what this was like.

I stood in the center of the rain, my arms hanging by my sides, and breathed in hot steam as the spray slid over my face, my shoulders. I could feel the ache in my arm draining with the water swirling around my toes. Even the tension in my shoulders eased.

For the first time since waking up in that lab, I completely checked out.

I blame the sheer shit of the past few days. I should have known better.

"Delighted you're enjoying yourself."

Malik Reed's even, unmistakable baritone cut through the noise of the shower, ripping me out of my fresh water fantasies. I jerked my face out of the spray, flipping my streaming hair from my eyes even as I rocked back on my left foot, stepping into a position that would give me the best leverage in the enclosed space.

I should have followed through with the straight-legged kick I geared up, should have ignored the jolt of surprise as it stole my momentum.

I didn't. Idiot me.

18

Malik lounged in the steam, his athletic body not so much filling the space as angled to make the most of the room he had. His hands tucked casually into the pockets of his slacks. Water spread like a black stain across the front of his vest. Droplets slid down his jaw, courtesy of my shake, but he made no move to wipe them away.

Sexy. Something about men, suits and water. No way I entertained that fetish alone.

His features had settled into hard lines somewhere between determination and implacability, and if it bothered him that his left shoulder was soaking up condensation from the glass he leaned against, I couldn't tell. His gaze, black in the murky bathroom, wandered down my naked body in blatant scrutiny. It hooked on the glint of metal at my left nipple.

He looked like a man poised to admire what was his. A thing in a prized collection.

I shouldn't have found that delicious. I totally did.

Big fat red alert.

I half-turned, lifting my hands to the hot spray. The fact that my pussy was throwing me a hungry tantrum irritated me – I liked sex, but I wasn't into corporate dogs, and definitely not into sadists.

Kind of into provocation, though. Although I looked out

of place in all this soft-finish chrome, I was confident enough in my sense of self to feel sexy about it, and I knew he was looking.

"Are you here to join me?" My tongue had no problem with the words, it was my voice that got carried away. Husky and low, like an invite. "'Cause," I continued, stepping out of the waterfall, "you're way too late. I'm done."

He didn't say anything. Not even when I walked forward, bare feet splashing in the patterned water swirling the drains. I halted just shy of plastering myself on him, bracing myself with one hand against the same panel he leaned against.

I raised my eyebrows in mock-polite inquiry, didn't bother trying to cover myself. I didn't know how long he'd been standing there, but if he wanted to appreciate all the work I put in to keep myself in killing form, more power to him.

Malik made no effort to move. "Water off."

The water ceased. The ceiling panels slid shut, catching any drips, and silence descended on the warm, sultry bathroom air like a second shroud.

I narrowed my eyes, though I was forced to pull my sodden hair back from my forehead when droplets slid down my face. "You are in my way."

"You're missing an appointment," was his reply.

"Yes, I am." I'd known when I laid down the line that there was a chance I'd be called on it. "Hope gave you my message, huh?"

"I believe the invitation involved handling it myself." Malik didn't pull his hands from his pockets – a pose that made him look too much like some kind of adspace model. It didn't sit right on him. Part of me appreciated the raw masculinity of the man, but he was too hard, too cold to pull it off with any real polish. At least Greg's version gave him an impression of the scruffy boy next door.

Although I guess that was the difference between them. Greg was very much aware of his attractiveness. Malik didn't need to sell anything to anyone. He existed, independent of what anyone thought of him. That much was obvious.

I still owed him a punch in the throat.

I let my gaze slide over his features. Delicious, sure. But dangerous. Nothing softened it – not the water clinging to his warm brown skin, the way his shirt and vest fit over his athletic shoulders, not even the incongruity of his expensive shoes against the wet tile. It was a deliberate mockery of the study he'd afforded me, only he wasn't naked.

Good thing. I had no misconceptions about my willpower in matters of the flesh, and a naked Malik Reed would be the worst idea I could entertain.

"You're still in my way," I said huskily.

"And you're still missing an appointment."

"For a guy who started this by having his people kick my ass," I replied, "you're putting a serious harsh on our relationship."

He inclined his head. "Tell me why you won't allow my team to examine you."

"Okay, one?" I held up a finger under his nose, which scattered more water on his vest, soaking in like black ink. "I don't need to be *examined*, thanks. The data your people pulled off me in that fight is enough." Not even a flicker of acknowledgment. If he'd been recording my activities during that scrap, he wasn't going to tell me.

Fine. I'd work on the assumption that he wasn't an idiot.

I lifted another finger. "Two, get the hell out of my way so I can dry off."

"Will you continue our discussion?"

"Will you keep me in here if I don't?" I countered.

Shit. I shouldn't have asked. Malik serious was bad enough, but there went that smile again. A curve of his full mouth that didn't quite reach his eyes, not really. The closest it got formed those little crinkles beside them.

It also sent sharp, unwelcome fingers of heat through parts

of me still wet from the shower and getting wetter by the second.

Maybe I'd see about tech that could turn off my sex drive. It existed. Given the fact he'd ordered four assclowns to break me in a fight, to say nothing of the wedding band I was pretty sure meant he was more trouble than the effort was worth, I didn't need this.

My arms shot out, both hands connected with his chest and I straight-armed him out of the shower door. He didn't stumble so much as take a smooth, balanced step back, like he'd only ridden my momentum.

I swiftly recalculated my assumption of the man's setup. Reflex enhancers? Balance modifiers? Some tech was subtler than others. I'd rather naively assumed Malik had none.

My weight shifted to the balls of my feet, adrenaline spiking, but he didn't even take his hands from his pockets.

I wanted a fight.

Hell, I wanted blood. Skin. Something that would tamp this restless, anxious surge of heat and awareness down.

Malik didn't give me any reason to push it.

"Do me a favor," I said, a flat edge away from a snarl as I stepped out of the shower. "Don't ever try to keep me confined."

"Confine you?" Malik snagged a towel from a narrow rack, as gray as the rest of the suite and thick enough that his dark fingers sank into the plush. The gold ring on his hand winked as he held it out, his features once more unreadable. "I can't even get you to show up for an appointment. You won't take my card, a fact Mr Koupra isn't thanking you for right now—"

I winced. "Chum off."

"—and you haven't given me a valid reason why you won't let yourself be checked out," he continued over me, a level challenge.

I snatched the towel from him, unfolding it over my naked body so it covered me from armpits to knees, and shook back my hair. "Because my tech is mine to know," I said bluntly, meeting his gaze. "This is a one-off, Malik, a single run. What I've got going on is my business, not yours."

"Attractive as what you've got going on is," he returned, though with none of the warmth a compliment of that nature should have had, "you made it my business when you came looking for resources."

I tucked the towel in place over my breasts, my jaw tightening. "Does your wife know how much of a flirt you are?" Not even a twitch. The man was not the distractible kind. I bit back a sigh. "I put up with your bullshit ambush, Malik. I got you your evidence. You never said exams were part of the deal."

"Only a fool would send resources out with an unknown," he countered. "I am not a fool."

No. I believed that. If anything, he was cautious, calculated, and thorough.

Look at me. Lulled into complacency with a shower.

Fucking A.

I pushed past him, bent to pick up my pants and discarded shirt, and stalked out of the bathroom, trailing water as I went. "Look at it from my angle," I said over my shoulder. "You're a complete unknown to me. What am I supposed to do? Trust you?"

"Do you have a choice?" He followed me into the airy flat, apparently not at all bothered that I was still half naked and his sleeve was mostly soaked. "The data you brought me suggests I'm the idiot for trusting either of you without some kind of collateral."

Water beaded on my shoulders. Rolled down my back. I shot him a fulminating scowl. "You're the one who said you'd help."

"Never for free."

What. An asshole. "You're getting data nobody's ever seen," I pointed out, referencing the stuff he hired Digo to pull.

"That makes him integral. You," he said with emphasis, "are still only boots on the ground. One word, and Mr Koupra will no doubt dance for joy to hear you've been removed."

Well, that just flew in the face of what he told Digo in that office. I started at him, hands clenched in my towel. Water dripped off my nose. "And now you're saying you want a full scan of my setup or else no dice." He tipped his head. I snorted outright. "Or what? You and I can go in circles, but you yourself said I'm the only one who's seen it. I know how to find it. How to get in. Your people can search for hours, but the burn team will napalm the place long before they locate it. You willing to miss out on all that pretty intel just for a scan?"

Malik's eyes raked over the hem of my towel. "I'm willing to hear a counteroffer."

"Sure." Heedless of the windows, I dropped my towel.

Finally. He reacted, shoulders tightening.

"Oh, sorry," I said dryly, pulling my sleeveless shirt over my head. It'd catch some of the water dripping from my hair, but oh well. It'd dry. "I'm not on the table."

I knew he heard the phrasing, had processed it, but if there was even an ounce of interest under all that unflappable polish, I didn't have the faintest clue. Just the rigid set of his shoulders. And a wedding ring.

Go figure. The first faithful husband I'd met in the corporate sector, and I found him interesting. And a rabid pain in the ass.

"I bet your poker face is killer," I muttered.

"I'm waiting." The way he said it, like I was some kind of kid getting sent to time out, flicked away the last vestiges of my strained amusement.

Fine. I could play the game, and I didn't *always* have to stroke my cock. Just like I didn't *always* have to kick teeth in. Both men were wrong.

I stepped into my pants. "You saw me fight once, you know

I'm physically fit." This was why I didn't go for skintight club wear when I hit the street for a run. Any item you had to wriggle, hop and strain your way into was going to end up wedged into your crotch at the worst possible time. Fortunately for me, my BDUs slid on like a dream, wet skin or otherwise. "The data you lifted off me in that fight can easily fill in any blanks. Extrapolate, and that should be all you need."

That I didn't want anyone poking at me, scanning me, or otherwise trying to get into my head to tell me how screwed up I was went without saying. If he didn't get that, I wasn't going to give him the opportunity to pry.

It bothered me that he just stood there, watching me dress and listening to my argument like it was perfectly reasonable to be doing both at the same time. The man was a robot.

Except then he opened his mouth, and there wasn't anything machinelike about that baritone. "Give me something that matters."

"Does your wife let you use that voice in the sack?" I inquired, widening my eyes at him with fake interest. "Does it work?"

He lifted an arm, wiping traces of drying water off his jaw with the back of one hand, and waited me out. Again.

"For all the fucks in – Look. It's easy," I said, though it was anything but. "I woke up in a lab-like prison with no idea how I got there. I got out, but I had to leave behind my–" *Shit.* "A teammate," I amended, "to do it. Who the fuck even knows what's behind it all? We're saints, Malik. SINless. We don't trust."

"Congratulations. That's one thing we have in common."

"Oh, good. Do I get a sweet little vest and a tie, too?"

A muscle in Malik's jaw went taut, then eased. One thick black eyebrow climbed on his forehead. I refused to look away, even if the words had slipped out. Authority, remember? I firmed my jaw.

I was tired of giving up my shit to other people. My file to Greg. A favor to Jax. The only sanctuary I had in this godforsaken hellhole of a city. My memories. My linker.

Losing more – giving up the fundamental secrets of my personal tech – hit low and hard. I didn't want to do it.

Chunking hell, I was so bad at this whole relating to people thing. If I were any more terrible at it, I'd be ambulatory meat on a stick. Just a flailing blender of death.

Indigo was right. I sucked at the game. That's why I needed a linker who didn't.

And he hated me, too.

No. I was done giving in. This was my line in the sand.

"I'll lay it out plainly for you." Malik raised a long, manicured finger, direct mockery of my own earlier emphasis. "Without my resources, you're going nowhere." Another finger. "Without a workup, you don't get my resources. The choice is yours."

And just like that, my line in the sand became a choice between my tech and my cred.

Fuck me.

19

He was seriously pissing me off. But what could I do?

Play the cunting game.

I raked a hand through my hair in sheer frustration. "You are such a bastard."

"Your counteroffer left much to be desired."

"Your face leaves much to be desired," I shot back. Childish, but he could blow me.

Malik shrugged, an effortless roll of his shoulders that tightened the shirt across his tapered chest. Personally trained into shape, I'd bet. Not like me, or the people I ran with. We were all beaten into shape by the life we led.

A life he wanted to screw with.

Ass. He was right. I had no options.

I bared my teeth. "Fine," I snarled, and gave it a shot. "A general exam only. *No* invasion."

His expression didn't change as he turned away, idly brushing at the fading stain the water had left on his sleeve. "I assure you," he said, "I have zero interest in invading you."

"Ha fucking ha."

Wait. Was that it? That seemed remarkably easy. Much easier than I thought it was supposed to be. And, oh, yeah, now I was back to wanting to rip his throat out.

"Once you have the exam data," I told his back, pushing

and I knew it, "I get to review it."

He didn't even hitch. "Follow me." He also didn't wait for me to get my shoes.

"Spunkmunch," I grunted, abandoning the boots to follow before he vanished into this corporate jungle. Not because he ordered me to, no way, but because glaring at his back and imagining all the creative ways I could tear out his spine and beat him to death with it provided enough entertainment to get me past raw anger and into sulky resignation.

A long elevator ride, a handful of corridors and an interminable silence later, and he halted outside a wide set of double doors with *Authorized Personnel* emblazoned on the front in bloody red.

We'd gone from open, airy halls to enclosed walls, harsh lighting, and the occasional blocky text imprinted on the corridors we passed. Eerily – uncomfortably – familiar.

"In there," he said, nodding. "Ms Ramsay has already taken the liberty of requisitioning your gear to Mr Koupra's specifications."

"Why don't I get to specify?" I frowned at the doors, trying very hard to ignore the fact that the hair on my arm had lifted. A low, thrumming warning simmered underneath my skin.

It felt wrong to go marching back into the same kind of place I'd escaped from. Wrong on so many levels.

"The obvious answer is that he's going to be reasonable about it."

I shot him a hard glare, briefly jarred from my trepidation. "You're a judgmental bastard, aren't you?"

"I appreciate that you're attempting to stick to apparent facts," he said mildly, "but I do know who my parents are."

It surprised me that I wanted to laugh. His level retorts – delivered with the same polite command he delivered everything – should have annoyed me, but I couldn't help a brief affair with his wit. It was there. Buried under ice and irritation, but there.

I did not want to find him amusing. It annoyed me.

"Do I at least get to req my own weapons?" I asked instead.

"If you have specific tech needs according to your synthetic model, then the lab will let me know."

"That is *not* an answer."

"Not true." His gaze touched mine. "It's simply not an answer you want."

It didn't help that I couldn't make up my mind. Laugh at him or kill him? Chuckle, or eviscerate? Decisions, decisions.

I'd play it cool. If I made it through the next hour without losing my shit, I'd take it from there.

Squaring my shoulders, I stepped closer to the doors, bracing myself for the *whoosh* of activated servos and the faint blast of sterilized air as it washed over me.

The back of my neck tightened. Cramped.

Afraid. I was *afraid*.

"One last thing."

I hesitated, my palm already damp with the effort I was making to ignore the instincts screaming at me to get out, get away. Run far and fast.

I glanced at him, teeth gritted. "What now?" I bit out.

Way harsher than even a second ago.

He didn't blink. "This isn't a game," he said, like I was a six year-old who needed the reminder. "One wrong move – you so much as twitch a nanometer out of line – and I'll pull the plug."

I turned slowly, stepping backwards into the cool air and out of the sensors. "Malik." My voice was steady; thank you, pride. "When this is all over?" I smiled. "I'm going to tear your throat out and shit in your chest."

The doors came together, sealing him on the other side before I could register anything but the answering glint in his eyes.

Amusement? Anger?

Whatever. He could take his line and shove it.

I turned around, fear a sour taste in my mouth, and faced a large room filled with monitors, machines, and a handful of staring personnel in white coats.

I guess they'd heard that. Way to go, first impressions.

It'd work. "I'm here for an exam," I said by way of greeting, loud enough to send my voice echoing back through the austere lab. "Just a friendly warning? Go beyond a basic scan and I'll start breaking limbs."

One of the employees in white, a copper-haired woman with a mass of freckles that did for her what they didn't for Malik, approached. "You must be Riko," she said cautiously. "I'm Orchard."

"Orchard?"

"Yeah, I know. If it helps, my last name is unpronounceable by nearly everyone." She smiled uncertainly at me. "If I offer you a hand to shake, will I get it back?"

I showed her my teeth.

"Right." Her smile turned a little sickly. "Let's just get you checked out, then."

"Will it take long?"

"Can I say anything that would make you happy *and* let me keep my job?" she asked.

I shook my head.

"Then yes." She pointed to my right. "Yes, it probably will."

I admired her honesty. And her general sense of survival. "Basic exam, Orchard. Very basic."

"Oh, trust me." She gestured me ahead, her pale blue eyes filled with wry humor. "I need my arms to work."

"Funny." I shrugged my dimly aching shoulder. "I said the same thing."

Her glance fell on my arm. Sheepish dismay filled in all the spaces behind her freckles. "Sorry." She showed me to a curtained section of the lab – white plastic drapes on white tile – and I stripped out of my still-damp clothes. "This is pretty easy stuff," she called as I tossed my clothing through the seam in the privacy drapes. "Nothing invasive."

The whole damn thing was invasive. Malik's insistence on getting a read on my stats, the scans, the corporate prison I'd woken up in, all of it.

I shivered. It had nothing to do with the chill in the cool lab. Anxiety seized my throat, squeezing down until I wasn't sure I could breathe without gasping for it. I'd been here before. Different, but close enough that it didn't matter.

Pristine white. Cold, sterile air.

Blood on pale tile.

Time of death: 14:37.

Naked and shuddering, I crouched down on the balls of my feet and wrapped both arms around my head to block out the light. Clenching my eyes shut didn't help.

All that white searing my retinas turned to gray. My vision went spotty around the edges.

"We're looking at a general scan and basic MRI," Orchard continued, completely unaware of me as I lost my shit in here. Her cautiously cheerful tones collided with the rabid panic clawing at my chest.

Fight or flight was an instinct every saint learned. The lucky ones, the ones that survived, learned *fast*. I'd honed mine into a killing edge, but there was nothing here to fight. Nothing to bleed and take down.

"We're also going to make sure your arm is working up to spec, though we can't deal with any recalibrations if we've got to keep it basic."

Her voice juddered through my ears, triggering a flood of adrenaline that tore my balance out from under me. My hand dropped to the tile, scored a flat echo that cracked through the quiet lab.

Orchard halted mid-explanation. "Riko? Are you okay?"

Shit. "Fine," I grunted.

I lied. I wasn't fine. Every breath lodged the sharp needle

of disinfectant into my brain. With it, I heard voices. Some quiet. Some yelling.

My head throbbed – a fierce knot of pain that started in my forehead and spiked through the rest of me. I blew out a hard breath.

Hands grasped my shoulders. *Sedate her, quickly!*

I reached up, fingers clenched in white fabric, and shoved myself upward as I pulled hard and fast. Gray and white faded to a streaming halo of carrot red, and Orchard's surprised shriek as she went sailing over my shoulder cracked through my waking nightmare.

The curtain swayed, the plastic wall she collided with juddered, and I gasped for breath in a lab that wasn't the same as the one I stood in.

I wasn't stupid. Just... fucked.

Very slowly, eyes closed, I put up my hands and waited for my shit to settle.

20

A second lab tech handed Orchard another ice pack. I winced as she tucked the flexible pad between her ass and her chair. Her tailbone would be sore for a little while, at least until the nanos eased the bruising that over-the-shoulder takedown gave her. She struck me as the delicate type. Landing on unforgiving tile sucked.

I didn't remove my hands from under my legs. I wasn't sure if my right hand would shake, and I didn't want to risk damaging anything with my left. The paper gown I'd put on did nothing for the cold air, but at least my fingers warmed beneath my bare thigh.

"I'm really sorry," I said again.

Orchard let out a long, slow breath as the ice did its job. Her sky blue eyes weren't quite so wary now as she studied me from what I'd still call *too damned close*. The tech had no sense of self-preservation.

I expected some kind of lecture or even an insincere, "Don't worry about it," like I'd given her. Instead, I got a long, slow appraisal. Unlike Malik, she didn't rely on projections. The tablet in her lap was clear, lightweight. She glanced at it once.

"Have you considered seeing someone, Riko?"

I almost laughed, but managed to clear a cough at the last moment. Landing her on her ass was one thing, but hurting her feelings was just mean. "You mean some kind of therapy?"

She nodded.

"No," I replied, my lip curling. "I get all the therapy I need on the job. Nothing like filling a shitwagon full of·bullets to make a girl feel like she's on top of the world."

My levity rounded her eyes. She shifted, wincing a little.

Ouch, my guilt. "Look, I'm sorry I scared you," I admitted, a resigned kind of sincere. "But I don't need therapy. I just don't like being poked at." The back of my neck still felt like fingers had clamped into the muscle, and all I wanted was to get out while I could. Instead, I sat very still on the pullout table, fingers flattened under my thighs.

Orchard nodded, like that wasn't a load of bullshit. The girl was sweet, but I couldn't call her stupid. I was getting the impression that Malik Reed did not hire brainless people. "Can you tell me what you experienced?"

Not if she put hot screws under my nails. I held her gaze silently.

She nodded again, like she expected that. She half-turned. "You guys take a quick break, would you?"

Both techs – including the round brunette who'd slanted me a wary stare as she handed Orchard that ice pack – stood up. "Are you sure?" the tall blond guy asked.

I met his inquisitive study with a shrug.

"Give me ten," Orchard replied. Her smile was cute. Earnest, too.

They left, but I doubt they went far.

Chair creaking, Orchard spun back to face me, sneakered feet dragging along the tile. It squeaked loudly. "Look, no witnesses," she pointed out. "It's just you and me."

And more tech than I had trust.

I cocked my head. "You think it's that easy?"

Her smile faded. "I think you need to talk to someone." Not really an answer. "I promise you, there's nothing recording here. Just us and a bunch of silent machines. Mr Reed doesn't allow recording devices in here, it's too easy to lose control of footage like that."

I wondered if he'd told her that himself. Somehow, I didn't think so.

"Riko." Orchard leaned forward, flinching when the ice shifted underneath her. "Ow. Ignore that," she added quickly. "Look, it seemed like you were going through some kind of re-living process. Classic anxiety, hyperventilation, vertigo. You weren't *here*."

My back stiffened, hiking the hem of the paper robe higher up on my thighs. "It's none of your business."

It said a lot about the company I kept that I expected her to argue that, even force the point. She nodded. Again. "I know that. And it's not like you know me. I mean, I'm the enemy, right?"

The cutest, most freckled, most impish looking enemy I'd ever had. I rolled my eyes at her.

"I just think that you're showing signs of post-traumatic stress," she continued gently. "I want you to know that you're not alone, okay? If you don't have anyone to talk to, you can talk to me." Her sincerity practically hammered at me, she was so serious.

Where the hell had Malik picked this one up?

And why hadn't life broken her yet?

Except for the fact that I knew jack-all about living in C-Town. Sure, most of the sinners I saw were the lower class mutants who wandered around pretending everything was exactly the way they wanted it, long as they could get the latest limited edition cereals and fashions and whatever the hell else, but word was it got pretty good up here.

Insurance, doctors, nice condos, guaranteed pay, sunshine that didn't burn... Security looked a lot like Orchard's gentle smile, and it pissed me off that I thought so.

I removed my hands from beneath my thighs, scraped them both through my hair. The shorn sides were soft against my flesh fingers, getting longer every day. I'd have to decide to cut it back or let it grow soon.

Too bad that wasn't the worst of my problems.

"You're very good," I said, as diplomatically as I knew how. Her mouth pulled to one side, skewing the freckles on her cheek to a blotch of pale brown. I bit back a sigh. "And maybe you're right," I added, before I made myself shut the hell up. "Maybe I do need to talk to someone." Because if I wasn't dealing with screwy tech, I was dealing with fucked-up brainmeat. That seemed somehow worse.

Orchard stood. The chair didn't make a noise, but her sneakers kept catching on the tile, sending shrill reverberations through the lab. "You just can't do it now," she finished for me.

Surprised, I braced my weight on my tech arm. I didn't bother to hide my blatant study.

She flashed me a faint, sheepish grin. "You're not my first... what do you call it? Fighter? Agent?"

"Mercenary." Also known as *illegal fuckhead* in corporate speak, in the same way coordinators were corp versions of linkers and enforcers their muscle. There was no word for splatter specialist – fuck-all if the suits would publicly admit to using trained killers – so I defaulted to mercenary.

"That, too." Orchard waved the distinction away with the clear plastic tablet. "I've worked with a lot of your type. No weakness before a job, right?"

Something like that.

She gestured behind me. "Lay down so I can get the scans started."

I obeyed meekly enough, but my eyebrow climbed. "You going to tell your boss?"

"Tell him what?" Orchard leaned over me, her figure shapeless beneath the white coat and a loose blue sweater. Unlike me, she dressed for the sterile lab air. "Assuming you check out physically, I don't have the authorization to do anything more invasive." She keyed in something to her tablet, then swiped at thin air. Over my head, a projection screen lit a square of empty space.

I grinned at her. "You're okay, Orchard of the unpronounceable last name."

"I'm going to tell everyone you said so. My... What do you call it? Rep?"

I snorted. "Cred."

"My cred should shoot right up, right?" And mine would probably tank even farther.

I didn't even engage.

The tech's spindly fingers slid through the light screen at precise notes. "Now, prepare to hate me for the next hour."

I groaned. "This thing takes that long?"

"No, it only takes five." She patted me awkwardly on the shoulder. "It's the physical you're going to hate."

She was right.

Any goodwill Orchard managed to foster vanished. By the time I'd been measured, poked and prodded on the outside, bent to test my arm joints, scanned, put through a few paces, and otherwise examined to death, I was fed up with her, the other techs, the lab itself, and Malik Reed.

Most of the exertion stuff he could have gotten from his damned readings at the Key. Dick. The whole thing. Every last one of them. A composite of dicks.

The only thing that made it even remotely tolerable was Indigo. Which surprised me. He came in for his physical halfway through mine, which meant by the time I was done, I got the pleasure of watching his systems tech – a tall guy named Gunner Leto – put Digo through his paces.

"Go away," Indigo growled, sweat gleaming on his chest as he ran the stationary track I'd already completed. Like me, he'd been given a pair of shorts and a tanktop. Both white. The sensors hovering around him flickered green periodically, clocking his vitals.

I grinned at him, leaning against a bank of monitors. "Can't. I've got a bet with Orchard."

"I'm not interested in beating your time, Riko." He spoke with effort, but he wasn't panting. Not yet.

"You're not?" Damn. I wasn't counting on that. I sighed, already calculating the cost of a good lunch. Orchard didn't bet cheap.

He glanced at me, blue eyes flashing in irritation. "You bet I would?"

"Hell, yeah, I did." I could hold my own in a fight like nobody's business, but Digo was a natural runner. Pound for pound, meter for meter, he'd outstrip me in stamina and speed any day.

"Hunh." With that mystifying sound, he turned his attention back to his run and said nothing else.

I watched him for a moment longer, not sure if I should say something else or leave him alone. This was weird. Normally, I'd stay and tease him. Now, I was pretty sure that any attempted flippancy would push him right back over into prickly anger.

I'd never actually been at odds with him before. Short of punching him until he stopped being so angry, I didn't know what to do.

It didn't seem the right time to give him the flowers. I mean, the detective.

Right now, he seemed to be tolerating me okay, focusing on his numbers rather than on how much he hated me. As he ran, his swarthy skin rippled with lean muscle – a fact I had no trouble admiring from this distance.

Rocky ground or not, I could appreciate a good physique. I still thought he'd lost too much weight, but the scrappy jackal frame was starting to grow on me. Ropey muscle flexed in his back as he rolled his shoulders. It wasn't the same kind of attraction – I'd never considered throwing down with Indigo, not honestly – but I liked looking at him the same way I liked looking in general.

The fact that nothing was the same between us really blew chunks. I missed our easy camaraderie. Now, I couldn't look at him without being reminded of everything I'd lost.

Ignoring the pang in my chest, I turned away. "I'll leave you to it," I said lightly.

"Hey, Riko."

I glanced over my shoulder. "What?"

He didn't look at me, brisk pace steady. "What was your time?"

"Fourteen, twenty-seven, twelve."

I couldn't see his expression from the back. His braid bounced against his shoulders as one hand lifted. "Noted."

He said nothing else.

As the door closed behind me, I shook my head. Why he wanted to know, I had no idea. Except Indigo was a tricky bastard.

A fact cemented by the personal note tucked into the file Hope delivered to my quarters the following hour. "Briefing on the helo," she told me, "wheels up in ten. If you want first pick on reqs, you'll be on time." She left me to get ready. I sat on the surprisingly comfortable couch and scanned the tablet, checking my numbers for anomalies. Everything seemed more or less the usual. Orchard expressed some concern for my shoulder girdle's structural longevity, but signed off on the exams.

At the bottom, she left an additional note.

00:14:28:07. You owe me lunch.

One second? One chunking second. I slammed the tablet to the coffee table beside me. That son of a bitch. Compared to the fact I'd lose a bet with an outsider, his loss of face by losing to my time was nothing. That I'd have to shell out to pay it off was probably just frosting.

Oh, yeah. He'd just flipped me an Indigo finger.

I glowered at the tablet. Kicked it out of reach when it said nothing to soothe my rankled pride. It slid off the table edge and thudded twice.

Reaching for my boots, I couldn't decide if I wanted to laugh or kick him square in the ass I'd admired.

It wasn't a truce. Not even close. It was just another subtle bit of calculus in his version of war.

And to think I'd even gotten him a blue bouquet.

What a cunt.

21

Of all the things I'd done, dropping from a helo with five other heavily armed and outfitted people to a filthy rooftop ranked among the most fun. It wasn't that difficult. The sleek black vehicle came in close enough that it was an easy step off, and one by one, we all landed on the rooftop in a cloud of whipped-up smoke and debris.

The first two to hit the roof spread out, each covering opposite ends of the long but narrow expanse, clearing the territory. As the last one of us hit the gravel, the cargo bay closed. The vehicle rose up and away, firing an oppressive backdraft of heat and smoke over us. Fortunately, our helmets came equipped with filters.

"Bye bye, sanity," the woman beside me murmured, her voice crystal clear in my earpiece.

Carter, she'd called herself. No first name given. Or maybe it was her first name. I didn't pry. She was one of two other women on the team, short enough that the top of her head just reached my chin. She also happened to be our heavy weapon specialist, which I appreciated. I liked a woman who could carry more than her own weight in armaments.

When Malik had mentioned funding, he hadn't been dicking around. Reqs had gone like clockwork, and I was given a workup of the gear I could requisition from Indigo's list. A few had been marked off with personal recommendations.

Hope was a sweetheart. Statistically accurate and perceptive to a scary degree, but a sweetheart nonetheless.

I chose something similar to the rest of the team, though I'd packed a little extra in ammo and guns. The body armor was lighter than I was used to, plated at the vitals but loose at the joints for mobility, and the skinsuit underneath actually my size. Comfortable *and* stylish. The helmet I'd chosen allowed for near-total visibility, with a heads-up display over the faceplate coming through as a blue overlay on the hardened plastic curve. Map, location, distance to the target my focus locked on, and a handful of vitals, including my own. It came equipped with thermal imaging, night vision, and its own air filters.

The fact that all this sturdy gear bore a logo – a white letter M, the tines on each end slicing downward in stylistic aggression – pretty much put the bow on my shit-wrapped day.

"I should have requisitioned a Valiant," I said to no one in particular. My own voice sounded compact, fed through the communications system and piped through to each individual feed. The comms were earpieces, rather than helmeted. Smart move; helmets busted. I'd broken more than a handful of my share. "If I'd known Mantis Industries was funding this party, I would have totally asked for one."

"Good fucking luck," Carter said beside me. "After TaberTek went balls-up a few years back, they're rare as virgins."

Yeah. I liked her already.

Mantis was known more for their armor lines and integrated tech defenses than they were for their weaponry, which made their crossplatform Valiant all the more coveted. I figured Malik as a corp exec, I just never figured it was Mantis he worked for. Some sort of department director, maybe? Corporations operated on so many levels, it was hard to tell middle management from a hole in the ground.

"Riko, get your head on straight." Indigo's voice, already weary with me.

"Downer," I replied, unperturbed. "Don't think I don't know you cheated that run, you *lazy* bastard."

He snorted. Carter mirrored the sound.

"Vid Team, listen up." A woman's voice piped through the line, and all of us stopped. "You're now two blocks west of the target. Something in there is on fire, which is providing the smoke currently obstructing the helo's drop pattern. You're going in on foot."

Hoofing it through a necro quarantine wasn't the part I'd call fun.

"You have three hours to complete your goal," she continued, her voice as calm as if we weren't currently standing in death central. "That's three hours to get in, acquire your goal, and get out. There is zero leeway."

Indigo swore. "That's cutting it close."

"No kidding," I muttered, picking my way across the gravel-encrusted rooftop to look out over the nearest ledge. Smoke curled along the street, spreading searching fingers through every nook and cranny like it was looking for a place to hide from the setting sun. "And we're losing light."

"Three hours is all Mr Reed could get from the burn team," she replied. "It's not a guaranteed lock, so make this happen faster."

"No problem," I said, saccharine as poisoned candy as I eyed the abandoned street with serious skepticism. No part of this city should be abandoned, not like this. "What could go wrong?"

"Is she serious?" asked the youngest on our team. He wasn't asking me. Probably was talking to the broad-shouldered heavy beside him.

"Shut up, Riko," Indigo said, but without heat. "Control, is the smoke interfering with your visuals?"

"Affirmative. We'll provide what intel we can, but we'll

be relying on your video feeds." She ignored my sarcasm entirely. Smart broad. "Remember your check-ins."

"You heard her," Indigo said, his voice in my ear making it seem like he wasn't on the other side of the roof. "Three hours on this crazy train. Check in every quarter, stay together, watch each other. This is not the place to go off your game."

"We know that." The other female. What was her name? Angelica. Angelina. Angie? Crap. "*We* trained together. What about you?"

"We've got your backs, too," Indigo said, his voice mellow enough that I briefly resented the fact he didn't waste that tone on me. "I know briefing was short and we didn't get any real shot at a meet and greet, but I promise you that we're all in this together."

I couldn't see her face behind the helmet, but I had no trouble imagining the expression she made as she sneered out a sharp, "How sweet."

"Ange, come help me secure this pack," the heavy cut in, his voice surprisingly light for such a big guy.

Okay, I was close. "Ange" was sort of like the lazy version of all of them.

I didn't look back to watch them work their shit out, my gear already checked, stowed and prepped.

They'd given me a Sauger 877 – no surprise there, it reigned supreme for a reason – but with one small modification. Nice as it was to drop a little under a thousand rounds in less time than it took to sneeze, it was hard on the barrel and shit for accuracy. If I was going to be shooting, I wanted something more reliable than spray and pray. The model I requested came with a small catch, reducing the rate of fire by nearly half but vastly improving accuracy.

Carter approached the ledge beside me, her features hidden behind her helmet. Didn't need to see her face to know she had a sharp mouth on her. From our initial meeting, I knew she wasn't the kind of woman anyone picked up on a whim.

Broad nose, wide jaw, a crown of tightly braided black hair, and enough muscle under her skinsuit to make even a heavy think twice.

The munitions didn't hurt, either. They backed up every word. Barring the right pay? Even I wouldn't mess with her.

"So," she said, fingers flying over her own assault rifle with near-blinding speed. Checked and prepped. "What do you suppose are the chances we'll run into anyone in here?"

It gave me the creeps to look down at the ghost town beneath us. I'd never seen anything like it. Even the shittiest holes I'd been in still had life of some kind. Kids, bums, fuckheads with nothing better to do than prop up on a curb and assault the unwary for credsticks or kicks. The animals, rats and feral strays, would be starving to death or scrapping for food, but there would be *something*. "The reports said twelve necros," I said slowly. But my gut said they'd dicked out too fast to get the full measure. City blocks didn't go silent like this. Not unless something goes *seriously* tits-up. "Honestly?"

"Prefer honest when I can get it."

My mouth twisted. "Slim to nothing."

"You think they all got out?" The young voice again. Hooker, I think. Calvin Hooker. Unfortunate surname, but I'd let it slide once already and it seemed too late to joke about it now.

I rolled my shoulders, not quite a shrug. "I think the lucky ones did," I said bluntly. "The rest will end up burned out of hiding." The kid sucked in a breath. "And when they do, the necros will get them before everything goes up in smoke."

"So, we just leave them?"

I nodded. "Hope they're already dead. If not? Hope the fire gets them first." Shitty reassurance, but it was the best I had.

Carter turned away from the smoky street below us. "Hey, Koupra."

"What's up?"

"You know our orders if we find corrupt, right?"

"Kill on sight." He said it like it was no big deal, and really, it wasn't. Sure, corruption could be tended, but not here, and not on this big a scale. We all carried handguns for the possibility.

My handgun of choice barely qualified as small arms, earning an appreciative whistle from Carter when the Mantis crew delivered it. The M422A Tactical Revolver's benefit was its massive .525 caliber, which is exactly what I wanted between me and any necro that might actually get past the initial storm of bullets we'd geared up for. It'd even punch a hole through dermaplating.

The downside was the old-fashioned chamber, but I was carrying extra ammo for it in several pockets slung in my belt. Frankly, I'd be lucky to get off three out of the chambered six if a necro got that close.

Street specs called it the Adjudicator. It was a gun I could only hold steady because of my synthetic arm; it'd blow a hole the size of my fist through practically anything.

Overkill on fleshbags, but I doubted the odds of finding any. That was one thing all the stories had in common. Necros killed. Twelve necros sounded like a situation that made for a lot of bodies.

"Two hours and fifty-five minutes," Ange said. She waited by a rusted escape ladder, its twisted arms hooked over the roof's ledge. "Shall we get this show on the road, ladies?"

"Locked and loaded," Carter confirmed.

"Weapons ready," Hooker said.

The heavy rolled his wide shoulders, his armor much thicker and bulkier than mine. "Ready."

"Good," Indigo said, and he half-turned towards me. "Riko? Set?"

I had a few other weapons stowed in my harness. A Phelps & Somers CounterTech II for backup, though I wasn't sure its 9mm rounds would do more than piss a necro off. I stored that ammo in the slot in my arm. I also carried an assortment of knives. Including one Hope had delivered personally to us all: a tethered switchblade packing an EMP charge on delivery. At worst, it'd slow a necro down long enough to get the hell away.

At best, its head would explode.

"I hope to see exploding heads," I said by way of confirmation. "I *really* do."

"Girl, you are weird," Carter told me.

I grinned. "Says the woman packing a grenade launcher, three mines and a Bolshovekia." My assault rifle would leave twitching necros in its wake. Hers looked like a custom job that wouldn't leave much of anything at all. "Hey, can I fondle your gun later?"

Carter's snort cracked on a laugh. "Get us out alive, and you can fondle anything you want."

"Oh, for fuck's sake," Ange cut in. "Koupra, get a handle on her."

I expected him to say something about how he didn't want to be here. That I wasn't his to handle, much less that he didn't answer to Ange.

What I didn't expect was a mildly amused, "Which one?"

The heavy chortled.

Ange's shoulders tightened beneath her racked gear. "*Your* enforcer," she clarified, like there was any doubt. "If all she's going to do is fuck around–"

"She'll be ready when she's needed," he cut in. "I suggest you keep yourself focused."

Aww. That felt good. Even if I was pretty sure he was only saying it to settle Ange's spiky attitude before it tried to make a play.

Too late.

"Bullshit." Ange braced her shoulders, like she was squaring up for a fight. "Nobody even explained why the hell you're supposedly in charge."

Busted.

Indigo didn't look at her. "How's your processing speed?"

Carter's hand palmed her helmeted face, and I watched Hooker's faceplate turn from Ange to Indigo in what was probably bewilderment.

I grinned. "Pissing match out of the way first, then?"

"Shut up," Ange snapped, then added pointedly, "Faster than average."

I watched the heavy instead of Hooker, because I expected the kid to shift closer to Ange in some kind of solidarity move. Carter didn't move, and I couldn't tell if the heavy was even paying attention. His name was Falk, just Falk. I'd stake a bet on ex-military. He stood with his feet wide and his arms folded around the barrel of his Sauger. Just waiting.

Indigo's gloved hand adjusted his helmet, almost idly. "I can process at six times the speed of the fastest human recorded."

"So wh–"

"Which means," he said over her, his voice feed sliding though hers, "by the time you've realized there's a new condition, I've already included it into the workup and halfway through calculating new orders." *Click.* His clip slotted into place, and he slung the weapon to his harness. It seemed like an absent move.

It wasn't. Without fuss, he'd unarmed himself, forcing Ange into the position of aggressor if she jumped him.

I didn't move from my vantage point, mostly because Carter was at my back, but I watched Ange closely. If she did pull something stupid, I wasn't sure I'd be fast enough to stonewall Carter and keep Falk from smearing Indigo's face into paste.

I could imagine the long-limbed woman setting her jaw beneath the tinted faceplate.

"So, what, just because you slapped some metal in your head–"

"It's more than metal," Indigo said, again cutting her off.

Carter shook her head. As long as Ange kept shutting up

when he spoke, she'd already lost. We all knew it.

"He's a linker," I said, exasperation sharp on the feed. "You call 'em coordinators. He's hooked in to where we are at any given time, has a bird's eye understanding of the area *and* doesn't need to rely on verbal cues to get it."

Ange's shoulders tightened beneath her racked gear. "What does that make you?" she demanded. Like it mattered.

"Not sure there's a word for it in c-speak," I said, going for serious but ruined for it when Carter snorted again. I grinned inside my helmet. At least someone here knew the jargon.

Indigo let it go. "Are we done? Can we move on or do you want to waste another five of our hundred and seventy-two remaining minutes?"

I watched Ange, watched her wrestle the fight back into a closet, out of the way until it could be addressed later. It was a very good trick to learn on the street. I had *no* doubt it would be brought up again. "We're done," she said tightly.

"Good. Falk on point, Ange, back him up." Indigo pointed to the side of the ladder, where she'd have vantage while he climbed. "Hooker, stay up here and keep them clear until we're all down, then shack up with me. Riko, stay on Carter in the rear. Keep strays from getting too close to our munitions."

"Sloppy makeouts for everyone if we get out of this," I said lightly. Taking a deep breath, I slung the assault rifle into place – hand curled lightly around the stock in case I needed to move fast – and joined the rest of the team at the ladder.

"Riko." An easy breath from Indigo, but my only warning. And I knew it. Fair enough. "Move out on three... two..."

Falk draped his Sauger across his meaty shoulders, swung out over the ledge and dropped, using the rungs between his hands and feet to slow his fall. The sounds were hard to conceal, but even if he'd gone rung by rung, the metal still creaked.

Ange was on the ladder before he hit the ground.

"So," Carter murmured, the quality of the sound changing

to one ear. Single-line in. "Was that *c* for 'corporate' or 'cunt'?"

My grin colored my voice. "Sorry, is there a difference?"

"Sainted bitch," Carter replied, but there was amusement there. I laughed softly.

"We got movement," Hooker warned.

Carter flipped back to main feed. "I see them." All humor faded as she raised the scope of her rifle to her eye. "One... no, two necros shambling down the center of the street. Drawn by the noise of the ladder, probably."

"What are the odds we just happened to land near two of the twelve?"

I shuddered, the visual knife of Nanji's disjointed scuttle across that uplink lab floor less than an eyelash flicker away.

I focused the other direction as Indigo took his turn at the ladder. The helmet specifications filtered out much of the lowering sunlight merging with the smoke across the street, which made spotting motion in the darker pools of shadow easier. Once night fell, that's when things would get interesting.

"Make that one more coming in fast from the north," I said. "What'd they do, spam invites?"

"All weapons at the ready. Riko, you're up."

Like I needed the reminder.

Slinging my Sauger when I knew there were necros bearing down on me went against everything I was. I shuffled up to the ledge, looked down at the tight ring of the team, each faced outward to provide a circle of support.

A crackling pop through my right ear shot a wincing jolt straight to my spine.

"Riko?"

Biting back an impatient curse, I turned, slung my feet into the rungs, and skimmed down the ladder with as much speed as I could.

Gunfire peppered the silent street before I hit the ground. Amid the rapidfire spray of the Sauger 877s, a particularly solid *thoom* cracked through the cacophony.

Hooker's sniper rifle, a Sauger H2, sacrificed range for accuracy, and the kid didn't disappoint. By the time I turned away from the ladder, gun already in my hands, one of the necros had collapsed into a twitching heap.

My pulse hammered in my adrenaline-fueled, buzzing skull as I joined the outward circle.

This sound? Not what I'd hoped to hear again. I heard it, felt it, like insects crawling through my brain.

The sight in front of me didn't make it any better.

Necros up close are something nobody in their right mind ever wants to see again. A lot of everyday sinners assume going necro looks like a body just twitching out and going postal. Not even close. The thing is, when the tech takes over, there go all the feelings of pain and survival instinct. A body gets thrashed, and sometimes it gets fucked up by its own tech.

The body splayed ten feet away, still convulsing as sparks shot from what looked like nerve threads laced through its limbs. A female. The stringy hank of hair clinging to her scalp was black, although I couldn't tell if it was filth, blood or naturally dark. She still wore the remains of a pair of shorts, one untied boot and the shredded ruins of a tanktop to beat the heat. One earring still clung to the torn flesh of her ear, winking obscenely amid the carnage.

Not the clothing or the location I'd have expected to find nerve tech in. That was expensive stuff.

Blood coated her flopping, jerking limbs. Smeared the ruinous cavern where her mouth had been. For all her limited visual tech, I couldn't imagine what the hell put her in this condition. Did necros fight each other?

Teeth gleamed, bared through her torn cheek and crusted with gore. The sound coming out of her wasn't human. Just the frantic, dying gurgles of a set of lungs that wouldn't function around the double-fisted size hole Hooker had left in her chest.

Not that it was strictly necessary for a necro to breathe.

Not far ahead of her, closest to Ange, a boy – maybe sixteen – had been cut down. His leg from the knee down was tech. Not anything sleek like my arm, but base model functionality. If the rest of him had been augmented in any way, it was lost to the butchery he'd become. Most of it couldn't even be blamed on us.

At least that one stopped moving.

Grimly, I lowered my weapon and riddled the convulsing girl with half a clip, obliterating her still-struggling body until there was nothing left for the tech to operate.

When the flesh no longer trembled, a surge of relief filled me. And with it, a stab of pain through my temple.

Fuck. My head felt stuffed full of glass. Angry wasps and glass.

"Search me this," I said, slow and thick through the noise. "Why are teenagers staggering out instead of lab techs or security?"

"A damn good question," Indigo said tightly.

"Heads up." Falk, nice and calm. Good man.

The others moved, shifting focus as a strangled, wet gurgle announced the arrival of one more necro – a body not so much crawling as pulling itself out of the shadow-dipped alley between two complexes.

It grabbed the ground with torn, ratty fingers seeping brown fluid, dragged itself towards us, its mouth moving like it would have begged for help if it could.

I squinted through the mental fuzz. "Is it missing legs?"

Hooker touched down in our circle.

"They must be drawn by the gunfire," Indigo said. "Up the street, then head west. Let's go!"

As one, Falk and Ange filled the dragging, writhing tech-fueled corpse with caseless bullets. The others sprinted away from the landing zone. I hesitated, my gaze pinned to the juddering, pathetic figure, its toothless, bloody wound of a mouth wide in a soundless scream I felt to my bones.

I didn't understand. Nanjali had looked like her usual self, give or take lost weight, hair, and the shit they'd spliced into her back. What had damaged these necros so badly?

"Hey." Falk's big hand enveloped my shoulder and most of my bicep. "Come on."

I looked up, saw nothing but broad faceplate.

Did he see the boy scream, too? Did he hear it, fill in that awful silence as easily as I did?

Or was he numb to the horror already?

"Move it." Ange's voice, and a sharp slap upside the back of my helmet.

I turned wordlessly and followed the others, Ange and Falk keeping pace.

Smoke enveloped us in a gray, clinging cloud. Even the filters couldn't sift it all out – ash and melting paint and a sweet, smoky fragrance that made me think of the Rat Cafe.

My footing skidded on nothing.

Carter caught me by the synthetic arm I windmilled in frantic over-correction, righting me as if I weighed nothing. "You okay?"

"No," I said tightly, but didn't explain. Stopping was not an option. Taking a moment to share some hard feelings was definitely out of the question.

My first run-in with a real necro and I was losing my shit. Nothing was what I expected. Three of the known twelve necros were *people*. Not sec monkeys. Not lab techs likely to catch the virus from a wire.

Just people.

The crackle lancing through my ear leaked into the other, stacking uncomfortable pressure behind my eyes. Gritting my teeth hard enough to compress my jaw seemed to ease some of the tension, but this was not the kind of sign I needed anyone to pick up on.

We ran for five minutes, hauling ass and our gear as the

last of the daylight faded to a thin seam. Indigo led the way, led by the data uplinked to him from the contact team, and Hooker took up the rear.

The farther we ran, the thicker and angrier the wasp nest in my skull got.

"Heads up!" Hooker called. I turned, too late. Gnarled fingers skated across my chestplate, and I looked into the empty, staring remains of gelatinous eyeballs boiled over onto clawed cheeks. The shriek inside my brain maximized the softer echo of its nails across diamond steel.

Carter cursed as she swung her gun around, but another cracked *thoom* and the necro's head erupted like rotten fruit. Gobbets of brain and the hard crackle of teeth pattering my armor didn't bother me nearly so much as the juddering, frenetic seizure gripping the thing as it splattered to the street at my feet.

I hadn't even seen it coming out of the alley beside me.

"That sniper rifle is a thing of verifiable beauty," Carter panted as she half-hauled me back in line. "I'd kill to get my hands on it, but Hooker's a jealous bastard."

Rattled, I could only nod.

Indigo rounded a corner. "Vid Team, checking in on the quarter," he said, his voice winded but steady.

Carter let me go. "You need a minute?"

"Copy, Vid Team."

"No," I grunted. Yes. But we didn't have one to spare. I felt like there were a thousand whiskey-raw voices shrieking at me. Adrenaline never used to hit me this hard. "My head just–"

"*Shit.*" Indigo's voice cracked. He came hauling ass around the corner he'd taken. "Back up, back!"

Like the well-trained group we were, we fanned outward, Hooker and Falk facing back the way we came and leveling ground fire as Ange called, "Carter! Twenty-five degrees!"

I could hear her grin through the helmet feed. "You got

it." She unhooked one of the mines from her heavy harness, armed it and darted out into the street. Ange fired over her head, giving her space from something I couldn't see as I concentrated on the second figure creeping along the same alley its shredded pal had briefly occupied.

"Don't do it," I told it. "This is *not* the best idea of your... uh?"

"Unlife?" suggested Hooker, a nanosecond before his gun fired. Damn, that sound. Like a fist to the chest. I was surprised it wasn't blowing him off his feet the same way it obliterated the heads of the necros he dropped.

Smart move, too. No chipset, no working tech.

"Three!" Carter barked into the headsets. I didn't need training to know what that meant. I darted closer to Hooker, away from the corner. "Two!"

On a soundless *one*, an auditory detonation lashed through the streets, now full of the rasping, laborious grind of desperate flesh still trying to function and the intolerable hum in my helmet.

The ground shuddered. A sonic wave only bumped us where we were standing, which probably sucked more for the critters nestled around that mine.

"Timer?" I asked.

"Wireless detonation." Carter's amusement crackled fiercely through the feed. "Can control it on the bandwidth. I love it so."

"And I'm weird?"

She laughed.

I didn't.

Five. I'd seen five. There were more than seven around that mine.

What the fuck had happened in here?

"Move," Indigo ordered. "Before any more come running."

Falk took point, leading us through the carnage the mine had left behind, heedless of the splashing, viscous pool of brilliant red picked out in the last vestiges of a dying sun.

My gorge rose as my feet found passage through the grotesque tangle of limbs, scattered tech parts, and still-twitching bits I couldn't identify.

The pressure on my head had eased, but not by much.

"Two blocks, huh?" I gasped.

Ange crowed, "Pussy," and I briefly considered kicking her helmet in.

"Why are there so many?" Falk, unlike me, showed no sign of slowing, distaste, or effort. He jogged like he could do it all day long, gear or no gear, through blood and guts or mud and rain.

Indigo replaced his clip smoothly while running. "That was, what, fifteen all told?"

"Eighteen," Carter piped in.

Fuck me. "I thought conversion was rare," I said through measured breaths. "What the shit happened to twelve?"

"Yeah, it's supposed to be rare." Falk slowed. "This many people aren't likely to wire in at the same time." He paused. "Soon as the light goes, we're going to have to switch to night vision. Seeing these things come at me from the dark is going to give me a damned heart attack."

"That's why we're all together," Indigo said, one hand adjusting his helmet as we ran, like it bothered him. "Keep it up, five minutes and then we'll rest."

We forged on, making our way through the smoke and lengthening shadows. A thick, cloying silence fell over us the deeper into the zone we moved, until the creep factor had my skin itching and my brain humming. Paranoia set in after three minutes of silence.

I was gritting my teeth when the sun sank beyond the skyline and the sky turned brilliant, breathtakingly purple.

An orange glow lit the sky faintly to the north.

"We'll stop here," Indigo said, slowing. "Falk, Ange, keep watch. The rest of you, night vision up and take a breather.

We won't get another until we get out."

Ange stepped out onto the street a few paces, her helmet tipped skyward. "Think we'll see stars with all the lights off?"

"Not in this smoke," Falk said, joining her to face the other direction, Sauger at the ready.

I kept my back to the others, fighting the urge to open my faceplate, knuckle at my eyes until the nagging, droning sense of paranoia – of being watched, followed, *hunted* – went away. Sweat didn't cool on my skin so much as absorb into the skinsuit, keeping me comfortable and dry, but I was beginning to seriously resent the enclosed helmet. Even with the night vision I turned on, turning my world to shades of black and green with the heads-up display turning red, I couldn't shake it.

"We should be, what, thirty minutes off?" I asked. "If we make time to shake any tails."

Indigo had flipped open his wrist-mounted integration unit; a pad that allowed him to treat his own helmet like a monitor, and when he needed to, project a comp screen on just about anything. "About that exactly," he said. "Nicely tracked."

The Vid Zone was more or less new ground for me, and running it at night seemed like a bad idea, but we couldn't have gotten that far from the landing zone. How I'd known the time was beyond me. Lucky guess, maybe.

"So, if there are more than twelve," Carter mused from her crouch, "what do we figure?"

There was silence for a moment. Then Ange, more a question than a statement. "I guess that depends on how many converted?"

"And how," Indigo muttered. "Jesusfuck."

My sentiments close enough, only with less Jesus and more *fuck*. Twelve necros. *Twelve*. I'd swallowed that because, sure, maybe there were people in that lab who were plugged into the system when it all went to hell. Why not? Fucked if I knew.

But this wasn't that. This was kids crawling out of the dark, gasping mouths hanging open and saliva dripping from half-mangled throats.

We crouched, sat, or stood warily, arranged in a crooked circle, and waited for Indigo to tell us to move again. Most of us faced the darkening streets, weapons held not so much loosely as in easy firing position. This time, I didn't have it in me to break the tense silence with a joke.

It was all I could do to force myself not to flinch from the wasps in my skull.

After only five minutes, Indigo finally spoke. "It's time."

None of us jumped. We were too relieved. Anything was better than silently waiting for the necro shoe to drop. Falk stirred, shifting his weight, as Ange unfolded from her crouch and clapped him on the arm.

"Finally," Hooker sighed.

Carter's boots scraped on the street as she stomped, like she needed to get feeling back into her toes.

"I'm picking up a serious obstruction between us and 35th," Indigo continued. He pointed back at Carter. "You can detonate those through the bandwidth, right?"

"Within about half a standard block."

"C-town or...?"

She chuckled. "Quarter of a mile." So, a corporate sector block. The city blocks in other wards tended to be a fuckingly chaotic mess, and less *blocks* than war zones.

"Ange."

"Yo."

Indigo turned to glance at her. "Can you plant one of those mines?"

Ange snorted something amused and not even remotely modest.

He let it slide. "Carter, you'll blow it on my mark."

"Can do," Carter confirmed.

He gestured to Hooker. "You, can you see enough to

cover her from here?"

"Why aren't we going around?"

"Because out here, we'll see them coming," I answered, scouring the looming shadows between walls. "Or at least enough that we have a fighting chance." There was no telling what forging through the checkerboard string of back alleys would net us.

"If we go around," Indigo added, "it adds time we can't afford to waste. Can you do it or not, Hooker?"

The kid nodded. "Pretty sure. The smoke is tough, but if Ange calls out markers, I'll make sure not to shoot her."

"I'll buy you a drink if you manage not to," Ange tossed back.

As plans went, not a bad one. "Everyone ready?" Indigo asked.

Ready as we could get.

Ange took the proffered mine – a plate slightly bigger than Falk's hand, disc-shaped and concave – and slipped into the street. I was intensely aware of the faded blue dot mapping her progress, long after she vanished to green-tinged shadow and smoke.

"What's the obstruction?" I asked.

"Not sure, but it looks like a carrying truck."

Carter nodded beside me. "That mine will at least shift it so we've got enough room to maneuver, and if there's any fuel left, it'll burn."

"Necros don't like fire?" I hazarded.

"Would you?"

Good point.

"I've got her," Hooker said, crouched in front of us, his eye plastered to his scope. "I don't see any movement nearby, so–"

"Do you hear that?" Falk demanded, staring up into the sky.

The only thing I could hear out there was that brain-wrinkling whine, and it wasn't even out there I heard it. I felt half deaf, like a cacophony filtered through too many layers, but a low hum – whirring on a completely different frequency – suddenly cut through even that. We all looked up, weapons out, scanning the open sky.

There was nothing to see.

"She's ten feet out," Indigo said. "Hooker?"

"So far, no ticks."

"Maybe we got all of them." But even Digo didn't seem to buy it. I didn't have to see his face to know he was worried. He was probably triple-checking the overview even as he spoke.

"Falk?" I waved him over. "You ready to–"

"Heads up!" Carter shouted, her weapon tracking something round and black, nearly invisible against the sky. We all ducked; I flinched as it narrowly missed Falk's head. A metallic *thunk* crunched into asphalt.

Indigo's helmet jerked. "Cover!" he ordered. "Ange, withdr–!"

Bullets ricocheted off the street in a shower of white sparks, and Falk staggered beneath the impact. They scored his heavy armor, spattered a narrow ream of blood where a lucky round clipped his elbow. Falk grunted, turned, big body angled to leap out of the way of the trajectory pinning him down, but too late.

A white-hot ball blossomed from the black globe three feet away, enveloping Falk in a fiery arc that saturated the smoke-laden air with the stink of melting armor and charred flesh. His screams blasted through the feed, brutal and mercifully brief.

The column seared through the night vision in a painful white flare that left wicked afterburners floating in front of my eyes. The blast slammed into us a breath later. Indigo grunted, staggering, and Carter yelped, but it swept Hooker into the building's façade like he weighed nothing. Windows exploded overhead, shattered into a rain of glittering orange fragments, and the only reason I didn't kiss the pavement came down to sheer luck.

Carter's voice crackled across our feed. "I've got unknown processes activating my trigger–" A beat. "Ange! The bandwidth is lighting the fuck up, *drop the–*"

"*Shit.*" Ange's line fuzzed with static. It figured she'd sound more pissed than worried.

Too late. A second detonation echoed from the street beyond us. Ange's comm signal winked out.

"*Falk.*" Hooker stumbled, the rifle clutched in one hand by habit. Somehow, half blind, I caught him around the waist, halted him before he lurched after a man whose twisted shell was still glowing white hot in the center of the green street.

"It's too late." I wrestled him back from the open street as Indigo shouted at us to get our asses out of the crossfire.

"Dios." Carter's voice, high and tight. "Ay Dios. It went off. It's gone, ay–"

"Carter," I barked, struggling to keep a hold of the kid trying to brain me with his weapon. I don't think he even knew how close he came, but I was suddenly grateful for the protection of my helmet. "*Haul it.*"

Carter's comm went silent. We withdrew fast, me wrestling with the kid until Indigo fisted one hand into Hooker's harness and dragged him, twisting and howling, back into a dingy, narrow avenue.

He was still fighting a sweat-drenched adrenaline high seven minutes later. We stopped, gasping, and Indigo shoved him hard against a peeling metal facing. "If you don't want to be necro bait, shut up and don't move." Hooker sagged. "Control, what the *fuck*?"

It was like the distance had pulled the plugs from my ears. The whine faded to a muted thrum, a low-frequency signal hovering at the edge of my hearing, though my head still felt too full.

Some kind of jammers? Or an active power line packing serious juice? Maybe I was sensitive to a certain frequency out here, or this damned helmet was giving me claustrophobia issues. I'd take the thing off after we got out of here and see if that helped at all. I wasn't used to working in a full suit. Decent visual capability, sure, but it was too confining for me.

Which was all much better shit to think about than what the hell went sideways out here.

"Control!" Indigo snapped.

The operator's voice clicked over the feeds. "We're working on it," she said calmly. "What just happened?"

"Assault out of nowhere. And way fucking more than twelve fucking necros!" Leaving a shaking, cowering Hooker, Indigo gripped Carter's shoulders and stooped to peer into her helmet, faceplate to faceplate. "Carter, you with me? *Carter*."

"I didn't..." Her voice was hoarse. She stood there, Bolshovekia hanging limply from her hands, and let him shake her like she didn't have the strength to shrug him off. "The mine triggered. It was still moving, I could track it on the bandwidth. She still had it. It was in her hands, she was– she–" The words cracked.

"Shit." Digo glanced at me. "Riko, I need eyes."

It was him or me, and I didn't have the patience for two corp enforcers losing their collective shit. I nodded, glanced around and spied a fire escape barely in reach.

"Ange and Falk are paste," Indigo told control flatly.

"Noted." Two peas in a pod, except I could hear the anger stomped thin in Digo's voice. Control sounded like she was taking notes, disseminating information. Cool as ice. "We're gathering data."

And orders, probably. Protocol demanded she call in Malik, at least update him.

That was going to be a fun conversation.

I jumped for the bottom rung, gloved fingers wrapping around the rusted, pocked metal. Hand over hand, I pulled myself up, shoulders and back aching with the effort. I was halfway to the roof before control's voice clicked back on to my feed.

"Drone activity was marked over parts of the Vid Zone moments before contact. You're not the only team in there, but it's unclear who's in the lead. Riko, your vitals are running high."

I leveraged myself onto the ridge encircling the rooftop, my gaze on the green-shaded, too-dim environment but my attention on the sinking pit her question opened up in my stomach. "You can track our vitals, too?"

"Yes."

Fuck me. "Which? Blood pressure, brain activity?"

"All of them," she said patiently.

Just what I needed. "Any hope Ange made it?" I asked instead, ignoring her question.

She didn't miss a beat. "No. Your brain activity is still hitting high ranges of activity, is that normal for you?"

"I'm just peachy," I said dryly. "Shot at by unknowns, lost two teammates, looking at a shitstorm of more-than-twelve necros, *hey!* What's not to be freaking about?"

"Point." She was reasonable, at least. "If there's anything abnormal, the techs will pick it up later."

Oh, good. Brain techs. Maybe one of them could be Orchard and I'd have to go put the squeeze on her after all. "This other team," I said, changing the subject. "We playing capture the flag?"

"It's unclear what they want."

"Find out," Indigo cut in. "I can't do my fucking job without all the data."

"Understood," she said, surprising me. Go, professionalism.

I let the data dweebs talk around me as I made my way through the metal rigging bolted to the roof. Some kind of signal tower, maybe. Aside from the far distance on the outskirts of the quarantine, no lights gleamed in the dark, which made details fuzzy in the night vision. So far, I seemed to be alone.

"The data indicates an enormous heat signature moments before Falk and Ange died," the woman continued. "What created the heat source that killed them?"

"I think it was a drone," Indigo said slowly. "No identifiable logo."

"Both of them?"

"No." He spoke very softly, like he was making an effort to keep Carter or Hooker from hearing him. Closed-feed, then, between us and control. "Ange was twenty meters away. One of Carter's mines detonated early. She claims her frequency lit up with the trigger command without her."

There was a short, charged silence. "According to the extensive data I'm looking at, that shouldn't happen."

"Yeah, no shit."

"I'm at the roof's edge now," I told them. I peered over it, down at the street we'd run across and both ways. Nothing moved, no creepy crawling psycho machines, no drones humming. Only the slightly less irritating pressure behind my eyes.

"Marks?" asked Indigo.

"Nothing."

"That's one thing going right, anyway."

Or was it? I crouched on the ledge, cradling the Sauger with one hand, balancing myself with my left. "Zoom in twenty-five percent." The heads-up acquiesced, turning the faceplate into a telescopic lens and magnifying my view. "Digo, you saw Falk get hit, right?"

"Yeah."

A nerve twitched in the curve of one shoulder. I resisted the urge to rub at it. It wouldn't help. Paranoia was settling over me in a big way. "So there shouldn't be nothing," I pointed out. "Unless there's a necro we missed with weapon enhancements. Not impossible, I figure, but how probable?"

"The Vid Zone doesn't have a runner shack that I know of, but who knows what that chopshop was doing?"

Too many what-ifs. I wrinkled my nose. "Thermals on," I said, a low voice command.

This would be so much easier, and quieter, if I was actually wired into the armor, but I didn't have the appropriate tech and that kind of long-term commitment to Mantis made my skin itch.

Obediently, the night vision faded, coloring the world in an eerie black, contrasted by ghostly outlines of the metal towers surrounding me. Glancing down at myself turned my silhouette a somewhat less ghostly white, but not the stark contrast I expected. Shielded and temp-controlled armor. Nice.

I turned my focus out over the ledge.

And nearly went ass-end over it. "Fuck me." That *wasn't* quiet. What little calm I'd scraped together filled in with ice-cold terror.

"What do you see?" Indigo demanded. "What's going on?"

Where the hell to start?

22

White. Packs of it, blobs of it marked by the heads-up display and labeled as unidentified, some faded to a fainter shade of gray, some still stark against the black. The bigger the knot, the denser the silhouettes.

I backed away from the ledge. "They're everywhere," I whispered. "We're surrounded, Digo. Go thermal, but brace yourself."

"That's impossible," control said tightly, and for the first time, her calm cracked. "There's no way there's that many converted in one place."

"Then what the *fuck* are you seeing on my feed?" My anger came out a harsh hiss. Pain throbbed in my forehead, right over where I suspected a blood vessel threatened to burst.

"I... It's got to be some kind of..." Her voice trailed away, a masculine murmur filling the silence. As if she'd forgotten her mic was on, she yelled, "I don't give two shits if he's banging the CEO's wife, get hi–" The feed cut off.

"Riko, get back here," Indigo demanded, and I didn't even bother with a quip. I obeyed.

When I scaled the ladder, landing beside Carter, I knew Indigo had followed my suggestion. There was a set to his shoulders, a watchful energy to him that was totally different than the usual run awareness I was familiar with.

He was spooked. Hard.

"You tell them yet?" I asked, open-feeding it.

He shook his head.

"Tell us what?" Carter asked, her voice dull.

I opened my mouth, but nothing that came to mind sounded gentle. I liked Carter. I didn't want to see her crack any more than she already had.

But, damn it, I needed these people on their feet.

Indigo ripped the scab off without my help. "We are surrounded by necros," he said quietly. "They're in the buildings, not so much in the street as far as I can tell, but there's at least thirty in my immediate field."

Hooker moaned. The kid was a mess, huddled over his drawn-up knees, rifle forgotten beside him. He rocked back and forth, his helmet wobbling like an overlarge knob on a pike.

He'd watched things go to hell for the first time, I bet. Lost a buddy, lost his cool.

I glanced at Indigo.

His helmet tipped in Hooker's direction. At least on this, we ran in synch.

I crossed the tiny alley, knelt, and rapped on his helmet with my knuckles. He jerked. "Earth to Hooker," I said sharply. "You in there, kid?"

He shuddered, the sound he made not quite acknowledgment.

This time, I brought my fist down hard. *Thud.* The plating rattled.

His body unfolded, one foot catching me in the knee. "S-Stop!"

"I will when your balls drop," I said, ignoring Indigo's sigh behind me. He didn't try to stop me, though. Hooker obviously hadn't responded to sympathy, which made it my turn. I smacked his helmet again. "Look at Carter. She's still standing. You going to let a chick's nanosteel dick outshine the real deal?"

He shook his head. To clear it or to deny my jibe, I couldn't tell, so I raised my hand to lay down another knock.

He threw his left fist up to block me. "Okay!" His voice sounded tragically young, but hey, at least I detected a note of determination. Finally. "Okay, I'm here. I'm focused. I... I just..."

This time, when my hand slipped beneath his guard, I laid my palm flat on his helmet. It wasn't exactly touchy-feely, but come on. I wasn't wired for tears and soft words of wisdom. "I get it," was all I knew how to say.

Maybe it'd be enough. I'd operated on less.

When I rose, offering him that hand to help him up, he took it. I didn't know if he'd hold together, but I had to believe he'd try. It was the only way we'd all get out alive.

Carter sucked in a deep breath and let it out on a long, drawn out, "*Fu-u-uck.*" That cleared, she added, "What now?"

"Now," Indigo said, "we do our jobs."

"Still?"

"Still."

I rubbed my hand across the faint seam at my shoulder. It wasn't aching; or if it was, I couldn't tell beneath my throbbing headache. Everything just felt *wrong*.

Indigo's faceplate rotated left to right, a slow, steady survey. "They're not moving. Why?"

"Let me go knock on a door and ask one," I said dryly.

Hooker cleared his throat. "Are they... Do they only hunt at night?"

I shook my head. "That wouldn't make any sense."

"They're just scarier at night," Indigo said, candid but calm. "Theory time. Are they dead?"

"You mean besides the obvious?" I pointed a thumb back the way I'd come. "I saw a few milling around in small pockets, but most were immobile. I don't know that I'd count them out, though."

Click. Carter replaced her clip, her words carefully even.

"Maybe they're hibernating."

"Job's done, nothing left to rend, power down?" My attempt at levity fell flat, even to me. We were all feeling it. Paranoid. Cornered. Were they hearing the crackle, too?

I didn't dare ask, not as long as control was listening. I couldn't risk them pulling the plug, especially now that I bet Malik had been called in.

My jaw shifted.

"Any sign of that second team?" Indigo asked me.

Again, I shook my head. "If they're out there, they're just white blots in a sea of them."

"Then we move out."

Given our choices – stay and wait to be picked off when those things finally realized we were here or go, finish the job, and get the hell out – I couldn't agree more.

Carter visibly squared her shoulders. "Koupra. About the mine–"

"It's okay, Carter." He didn't look at her, focusing on the Sauger he ran his hands over. "It wasn't your fault. Can you change the sec on your setup?"

"Yeah. Already did."

"Then we're square. Hopefully it'll confuse whoever triggered the last one."

And that was Digo. All around nice guy.

I bit my tongue before I said something stupid to ruin the effort.

"Hooker?" Indigo asked.

"I'm here."

"Good." His faceplate turned to me. "Riko? What's up with your vitals?"

Yeah, yeah. "I'm pissed."

"Un-piss, I need your focus," he said, and then let it go. "Here's the plan: we have two and a half hours left to get to the site and get our shit." I refrained from pointing out that his sister had been filed under "shit". I was in enough trouble for it already. "We stay low, we stay quiet. No noise."

"What if they come at us again?" I asked.

"No noise," he repeated. "Melee weapons first."

"Balls." As a word, it didn't quite do my incredulity justice. "You want us to hand-to-hand these things?"

Indigo nodded. "That's exactly what I'm saying. Use the EMP if it gets tough. Quick, clean, no shot to wake the dead."

I winced. "Thanks for that. Now I'm picturing a wave of necros shuffling down the street."

Hooker's laugh was wan. "Maybe they just want our brains."

"Shut up," Carter snapped, shrugging like her skin was trying to crawl off. I sympathized. "I hate zombies."

"Zombies are fiction," Indigo cut in, his tone sharp. "*This* is a virus hacking hardware that doesn't belong to it. Let's get the hell out of here so the burn team can make it right."

I preferred the zombie analogy to walking tech. Shuddering, I said nothing.

"We clear?" Indigo asked.

"Clear," Carter said.

Hooker nodded. "Yes, sir."

"Riko?"

"Why am I always singled out?" I groused. "I shitting heard you."

"Because you're a pain in the ass on a good day," he replied, striding for the alley mouth. Hooker fell in behind him, the better to cover Digo if anything crawled out of the thermal dark, and Carter and I took the rear.

We all made an effort to keep quiet as we left the alley, sticking to the open street.

It was hell.

Under the thermal scanners, white shapes hunkered behind ghostly walls, huddled in knots. Most were still. Some shifted.

At least one darted suddenly from one point to another,

causing my heart to lurch up into my throat, then splash down into the pit my stomach had turned into. Carter's hand spread on my shoulder, a sure grip that still shook.

She'd seen it too.

Every hair on my arm, the back of my neck, stood on end.

I'd never heard of anything like this. Necros were supposed to be rare, converting those caught between hookups, not districts.

We all expected them to jump out. To perk up like dogs scenting raw meat. Any moment, they'd come roiling out from the structures housing them, and my imagination wasn't doing me any favors.

"I hate you, Hooker," I muttered.

He shrugged; I pretended it was an apology.

"Shut it," Indigo said softly.

We managed quiet for another five minutes. Then Carter whispered, "Do you think any of them are just people hiding from the necros?"

We didn't answer her. Not even Indigo.

Somehow, that thought was worse.

The farther we walked, the uglier the droning noise in my head got, until every step was emphasized by the throbbing ache behind my eyes. I could see fine, but my hearing was taking an audible beating again.

"Anyone hear that?" I muttered, shaking my head and raising one hand to tap against the side of the helmet.

They all froze. Then, Hooker's shaking whisper. "No?"

Shit.

"What are you hearing?" Indigo asked me.

"A whine." Again, I tapped my helmet. "Probably just some interference. Let's keep going."

"What interference?" Hooker glanced at me over his shoulder. "The power's out."

"But the bandwidth isn't," Carter noted.

I squeezed my eyes shut, dragging my armored forearm

across the faceplate. It didn't help. Despite the suit's temperature regulation, I was perspiring hard enough to taste salt on my lips. "Thermals off," I muttered. The faceplate visuals faded to empty streets and wisps of smoke, all the lines outlining the silhouettes of my team turning green again.

With all the white blobs gone, I could almost trick myself into breathing normally again. Almost. My back teeth ached with the strain.

A breeze scattered the smoky drift, clearing aspects of the street as we forged through. Eerie as it was already, seeing the distant halo of the city lights thrust into the sky only made it worse.

So close to normality. And yet so fucking far.

The smoke moved in the corner of my eye, skated at the edge of the helmet's visibility range. Out of habit, I glanced left.

Fuck–

"Drop!" I shouted.

Merc or enforcer, everyone here knew that tone. We hit the pavement. A dull *whump* echoed us. I expected bullets; heard nothing but a whoosh of something sailing through the air and the distant clatter as it hit the building to my right. I was already rolling out of the way when someone – Carter, I think – opened fire. The Bolshovekia's report runs slightly sharper than the Sauger 877's.

In the orange flare of the muzzle flash, I caught the outline of two silhouettes, each wearing armor and darting back into the shadow.

All hell broke loose.

Another rapidfire hail of bullets, and whatever had taken root in my head detonated. Wave after wave of noise filled my aural synapses, blocked my ability to hear, even to see, as I staggered to my knees, swearing violently.

Hands gripped my shoulders. If their owner was talking to me, I didn't hear it. I couldn't hear it. Buzzing, ragged and nerve-shatteringly raw, filled my senses. My eyes crawled, my sinuses felt shoved full of static and pressure. If I opened my mouth, I didn't know if it'd be my voice or the pressurized drone escaping.

The hands yanked me to my feet. "Get– ... –ko!"

I blinked hard. Darkness filled my vision.

Something cracked against my helmet, rocked my head back on my shoulders and I flailed for balance before another set of hands grabbed my shoulders. Orange flares spattered the darkness.

I wasn't blind. I was just in the dark.

"Thermals," I gasped.

The darkness transitioned to ghostly gray and I stared at Carter's silhouette as she dragged me at a dead run. The heads-up traced her outline, thin and red, and put her vitals in the stratosphere.

I found my feet with effort, forcing the words through my aching jaw. "They don't show." My voice rasped. "They aren't showing in thermals!"

Indigo turned, his gun pointed at us, but he waited until we'd managed to sprint past him before laying down enough cover fire to empty his clip. I heard it clink to the ground. "And they're carrying monofilament nets."

Carter let me go. "What the fuck happened?"

"You opened fire," Indigo snarled, "and woke the goddamn host. Go!"

"Where?" Hooker asked, sounding more and more like a frightened rookie.

I shook myself hard, glancing from left to right and left again. "This way," I shouted, and darted left through a sagging fence with rusted, broken metal sheaves.

"What's that way?"

I didn't know. I mean, I did, but I didn't. Somehow, I just knew that darting left through a sagging fence with rusted, broken metal sheaves was the way to go.

Behind me, the necros turned into flies, darting wall to wall, trapped in their little honeycomb of tenements and flats. Some had found a way out. I imagined I could hear them gurgling, gasping; sniffing our trail, hot meat and sour sweat.

"Follow her," he ordered. "Go, go, go!"

I ran down a narrow passage between two sad little tenements, ducking under low-hanging laundry lines strung between the two. Hooker's rifle snagged in one, abandoned shorts wrapped around it, and he wasted precious seconds untangling the barrel while Indigo whirled and laid down another line of cover fire.

I didn't have to see them to know they were there every step of the way: necros. It seemed like thousands, but that was my imagination ruining my shit. If even ten of them came out with all the fuss, it was more than enough.

We could not handle ten, much less thirty, fifty, or however many there actually were.

And we sure as balls couldn't handle them while a team of unknowns took potshots at us from the sides.

"Either necros are learning how to hunt as a team," Hooker gasped, catching up to us, "or we're being flanked by that second group."

"I will pay," I panted, "good fucking cred if they're human."

"Pay up," Indigo said grimly. "Control, we've got the second team on us!"

Control flicked the feed on, but whatever calm she'd managed to scrape together had obviously frayed. "What's your position?"

"Past *oh, shit* and two blocks into *fucked*," he snarled. "We need support, lady!"

"We're waiting–"

"I don't care what you have to do, but you do it and *you do it now*."

A brief pause. "We'll do our best," she said, and the line clicked off.

Not soon enough.

I ran. Bullets pinged off the brick and metal frames surrounding us, but I didn't stop. None of us stopped. Indigo held the rear, and he didn't ask me where I took them. I could imagine his features, hard planes locked down to petrified determination. This was not the point in which a runner lost his cool. This was the point that separated the chrome from the diamond steel.

I didn't know which one I was right now – jumpy enough for chrome, pissed enough for diamond steel – but as I led the team through a maze of alleys, my heart pounding a bloody, ragged beat in my skull, I refused to end as a nameless statistic. I needed to zen it, and I needed to do it fucking now.

"There's a team on the rooftops," I said through stretched, bloodless lips. My feet pounded the asphalt, jarring every bone in my body. "Another flanking us. How do they know where we are?"

"And why aren't the necros chasing *them*?" demanded Carter, with a righteous indignation that made me gasp out a laugh.

Indigo wasn't amused. "I've tried every frequency, I can't register them. How do *you* know where *they* are?"

He couldn't? I didn't look back at him; Hooker and Carter were in the way and I couldn't see through his faceplate anyway. "Angle of the bullets," I lied.

I didn't know how I knew. I just did.

"Then what– *Fuck!*" A spatter of gunfire peppered the alley, and Carter went down on a ragged curse. The smell of blood – sharp, coppery, wet – filled my nose, even through the filters.

Fuck, shit, fucking spunkchucking *fuck*. "Move!"

"Carter!" Indigo slowed long enough to grab her arm and haul her to her feet. The Bolshovekia clattered to the asphalt.

The iron-rich fragrance of wounded flesh impaled itself into my senses.

My fingers clenched over my Sauger so hard, I saw the

numbers spike under my personal visual display. I don't think it was strong enough to bend a nanofactory diamond steel rifle, but my arm had surprised me before. Swallowing hard, I forced myself to raise my weapon, aim into the black above our heads, and lay down cover fire.

I heard nothing; no return fire, no movement.

Even the white shapes had faded, far enough in our dust that my sensors couldn't pick them out anymore.

"You okay?" I managed, a semblance of together.

"Yeah." Carter's voice was tight with pain. She hobbled against Indigo's shoulder. "Fuckers got me in a seam. Armor took the brunt." But not all of it. The full-bodied fragrance of her blood made me want to puke.

That was a first.

"Riko, where the hell–"

I cut him off with a gesture to the right. "This way," I said. "I have an idea."

I didn't give any of them time to argue.

They followed after a beat, and I didn't run so fast that Carter couldn't keep up – but I knew it was a struggle. She wasn't dying, not yet. Not that it cleared her. If we didn't bandage that wound up soon, her nanos might not have the juice to keep her on her feet. Gritting my teeth, I worked my way through narrow lanes and thin alleys, some so constricted that I spent the whole time coiled, overclocked and waiting for the hail of bullets I expected from above.

It came instead from behind.

Sparks pinged off the walls by my head, so close I could see the flecks of brick skate off my visor. The echo of automatic fire slammed wall to wall until it felt like my head was wrapped in a vise and only getting louder. Tighter.

Indigo grunted. "They can't get a good angle."

"Neither can I!" Hooker wasn't great at holding it together, but at least he kept up. "They're getting closer!"

What the *shit.* "Climb over me," I ordered, and dropped to the ground.

"What—"

"*Climb over me,*" I shouted. Too loud, given necro senses, but I didn't care. Indigo hesitated. Hooker was ahead of him and didn't. I gritted my teeth as booted feet stepped hard on my shoulders and over. "Keep going," I added, in case that wasn't clear.

"You better…" Indigo's voice hazed into background noise as another set of boots planted on my armored back. It wasn't the weight. Carter was unsteady, but I was strong enough. It was the noise. Crackling, shimmering, strident. I banged my helmeted forehead against the asphalt, but it didn't help. All it did was pop something in my nose.

I tasted my own blood.

This wasn't the first time.

Blood in my mouth, pressure in my head. The flashback struck hard and fast, just like in Orchard's lab. I spun in a mental vertigo, struggling to slog through shattered memories I couldn't grasp.

There was no white tile here. Just asphalt and filth.

"Go," I gasped, leaping to my feet. Hooker's shoulders scraped against the wall as he sidled ahead, but I wasn't as wide as he was. I had room to move, to pull the Adjudicator out of its holster and sight, straight-armed, down the alley.

Nothing moved in my thermal vision, but I knew they were there. I knew where they all were.

My skin prickled. *There.* As if I had a map of the area, I could see them. Sense them. I jerked my arm up, sighted once and pulled the trigger.

The echo of the shot cracked through the dark, the muzzle flash flaring white.

Something scraped. Clattered. A man-shaped blur hazed into a white silhouette as it fell from the roof. It smacked the asphalt in a tangled knot of splayed limbs, bounced off the ground with a sickening crunch and fell against the wall.

Ange may have had stealth tech, but theirs? Way better.

No more bullets came out of the alley behind me. "Thermals, off," I said.

The ghostly shroud faded.

Black shapes solidified into view.

"Fuck!" I grabbed a hand splayed inches from my faceplate, held it fast and smashed my metal fist into my assailant's elbow. The fact I carried the Adjudicator in it only added to the impact. Before he managed to wrench back, arm momentarily useless, I turned, slammed a straight-legged kick hard into his plated chest and left him colliding into the other guy on his heels. Assmunch. Choke on that.

"Go!" I shouted, just in case my team needed the reminder. If they said anything, I couldn't hear it.

I was angry wasps and pain and blood thick in my throat. My vision flickered under the strain, but I didn't stop. Didn't dare slow. For whatever reason, the bodysuits on my tail didn't open fire again.

Small smegging favors.

I holstered the Adjudicator and sprinted after my team, certain the bogeys would follow. They wanted something. They weren't after the necros, that wouldn't have put them on us. They wanted something we had. Knowledge? Our gear?

If they weren't looking to shoot on sight, that made it unlikely they'd hacked Carter's mines. Which meant something else had gone wrong.

Hands grasped at my rig and I wrenched away, lashing out another kick that didn't connect with anything but brick. The jarring pain rippled up to my knee.

"Come on!" I snarled, almost blind with it.

"Oh, *fuck*," Hooker squeaked, voice cracking on a raw note of terror. "Necros!" He stopped at the alley mouth.

"Everyone, back–"

I didn't let Indigo finish that order. Barreling on them, I rammed my shoulder into Indigo's back and forced him and Carter to collide with Hooker. We stumbled out of the maze, all of us gasping, two of us screaming.

Hooker.

Me.

The sound was unbearable now. Blood vessels ruptured in my eyes, something I didn't know what to name ruptured in my awareness, and the world went red, then black.

23

"—ass to get *up*."

I jolted into awareness on the heels of an order lined with ice, sharpened to a bloody edge. I was already lurching into movement, but as my vision cleared I stumbled, unsure of where I was going. What I was doing. My boots skidded on slick ground.

I tried to speak, but blood turned it into a mucus-thick gurgle. It took effort to clear my throat. "Malik?"

"Clock in."

I shuddered, somehow gasped, "I'm here." My helmet was gone, which made checking the faceplate worthless, but the display on my bracer told me I'd lost time. Four minutes, give or take.

Talk about losing my shit. Smoke and blood and the tang of decay filled my senses. My muscles ached, body thrumming with pure adrenaline, but I felt rooted. Hazy.

Everything but zen.

I could all but taste the seething fury on the line. "We are going to talk about this later. Get eyes on your team."

I frowned, shaking my head. "Indigo?" I turned around.

Red. Black. Gleaming, textured, gorge-inducing.

I blinked, trying to clear my vision, but it wasn't my disorientation painting the street.

I didn't have the vocabulary to punctuate the carnage around me.

Limbs. Guts, intestines, chest cavities gutted and heads blown clean off where they weren't a scattered mass of gobbets and brain. My EMP knife still hung loosely from my hand, blood dripping from the serrated edge, charge emptied.

Did it explode a head? Did I miss it?

I swallowed back a nauseating need to laugh.

A black-clad arm lay limp and discarded by my feet, leaking blood at the severed biceps. A crisp white logo glowed obscenely clean on the sleeve.

"MetaCore?" I asked, my voice sickeningly steady. My brain shut down the colors around me – red so heavy and dark it was nearly black; the brown spatter of thicker things my subconscious quietly shoved into the dark recesses of memory to be drowned in drink or slank later – and focused instead on the logo. "It's MetaCore in here."

But why? Was it me, after all?

Had I led them in here? Or were they after the same data?

"Thank you," Malik said, anger and ice packed in to absolute calm. As if I wasn't standing in a circle of butchery so complete, I wasn't sure how I wasn't screaming. Maybe he couldn't see it. My helmet had vanished somewhere. "I'll figure out why. Get your team somewhere safe."

I raised my gaze from the mess around my feet, skimmed the rest of the street in either direction.

Indigo watched me from his splayed position against the front door of an empty junkshop, his helmet cracked and faceplate shattered. Blood smeared the side of his visible mouth.

To my left, Hooker was bent over the remains of something in black armor.

I didn't see Carter.

Or maybe I did, and I wasn't putting a name to the mangled remains.

Slowly, I picked up one foot. Put it down.

Gobbets of something milky and pink squelched underneath my boot.

Another step. This one made no sound.

The third splashed. Bile rose in my throat, burned a hole in my chest, but I forced myself to clear the street – *squelch, squish, crunch, snap*. The things I stepped on defied description.

Indigo's eyes closed as I knelt beside him. "I forget," was his resigned greeting.

"Forget what?" I put the knife down, searched his helmet for the clasp underneath his chin that would release the seal.

"You're a hell of a splatter specialist."

My smile felt too tight. I pulled his helmet off with care, caught his head when it would have fallen back against the shop's rusted facing. The thick strands of his loosening braid clung to my blood-drenched fingers. "Obviously, you've been taking us on the wrong runs."

Indigo looked like death. The quiet sort of death, not the ruinous mess of necro and corporate carcasses behind me. I couldn't tell how much was pain and how much was terminal.

"How bad is it?" I asked.

"Bad. Gut wound." His teeth bared in a smile that indirectly reminded me of mine. Too much edge. Not enough warmth.

I was a terrible influence.

I tilted my head. "Malik?"

"Vitals won't read without the head unit," he said in my ear, as cool as control had been until shit hit the fan. "But if you patch it and down a recharge, your nanos will handle the rest."

"You know what?" I put a hand on Indigo's shoulder, forcing him to lean back until the bottom edge of his chest plate shifted out of the way. "So far, your armor sucks. Infrared that doesn't see through stealth units better than yours, night vision without filters for near-zero light. I've seen scrap gear with better systems."

"Noted. I'll pass it on to tech the desk. When you return," he continued on the same even note, "we're going to talk about why your vitals just went apeshit."

If it had anything to do with what happened in the four minutes I'd lost, that was not a conversation I was going to have. Maybe there was a good reason. Adrenaline, berserking haze, whatever. All I knew was that I'd led my team into a necro knot to shake MetaCore and barely come out in one piece.

Carter didn't come out at all.

This shit scared me.

"Shut up, Malik," I said, my tone making it clear I wasn't paying any more attention to him. "I'm busy saving Indigo's life."

He said nothing, but Indigo sucked in a sound that might have been a laugh.

I peeled back the curled remains of the plating covering his gut and saw nothing but a bloody tear. "What the hell did this?"

"A necro," he said tightly. "Tore through the armor like it wasn't even there. I don't know what the hell he'd been wired with, but it was sharp and fast and it sucks."

"Yeah, well, sucking abdominal wounds, am I right?"

"Fuck you, Riko."

Everybody was a critic. I stood. "We need to find somewhere safe. Can you walk?"

"I can lean," he managed, and took my hands. I braced myself, hauled him upright, and flinched when he locked back a groan. Shoving my shoulder into his armpit, I stabilized him the best I could.

"Hooker!"

The kid jerked, scrambling for his discarded weapon.

It took everything I had to gentle my tone. "Come on, kid. We're going."

For once, nobody flipped me any shit. Tearing himself away

from whatever he saw in Carter's devastated remains, Hooker dragged himself to his feet, turned, and trudged after us.

At least the wasps in my head had settled to a mellow buzz.

We walked in silence, punctuated only by the crunch and squish of our boots dragging through obliterated corpses, and very deliberately did not talk about what happened.

I wasn't sure any of us even knew.

24

We settled on a rooftop, high enough that it towered over its neighbors and lacking in any cover for necros to hide behind. Hooker's eyes were starting to go glassy, so I set him on watch.

Not the kindest thing I'd ever done to a kid in shock, but he'd stay alert. If only to make sure whatever happened down there didn't happen again. I was pretty sure that if I let him settle, he'd check out for good. Watching a teammate blow herself up with a mine still strapped to her back did that to a brain.

At least she'd taken out half the clot with her.

Heh. *Clot.* I was a grotesque riot.

It beat the alternative, though. I wasn't going to die down here.

I stripped off my gloves, then helped Indigo out of his ruined chest piece and peeled back his skin suit. His flesh gleamed gold in the faint circle of light cast off from the glow rod propped on the ground beside us. Gold and bloody red. The edges of the wound curled out like a gaping flower, and blood oozed thickly with every panting breath he took.

I steeled myself. "Shit, Digo, that's nothing."

"Riko?"

"Yeah, yeah." I flashed him a grin I didn't feel as I peeled open the first aid bandages. "Fuck me."

"Not even on my best day, sugartits." But there wasn't any laughter in his tone. Just pain, tension, and more resignation than I liked to see from a guy who'd been my linker for more of my runner years than not.

I packed the wound with a lot more care than his jibe warranted. "Been taking cues from Jax, huh?" He didn't answer me, and I didn't push. The skin around his mouth went yellow with strain. The harder I pushed, the paler he got, until sweat watered down the blood and he gasped out a harsh word racked with pain.

"I know, I know." I firmed my grip. "Drink your recharge."

"If I throw up on you," he managed from teeth clenched so tight, his jaw stood out in harsh contrast, "you deserve it."

I nodded, but I had nothing clever to say.

He was right. I'm the one who'd fucked his sister, vanished with her, and then left her behind. Whatever the reasons, whatever we found to explain what was going on here, I deserved whatever he put on me.

But I'd find out who betrayed Nanji first. Maybe if I offered that asshole's head to Indigo, I'd make some amends. Maybe.

The fresh bandages under my ungloved hands slowly turned red.

Indigo drained the recharge pack, sucking out the thick green sludge until the plastic crumpled in on itself. I waited a full two minutes.

When I raised the bandage to look beneath, I couldn't tell if the bleeding had slowed or if I was used to the warmth of it on my palm. "Nanos kicking in?"

"Feels like it." He spoke thickly. "It itches."

"Itching is good." For the really bad wounds, itching meant healing.

"Dunno. Never been hurt bad enough." His blue eyes gleamed at me. "You itch when you reconstruct?"

"Fuck, yes." Of the two of us, I was most likely to walk home with a bullet or worse. As a rule, we banded around our linkers. Runners didn't get far when a linker's death blinded them. "First time I ever got a gut wound like that, I kept shoving forks down my pants to get the bottom edge of the scar."

A ghost of a smile shaped his mouth. "Kinky."

"You only wish."

We fell silent again, only the hum – softer, much less painful – and the thickening dark to keep us company.

This was the perfect time to talk to him. To tell him all the things I hadn't yet – about me, his sister. About what we'd find down there, or at least what I was scared shitless we'd find.

I didn't. I could claim it had more to do with Indigo's need to knit without straining it, but I'd be lying.

The silence turned to an accusation, and I sweated it out in grim silence.

After ten minutes, I checked under the bandage again.

"Looks like it's slowed." With effort, I straightened from my huddle, flexing a hand that had cramped from the pressure. "Give it a few more for the worst of it to seal and the boost to kick in."

He didn't answer me, eyes closed. But his breathing had steadied, so I withdrew to a comfortable distance and took up watch on the edge of the roof. Hooker, with his longer range, had a vantage point of the street. I kept an eye on the rooftops closest to us.

"Hooker, down a recharge," I told him, and watched for the movement of his back that said he obeyed. I fished out my own recharge from my belt.

My whole body ached, a lowkey throb.

I focused on twisting open the seal, on swallowing the slightly salty mix with more care than needed.

If I didn't, if I let myself think about what had happened back there, I was afraid I'd end up like Hooker. Traumatized. Questioning everything. Glassy eyed and shellshocked.

Zombies? I wished. Every zombie shock vid I'd ever seen had seemed sad and pointless to me. None of it mattered: dead was dead.

This? This was insane. This was a tech virus infecting meat; killing the brain and replacing it with its own programming. It wasn't right. Machines had killed before – ask any idiot who wasn't paying attention on the job – but they didn't have the *right* to kill. It shouldn't have been a choice.

Tech infection seemed too damn close to a mechanical choice for me.

Who was the fuckhead who'd risked the corruption and didn't tell anyone?

Was I the cause of all this? That didn't seem likely. I'd missed going necro. But Nanji hadn't.

Wouldn't that just be *perfect*.

I sucked a gob of green sludge out of the squeezable plastic tube and stared out into the light-speckled distance.

"Do you suppose we'll die in here?"

I looked back, surprised out of my silence. "Uh…" Brilliant. I tried again. "Sorry, but is this Indigo Koupra I'm talking to? Exceptional linker, brains behind the best operations on the street? Maybe you've heard of him."

He didn't open his eyes. "I'm serious, Ree."

I held my breath for a moment.

What did he want me to say?

"Maybe," I said, exhaling the word. "MetaCore on our ass, necros infesting the neighborhood like some kind of disease…" I shrugged. "Not the best odds we've ever faced."

"Probably the worst."

"Yeah." I squeezed the plastic in my metal hand gently. The recharger squelched. "Probably."

"You want to tell me what went down with you and my sister?"

Now it was my turn to close my eyes.

No. I really didn't. Fuck. I still regretted not being the one to put a bullet in her. I didn't know if we'd find her shacked up in the middle of all this carnage, the patient zero of the Vid Zone blight.

There was a lot I hadn't worked out yet.

What if we died before we made it anywhere?

I opened my eyes to find him watching me.

I looked away. "What do you want to know?"

"Did you love her?"

"Does it matter?"

"It does to me." He paused. "And it would to her, too."

Guilt opened up like a bloody wound in my chest. My fingers twitched on the plastic casing, forcing a rim of green around the narrow strawlike tube. I took the moment to suck it clean, working over what I could say – what I *should* say.

The truth?

I guess I owed him some truth. "No," I told him quietly. "Not like you want me to." I met his gaze across the dim lighting. "I liked her, though. She was fun, friendly. I liked being around her. It was like..." I looked up at the low-hanging layer of smoke. "It was like the opposite of hanging with Jax, you know? She kind of had this thing, this quality that made you care about stuff."

"Is that why you left us?"

I winced. "That's... different." Completely different. Without my memories, I didn't know the first thing about why or how. Obviously, I'd left, then somehow ended up at that lab, but why?

He watched me, the skin around his eyes pinched. Anger, maybe. Pain.

"I didn't mean to leave you." I gestured at him with the boost. "I've been kind of fucked up lately, okay?"

His mouth tightened, that muscle ticking in his jaw. "Fucked up," he repeated. "That's it? That's all you got?"

I didn't have it in me to get mad. "Please don't work yourself up," I said instead, wearily. "You still have a gaping hole in your gut."

"Fuck you." He elbowed himself up, until he managed a semi-recline that let him stare me down. "You have a problem, Riko. You leave everyone who starts to like you, and it always screws it up for the rest of us. Why the fuck couldn't you just leave Nanji? Leave her with *me*?"

I got it. Angry older brother. I couldn't begrudge him the effort. He was even right, sort of. I left my folks without much of a backward glance. I'd left Lucky. Sure, I saw him time to time, but I didn't really visit much.

I left Jax when things got too messy. Liked my fuckbuddies sexy and uncomplicated. I liked being wanted.

I didn't see how any of that was wrong.

But I couldn't drum up the energy to try explaining. I didn't even know if I could. I was just too... tired. And it didn't have anything to do with why I was here, anyway. That was my business. Not his.

He could go fuck himself.

I turned away, gazing out across the empty rooftops. "You're right."

"Damn it, Riko."

"Yeah, that's cool." I shifted my grip on the Sauger, resting it across my lap for better access. Always one part of my brain on the job; the same trait that he was tearing at now. Guess it was okay when it was his ass I was watching out for.

"Yeah, I'll bet it's cool," he spat. "You really don't give a fuck how I feel, do you?"

"Right now, Digo, the number of fucks I have to give are rapidly shrinking."

He glared at me. "And that's why I don't trust you anymore." He leaned back, like he'd scored a point. "I thought you'd change when you hooked up with us, but you didn't, did you? You don't give a shit about any of us."

That wasn't true. These were my mates, my runners. I'd worked with them for more than a handful of years. Of course I cared about them. I trusted them.

"I'll prove it," I said to the thinning, smoky night air. "We'll find her, and I'll prove it."

"You realize that's another of your problems, right?"

My teeth clicked together. "Digo," I said, all pretense at patience snapped, "I have a metric ass ton of problems, but I am *not* the one with a sucking abdominal wound."

Okay, my turn to score a point. Never argue with a splatter specialist if your ass isn't ready for a throwdown of the physical kind.

Maybe he remembered that unspoken rule of the street. He was silent for a long time.

Then, quietly, he sighed.

"For fuck's sake, now what?" I snarled.

He shifted – his armor scraped the rough ground. "How fucked up?"

I stared out over the dark street.

This was it. An opening. I couldn't ask for a better time.

Or a worse one.

"Talk to me," he said. Not soft. Not quiet. But steady. Like he was making an effort.

He owed me that much. Just like I owed him. Trust, huh?

I sighed. "Very," I said tightly. "Very fucked up. A lot of..." I hesitated, frowning at my weapon. "Most of that month after that MetaCore run is a blur." Sort of a lie. "Whatever I did – I don't know. It's all gone, Digo."

"You don't remember?"

I knuckled at my eyes with a grimy hand. "Not really. It's something I've been trying to figure out. Retrace my steps."

"And Nanji's part?"

Damn it. I winced, shifting on my perch. "Part of the blank." *I'm sorry.* More than he'd ever know. "I don't mean all of it. I was serious when I said I liked being with her. It's just..." I blew out a harsh exhale.

"You lost a month?"

"I lost three. April to July, man. Anything after that MetaCore run put me on Lucky's table. It's like I went under and never woke up until that lab."

He went quiet. Processing, maybe. Swallowing it down with the same effort I still couldn't muster.

I lived it, and it still sounded like bullshit to me.

"Did Lucky clear you?"

"Yeah." Mostly.

"Do you trust him?"

Any other time, I would have clocked him for the suggestion. Now, I couldn't fault his logic. But I couldn't go there. Not yet. "I do," I said grimly. I had to.

Digo grunted a wordless acknowledgment. For another few minutes, silence hovered like a smoky shroud. Then, "Is that why you're here? To figure out what happened to you?"

"Yeah." I tilted my head until I could see his silhouette out of the corner of my eye.

His armor scraped cement. "What if I said I believed you?"

"Do you?" When he hesitated, I shook my head. "It's cool. Whatever we'll find, it'll answer both our questions."

That was about as zen as I could manage.

"Yeah. Well, listen," he said to my back. "While we're being all touchy-feely here."

I snorted.

"I guess I should mention that I sold you out."

It took me a moment to register. A moment longer to work through the arrested hitch of my thoughts.

What the shit? I tell him I lost my goddamn mind and he comes back with a casual note of betrayal? I turned, my feet sliding off the ledge and hitting the rooftop ground so hard, dust puffed out from underneath the tread. "Sorry, what?"

Behind Indigo, Hooker stirred, his shoulders shifting as if he'd only just tuned in to the tension.

Digo ignored him. His eyes, the set of his jaw, even the hands fisted against the ground outlined defiance. "About a day before you showed up at the Mecca, Reed introduced himself."

I expected the man himself to cut in on the feeds, but the line was silent.

Indigo looked away. "Mantis was offering a bounty for you. Paid in full on delivery. Said if you showed up, give him a call." His laugh was harsh. "You were still AWOL, so it didn't matter. I was done. At least I thought I was until you came back like nothing had changed."

Very carefully, I set the dregs of the boost down on the roof ledge. I wanted to smear it. Wanted to turn on Indigo and kick the stupid right out of him.

Instead, I stood. "So you sent me to him in the guise of finding a team."

He shrugged.

"I *knew* it," I hissed. "Don't say you never gave me anything? You spunkchucking son of a *whore*."

Another shrug. "Turns out, you were worth getting paid for twice." Amusement, sharp as a knife, cut me nearly to the bone. "Assuming we survive this."

So that was the first payment owed. I could barely breathe around my fury. *Betrayal.* That hurt. "You just sold me out to the first suit who came looking."

He nodded.

"Without hearing me out?"

Another nod, but the sharp amusement slashed into his features twisted. He didn't explain himself.

I wasn't interested in hearing it. My throat ached around a lump I didn't know what to do with. I turned away. "Is this true?" Silence. I lifted a hand to my ear, as if it would help. "Answer me, you scumeating failure of an abortion, *is he telling the truth*?"

Malik didn't bother with preamble. "Yes."

The lump hardened. Anger replaced hurt and I let it. So much safer. So much less painful. "Why?" I gritted out. My fist clenched, unclenched; clenched again as it locked around the Sauger. "Tell me why I shouldn't put a bullet in the last two men here with me and then come for you."

"That would be counterintuitive," Malik replied.

Behind me, I heard Indigo say my name.

It scored another notch into my rapidly fraying temper.

"Here's what's counterintuitive," I said, my voice low. It shook – strain and fury. Betrayal, achingly sharp. "When I get out of here, Malik Reed, you're first on my list."

"I don't doubt that." His deep voice remained calm, a soothing counterpoint to my vibrating rage. I hated it. I hated him.

Nothing in this world would give me as much pleasure as sinking my fingers knuckle-deep into his eye sockets and watching his brain ooze out.

He used me. Right from the start.

My vision turned red. Bloody, furious red.

"Use your brain," he said, the admonishment so sharp, I stepped back. "You're in necro-infested territory and it's only going to get worse. Do you want answers or not?"

I did. But did I want them at the expense of the payback I desperately wanted to deliver?

Fuck. Fucking chumsucking *twats*.

"Fine," I hissed. "But tell me one thing."

"One."

How damned magnanimous.

"Why did you come looking for me?"

There was a pause. Then, simply, "I've been trying to get a lock on this operation for months. Sources pointed me to you."

"What operation? This one?" Malik's silence was telling. Just. Fucking. Awesome. "So you *knew* about this? The *whole time*?" And he'd used me to get the evidence he needed.

His tone didn't shift. "Get out of there with the intel we need, and we'll talk."

Not if I murdered him first. The knuckles of my flesh hand cracked. "Did you–" It broke, and I swallowed hard before it all came out on a surge of bile.

Somehow, he knew. "Did I know about the number of necros?" Malik's voice didn't soften. I would have believed him less if it had. "No. But I wasn't surprised. Keep the rest of your team alive, and we'll find the truth inside."

Every cell in my body went nova as my temper cracked against what little restraint I had left. All I could do was slam my fist against the wall beside me. It hurt like hell, but I notched it in with the rest of the bullshit I carried.

Hooker's voice, still wired inside his helmet, filled my ears. "Chum," he said, shaken and sounding every bit the kid I kept calling him. "That was not cool."

Indigo closed his eyes. "Fuck you, Hooker," he said wearily. "You're named after a low-rent occupation."

But he kept one hand on his Sauger.

25

Silence – stillness, anyway, and that dull disharmony –
reigned. I let it. If it bothered either of them, relieved them
that I wasn't engaging, I couldn't say. We approached our
final destination without speaking, and I let them drown in
their own thoughts.

While I drowned in mine.

So, I'd vanished after his sister's death. I went missing for
a couple months. I couldn't remember any of that, and so
what? *Amnesia*, motherfucker. What was his excuse?

Nanjali.

Everything kept circling back to her. Her face, her name,
the sound of her laugh.

I hated this. The uncertainty, the anger. Maybe I couldn't
remember what had happened – maybe I was innocent of
any wrongdoing – but she was Indigo's *sister*. His only blood
family, far as I knew.

That made up for a lot of shit decisions on his part.

Which meant my head of steam cooled faster than I wanted
it to.

In the end, Digo and I were the same kind of asshole. A
part of me understood that.

The rest of me – that part trained by the street and a
runner's survival instinct; the hard killing reflex conditioned

to give no second chances – was growling that Indigo Koupra could eat me.

What the hell had happened to us?

"Pick it up," Malik said, breaking the long silence with his relentless calm. "You have one hour and twenty-five minutes to get what you can and get out."

"Got it." Indigo's confirmation, not mine.

Malik Reed could eat me, too.

The place didn't look any different than any of the other structures surrounding it. Hemmed in tightly, it was nothing but flat metal facing shored up by rusted plates here and there, worn veneers and the occasional busted and boarded window. It smelled too much like smoke to get a clear scent, but I thought I smelled sour refuse underneath it. Stale and rotting.

"Hey, jackholes." I pointed. "I think this is it."

Indigo didn't bat a pretty black eyelash. He looked like hell without his helmet, but we all did. Around the soot and dirt and blood, anyway. "According to the fixer's notes, it is. I take it waltzing through the front door won't work?"

If my patchy memory wasn't playing tricks on me, it wouldn't. "Nope."

"All right. Hooker, stay sharp. I'll do a circuit and–"

"Wrong." I frowned at him. "One more hit like that gut wound and your nanos are toast. You know that, right?"

"Aw." His lips quirked faintly. "I didn't know you cared."

"I'm one bullet away from it, Indigo."

He was silent for a moment, his study weighing me as if trying to decide if I was serious. Then, "You have it together enough to finish this out?"

"She does," Malik said in my earpiece, putting words in my mouth I wasn't ready to deliver.

I gritted my teeth. "Who asked you?"

"You did, when you asked me to fund this field trip." His tone hardened. "Now get your shit together, all of you, and get this done."

Over and *fuck you, too.*

Hooker said nothing.

I bent my irritation to the task in front of me. One thing at a time. Do the job in front of me, and I'd handle the rest later.

Better I blow my anger out on this, anyway. Maybe once we got out, I'd be ready to talk.

No smegging promises.

"There's another way in," I finally said, surveying the street in both directions. "I just have to figure out where the door is."

"Make it quick," Indigo said, his gaze on the street behind us.

Advice I could agree with. Maybe we'd gotten all the MetaCore enforcers, or maybe they were out playing tag with the rest of the necros, but whatever the reason, the relative quiet didn't sit right.

The smoke thinned, shoved along by a breeze cooling my sweat and blood-streaked cheeks and easing some of the heat I felt keenly now that my suit's templock had broken. The draft felt good.

A narrow crevasse sat like a black seam at the far edge of the faceless structure, as good a place to start as any. Without a word, I strode for it, withdrawing a flashlight from its band at the back of my belt and twisting it into the notch at the base of my Sauger. It weighted the front more than I liked, but with my helmet gone, I was almost blind out here.

The fact I knew about the door in that alley came down more to memory than sight, but I didn't second guess myself as I stepped into the dark, weapon at the ready.

"Torch up," Indigo told Hooker. "Keep an eye on our asses."

Refuse greeted the searching light, piles of garbage left in torn plastic bags and crates tipped over by hungry animals, bums, or worse. The smell was nauseatingly thick.

"Ugh." The first sound Hooker had made in almost forty-five minutes.

I didn't blame him. Gritting my teeth, I forged through it, my light cutting through the pitch dark to glance off sharp edges, stained paneling and worse.

I stopped in front of a section of mottled wall, flanked on each side by tilting, bundled plastic.

"What?" Indigo peered over my shoulder, so close I could smell the lingering tang of dried blood.

I rolled that shoulder back hard enough that he backed up a step. "Scan here."

He flipped open the arm unit, squinting at the narrow screen. The text on it scrolled at a rapid rate; his dark eyes reflected back the amber glow, missing nothing. "There's a signal coming right below our feet. It's faint, I can't lock it, but something down there has power."

"Which means you'll lose this signal when you get in there," Malik said over the feed. "Step it up. The burn team's getting impatient and I can't keep pulling favors for you."

"You mean for you," I muttered, but didn't give either of us time to get into it. I flattened my metal palm against the wall's cool facing.

Pretty typical stuff. Pocked metal over brick. Standard durability. I doubt anyone considered reinforcing it since nobody could tell it was here.

"No grenades." I grimaced. "No mines, no heavy."

"No problem." Indigo palmed my shoulder. "Out of my way." I tensed, but he dragged me back a step. "My job, Riko. Get lost."

Lost wouldn't be helpful to any of us, so I settled for shaking off his hand and folding my arms, Sauger cradled. I did not call him any of the names that came to my humming mind.

Strange. It was, I don't know, like the more I listened to the buzz, the less it bothered me. I could focus, even hear through it. Maybe I was getting used to it. The pressure hadn't faded, but a headache only gave a body two options: ride it, or drown. I was tired of drowning.

Indigo pulled two twisted cords from his belt, slipped them into place in the arm unit, and ran his fingers over the facing. At two separate places, he affixed the pads to the wall and tapped the arm unit's keypad. He worked quickly, silently, running whatever programs he had stored up for the job. Once in a while, he shifted a pad. Then the other.

"Why are you using hardware instead of a projection?" Hooker asked.

"Trying to keep everything locked down to this single unit," he muttered, but absently. After another long moment of trial and error, he smiled. The curve of it as he glanced at me was like a fist squeezing in my chest.

For one second, it was the Indigo I'd known for years; a stark echo of his sister, right down to the faintly pointed incisors giving their smiles an impish charm.

My guts twisted. By habit, my lips tilted up in return.

Reality didn't let that slide for long.

His smile faded, replaced by the same wary tension infecting us all since we'd arrived inside the quarantine. "Got it," was all he said.

As if something reached in and plucked a tight chord inside my skull, the hum I'd gotten used to shifted faintly. A note of harmony in the dissonance, here and gone again so fast, I gingerly tipped my head.

No shit. Was it that simple? I rubbed the base of my skull with one hand, nearly laughed out loud before I swallowed it on a grunt they ignored. The wasps in my head, the flicker I'd felt when Indigo's tech cracked the system, were they just frequencies?

Just like the nanos needed to be calibrated, the chipset needed the same kind of calibration. By design, each chipset was supposed to be unique to its specific user and nanos, but any number of things could knock it out of sync.

Obviously, I was picking up on some serious interference, which translated to something my hardware – my brain –

could understand. White noise.

Lucky had said I needed to recalibrate. This must be why.

Relief filled me as a seam hissed out compressed air. The unlocked panel slid into the wall, revealing an empty elevator smelling like the same air that filled the alley. And something sharper. Acrid.

Smoke, burning plastic and disinfectant.

The lights flickered inside. "Well," I said, manically cheerful. "At least it has power." And I wasn't losing my mind. Total win.

"One hour and thirteen," Malik reminded us. "Work *fast*."

No problem.

We filed inside. "If I'm right," I said as the door closed behind us, "the uplink lab will be two doors down to the right. We should be able to tap in, see if we can find traces of Nanji, get the data, and get out."

"Sounds easy," Hooker mused.

His tone mimicked my thoughts – and Indigo's, I'd bet. It was going to be anything *but* easy. We just weren't that lucky.

The car shuddered, lights wavering rapidly. Every shock vid I'd ever seen came to settle inside the narrow space with us, filling up the air with cold, nervous sweat. I gripped the wall with my flesh hand. It slipped, leaving clammy streaks of dirt and congealed blood.

Malik, probably nursing a hot coffee in one hand and counting stacks of credsticks with the other, didn't sound the least bit worried. "Mr Koupra, is your isolated unit still in one piece?"

"Yeah."

"Good." The line crackled, streaking Malik's feed with juddering syllables as the elevator sank. "Do not interface with anything else. The chance... –ecro infection could... team won't–"

"Bye bye, asshole," I said, way perkier than the environment demanded. I shrugged at the two men staring at me – though of the three of us, Hooker still had his helmet and he could be sleeping on his feet, for all I knew. "He *is* an asshole."

Hooker stirred. "What was he saying about interfacing?"

Digo didn't argue with my take. "You get that the necro code moves tech to tech, right?" He pointed up at nothing in general. "Computer systems, wiring, servers. If it's wired to a network or even a single drive, it's fair game."

"So... it's... It's alive?"

Fucking A. "No," I said, all pretense of my fake cheer dropped. "It's not alive, Hooker. It's a machine."

"Think of it more like a computer virus," Indigo clarified. "This place still has power, which means it's on a closed circuit. It could have active sectors of necro corruption in its databanks. Linking other systems to it provides a pathway for the virus to spread, you follow?" He closed his unit, tamping the plate down carefully on his arm brace. "Stay on your toes, watch out for each other. I'll use the isolated system to pull whatever info I can from the place and we'll get the fuck out."

He did not, I noticed, mention his sister.

That made him the levelheaded one here. Even if he didn't say so, the odds of Nanji's survival in this mess had exponentially dropped the longer she remained in this shithole.

All I needed to know was how she'd died. If she was still dragging herself around down there, full-on necro.

Not that it'd matter. Dead was dead.

Was it for her?

No. No, it wasn't. It was for me. I couldn't let her corpse go because if I did, I'd never know what put me down here. What I'd done in those months I couldn't remember.

I couldn't fix my cred until I knew, and *that* was the simple fact of this whole fucking mess. It wasn't *about* Nanji.

But unlike Indigo, who would go through his grieving stage, I just wanted to get the intel and move on. There was no other way to cope.

Yeah. This was going to be one hell of a hot mess.

"But..." Hooker paused while he unscrewed the barrel from his Sauger H2, decreasing range even further but allowing for tighter full auto in enclosed spaces. He worked fast, despite his hell of a day. "I mean, if you link in, won't that bring necro infection with us?"

"Yeah, but there's ways around it once you're in a secure link zone, like a prepared lab on its own closed circuit." Digo gestured me forward, to stand in front of the door while Hooker covered the rear. Linker in the middle because without one, a team was blind.

"It opens behind us," I told them, gesturing at the wall opposite of the way we'd come in.

"So, we're, like, carrying a techno plague?"

"If it helps, sure," Indigo said patiently. "Only it'll be trapped in the isolated comp unit, with no way of getting out."

The elevator thudded as it came to a full stop. The lights blacked out, leaving us in the dim luminescence given off by our torches. Hooker grunted something I think started as a yelp before he got a handle on it.

"Easy," Indigo said softly.

The new set of doors creaked open, the screeching of metal snagging on metal tearing through the mental gauze I'd managed to pull over my aching head. I flinched under the popping pressure, but it ended as quickly as it began.

A thin trail of smoke drifted into the elevator unit, backlit by the dull red glow of emergency lighting. Sparks shot blue through the foot-wide seam.

We were stuck.

26

"Nobody panic," Indigo ordered, probably more for Hooker's benefit than mine. My ears were ringing like someone had clapped both hands over my eardrums, but I was otherwise fine.

Nervous, but fine.

When I got out of this, I needed to find a reputable doc willing to work with me long enough to do a full chipset replacement. This kind of feedback wasn't normal. A replacement was going to suck for time, but I didn't see any other way. It was delicate work, brain integration.

I patted my harness, briefly checking on my backup arsenal by habit. "Before we crack this, how are you all on gear?"

"Half ammo," Hooker said, "but still have my backup. Suit's running fine."

"Three clips and a CounterTech," Indigo said. "You?"

"Down to my last two clips, but I've got a CounterTech and extra ammo for the Adjudicator." I grimaced. "Smegging shame our munitions got slagged."

Hooker cleared his throat.

Indigo glared at me. "Seriously?" His tone made it clear I wasn't earning any magical friendship points.

I bared my teeth. "I'm sorry, fuckholes, did you want me to keel over in tears right this second? They're gone. We're alive." I snapped twice in front of Hooker's faceplate. "Focus on getting your ass out before you start worrying about others."

"Yeah." Hooker's helmet bobbed. "I'm on that like you wouldn't believe."

Good.

Indigo growled through his teeth. "Just get the door."

"I'll take one end," I said.

"Hooker, keep us covered."

The kid raised his Sauger to his shoulder, sighting down the middle of the open crevasse as I wedged my fingertips into the seam and waited for Indigo to give the okay.

On his word, we pulled.

The doors wanted to give. I could feel it. They rocked an inch, caught on loosely wedged resistance. My metal arm flexed, biceps tightening. Another inch. It shrieked. "Stay on it," I grunted, pulling hard.

Indigo's jaw clenched with the strain, his fingers yellow around the door's edge. The whole shaft screeched an echoed refusal that set my teeth aching.

When it sheared through whatever blocked it, Indigo and I both hit the sides of the elevator, rocking it. My metal arm thudded against the panel, sending a snap and crackle through my joints. I hissed. The lights flickered on, then off again.

Hooker didn't lose sight of the open door. "Clear."

Indigo shook out his hands, grimacing. "Let's go."

We'd worked together long enough to fall back on routine – we stepped out as a unit, back to back. Indigo faced left, I faced right, no blind spots while Hooker covered from his vantage.

Nothing rushed us. No movement. In the burgundy shadows of the backup illumination, the corridor looked empty of all but a blood-red gleam of shattered glass. Our flashlights knifed through it, narrow beams patterned by wisps of smoke and fluttering dust motes turning gold and blue. Creepily serene.

"Clear," Indigo said.

"Same," I replied, and Hooker stepped out behind us. "This way." I proceeded down the hall, the rhythmic clunk of my team's boots behind me. "They called it the uplink lab. Whatever it is, I saw a lot of computers." I hesitated, my pace hitching. "It's... where I saw Nanji last."

Indigo's pace didn't hesitate. "Was it the one on fire?"

"Yeah." I didn't know what else to say; how else to go there.

"She was still alive?" Hooker asked me.

"She was... moving."

Neither questioned my choice of words. Digo already knew why.

We approached the pile of red-lit glass and I took a deep breath. Anxiety twisted around crushing disappointment as I edged out in front of the window whose tempered glass had exploded outward, showering the floor with fragments. It crunched underfoot. "Fuck," I said, because there was no other word for it. "Just *fuck.*"

"Nothing but slag." Indigo studied the inside of the lab, strangely calm. He didn't approach the blackened, scorched frame, but there wasn't much need. Anything that had been in there had melted down into unrecognizable residue. Twisted metal, hardened globules of liquefied plastic. Any corpses I'd seen were nothing more than ash and a memory now.

"Some fire," Hooker said, and whistled in his helmet. "Look at the tables." They'd bent in, softened to the point of curving under their own weight until the legs formed perfect arches.

If metal couldn't even hold, how long had Nanji?

I closed my eyes.

Had she screamed? Did they kill her before it consumed them all?

Had she torn off their chumsucking heads and spit out their entrails before she died?

I really, *really* hoped so.

Indigo touched my shoulder. "Let's find another source."

Damn it.

I stepped away. "I don't even know where to begin." My throat ached. My chest hurt. My head pounded – anger, frustration, shorted tech, I couldn't even tell it apart.

"Security is usually wired through most of everything. I'd be surprised if they didn't have cameras set up in every room. We'll start there." Same old professional linker. On the job, on the clock.

Off the emotional grid.

Usually, that was me. He'd accused me of just that, right?

I needed a grip. "Fine." I took a deep breath, digging the heel of my synthetic hand into my aching forehead. "The security force came from that way." I gestured with my Sauger, the barrel pointing further down the hall. "Past a set of doors. Maybe they mustered there."

"Without a map," Hooker said, "seems as good a place to look as any."

"Riko."

I glanced at Indigo, but I couldn't read his eyes in the dark corridor. They were shadowed, framed in black and bloody grit. "What?"

"Are you okay?"

"Fine." A blatant lie, made all the more apparent as soon as I snapped it. Hell, even Hooker didn't buy it. He hummed a question. I grimaced. "My head hurts," I added when neither of the men moved. "I think my chipset took a knock. I'll have it worked out when I get back." By someone. Maybe.

"You okay to keep going?" Indigo asked, his light shifting to my feet.

I frowned at the reflected glitter, some painted with flecks of black and gilded red by the emergency lights. "Better question," I suggested evenly. "Can you force me not to?"

Indigo's mouth tightened. He couldn't, and trying now didn't promise anything but grief.

He surprised me. "Just be careful," he suggested, as gently as the environment allowed.

Another knock to my calm.

How, exactly, was I supposed to do that? Should I ask my chipset to stop misbehaving? Should I ask my brain to scrub every reminder of Nanji's ghost from my mind?

"I'll get right on that," I muttered, curling my fingers more firmly over the Sauger's stock. "Let's get this shit done and out."

"What was that?"

We both turned to frown at Hooker. He wasn't watching us; his faceplate was focused on the slagged lab. His flashlight burned a stark hollow through the dark, picking out rippled metal and streaks of charred black.

I glanced inside impatiently. "What?"

"I thought I saw–" He stopped. Thought about it, I bet, because he shook his head. "Never mind."

"You sure?" Indigo asked.

"For fuck's sake, Digo, stop second-guessing everything," I snapped, and stomped away from the men, long stride carrying me past the window – past the ghostly memory of Nanjali Koupra, eyes wide and fearful as she hammered on shattered, nonexistent glass.

I'd be carrying that one for a while. Even when I'd do my damnedest to walk away.

They followed me down the hall in silence. The lights hummed faintly, thanks to the backup generators feeding the place around us. Unlike my earlier visit, they didn't turn off and on, and there was no echoed sound of booted feet sprinting for the uplink lab we left behind. I led them through wine-red shadows and endless, stark halls, turning left when we passed through automatic double doors imprinted with text on the side that closed behind us.

B L O C K – C.

All personnel to be armed beyond this point.

Right direction.

"Oh, good," Hooker said, grasping at whatever humor he could. "Does that mean we can put our weapons away now?"

"Be my guest," Indigo offered.

"Heh." He rolled his shoulders uneasily. "No thanks. This place gives me the heebie-jeebies."

So cute. I just wanted to pat him on the helmet.

"I don't know where this hall leads," I began, only to lock it down when Indigo's hand jerked sharply up, fingers straight and together. *Silence.* His head cocked, cheekbones gilded red and thrust into sharp contrast as he stared at something – nothing – past my head.

I listened, straining to hear anything over the crackling in my skull.

"Damn," he finally muttered. "I thought I heard gunfire."

"I didn't hear anything," Hooker offered.

Neither did I, but I didn't bother saying so. My whole setup was suffering.

"All right, let's go," he said instead.

"Are you sure?" I asked, sardonic as all hell and completely failing to hide it.

"Go find a necro cock to suck, Riko."

It wasn't as sharp as I'd expected. "Let me know if you start feeling techish," I shot back, but I was talking to his back. He moved ahead without me, ignoring protocol just to leave me in his wake. It didn't sting. Not like everything else. This was just funny.

"Um…" Hooker hesitated.

I snorted. "Go on," I told him, amused. "He'd probably prefer you on his ass than me."

"Okay. You can watch mine," Hooker told me, and without an expression behind his faceplate, I could only assume he was being serious. He followed Indigo, Sauger H2 up and ready.

I took him at his word.

Hooker's ass wasn't all that bad in that armor.

Indigo followed the corridor, gray panels occasionally dotted by stains I didn't have time to check out. Probably better we didn't, anyway. The knot in my head thickened until I was sure my brain had wrapped corded nerves around my chipset.

When a door slid open at Indigo's passing, we all jumped. The gun leaped in Hooker's hands; the light slid over the black entry, picked out more gray flooring, and he laughed nervously.

Indigo's shoulders visibly eased. "Automatic sen–"

Hooker's jumpy chuckle died on a strangled scream.

I didn't even see it move. It was on him, human-shaped and wearing the remnants of scrubs that used to be white before blood and putrescence had stained it. It rode Hooker's chest, tearing at his helmet. Thick, wet sounds escaped from its discolored mouth.

I raised my Sauger, my heart slamming hard against my ribs as adrenaline rocked through my veins – my head – but Hooker's weapon arced, spraying bullets wildly across the hall. It scored the wall beside me, the ground at my feet. I jumped back, screamed a warning.

Too late. Pressure spattered my right leg; pain sheared through my awareness, blossomed like a river of rusty razorblades into my synapses. I strangled on my words, fell to the hall floor.

Indigo reached for Hooker's flailing arm, but the kid spun violently, his screaming magnified in the feed. *"Get it off!"*

"Hooker!" I tried again through clenched teeth. "Stop flailing before–!"

No use. Terror rode him. He staggered backwards; his shoulder rebounded off the door jamb.

I tried to lurch to my feet; I screamed Hooker's name as seven more hands reached out of the room. Stained, twisted fingers dug into the seams of Hooker's armor. Two necros fell into the light, yanked into view by Hooker's writhing panic, and I saw veined skin flapping loosely, foul teeth bared, and milky eyes staring emptily from sockets turning black with necrosis.

Whoever they were, whatever they'd done, it was too late to help them. To help any of us.

Clawed fingers found Indigo's arm, another grabbed at Hooker. Digo shouted, wrenched back so hard that necrotic fingernails tore free and splattered blackened blood against the wall. Rich, vibrant crimson lines blossomed from pale furrows carved into Indigo's arm, just above the thicker plating.

He swore, over and over.

I tried to stand, to reach for Hooker's spastically thrashing limbs. He careened into the other side of the door.

The hall echoed with the soggy, juddering rattle of clashing tech and failing organs.

Hooker was still screaming as they dragged him into the room.

The door slid closed.

I stared, wide-eyed and shaken, and listened to them peel back armor like it was nothing; listened to Hooker's gagging, sobbing, hysterical screams – saw it happen in my imagination with effortless clarity.

The salty, coppery odor of blood and the sour flush of voided intestines filled my nose.

Indigo hauled me to my feet. "*Run,*" he ordered grimly, his dusky skin sallow. The whites of his eyes were clearly visible as he slung my arm over his shoulder and forced a pace that sent knives of agony up my bleeding shin.

A desperately long thirty seconds later, gunfire shattered through the feed; echoed faintly behind us.

Hooker finally stopped screaming.

27

"That wasn't his H2," I gasped, hobbling with every ounce of determination I possessed. No way – *no way* was I going to end up as some necrotic fuckhead's lunch. I'd shoot myself first. I'd take every last necro down with me.

Indigo slapped a palm against the door that closed behind us. "Cover me."

I sagged against the corridor wall, blood only one part of the thick soup of odors filling my nose. Decaying flesh, the stench of fear and rot, stale air – I gritted my teeth, head churning, guts roiling.

Indigo slapped a disc against the panels, a startlingly bright green flash sealing the seam.

My chin jerked, though I didn't take my eyes off the hall. "Did you hear me? That wasn't an H2!"

"I heard you." He thumbed the small black patch inset over matte black keys – he'd always painted over his tech, even the keypads – and turned to look at me.

It wasn't a calm regard.

Terror flared his nostrils, filled his wide-eyed stare. He breathed heavily, sweat a dull sheen matting his dark hair. In that fear, I found the same kinship I'd learned to recognize over the years of cock-over-sideways runs and surprises.

I felt the way he looked. Worse, maybe, because I had to

sit here and juggle the crossed frequencies turning my skull to a mix of dissonant chaos. If I could do it? I'd be damned if he gave up on me now.

I exhaled slowly, forcing a measure of calm.

"Plan?" I croaked, my sweaty grip sliding inside my glove.

"They'll have to weld through or bust the freq." He sucked down oxygen like a drowning man, sweat beading down his filthy jaw. "Can necros do either?"

"How the fuck should I know?" I snarled, swiping at the sweat plastering my hair to my cheek. "I thought they only spread through wires."

He nodded like he'd thought the same thing. "You. You sit."

"Is here the–"

"Before you bleed out," he added. Flat. Desperate.

If I died, he was on his own.

It wasn't friendship, exactly, but survival had a way of evening the odds. Guess we were on the same page, after all.

Supporting the wall with my shoulders, I slid to the floor. Pain ricocheted up my leg. "Bleeding's already slowed," I managed between clenched teeth. Sweat popped, a clammy grip across my forehead, my shoulders. "Think there's a few bullets lodged."

Indigo crouched by my extended limb. "Fuck." Not the most encouraging word, but I couldn't blame him. My leg below the knee had turned into so much shredded armor, the brutalized flesh mushroomed through the savaged metal. This armor design wasn't made to turn away bullets shot from that range, and definitely not from that caliber.

On the other hand, I hadn't lost the leg.

I sucked in a hard breath. "I can walk soon as it's done dripping." It'd hurt as long as there was lead rubbing against the bone, but it'd hurt less than getting torn apart by necrotechs. Of the options, I'd take the first.

Indigo nodded, sitting back on his haunches. He stared

down the hall, his pulse visible as it hammered through his neck. "Right." He pushed strands of sweaty hair back from his forehead. "My guess is that MetaCore came down the same way we did."

"So we've got necros infesting the place, and a corporation on our ass. Sounds like a dream."

Indigo looked up at the ceiling, his jaw tight with effort.

I knew what he was thinking. I knew, because if I were in his shoes, I'd have done the same damn thing.

But I wasn't. "We have to keep on."

"The hell we do." He stood, one hand clamping around the furrows in his arm. "Anything we find, and gods know where we'd find it," he added grimly, "isn't going to be worth the losses."

"It will be."

"Riko." He rounded on me. "This fuckup is not worth our lives."

I hissed. *"It's not a fuckup."* I elbowed back against the wall, struggled to get to my feet – gave up when he swore fluently in a mix of street and his pidgin family blend. He stepped in to flatten one hand on my shoulder.

He only did that, brought in the bits of the language bastardized on the street, when he was really scared.

I don't know why I didn't knock him on his ass. Maybe because I recognized the gesture for what it was.

I sat, obeying the pressure he applied, but I gripped his wrist with my bloody hand. "I'm not walking away."

"Riko." Indigo's laugh bit. "You aren't fucking walking, are you?"

"I'm serious!" My voice rasped, harsh and grating, but I couldn't let this go. I couldn't live with it – wouldn't be allowed to. "If I leave this hellhole without that info, my cred is shot for life. Do you get that? I. Will be. *Fucked*." And then I would be dead.

I was good, but I wasn't good enough to survive the kind

of shitstorm that a bad fall from good cred could net a runner. Not alone.

And I didn't kid myself. Until I had more to bargain with, I was totally alone.

He said nothing, staring mulishly at my gloved fingers leaving crimson streaks on his own wrist.

"Digo." His name hissed between my teeth.

It was as close to a *please* as I ever got.

His grip eased on my shoulder. Muscle and tendon flexed beneath my fingers, but he didn't pull away. When I turned, his gaze touched mine. Achingly tired, faded with pain and a fatigue that went deeper than tech and bone. "Is it worth that much to you?"

He wasn't really asking me that.

Could I live with myself if the data proved what we both were afraid of? That I was at fault?

That this was my mess? Nanji's mess?

I nodded, letting him go. "We have to keep on," I said grimly. As good an answer as I had. "Whatever is going on here, Malik wants it and I'll bet someone else will pay top cred to get it, too. Like them," I added pointedly, tipping my head back toward the sealed doors. "You think they'll pay us or just kill us?"

"What makes you think Malik will pay us?"

A fair point. And a logical one – a smidge of relief filtered in through the chaos. That was Indigo Koupra. Paranoid as shit.

"Simple," I assured him, and this time, I didn't let him stop me from dragging my sorry ass to my feet. "I'll kill him if he doesn't."

"And me?"

No, I didn't forget that he'd betrayed me to that same corporate toolshed he accused me of handing his sister to. But I'd be damned if I let him follow his sister to the grave. I put pressure on my leg, hissed in a breath when it flared, but it held my weight.

"It's like this," I finally told him. I eased my weight off the leg, then on. Every shot of pain, every twang of abused nerves, made it easier to get used to. I met his gaze over the incandescence of our lowered torches. "Right now, you need me to get your ass out of here alive. I need you to get my ass into that security system. It's a match made in heaven."

"Or a one-way road to hell."

"Yeah, well." I stripped off my useless gloves, dropping them to the floor. They landed with a damp splat. "If you wanted an easy payday, you should have listened to your momma and joined a whorehouse."

His laugh surprised me. It wasn't warm, not even amused, but it did something to ease the tension. Made the air breathable again. As the crack of sound faded away, he caught my shoulder again, his bloody grip tight.

It was a move that stole a little bit of my anger. Turned a little more of my fear into something stronger than nerves.

This time, it wasn't hatred between us. Solidarity had finally snapped into place. Familiar, instinctual.

I didn't know how long it'd last, but as long as it got us through this shitstorm, I'd take it. "I'd kill to have Boone down here," I said ruefully.

"Yeah. Me too." He didn't push it any farther than that. Letting me go, he gestured down the hall. "Stay to the center, try not to trigger any of those doors."

"You got it."

I took the lead again, keeping as close to the middle of the hall as I could. I covered the left side, Digo covered the right, Saugers held at the ready. For almost ten minutes – endless, nausea-inducing long minutes – nothing else moved. I heard no outside sounds, saw no movement. If dead eyes watched us from the black windows, I couldn't see them.

But I was positive they were there.

I jerked as something in my neural frequency cracked a warning, a single second before Indigo checked his arm plate and said tightly, "They broke the lock. Haul ass."

The stomp of booted feet echoed from somewhere behind us.

I took off in a dead run, struggling and failing to stay in the center. Digo didn't try. He sprinted like a man on his last legs. I didn't stop, not even when the mechanical *whoosh* of two doors whirred open in our wake.

I picked up my pace, locking back groans of effort as it rocked my wounded leg. Indigo followed, but he said nothing, probably thinking the same thing I was: if the necros were attracted by noise, maybe they'd give us a miss and go right for the corporate boots pounding behind us.

It probably would have worked, too, if I didn't round a corner to find myself swallowed by pitch black. My light picked out open floor but nothing else. The quality of the space changed – it felt open, wider. I stopped. Indigo collided into my back and I grunted a shushing warning before he could ask why we'd halted.

The shadows sucked the sound away, bandied it around like a toy before eating it completely.

Our lights crisscrossed into the black space. No walls on either side of us, but I picked out the faint outline of what looked like chairs. Tables. A kind of commons?

I hesitated.

Anything could be waiting in here. Necros, corpses, hell, munitions that could blow sky-high, rigged by survivors. Calling out would be a death warrant; staying silent could get us as dead, just as messily.

I lowered my weapon, highlighting stark gray flooring in front of my feet, and a streak of white tile angling left.

Gunfire erupted from the hall behind us. Lots of it. Guess our necro surprise party had done the job.

Indigo tapped my left shoulder. I turned left, took one step and hesitated again. My gaze slid right; the short hair on the back of my head prickled.

He prodded my shoulder.

I reached back, caught his arm and pulled him right.

"What–"

I squeezed in warning. I couldn't explain. It wouldn't make sense anyway. I had a gut feeling.

If we moved left, we were dead.

Although, as we walked as fast as we dared through the empty chamber – stepping around overturned chairs and scattered containers revealed by our laughably thin lights – I reasoned that we may just be dead a different way.

Necro rending. MetaCore bullets.

Whatever.

The echoes behind us gained in intensity.

My guts turned to a frozen knot of dread – no, of *panic*. Something felt wrong; getting more wrong by the second. Something bad was happening and I didn't know what to call it. Where it was coming from. Paranoia jammed spikes of terror into my eye sockets and *twisted*, and I stopped dead as the first tinny reverberations of bullets spattering the walls behind us sent shrill echoes through the room.

I sucked in a shuddering breath.

Ting. Metal skated across metal. Bounced once.

Indigo's body crowded mine, his arm wrapped around my chest and hauled me hard to the right. We hit the floor as a column of orange flame turned the dark into a searing flare of eye-scalding light. Heat licked over us, too far away to cause damage but close enough to smell the same acrid stench of chemical-laden fire that had swallowed Falk.

Ting, ting. Ting!

"Move!"

We pushed off the floor with street-honed speed and instinct, tearing across the chamber as two more gouts of flame roiled up in our wake. In the blinding flash, I saw the remains of tables and chairs, discarded armor and bodies. Chains of them. Row upon row of corpses laid out along the right side – exactly where that pale path would have planted us.

The last grenade erupted too close to dodge, closer than I expected it to flare. The detonation stripped what was left of my night vision. The blast wave pummeled into our backs, sending me ass over elbows and shoving Indigo out to the middle of the open chamber.

I hit the ground, propelled so hard that my teeth bounced off the floor and my feet tried to rebound off my head. Things stretched, popped. Pain didn't even rate against adrenaline. I rolled with it best as I could, collided ribs first into an overturned table, and grabbed at its edge as lights filled my straining vision.

Three, four, no... *Fuck*. Ghostly afterimages peppered my sight as I struggled to count them. Four? Six? More than two.

I heard no communication, but that probably meant they had the same kind of sound-dampening helmets we'd been using before we broke them. The grenade fires died, leaving glowing embers where flammable materials had taken in the heat.

Pop. Light bloomed, a blue nimbus struggling against the dark and fed by more glow rods. They hit the ground, thrown from the entrance. I peered around the table, hauled my Sauger up and sighted down the weapon – nice little cluster of corporate fuckheads they made.

Just in time for something in my skull to go *snap*.

A gasp wheezed to my right.

My finger froze on the trigger.

The wheeze turned into a rattle. Moist, pulpy.

Oxygen turned to ice in my lungs. Very slowly, I turned my head. Sweat slid down my temple; fear turned it clammy in my palm.

The corpses rippled.

Noise, fire, the blast impact. Enough to wake the dead.

Or the converted.

Something thick and... and *wet* popped inside my consciousness. Something I didn't recognize, that didn't live inside my head but left me reeling, feeling as if my skull had peeled back and exposed all my nerves.

Eradicate.

A directive. A warning. A *need*. It swallowed me whole.

Limbs trembled in that row of corpses, slack mouths gaping and heads flopping as silhouettes thrust upward from the bloody, gory swell. They didn't stand; they erupted, flowed into position, and they took no time to calculate. As if they already knew exactly where the food stood, blobs of flesh peeled off the shuddering pile and turned to lethal hunters.

MetaCore fired first. Muzzle flash sparked like fireworks in the blue glow, and one necro's legs were suddenly splayed awkwardly three feet behind its body as it skidded to the ground, smearing blackened blood in its wake.

Another darted past it, leaping at the fan of enforcers in sleek armor.

One came for me.

Eradicate.

I turned just in time, bracing my back against the fallen table and locking the trigger. The necro had been female, her slack face still wearing traces of lipstick and lurid blush. Her eyes flashed at me, ocular replacements dilating as my clip emptied in less than a second. It shredded her chest, forcing her to come in lopsided, one arm dragging. It didn't stop her.

Over her shoulder, Indigo sprinted for a door at the far end of the chamber. *S E C U* gleamed in large white letters, the rest charred beyond recognition.

I set my jaw, rolling out from behind cover as she threw herself at me, once-manicured talons extended. She'd cared about her appearance while alive. Her nails were still bright red, though congealed remains swung from one hand like snot dried into a clinging web.

She caught herself gracelessly, lacking the wicked speed

I'd seen in Nanji and some of the other necros. I dropped a kick to her shoulders that forced her face into the underside of the sideways table, then pounded the stock of my Sauger 877 into the back of her head. She screamed, ragged and breathless, fingers scrabbling at the floor, the table. Again and again, I hammered at her, until the chipset buried in the base of her skull tore out through her jaw, falling with a wet *splat* on the floor beside us.

She convulsed, then went still.

Gasping for breath, I looked up. MetaCore had knotted, and necros closed in with the single-minded determination of extermination.

Some had seen me.

Fuck.

I turned, dropping my gore-plastered Sauger, and sprinted for the security door.

Gunfire filled the chamber, sparks lit the ground beside me, but if they were firing at me or the necros between me and them – or if the necros themselves had any security upgrades; a terrifying prospect – I didn't know. I ran with blood thick in my nose, my skull hammering. I raced across carnage-slick ground, skidding more than once, and caught myself on the door.

It wouldn't open. The panel beside it hung open, circuits blackened.

I hammered on the door with my synthetic fist. *Clang!* "Indigo!"

I heard nothing on my feed.

That son of a bitch. If he wasn't dead, I was going to kill him.

"Indigo!"

I reached behind me, pulling the CounterTech from the harness and plastered my back against the locked door. My hands shook – rage. Bitter, vicious. A necro wearing the black BDUs of security barreled down on me.

I sighted down my arm and pulled the trigger. Once, twice. A third time as he staggered. His skull collapsed.

He hit the floor. Twitched.

And dragged himself slowly across it.

Fuck me. A 9mm wasn't enough to take out the base of his skull. I'd need precision sighting, and I wasn't equipped for that kind of aim.

Surprise, more tech I didn't have.

I dropped the useless firearm, turned and wedged my metal fingers into the seam of the door. "Open," I told it, straining to override the bearings holding it in place.

It didn't budge.

I widened my stance, sucked in a breath and pulled with everything I had. A woman screamed to my right, muffled but jagged; I didn't look. I blocked out the necro dragging itself towards me, the gory scene behind me, and *pulled*.

I heard the servos in my arm spin. *Felt* my shoulder girdle snap taut, then strain. Pain lanced up my shoulder, into my back. The muscles around my scapula twanged, popped. White-hot agony dragged across my senses as the reinforcement in my biceps lengthened, hit max, and then detached from the muscle holding it together. I screamed. The filthy claws of a necro gouged into my thigh, dug in and held fast. Pain on pain.

The door opened an inch. It was enough.

All at once, the bearings broke, the lock gave, and the panel slid open. I fell inside, my left arm hanging useless and limp as I smeared the ground with my face.

The necro clawed at me. I kicked hard, my boot tore off his jaw with a sickening pop. He still advanced, nothing in his empty, milky eyes: no hatred, no fear. No pain.

Scrabbling for the .525 caliber pinned between me and the floor, I rolled, trying to shake off the necro's grip; flesh gave before he did, and I shrieked as he fell off me, a hunk of my thigh in his bloody grip.

If I survived this, I was going to school Malik on what armor was cunting *for*. Bullets were one thing, but it didn't hold for shit against whatever these necros had going for them. Mantis should've been better than this.

I struggled to sit up, abs cramping with the effort, and clocked the necro with the heavy gun. It reeled. Taking advantage of the second it gave me, I shot it pointblank. The recoil nearly popped my elbow inside out. The report tore through the chamber, bounced back on a riddled sea of echoed assault rifles.

In eerie, surreal echo of the first sec goon I'd killed down here, its head burst.

Finally. I got to see an exploding head.

Laughing seemed inappropriate. Hysteria, on the other hand, battered at my mental faculties like it didn't give a damn.

I dragged myself upright, shaking off the limp, twitching body. It took effort – so much energy – but I staggered to the door. Slamming the hand holding the gun against the panel beside it shoved the doors closed again.

There was a click behind me.

I turned, Adjudicator barely up, and sighted between two familiar blue eyes.

Dark. Focused.

Tinted too far into gray to be nothing but shadow.

My linker was fighting nanoshock, and at the rate this shithole was going, he'd hit corruption before we got out.

What did they call this?

Oh, yeah. Déjà vu. That feeling like I'd done all this before.

Indigo froze, his Sauger pointed at me. My revolver pointed at him.

Stalemate.

I looked at the weapon, at the flashlight centered on my chest. Blood ran steadily down my leg, seeping into my boot. Putting weight on it squished. It also hurt like a motherfucker.

My left arm hung limply, ignoring every effort to move.

I'd snapped something. Or everything.

"This would be a lot funnier if you had any Mexican in you." My voice shook. Adrenaline. Pain. Nanoshock, too, maybe. I'd pushed them too far again; didn't rest when I'd had the chance.

Ass. It's like this place wanted me dead, and I was determined not to die according to script.

My arm dropped. The gun was too heavy for this kind of patience.

He stared at me. Hard. Then, jerking his chin at the door, he lowered his weapon and turned away. "They autolock," he said. "Come in. You want to see this."

I glanced at the doors. Looked back at his rigid, armored back as he vanished into another door at the end of the narrow room. A foyer, maybe. Some kind of waiting room.

Maybe they did autolock. Maybe he was full of shit.

I didn't have it in me to argue.

Wasted time, at this point, would see us dead. Chewed up by the things out there or gone necro ourselves.

No. Just no. I'd escaped this hell once. I'd do it again, *with* my Koupra in tow, or so fucking help me...

I followed him, limping badly. The door at the other end opened as I approached, so at least I didn't have to break my other arm to get in.

This room gave every impression of lockdown, security only. A row of tables took up one wall, the kind of tables bodies get strapped to, and a bank of computers took up the next. Lockers dotted the bare space in between, each labeled neatly. *Gomez. Jones. Dent. Rogers. Atwater.*

A wide viewing screen looked out into the dark chamber, where orange muzzle flash and gouts of flame briefly illuminated the struggling necros and the fuckheads they danced with.

Indigo hunched over a computer, his isolated unit already

wired in. He didn't look up at me. Didn't say anything. The blue text on the screen and the corresponding amber data on his unit lit his face, but all I saw under black grit and blood was an empty slate. Nothing. No *hey, sorry about that* or *sure glad you're alive*.

Nothing at all.

Then I saw the body laid out on the third table, dusky feet pallid in death, and it all made sudden, achingly logical sense.

"So," I said. Desperately nonchalant. "Guess you found Nanji."

28

I didn't know why she'd be in here, except maybe she posed some kind of security risk, even as a corpse. Maybe especially as a corpse, given the chaos outside that window.

Half of her face and most of one arm was charred, leaving one delicate ear untouched and most of her back and legs. Her skin, a softer shade of Indigo's brown, had turned gray in death. She was laid out on her stomach, leaving her ass exposed and baring the raw, ruined channels of her back. They'd torn out her spine. The back of her ribs.

The tech was gone.

I dragged myself to the table. "What did they do to her?"

He didn't answer. He didn't have to. It was obvious what they'd done. Removed everything, left her empty and spineless and alone.

I swallowed hard, unable to scrape the image of her as I saw her last from my mind. All that shiny chrome. The black tint to her blood. She'd still been alive. Fighting, and *alive*.

I'm sorry.

Necros didn't fucking apologize.

I was too late for her then. Too late to save her, too late to be the one to end her misery.

Just another fuckup in a fantastic array of them, wasn't it?

And now her brother looked on, that same gray tint to

his eyes. The same thickening black smear as his nanos overcompensated for the hell I'd put him through.

The ache in my skull pounded in time with my heart. A vise wrapped around my head as I reached out with my shaking hand, the Adjudicator throwing back trembling glints of flickering blue light. My knuckles skimmed over ragged, blackened flesh. The smell of necrosis hung thick and rank in the air.

Indigo stood, the chair creaking as his weight left it. Dimly, the crackle and echo of repeated gunfire peppered my awareness, but it was the small handheld he thrust into my face that grabbed me.

The vid screen filled with silent footage.

A chopshop. Maybe the one upstairs. Nanjali lay on one of six tables – tables remarkably similar to the one she occupied now. She was asleep, a mask banded over her head. I stared, empty and cold, as I recognized myself from behind. Bleached hair swept to the side. Black long-sleeve shirt, black pants, boots hidden by the frame.

A man gestured from the other side of my girlfriend's naked body. He wore black BDUs, a black T-shirt. I couldn't see his face, but he carried a small tablet. I gestured with my metal arm.

Imprinted my good thumb on the tablet.

My guts twisted. I felt as if I'd been kicked in the stomach.

As soon as the man powered down the tablet, I turned away. From him. From Nanji, quiet and sleeping so innocently. I didn't see my own face. I wanted to. I needed to know what the hell I'd been thinking. What my face looked like when I sold my girlfriend to this necrotic shithole.

The man in black gestured again. Four more men in identical clothes, eerily familiar, stepped into view from all sides. I turned, said something. Raised a hand and beckoned them.

Indigo turned it off.

I knew the end. Me, only a couple days ago. Waking up on a metal table. Blood in my head. Ghosts of nightmares.

I shuddered, something cold wrapped inside my chest. I remembered – didn't I? Did I remember waking up before that? Sluggish. Angry. Afraid.

So much pain in my head; so much noise, until I screamed and screamed...

The same sense of panic I felt in Orchard's lab clawed at me.

No. It was real. I refused to deal with post-traumatic stress based on a fucking dream.

I dragged my gaze to Indigo.

He watched me, the skin over his cheekbones so taut, his olive skin looked sickly yellow beneath the grime. I'd never seen him look so fragile, as if one wrong word would shatter him.

If I felt hollow, he looked it – between the two of us, I couldn't name anyone more fucked up than we were. He dashed one arm over his eye, smearing more blood. More grime.

Thud! The glass pane across the viewing room rattled.

I blinked, staring at him as if I'd never seen him before. As if I didn't know what my own skin felt like. Everything turned inside out on me. Questions turned into a screaming accusation inside my own head and I couldn't slog through any of it.

I couldn't force myself to function.

This was what it was like to have my world ripped inside out, huh? I chuckled. It broke on a ragged sound.

"Fuck." Indigo leaned over the table. "Are you seriously *crying?*"

"I don't cry," I snarled, but damn, my throat hurt with it. My chest ached. My eyes burned. My only working fist clenched over Nanji's cold, dead flesh and when I inhaled, I shuddered to smell her rotting flesh.

"Ah, shit. No payoff's worth this." Indigo rounded the table, gripped my shoulder and bodily turned me from the slab of his sister's corpse. He caught my face in his grimy hand, tilting it up so I had no choice but to meet his eyes. Blackening, dot by dot. "*Breathe*, Ree. Why am I the logical one right now?"

He was right. Indigo was professional as hell, but I was the splatter specialist. Those of us who get this far in the business don't get there because death bothers us.

But this was different. I couldn't explain how, it was just *different*. I squeezed my eyes shut. "Give me a smegging second."

Thud! The glass cracked.

"No time." The fingers at my cheeks tilted, forcing my face up. "Look at me."

Guilt slashed at me from every side. Hating everything about this – the weakness clawing at my guts, the wrenching uncertainty of my own reliability – I obeyed that thread of gritted command in his voice and clasped his wrist tightly before he wrenched me off balance.

He held my stare for a moment more, making sure he had my attention. When I didn't look away, when I made no move to throw him off – hell, maybe when he found what he was looking for in my face, his mouth twisted. "This is three shades of fucked up."

"I know," I croaked.

"Tell me that isn't you."

I couldn't. It was me. Right there, clear as day. My hair, my arm.

Indigo's wrist flexed beneath my grip, tensile muscles tightening. "Look me in the eye, and tell me that isn't you on that feed," he said tightly. "If you do that, I'll spend every waking second cracking this thing until I figure out where it came from. Do you understand me?"

I wanted to. Everything I was screamed that I'd never sell out my teammates – never betray Nanji and Indigo. Not like this. Never to *this*. I hated the suit sector. I despised authority.

I liked my team and the freedom they'd afforded me.

But how could I be sure?

Thud! Thud!

The echoes of the necro assault cracked through the small room.

I stared into Digo's blackening eyes, read the anguish there. Anger, hurt, yeah, but there was more. Something violent and desperate.

Something challenging.

My dead arm dragged at my ruined shoulder brace. It hurt. *Thud!* The glass cracked.

"Riko?" Indigo pulled me closer, invaded my space until I had no choice but to inhale the same air he breathed out, face the demons in his stare the way I wouldn't face mine.

Maybe I wouldn't do it for me, maybe I could pretend like I didn't give a damn, but Digo didn't deserve that. And hell, I wasn't enough of an asshole to try.

I owed him more than that.

"Tell me." He didn't sound angry. His voice unraveled, until I couldn't be sure what was fury and what was demand.

Indigo Koupra was pleading with me.

I closed my eyes, back teeth grinding. It was too late for Nanji – maybe it was too late for me. But fuck me if I didn't feel a little less alone. At least for now.

"I can't," I said sharply, and wrenched my face from his grasp, planting my hand against his chest to insert enough distance to breathe in. He had to dance back a few steps to catch his balance.

I steadied myself against Nanji's cold metal table. Cold, gray skin.

Beyond saving.

But I wasn't. *We* weren't. This was not the place I intended to die.

"I can't say for sure that's not me," I said. "But I can tell you right now that the me standing here wouldn't make that choice. I wouldn't sell my team."

Maybe I lied.

How the *fuck* would I know?

The glass behind Indigo fractured.

He jumped, half-turning. "Fine," he managed, strained even past fatigue. Any more highs, any additional lows, and a lesser man would have cracked. He was almost there; I could read it in his posture. Too tense. Fragile as fuck – I'd never forget it again.

Indigo cared in ways I'd only ever taken for granted. And it was that caring that might cost me his life, too.

Yeah. I was a real class act.

"I'll move heaven and earth to crack that shit wide open, so let's get it together," he said, eyes on the window, "'cause this isn't holding anymore."

"Done." I reached behind me, picked up the Adjudicator and forced my aching, shattered muscles to obey.

Indigo gave me an out. I knew it was only a matter of time before he regretted it, but for now, I had time to find out what the fuck had happened. All I knew for sure was that if that was me, I had *not* been in control of myself. Which meant somebody had.

Nobody set me up and lived to gloat about it.

Rage. It filled me. Carved a hole inside me and sheared through my defenses. Self-inflicted anger, chaos and regret; disgust and fury melded into a devastating conflagration.

This is why you don't piss off a splatter specialist. We have too much broken shit to burn.

Necros pressed against the glass. Beating on it. Hammering on it. One swung a stolen Manticore against it. Again and again. The tempered glass went white under the pressure.

Eradicate.

Wherever the word came from, whatever it meant, it was an order I'd happily fulfill. My way.

Spiderweb fissures spread across the whole pane, turning visibility to nothing.

I pushed away from the cold table. Turned my back on Nanjali for the last time. *Sorry, baby.* "Did you get what you needed from the network?"

For a moment, Indigo said nothing. I glanced at him, a quick survey to make sure he hadn't keeled over, and caught him studying me with an odd expression. Like he couldn't quite decide if he'd just made the best choice possible or the worst. Wary mistrust and a vicious kind of hope.

All kinds of fucked up.

I raised my chin. "We in this?"

He nodded, mouth pinched into a grim line. "We're in this. I need one minute."

"You have thirty seconds," I countered, and kicked over a locker. It crashed hard, spilling its contents – clothing and a woman's purse – across the floor. I shoved it into place in front of the door.

Indigo flinched as another section of the window shuddered, hammered beneath shapeless shadows. He checked his comp unit screen. "Twenty-five seconds. What are you planning?"

"To get you out alive." I refilled the Adjudicator, awkward as shit with one hand. "Whatever you do, don't stop running."

"You can count on that. But how do we *get* out?"

I smiled, brain crackling. I didn't know where the knowledge came from; maybe the same bank of ghostly images that remembered white-gloved figures shoving me down. The same memory that said I'd beat my head against a wall to make the pain stop. They flashed through my mind like the vid Indigo had shown me, grainy and small. Flickering mirages.

I'd sort out what was real and what was wishful cunting thinking when I got out of here.

"When it's clear," I told him, "go out and turn left. There's a narrow corridor just past the security arrow pointing back here."

"Riko?"

"Pay attention." I spared him a glance. Terror carved deep brackets into the side of his whitened mouth. His weight splayed on the balls of his feet, he looked half ready to bolt from the fracturing glass – and the comp unit attached to the systems in front of it.

That he stayed for that data said a lot more about him than it did me.

I hauled the Adjudicator into position. "Gather your energy," I warned. "You look about six fucks past nanoshock."

"I'm fine."

Sure, and I was the president of this shitshow. "Are you ready?"

"Can you be ready for something like this?"

Point made. I shook my head. "Promise me something, Digo."

His brow furrowed. "No suicide speeches."

"Shut the fuck up and listen," I snarled. "If I don't get out of this, you get to the bottom of everything." My arm trembled, screaming against the weight. "If that *is* me..."

His eyes flinched, jaw locked so hard his cheekbones gleamed sickly pale, but he nodded.

Fucking A.

"I'll find out," he promised. One long-fingered hand spread over the comp unit. "Vids have markers, patterns. I'll figure out where it came from, who made it, and then *we* will fuck some shit up."

All things considered, I couldn't ask for better.

"Hold on to your ass," I warned, and fired the Adjudicator into the window. A fist-sized hole exploded through the pane, tearing through a necro's head as the .525 destroyed fractured glass and bone like it was nothing. The cracks spread to meet the other knot of creaking fissures, and before Indigo could stop me, I sprinted, jumped, and barreled through the center.

I would not go down like prey.

The impact stole my breath, but not my rage. Glass erupted in a white shower of shards and dust. Bodies collided with mine, swept back by the impact of the shattered pane, and I rolled with the momentum until I hit a crooked bank of chairs. Springing to my feet should have hurt; it didn't. I felt nothing but frenzy – I needed to end this, to kill, rend limb from limb. These skull-fucking wastes of tech, these necrotic pieces of walking flesh, *would not* take me down.

I had shit to do.

I fired twice. I don't know what the shit was keeping my arm from tearing itself apart in the recoil, but I wouldn't question it. Two necros hit the floor, twitching.

Three more came at me.

Two others wobbled to a standstill, turned on Indigo as he clambered through the empty frame, the computer cradled under his arm.

I dodged the first gurgling necro – a man, thin and balding where his scalp hadn't been ripped away – and sighted down my trembling arm. Despite the knot of shamblers around me, the necro reaching for Digo earned a bullet in its spine.

The thing staggered back, splattered with blackened blood and glittering shards of spinal implantation decimated by the messy round. Fingernails found my exposed thigh and tore it open again; teeth locked onto my metal arm and splintered, a sickening sound that raised the hair on my body in visceral revulsion.

Another necro jumped on my shoulders. My knees hit the floor. Black spots floated in my vision.

"Riko!"

"Go," I snarled into the feed.

Nanoshock and I were old friends by this point. I could feel my nanos straining, feel my flesh surging, bloating with the little fuckers. Maybe I'd die here, but it wouldn't be alone. And it sure as shit wouldn't be with Digo – my linker had to get to the bottom of this mess.

When it came right down to it, I'd trust nobody else.

The necro on my shoulders fell off. I was struggling to pull away from the jagged fingernails in my leg, blood running fresh and wet, when the tech freak jerked wildly, screaming in a guttural, too-human exhale that echoed and re-echoed. It collapsed, blood seeping from its ears and nose.

I fired a fourth shot, dropping a crawler. The necro trying to gum my useless arm blew backwards in a gory spray. The ozone stench of frying tech filled the air.

Indigo left his EMP knife in the still-shuddering corpse and hauled me to my feet. Its head, I noted, did not explode.

I didn't get a chance to catch my breath.

Three more crawled from the hall we'd come in from. One stopped to bury its teeth in a black-armored figure, cutting off a short, sharp scream, but the others saw us first. Live prey.

I struggled to straighten. Indigo yanked me upright so hard, I nearly collapsed at his feet.

"Move!" he yelled, and hell if I know where I found the strength to do it. I leapt over the knot circling me, planting a boot in one's face to do it, and hauled what was left of my hobbled ass.

The door I'd promised was mercifully unlocked. Maintenance tools littered the narrow corridor, overturned crates beside a mangled body. Wild animals wouldn't do this much damage.

We leapt over it, sprinting – or, in my case, staggering – for the exit I'd said was on the other end.

Miracle of miracles, I was right.

The door on the far end opened to reveal an elevator exactly like the one we'd entered through. Exactly, except for the knot of spastic necros inside.

They grabbed Indigo, jerking him off his feet, clawing and tearing. He screamed; I didn't slow down, launching myself inside the elevator car to hammer on one with the butt of the Adjudicator. It turned, empty sockets glaring at me, mouth leaking dark plasma and exhaling decaying rot.

Digo dug his fingers into one's throat, surprising him when it tore like old cloth. The thing's esophagus came out in a dripping, bloody tube. The necro jerked. I kicked it out of the rocking elevator car, ducking under the first's sloppy grab, and jammed the barrel of my gun under my assailant's whiskered, slack-jawed face.

Firing the Adjudicator that close blew a hole through my eardrum. My vision turned red with it.

I howled, dropping my now empty weapon.

Another report dragged fiery streaks of agony across my hearing as Indigo filled the last necro full of bullets. As it staggered, blinded, he shoved it out with the other one and jabbed the command to close the door.

I reeled. He grabbed my shoulders.

"Riko!" I heard him through the feed in my right ear, mostly. My left, like my arm, was deader than shit. "Are you okay?"

I caught his wrist with my functional hand, prying it loose. "Let go," I rasped. "Hurts."

He obeyed without fight. "What the hell happened?"

"Blew out my ear." I bared my teeth at him. "Didn't see them in here. There's more above."

He looked up, then back at me. "How do you *know*?"

I shook my head. I didn't know how I knew. It was the same way I'd known about the elevator here. I knew because I knew.

Whatever he saw in my face – something behind gristle and blood and thicker spatter – it seemed to be enough. Wordlessly, he refilled his handgun, another CounterTech, and braced both feet.

"Other side," I managed.

He turned.

"– ear me?" The feed crackled, another note of disharmony in my sea of white noise and pain. "Vid Team, respond!"

"We're in range again," Indigo said, but that wasn't optimism I heard in his voice. It was warning. "Control! We're coming out with necros hot on our asses and more above."

"I read you." It was the woman again. "Do you have the data?"

"We're rolling out with nanoshock," he added flatly. "Is a medivac prepped?"

"Do you have the data?" control repeated.

Digo bared bloody teeth. "Yes."

"A rescue unit has been sent to your location, you need to meet it on open street."

I wondered what would have happened if Digo'd said no.

The doors slid open, revealing a road nearly pitch dark compared to the lights we'd come from.

I groaned my frustration as another wave of noise split my skull. The elevator echoed hollowly; I didn't realize I'd slammed my forehead against the side until Indigo swore and jerked me away from the panel. "What the fuck!"

"Hurts," I groaned, shuddering under the dual pressure – memory and reality. So much screaming in my head. So much pain.

I'd been here before. This awful noise in my head was more familiar than I remembered it being.

Indigo wrapped his arm around my neck, hooking me in a lazy man's headlock.

I didn't fight him. The added pain didn't help, anyway.

"ETA?" he demanded.

"Three minutes," control said calmly.

"Fuck me," he growled, and wrenched me out of the elevator. He turned right – I snagged his arm and dragged him left, deeper into the intersecting alleys flanking the building. "Riko, we need open street."

"You get open air," I rasped, and lurched into a staggering kind of jog that wouldn't outrun anything.

A juddering, gurgling grind of ruined flesh filled the alley behind us.

"Keep moving." Indigo's voice spiked with fear.

"Up. We need up." I blinked through bleary eyes, everything I focused on edged with black. I was reaching total nano meltdown.

Indigo grabbed my good arm, whirling me around. "Up!" he yelled, pointing directly over our heads.

I followed the line of his finger. It shook.

A fire escape. Just like the ones that dotted every building around us.

Relief quickly sank into despair. "Can't."

"Yes, you can."

Silhouettes filled the alley mouth. Hungry, searching. I felt them, knew they were there; drowned in hunger and anger and rage. *Eradicate.*

"Vid Team, this is rescue coming in," said a masculine voice. "What's your position?"

"Ass-deep in necros," Indigo snarled. He knelt, dropping his gun, and cupped his hands. "Bitch, climb!"

I didn't intend on obeying. He didn't give me a choice. When I didn't step inside his hands, he punched me in the bleeding thigh – sparklers of pain licked from forehead to heels and I staggered.

He grabbed me at the softened knees, braced me with his shoulder and stood so fast, it was fall or fly.

I caught the fire escape.

Silhouettes crawled, shambled, darted out of the shadows. Too close. Too fucking fast for me to get the damn ladder under me.

"Indigo!" I yelled, hanging by one arm.

He shot a hard look over his shoulder. "Find me another way up," he said in the feed. "I'll lose them."

"No!" He sprinted away while I struggled to pull myself up. "Digo!"

The necros turned like a unit, tracking him as he vanished deeper into the alley.

"Vid Team, we need a location."

"Fuck your location," I rasped. Muscles I'd never worked so hard in my life strained as I hauled myself up with one arm. I hiked a knee with bone-breaking effort, hooked it in the bottom rung.

It took everything I had, but I climbed, awkward as fuck, yelling for Indigo to answer me.

He didn't.

No. No, no, this would *not* go down this way.

I needed him, damn it.

I limped across the rooftop, ducked under the dead power line hanging over it, and checked the north side. The east.

"Indigo!"

"Shut up," he hissed in my ear, and I nearly fell over with relief. And blood loss. "Pinned. Get to the extraction and get out, I'll meet you at another rendezvous."

"The hell I will," I shot back.

"Riko, I trusted you down there." His voice hardened, thick with pain. "Now you trust me. You have the computer. Get out."

"No, I–"

"I put it on your rack. I need you out there kicking ass and making sure nobody leaves mine behind, you hear me?" His voice dropped. "You'd better come back for me." There was too much of a question in that demand.

He wouldn't last the burn, much less the corruption on the other side of nanoshock.

Fuck. That.

I slapped at my harness with one hand – the isolated system hung from my back. I didn't even notice him do it. That *ass*.

"Time is up." Malik's deep voice. It filled the feed like a lifeline. Just a few more moments, and I could be out of this nightmare. "Get on the transport, Riko."

I looked up at the sky. Black and empty, until it faded to something less thick beyond the quarantine. More welcoming.

A faded golden glow blushing with spots of neon, diamonds in every conceivable color.

I blinked hard. It didn't focus anything.

"That data is all-important," Malik said flatly. "Koupra knows that. The rescue team is coming in. We'll send a unit for him."

Lie. This data was all that mattered to him. Digo was a casualty – and so was I.

I looked down. The street remained dark, hiding anything that crawled on it. But I knew. I could sense them. Maybe it was the chipset; maybe I'd just figured out their tactics.

Maybe I was losing my fucking mind.

Indigo cut through my feed with a terse whisper. "Get on that helo. One of us needs to make it out."

"Both," I countered. "Both, or no deal."

"Get out, and take that feed to Jax."

Twin blue lights soared into view.

"Vid Team, we have visual confirmation," said an unfamiliar male voice. A light spotlighted me, shearing away my night vision. "Hold for recovery."

Fuck it with a jagged pipe. No lube.

"I don't leave without Indigo," I snarled.

The vehicle tilted slightly, backdraft so close I could feel the heat in my nostrils.

"Get on the transport," Malik said quietly, every word iced menace.

"Vid Team, step away from the ledge," the pilot ordered.

"Riko," Indigo hissed, "they're everywhere and you're going to burn out, don't–"

I blinked up into the light. "Hey, Malik?"

He must have sensed my intention. "Don't you *dare*," he said, all but a growl seething with cold fury.

Lifting my only functional hand to the sky, I extended a grimy middle finger and held it. When I was sure the spotlight had captured every nuance, I launched myself from the roof to the knot of necros below.

Malik swore.

I collided into two necros. They buckled under my weight, one snapping in places that bodies shouldn't snap. The other rounded on me like a rabid dog, but it was missing an arm, which made it easy to punch in its empty, slack face. Blood spattered the necros in front of me.

"Riko, you *stupid*–" A gunshot rang out over the street. Indigo rolled out from under the abandoned car he'd crawled under, CounterTech spitting a flare that peeled half the necros off me when they sensed easier prey. "You're going necro in the fucking brain!"

He had no idea.

I gritted my teeth, rode the pain – the shock from the landing, the blood loss, the hammering, sawing, wailing dysfunction prying my eyeballs out of my aching sockets. Was this what Indigo was feeling?

I couldn't process it.

"Get," I seethed, reaching for a necro, "out. Get out." I curled my hand around its face, yanking it off its feet. My fingers slid into the cold, damp cave of its mouth. Pulled. "Get out!" Flesh split, bloody strings tearing through my fingers. It flailed in my grip. I screamed. "*Get out!*"

I was banking on the fact they wouldn't leave us to fend for ourselves, and I was right. Malik's voice over the feed snapped orders to extricate us whatever means possible. Us. Plural.

Hell, yes. All we had to do was survive until rescue got us.

Easier said than done. Every necro body in sight rounded on me, and there was no more time to speak. To think.

No more room in my brain to think with.

Whatever it was that fried through my chipset, it stripped away my identity until there was nothing left but blood and bone; gristle and putrid flesh. I stood back to back with Indigo and fought with one arm, used the deadened synthetic to take blows meant for my exposed side. I tore and pushed and threw until it was all I could do to keep Indigo at my back as he gunned down body after body. I couldn't tell the difference between them and me – blood-soaked, gore-streaked, teeth bared and screaming.

A chunk of armor took flesh with it from my side. My leg reopened; I didn't give a fuck, tearing the arm that slashed me from its socket and spinning to slam the shoulder joint into another's head. They came again and again. Clawed for my vital organs.

I ripped one off my shoulders. Another one replaced it. I staggered, unable to tell if it was my blood pumping to the brightly lit street or theirs.

I was losing. *We* were losing.

I threw my head back, narrowly avoided losing my eyes to a bony swipe. Blinding white light filled my sight; burned out my vision. My foot came down on something that rolled, gelatinous and slippery, and I went down. Indigo tried to catch me, tangled up in my footing and fell on me instead. Something sliced through my chest.

The world went nova.

I'd been shot, stabbed, burned, caught in shrapnel, and – more recently – clawed up by necros. I never expected a trip and fall to take me out. That was fucking embarrassing.

Pride demanded I get up off the ground and shake it off. I struggled to open my eyes, to move, but all I saw was red and black. I couldn't breathe. I sucked in air, choked, coughed. Agony tore open my chest, bubbled from my lips.

"Lay down cover fire!" I heard. Real voices, not comm chatter. "Get them on board."

"Hang on, Riko." Something sharp punctured the skin on my neck, just over jagged furrows throbbing at my collar bone. I wanted to give the speaker the same courteous digit I'd extended to the helo, but my eyelids turned to lead weights.

"The burn team is sending orders for quarantine, sir."

"Tell them," Malik said, his voice sounding extraordinarily clear, "to go fuck themselves."

29

I sat on the edge of an examination table, rotating my synthetic wrist and listening for the telltale sound of servos in the joint.

"I replaced a lot of the mobility parts. Pretty great, huh?" Orchard, the redheaded tech I'd threatened with a broken arm, had repaired mine. The irony. It slays. "I had to make a few enhancements to the overall model, but you should feel back to normal in no time."

If "normal" meant feeling like an intruder inside my own skin, then yeah. I could fake that. As long as Orchard kept her pink fingers off my brain, I could probably go on faking indefinitely.

But I knew. Blindsided as I was, I knew that I'd lost my shit down there. That I'd nearly killed Indigo with my choices – killed myself – and I couldn't even say why.

I bent my arm. The matte plating looked a little worse for wear, but I couldn't find fault with the connectors.

"We had to reinforce your shoulder girdle," Orchard was saying, scrolling down a projected screen wide as one arm and ticking off the salient points. The floating numbers looked like gibberish from this side, but the fact she'd defaulted to a widescreen projection said she'd gone through a metric shit ton of data. "Your biceps bracing needed total replacement, so since we had pretty much full run of the budget, we fitted your whole arm and shoulder with a custom muscle weave that should make future separation more difficult to achieve."

I looked up. "Trust me," I said dryly. "I never plan on reaching that particular achievement again." Once was more than enough. Metal was durable, sure, but it didn't matter how strong the tech was if the flesh couldn't cope. I'd found the breaking point against that security door, and the memory of it sent fingers of oily sweat skimming down my spine.

And I didn't even have a SIN registry to score the achievement. Shitting bloody irony.

Orchard nodded. "I'd appreciate that. Your chipset was showing some serious wear and tear, so we replaced it entirely with an updated model. Don't worry," she added when I shot her a narrow-eyed stare, "I didn't mess with anything else. Promise. I patterned the new tech off your previous specifications. I added some upgraded filters that I'm not supposed to give non-employees, so *shh*."

I bit back a growling sigh. Leave it to Malik dicking Reed to take advantage of my unconscious state. I'd wondered who I'd go to for a full recalibration, and as it turned out, I owed him. Lucky me. I didn't trust Orchard far as I could fuck her – all signals were coming back at no-go – which meant I'd have to play this as cool as I could manage. "How bad was the chipset?"

"Hard to say for sure." Orchard flicked aside an array of screens until a multihued splotch in various primary and secondary colors filled the projected square. She tucked three fingers into the bottom edge and rotated it deftly. The projection flipped. "This is an average picture of your brain during most of the mission."

I eyed it, bracing my hands on the edge of the examination table to study it closer. "It looks like a mess."

"Brains are funny that way." Another flick, and a new picture took its place. She jabbed a finger into a large patch of brilliant yellow at the base of the blotch. "That's what was going on around your chipset right before you lost your helmet."

"It went supernova." I lifted my hand to the base of my head, testing the skin now covering the replaced set. No scars to show for it. No bumps. "Like it caught fire."

She framed the yellow glare with her hands, cupping the blotch through the screen. "Whatever was going on, it turned on every communication center in your brain. Like it was trying to account for some other handicap. It's no wonder you lost consciousness for a while." She looked up over her cupped hands, orange eyebrows high. "Anything to add here?"

Not unless I wanted to spend the next ungodly amount of time holed up in this stinking lab with its glaring white façade.

"What about corruption?" I asked.

She blinked at me, sky blue eyes crystal clear. "No signs. Your nanos needed a boost like whoa, but I suspect any oddness you felt was due to this." She gestured at the colorful brain scan. "So..." A pointed pause. "How do you feel?"

I folded my shoulders into a casual shrug. "I feel fine."

"How'd you feel *then*?"

"Like a cranked out teenager high on colordust," I told her. "How do you think?" I tried not to take offense when disappointment replaced eager curiosity in her features. "If it changes, you'll be the first to know, okay?"

You'd think I offered to clean her damn lab. She perked right up. "Great." Another one of those practiced gestures, and the screen swapped back to her chart. "I also took the opportunity to replace your netware applications." Another pause. "Uh, don't tell Mr Reed. The rest is good to go. You're in remarkably good shape, given everything."

I looked down at myself, checking my ink for any new scars. The fact I was wearing plain white underwear and a cropped tank bra bothered neither of us. Like I said, she'd been stunningly indifferent to my flirtations. "Any other good data getting pulled from the helmet feeds?" I asked.

"Don't know," she said, but without the same focus she'd given my brain. "That's another department's job. As for you and that other guy, the fact you came back from this mess at all is kind of fascinating, don't you think? I mean, we've never seen a necrotech spread like that. It's crazy interesting!"

"That's *a* word for it," I acknowledged, dry as bone. She grinned, but if she'd meant to ask any more questions, the double doors across the lab hissed open and cut her off.

Malik strode inside like he owned every piece of tech in it, Orchard and me included. Control freak.

He wore gray. Again. Surprise. This suit was darker than the previous, a single-breasted jacket over a matching vest. His dress shirt was a shade he probably convinced himself was *light red* but which I called pink. Again, a tie. Also gray. In one hand, he held a duffel. Black, though, not gray. Surprise.

Orchard launched herself from her stool. "Mr Reed, sir! Just running over the diagnostics with the patient."

I didn't bother sliding off the end of my table. I swung my bare feet idly, leaning back on my hands and well aware of what that did to my physique.

A girl didn't get killer abs by being soft.

Malik's gaze flicked to me, but didn't linger. "I've got it from here, Dr Gearailteach."

"Yes, sir." Slanting me a wide-eyed apology, she swiped the projected screen back to her desk's anchor unit. "Bye, Riko," she said cheerfully. "Don't forget lunch!" Without waiting for confirmation, she fled the scene, red ponytail bobbing.

Traitor.

The doors closed behind her, leaving me alone with Malik Reed, suited exec and all around cardholding member of the gaping assholes committee.

I owed him so much emotional backlog, I honestly didn't

know where to start. Or if it was even worth it to bother. It annoyed me that I didn't hate him as much as I thought I should. I guess a near-death experience with ambulatory tech did something for a girl's perspective.

I eyed him. "Her last name is what?"

"Ask her yourself." He tossed the bag at me. Without thinking, I caught it with my tech hand. It was heavier than I expected. "Good reflexes. How do you feel?"

I peered inside the bag to find an indistinguishable mass of black. "Like someone that should feel like hammered shit and doesn't. What's this?"

"Clothes."

I couldn't wait to see this. Ignoring him, I rifled through the pile of black, fishing out a pair of black pants that would fit like a wet dream with none of the imagination. Underneath, a halter top similar to the one his team had ruined at Plato's Key. Also black.

Malik Reed was a one-color-per-customer kind of tool.

I found a pair of black boots under it, sporting a two-inch tread and a four-inch, street-ready heel.

I raised an eyebrow at him. "What's this for?"

"Your other apparel was damaged." I noted he didn't claim responsibility for that one, either. "I took the liberty."

I eased off the table, my bare feet hitting the cool tile, and snapped open the pants. "Indigo get the same treatment?"

Again, I was hit with a lingering sense of déjà vu.

Malik made no effort to turn away. He watched me the same way he always did, unreadable as stone, arms folded over his chest. "Mr Koupra's nanoshock symptoms were too early to be of import. His wounds were also less... *extensive* than yours." Goddamn, they liked to underplay it around here. "He responded well to the treatment, his various injuries healed without scarring, and he was released two days ago."

I appreciated the detail. While Orchard had made it a point to fill me in when I'd finally been pulled out of the recharge tank, she'd kept it to "doing just fine" and "already headed home". As the med staff hosed nutrient-rich slime off my clammy skin, she'd told me that a four-block radius in the Vid Zone had been razed to the ground. Farther, even. With the burn team's proficiency and the chemical napalm used in a controlled burn, the structural integrity of the place hadn't stood a chance.

By the time anyone had gone through it, there was nothing left behind but a slagged crater. Indigo and I were the only witnesses to whatever went down in that hellhole.

So why the pause?

"Then to what do I owe the pleasure?" I asked mockingly. "Are you here to lecture?"

His dark head tipped, fluorescent overheads carving harsh planes into his implacable features. "You owe me a conversation, as I recall."

"Yeah, that's not going to happen."

"Why?"

I shot him an impatient shrug as I wriggled into the pants. I was right. They fit like a second skin, which made them sexy club wear and worthless everywhere else. "What do you want me to say? My whole team nearly died down there. I lost my cool, like the brain scans say." A mild stretch. "You set me up. Oh, and I cost you four enforcers. Don't you have a lot to say about the value of resources and shit?"

"You returned with data from the infested lab. That in itself is valuable." If the loss of his team bothered him, I couldn't tell.

And Digo called *me* cold.

"Are you going to tell me what you've learned?" I prodded. "Or am I going to have to do this dance for the next hour?"

He gave in with surprising grace. Damn it. "According to Mr Koupra and the footage taken from the suit cams above ground, the surge of necrotech infection spread to one-fourth of the quarantined population."

Ouch. That was a lot of walking necros. A whole lot of normal folk gone real bad, real fast. I zipped the pants up and stripped off the modest bra without looking at him. "Everyone said conversion only works via wire, and it's rare."

He didn't afford me the same courtesy. "It will take time to sort out the data." Without letting me pursue the topic, as though deciding it was done, he added simply, "You have questions."

I wasn't sure I did. Not the same ones I'd gone in there with. I frowned. "Did you pay Digo for his..." What would I call it? Selling me out? *Ugh.* "Blood price? For meeting your demands."

His head cocked, the glaring white lights turning his shorn hair to a dark shadow on his swarthy scalp. "What do you intend to do if I confirm that?"

"Thank you."

There. A flicker of his short, thick eyelashes. I'd surprised him. Finally.

The emotion didn't linger. "Mr Koupra has been compensated accordingly."

"Good." I was happy to leave it at that.

This time.

I shrugged into the halter, wrapping it around my ribs with deft ease. He must have modeled the shirt after my yellow one. The material was softer than I remembered, nearly sheer but for the layers. A good printer could reproduce the pattern as many times as needed, but I liked this quality fabric.

He wasn't inclined to let me get away with that. He raised his eyebrows, his full mouth hiking up ever so faintly at that crazily endearing corner. "You were saying?"

Oh, for all the fucks in the world. I shrugged my bare shoulders. "Thank you for paying him," I said, and slanted him a hard eyebrow from beneath the fringe of pale hair flopped over my forehead. "Next time you put a bounty out on my head, make sure it's to kill me."

The smile, small as it was – smug bastard – didn't fade. He switched gears without confirming my unspoken threat. "I understand Mr Koupra located some footage."

I stilled, black cloth stretched taut in my fingers. My gaze pinned not on him, but somewhere beyond his right shoulder. Desks, computers, examination grids flickering faintly between stations. I didn't see them.

I saw myself, negotiating with a man in black security BDUs over Nanjali Koupra's unconscious body.

I swallowed hard. "Yeah." A rasp. I cleared my throat. "But it might be fake."

His dark brown eyes searched my face. "Might be?"

I forced myself to loosen my grip. To finish wrapping the material and tie it in place. I wasn't sure how to frame my thoughts in a way that didn't sound desperate.

How did I explain that I was haunted by a memory that unfolded more like a vid screen recording than a recollection?

Echoes of panic still haunted me when I looked at white tile. The smell of disinfectant cramped inside my guts and chest and stole my breath. I didn't make that up.

Malik didn't cut me any slack. It wasn't his style. "Riko." His deep voice wrapped around the name I'd heard for ten years, and I shuddered. Regret? Aversion.

Who was I, really? What had happened to me in those four months?

What the shit was I becoming?

"What makes you doubt what you saw?"

Pulling my thoughts back roughly to the present, I turned away, pulling on one boot and kicking it up on the edge of the table to fasten. These tied, with real laces and everything. Quaint. "A few minor details," I said, forcing my tone into something close enough to calm to fake it. "Individually, no big deal, but all together, they don't add up."

"I'm listening."

I'll just bet. "That vid showed me imprinting my thumb

on a tablet. A contract, maybe, or some kind of employment record."

"So?"

"So, that's bullshit." I yanked the knot hard, surprised when my metal arm nearly snapped the lacing.

Enhancements. Right.

I went through it again with my left shoe. "I'm a saint, but I was born a sinner. There is *no* way I'd ever let my fingerprint end up on some corporate rap sheet. I may as well write home and tell them where I am."

"You don't think that you're setting up an elaborate lie to tell yourself?" His tone gentled, but only a fraction. "I'm not here to judge you. If you betrayed your team–"

"Suck my balls, Malik." I stomped both feet, surprised and gratified by the comfort, and turned again, hands propped on my hips. "I didn't do it. You don't just throw away a decade of conditioning."

"Anything else?"

I hesitated. "Nothing I can pinpoint."

"Why?"

I eyed him. "Because I can't, okay?"

"So you're willing to ignore visual evidence in favor of… what? A hope?"

"I don't know," I said, probably the first blatantly honest thing I'd ever said to him. I shot him a slanted smile that promised nothing by way of gentling. I still wasn't made for soft. "I risked my ass for all that information, and I'm not convinced the vid is real."

"You aren't convinced it's not." Eerie, how well he had me figured out. "What will you do?"

I focused on the question, ignoring the knot of anxiety threatening to lodge in my chest. "I'm going to do what I do best, Malik. Wreck everybody's shit until I get to the bottom of that hellhole. Whatever went down, somebody has answers."

He didn't move. He didn't lift an eyebrow, or look at me

like I was insane. Malik was a watcher, and as creepy as that should have been, it only made me very much aware of his gaze on me. "How do you propose to start?"

I shook my head. "I don't know yet, but I can tell you one thing. Whatever was down there, MetaCunts, Inc wanted it bad."

"Do you plan to do this alone?" he asked me, a furrow forming over the bridge of his nose. It pulled at his freckles – which wasn't nearly as disarming as when Orchard's did the same.

Malik's instincts, I decided, were scary as fuck.

I ran my hands through my hair, forcing it behind my ear. Until I found out for sure what was wrong with my memory, I wasn't sure about running with anyone – especially my team, who probably still hated my guts. Indigo and I had worked out a kind of mutual ground, but Tash and the others might be harder sells.

There was no shortage of mercs eager for corp targets, at least. The problem was sifting through the mess for quality.

"I'll figure out something," I finally said, glancing at him with a shrug. "Right now, I don't trust myself."

Something sharp glinted in his gaze, twitched that muscle in his jaw and was gone. "Why?"

My mouth slanted into a grim slash. "Chunk off, Malik, you know why. When my chipset shorted, I damn near lost my shit for good down there."

"Don't you want to find out what caused it?"

"And stick around here?" I swiped my flesh hand at the lab as I passed Malik, dismissing them both in one sharp gesture. "Ass, no. I've had my fill of labs to last me a long time."

He turned to watch me, and his tone dropped to a mocking octave. "So it's easier to run."

"I'm not running," I snapped, but I stopped dead in my tracks.

Yes, I was. Damn it.

I turned to find him still watching me.

"What the tits is your malfunction?" I snarled. Annoyance, frustration.

His lips curved into a deeper smile; an edge in it that battered at my already fraying sense of grounding. "You're running," he stated, like he was the authority on all things me.

I swiped my hair back from my forehead. "What do you want from me, Reed?"

His arms dropped, easing his silhouette from nonchalant patience to something harder, more aggressive. Like he prepped for a fight as he approached me, closing the distance I'd put between us in my rush to get the hell out. "I can respect your need for answers."

My gaze narrowed. I wanted to step back; screw him if I gave him that satisfaction. Instead, I raised my chin.

"I want answers, too." He stopped a mere foot from me, so close I could pick out the individual freckles on his nose and cheeks. He smelled like something custom manufactured and expensive, which shouldn't have smelled delicious and did.

Shit on that. I moved back, after all.

Satisfaction flicked a corner of his mouth.

"Yeah, well," I said tightly, "we all *want* stuff, big boy. Get used to disappointment." I turned away.

His hand lashed out, wrapped around my scarred metal arm and I was suddenly whirling, spun like a thrashdancer caught off guard and pulled close enough that half of my body was plastered against his.

I blinked into intense dark eyes, aware that my pulse had launched into a rapid beat. I was a tall woman, but I didn't realize how tall Malik was until I stood almost nose to nose with him in four-inch boots.

I inhaled tightly, which dragged my chest against his. My snatch clued in right around the time my brain went nova in warning.

The fact I found him delicious annoyed the hell out of me.

"Let me help you." It was practically an order.

I bristled in his grip. "What makes you think I want the help from you?"

"What makes you think you can afford to go without it?"

I could have shaken him off, probably would have enjoyed the chance to lay him out without his security team, but I didn't. His men had pulled me out of that hellhole and I'd already cost him four trained enforcers.

He deserved a warning.

I gave him *one*. "Let me go," I said softly.

He didn't. He searched my gaze for something I didn't know, so close I could see each individual whisker making up his shaped goatee. I bet his hair would be rough against my palm.

I bet his skull would cave in beneath my metal fist.

His fingers tightened. I couldn't feel it, I just watched the numbers in my lateral display hike.

Hell of a grip. Arousal dragged rough claws through my unstable restraint. So did snapping restraints of fury.

His grip eased, like he knew. "My apologies," he said, with the same level of calm certainty he did everything, and let me go.

I resisted the urge to rub the spot where his fingers had encircled cool metal. My phantom arm didn't need the encouragement. "Your wife must think you're a real catch," I muttered, irritated.

He ignored me. "There's tech and intel you're going to need if you're planning to wander blindly into corporate warfare." He cut me off before I could argue. "Don't delude yourself, it *is* corporate warfare. That lab was well funded, highly organized, and extremely covert."

"I told you so."

His eyes glittered.

Too late, I remembered that he'd already known.

My teeth gritted.

"Work with us, Riko. Mantis Industries has the funding, the tech and the resources to help you."

"Never mind that you'll get your espionage fix, right?"

"And then some." He shrugged. "If you need information on MetaCore, the tools to take them on, and resources you don't currently have, you're going to need a backer. I tracked you from that lab when no one else knew you were even alive. I have the means. You have the drive. Give this a shot."

Shit. I looked down at the floor in front of me, blindly cataloguing all the pros and cons I could think of.

Resources, sure. Tech upgrades that Lucky couldn't get – and wouldn't give me now, even if he could.

Better funding than your average merc group.

What was Malik Reed's game?

I eyed him with blatant speculation. "You used me."

"We've already had this discussion."

I was running out of names to call him. "I thought you suits didn't trust easy."

"You cost me four highly trained specialists. Is this your version of easy?"

Point well made.

Cons? The corporate world didn't operate by the same rules the street did. Working for a corporate's cred was one thing, but going on payroll was something else. It'd cost me the last of my hard-won street rep and then some

Oh, and there was that teeth-grinding fact that I found myself wondering if a married man's cock was as rigid as the rest of him.

Too many cons to list.

"I want to talk to your armor research team," I told him, testing the waters.

"Why?"

Compromise wasn't a word I think Malik considered often. "Because," I told him, "I've got first-hand experience on necro armaments that turned Mantis's suits to paste and chewing gum. If I'm going to be wearing the suit, it damn well better work."

Maybe he got off on facts. He didn't argue. "Done."

I pushed it. "And I want to freelance. No payroll, no paperwork, no news feed headlines."

"Freelancing comes with certain restrictions," he countered.

I shrugged. "As long as I get full disclosure on every offered contract."

He studied me. I returned his scrutiny with poker-faced challenge, but my hand came up to cover the patch of metal he'd grabbed. By the time I caught myself doing it, it was too late.

His gaze flicked to the movement. Lifted again to meet mine without so much as a glint of recognition.

Seriously, he bothered me.

"No," he finally said. "I get to choose what information is disclosed per contract, but–" He raised one dusky hand. "The final say on any job you're offered is yours."

Okay. I didn't want to admit it, but that was reasonable. Any information he didn't disclose, odds were I knew somebody who could hack it. Assuming they'd do it if I was the one asking. Fuck.

I rolled my re-knitted shoulder, testing its reinforced socket as I pondered how much farther I could push.

Well, why the shit not?

I rocked back on my heels, sliding two fingers into the waistband of my snug pants in lieu of pockets. His gaze flicked to my exposed navel, the ink decorating my hip, then back up. "I don't answer to your board." When he didn't immediately argue, I added offhandedly, "Oh, and I want a Valiant 14, fully loaded."

His mouth shifted into that aggravating little curve, like I'd amused him again. "That's worth more than a freelancer's salary."

I knew it, too. "Those are my terms."

"Expensive terms."

I grinned. "I'm an expensive date."

"Noted. Now hear *my* requirements," he replied, and my smile faded. "If you don't answer to the Mantis board, you answer to me. You'll have more freedom than most working under me, but only as long as I see progress. One wrong move, and I'll have your Mantis credentials pulled faster than you can say Jane Eyre." That smile tightened to a taunt. "Much less spell it."

My back teeth clenched. A little rough flirtation was one thing, but I did not like this whole control business. "It will be a cold day in the wastelands before I work *under* you."

His eyes glinted. "Mandatory exams." He ticked off a list on his raised fingers. "Training exercises and goals. You will work with teams and without."

"Hold it." I crossed both arms in front of me, a physical X of denial. "Fail. I am not your custom lapdog, Malik. I do what I do on my terms, or it doesn't work."

His eyes narrowed a fraction, short black lashes flickering once. He didn't like that? Too bad.

"I'm not a bottom-tier suit looking to scale the ladder," I said flatly. "I'm an asset and an equal partner or you can kiss this ass goodbye. And I'm not turning down outside runs."

"Then you turn down the ones that target Mantis."

"It depends on the pay."

His jaw moved. "I'll give you a list of Mantis units that are hands-off. Anything else you want to hit is fair game, as long as you give me a chance to counteroffer."

Okay, that surprised me. "Why?"

"Because other departments aren't my problem," he replied evenly. "Come after mine, and you'll wish you'd taken the opportunity to work under me first."

I couldn't decide if I pitied his wife or envied her. "Then we're agreed. I'm a freelancer, you keep your girly mouth shut about it, and I get a Valiant 14?"

"Acceptable." He held out his hand, palm slightly tilted. I stilled.

What kind of bullshit challenge was this? Daring me to take his hand willingly?

Or being a jerk.

I'd put cred on the latter, but even as I considered it, I recognized the position he'd just put me in.

His eyes didn't leave mine, way more self-satisfied than I was comfortable with.

If I did this, that was it. I'd be another sellout merc turned by corp money. Working for the capitalistic fuckheads of the world.

But if I played it smart, I could use Mantis to shore up my failing cred. Milk it for all it was worth, and put to rest all this bullshit. Once and for all.

"Fine." But I ignored his offered hand. Challenge denied, motherfucker. "You have yourself a freelancer."

For the first time, something in his dark brown eyes lit.

"Welcome to Mantis Industries. And since you're officially on the roster," he continued, like this was the most casual business meeting in the world, "you have authorization to know about the data you and Mr Koupra brought back."

"Oh, goodie. On the clock already." I patted my chest with mock concern. "Is it okay if I left my tie at home?"

He ignored my sarcasm. "Preliminary data is coming out of the undisclosed lab we've set up on an inaccessible system. What it's telling me is that there's more to that quarantine than your usual necro risk."

"As if a 'necro risk' isn't enough," I pointed out dryly. "What do you mean?"

"I mean," he said patiently, "the techs have found unfamiliar code encrypted in portions of the logs."

I wasn't following. Tech was tech. It was all predisposed on code. "So?"

"It means that whatever was going on in that place, they were working on something new. Possibly even an attempt to weaponize the necro virus."

I stared at him, his words echoing hollowly in my head. "Isn't that illegal?"

He raised a black eyebrow at me.

"All right," I allowed, "isn't that the kind of thing that's going to get a metric fuck ton of corporate napalm slapped on somebody's ass?"

He inclined his head. "Likely."

Weaponized necros. Son of a *bitch*. Was that what they'd been doing in that lab?

But then why use people? The code could just be...I don't know. Thrown together on a computer system, right?

Except Indigo had said the actual necro whatever started in a flesh-tech hybrid. Only then could it infect systems.

That had implications I didn't like.

"Is that it?" I asked.

He folded his hands behind his back, watching me with that unflappable calm I despised. "One thing." When I stared at him, waiting, he stared back.

This time, the glint in his eyes was anything *but* amused.

"We believe we know how the necros converted so many."

"And?"

A pause. "Infection."

I blinked. "Come again?"

"I mean," Malik said slowly, once again the very model of patience and condescending education, "they aren't spreading through just wires anymore." Again, he waited.

The realization, when it dawned, came slow. Icy. "Holy fuck," I rasped.

"Indeed."

He half-turned, as if dismissing me in favor of the wide, translucent screen showcasing all of my recent vitals. That made me nervous. "We're going through everything now, but initial impressions seem to indicate the code is in process of utilizing the nanos of the converted." He glanced at me. "Mr Koupra very nearly demonstrated this for us. You, however, escaped infection."

My knees buckled.

I locked them in place, fists clenching. "Impossible."

"On the contrary." His smile was a hard slash, grim and – in some weird little way – pleased. Maybe he saw it as a challenge. "The nanos delivered by contact with a necrotech's fluids are programmed to assault and convert host nano agents. If your little stunt had taken up any more time, your prized linker would be well on his way to – what is it you call it? – necro-land."

The teeth in my thigh. The blood everywhere. Ragged nails breaking into ichor. And that was the shit I'd survived. Indigo had been torn up just as bad.

Was that why we'd hit nanoshock so much faster?

But if so, why infect him and not me? Was it luck?

Prototype tech?

I hugged myself before I realized I did it. "So now you get hit with their converted nanos and they start cannibalizing your tech?"

"Precisely." Another inclination of his head. "We are," he said, dry as hell in a decade's drought, "working *every* angle. Until we know more, consider yourself brought up to speed. I want full reports on every move you make, beginning with any current leads that can locate the source of this... *mess*."

I had a few leads, all right. Specifically, the other chopshops listed in Fuck It Jim's records. I was rattled to the bone, but I shook my head hard. "I don't do reports."

"You will now."

Shitlord. "And what will you do if I turn out to be the source of all this?" I asked his profile. "I still can't account for my time in that lab."

He flattened one hand against the desk, idly rifling through the screens with the other as if searching for a specific one. "Are you a religious woman?" he asked, eyes on the display.

"No." Not even a little.

"Then praying will do you no good." As answers went, it was enough. "Hope to whatever guidepost you want that you aren't subject zero." His hand stilled. "Do you think you're at fault?"

"No." I paused. "Not intentionally."

"Intentions." Now, he looked up. His eyes, always dark, gleamed. "About as useful as 'almost' and 'should have'. Drop them."

Before I could decide how to address that, whether I should even ask how much of that he actually believed, he turned back to the translucent screen on Orchard's desk.

"Ms Ramsay will go over your verbal contract."

"Verbal?"

Amusement touched his voice, now. "I believe you indicated you'd never imprint your identity on paperwork. Or," he added with deadpan certainty, "work under me."

So he *was* listening. The thought shouldn't have warmed that icy knot in my chest. It totally did.

Then again, he did subsequently attempt to goad me into proving myself wrong, too. What a twat.

"Naturally," he continued with calculated nonchalance, "if you break your contract, verbal or otherwise, it's not court you'll have to worry about. Please don't cost me any more of Mantis's enforcers."

And there went the warm fuzzies. "You're a flaming bag of dicks, Malik."

"Keep that imagery warm," he replied, entirely unruffled.

Oh, the man thought he was a riot. I left before I decided to take a stupid decision and compound it with something worse. Like... I don't know. What could make selling out worse? Necrotechs spreading. Duplicating by infection.

Yeah, that'd do it.

I was halfway through the door when his deep voice called, "One last thing. Do you want your identification metrics saved as Riko or Risa Cole?"

My stomach clenched. I turned slowly, my pulse thick and heavy in my ears.

He hadn't moved, but his gaze lifted from what would have been my ass a second ago, up my navel, my breasts. They touched on my lips and my skin warmed in the same way my chest had, slapping suspicion with a surge of good old-fashioned libido.

"According to the data pulled from Mr Koupra's computer," he continued mildly, "Risa Cole died in that lab."

I fisted my hands at my sides. "Good. Let her rest in fucking peace."

He straightened from the desk, tucked his hands into his pockets. It should have made him look harmless; nothing Malik Reed attempted would ever qualify as *harmless*. The aggressive edge of victory shaping his smile snapped a finger of black rage into my thundering heartbeat.

"As requested," he said, like he was doing me a favor. "Now you know what I know." I very much doubted that. "I'll have your biometrics listed under your street name. *My* eyes only."

Anger and arousal. Knowledge and power. Fuck me, but I liked a man who yanked my chain.

Even while I wanted to shove my fist into his still-beating heart and make him watch me eat it.

Libido-checking tech. I was so on that.

"Very soon," I said quietly, "we're going to talk." Not now. Not while I couldn't get a handle on my shit.

Not until I knew more about my own role in this mess. The scope of the necro infection.

"I look forward to the occasion." Twatflapping son of a *whore*. The challenge inherent in that statement made me feel like he'd just slapped me on the ass. His gaze settled to my waist, and the pale band of flesh revealed between waistband

and halter hem. "Why the arrow?"

The question, innocuous as fuck after that epic reveal, threw me for a loop. When I realized he meant the bright pink light tattoo, a wide arrow at the small of my back pointing to the cleft between my ass cheeks, I turned away again. "Because," I answered over my shoulder. "Fuckheads like you need a reminder of what they're missing when I do this."

"Do what?"

I left him watching my ass as I walked away.

The doors shut on his sound of amusement; not quite a laugh, but I'd surprised him.

I wouldn't go so far as to call him human, but it helped. If he was human, he would bleed. If he could bleed, I'd be the one to squeeze it from his stones.

Eventually.

Hope Ramsay waited for me in the first intersection. She wore slacks this time, brown and nondescript. A clear plastic digital unit was cradled in her arm. No intangible screen for her. Another prim blouse, sleek bun, plain glasses.

She smiled. "I hear congratulations are in order." Something in my face must have warned her, because her smile faded. "Mr Reed get under your skin?"

Not just him. I folded my arms under my breasts. "How much of his information do you know?"

"Only what he tells me."

"What did he tell you about me?"

Her head tilted to one side, mouth pursing. After a moment, her smile returned. A little bit crooked. "That you're on the freelancer payroll starting now, retroactively dated to the quarantine extraction, which means you get paid for it. And that you're more than a handful, and I shouldn't let you bully me."

If she lied, I couldn't tell. She seemed sincere enough, but nobody got to be a suit secretary without swimming with predators.

"Anything else you want me to know, you'll have to tell me yourself."

I raised my eyebrows at her. "What if I said I'd tell you everything you wanted to know if you went out with me?" Okay, so yeah, that was pretty much out of nowhere. But I wasn't comfortable – I was fucking *un*comfortable – and I wanted someone else to be, too.

Of course, if she said yes, I could think of a few ways to settle my nerves.

Her smile really was pretty. It widened at me now, exactly the opposite of what I was after. "I'd say that I didn't get this far by skinnydipping in the water cooler." She linked her free arm companionably through mine. "Besides, you lack a certain feature I tend to enjoy."

"Dicks can be acquired, you know." She chuckled, but dismissively. "You don't know what you're missing."

"If I'm ever curious, you'll be the first to know. Come on, let's get back to civilized territory."

Civilized, huh? Balls to that.

I let Hope guide me back to the elevator, only half listening to her stream of introductory encouragement. In the paneled reflection, I looked at us together – my smear of mutable and vibrant color, her pale coloring and dark blonde head. Black and neutral tones. Tall and short. Metal arm and pliable fleshbag.

Corporate and... *fuck*. Corporate freelancer.

I had to draw a line somewhere.

As I heard her say the word "quarters", I opted to start there.

I covered her mouth with my hand. "New game, Hope. Let's find the splatter specialist somewhere else to live. A flat she can pay for with her own creds, in a zone that won't raise eyebrows or scream that I'm a corporate tool."

She looked up at me, her plain brown eyes sparkling through her glasses. "I knew you'd say that," she said, muffled but not at all deterred by my impromptu gag. "Here." She passed me the tablet.

I let her go. "Why didn't you just say so?"

"Because teasing you is fun. You're needlessly difficult."

I was going to be a difficult a lot. As the elevator lifted and Hope filled it again with cheerful, welcoming chatter, I looked down at the list of flats to rent and buy and wondered if anyone would notice that my stomach had stayed below.

Everything I thought I knew had changed. The answers I'd gotten weren't enough to cover all my questions, and hell, I felt like even more questions had been added to the mix. Whatever corporation had funded that lab, they had been playing with necro code. Weaponizing it, Malik said. Maybe. Maybe something else.

Not cool.

Somebody, maybe the same people, had screwed me in *every* way except the way I liked it. I owed Indigo an investigation into his sister's death; I owed a massive favor to an ex-lover who called me a rival.

I owed Nanjali's ghost some answers.

Hell, I owed myself some answers.

Somebody was fucking with me. Maybe I was fucking with me. I'd find out.

Indigo had promised his help. I'd already made a deal with Greg, and I was going to deliver that particular bouquet as soon as I could. Jax had my back – for the moment.

I wasn't as alone as Malik thought me, but now I had Mantis backing.

Was I in over my head?

Oh, yeah. If this new Mantis Industries contract got out, other mercs would see me as a sellout, and they'd be right. I'd have a whole new set of rules to play by, ones I didn't think I had the patience to learn.

Things were not going to get easier. Just the opposite. Hell, Lucky was going to shit a brick if he ever spoke to me again, and I couldn't blame him. In all my years as a runner, I'd never let anyone else touch my tech.

Now I'd practically sold my body to Mantis.

The mirrored elevator panels threw back a reflection that looked like me, but I didn't see the confidence earned after ten years on the street of a city that tried and failed to fuck me when it had the chance. I didn't see a qualified runner, or a saint.

I saw a fighter whose scars were carved somewhere deeper than skin and flesh, whose ghosts growled in the deep recesses of a memory I wasn't sure I could trust.

Eradicate.

Maybe. But not if I got to those tech bastards first.

"By the way," Hope said as the doors slid open. "Every contract includes absolute nondisclosure."

"Yeah, yeah." I slanted her a half shrug. "Don't talk about confidential stuff, blah blah." Like I cared.

Her eyes were serious behind her frames. "No, Riko." She shook her head. "You don't talk about *anything* Mr Reed's department handles. Period."

I couldn't help it. I slapped a hand against the sensors to keep the doors open and looked down at her. "Or what? I get sued?"

This time, her smile carried a deliberately sanitized curve. Utterly without emotion. "That's *a* word for it," she said coolly. Echoes of my own snotty challenge to Orchard.

I got why Malik hired her.

30

"Yeah, I know it's not the glam job you were imagining," I said across the stark metal table, "but it's what you get. Do you want the creds or not?"

Detective Douchedick watched me the way a puppy stared at a bouncing ball: torn between launching himself at it or waiting for the chase. I didn't flatter myself too much about it. It wasn't *me* he wanted, but the creds I could give him.

If he'd do the damn work.

"I hate paperwork," he said, barely shy of a complaint.

"Yeah, everyone does." Which is why I wanted him to do it.

He sighed, a real pity party, but rolled his shoulders under his leather jacket. The fact his persona still sported something that obscene in the height of summer's blistering heat said a lot about Greg's choices in life. "All right, fine. I'll dig up what I can on Vid Zone permits and surrounding tickets. I don't know what you're expecting to find in the mess."

I didn't either, not yet. "Connections, Greg." I smiled at him with a lot of teeth. "If I'm very lucky, someone fucked up and it's in your system. I'll be sending you a couple more addresses to check out for me."

He shook his head, a streak of dark blond sliding over one eye. He pushed it back with one sculpted hand. "Where should I send the stuff I find?"

"You know the Mecca?"

"Not personally."

I tapped the table. It didn't so much as budge beneath my persona's metal arm – it didn't even clank loudly, the way I'd hoped. Lazy filters. "Acquaint yourself. Leave the data with Shiva, she'll know what to do."

Greg shrugged again, and stood up with an easy confidence I didn't think was all styling. His gaze, when it met mine, remained steady. "Thanks for the opportunity, Riko."

Aw, damn. Sincerity, like a real human being. I was getting used to treating him like a thing. I pulled a wry face. "Don't thank me yet, detective. This is going to be a long, shitty road." His lips tugged into a rueful smile, and for fuck's sake, I didn't need that, either. I waved at him. "Go away. I'm a very busy saint."

He sauntered for that white door, obviously intent on using it to make a classic kind of exit. I half-turned in my chair to watch him go. I knew for a fact that his ass looked just fine in those jeans, in projected space and out. He needed no help there.

All of one day out of the Mantis medlab and I'd never felt lonelier. No real team to speak of. No girlfriend – no semi-permanent fuckbuddy, even. No mentor. And the crawling knowledge that necro-juice spread like the shits in a buffet left me feeling just this side of freaked.

One smegging day, and I felt like a hermit.

I left the projection shortly after he did, returning to the meatspace the rest of me occupied just outside the Mecca's front door. Shiva's reach didn't extend too far into the street, but only a total idiot messed with a saint outside her door.

Besides, projections didn't mask the real world. Just dimmed it some. Anyone shoved me, I'd feel it.

Then I'd make the asshole risking his hands feel it right back. I was feeling spiky.

I skipped the line, earning a few profanities, and pushed my way through the front door. The bouncer gave me a hard look – I raised both hands and shimmied my weaponless hips – but he didn't give me any sass.

Jad would have flipped me some shit for my trouble. I looked pretty damn good – lethal *and* hot in crimson pants and a white racerback tank, and I knew it. My black ankle boots sported four-inch spikes because I wasn't looking for trouble.

That and I could snap the heels off at the first sign of a fight. I'd done that enough times to be something of an expert.

Stepping inside the Mecca netted me the familiar bonedeep thud of thrashjam bass and wild color. The feel of it, the welcoming fragrance of incense and sweat, did something for my simmering tension that too many sleepless hours hadn't.

Threading through the crowd, immersing myself in the chaos, I made it as far as the bar when I heard my name.

I turned, scanning the tech-studded crowd.

Shiva leaned against the nanofactoried bar, a slender goddess towering over her flock with benevolent tolerance. Her nails were *caution, danger* orange, her hair pulled into a high, perfectly straight fall of gleaming purple. Under the right lights, the bar would be the same color. Most of the time, it looked black.

Aggressive makeup took Shiva's mixed features into the surreal, with harsh blue lines painted out from her uptilted eyes and killer orange lipstick shaping her lush mouth. Her nose was strong, cheekbones sharp enough to cut glass, and her slender body wrapped in blue and silver homage to her muddled heritage. Her shoes had heels that could put a hole through solid steel, designer brand to my cheap printed knockoffs.

She beckoned me, head tilted so her hair slid over her shoulder.

"Shiva," I acknowledged, once I was close enough that I

didn't have to yell. A beautifully stacked server with kinked black hair bypassed me, pausing to nod at her boss. Her gleaming red gaze raked over me, her wide mouth hiked into a smile, and she was gone.

I recognized cosmetic tech to give the girl a devilish vibe. I also studied the kind of lush ass designed to haul a train behind her. Delicious.

Shiva's tawny eyes danced over me, from ankle boots to gelled hair, and finally met my inquisitive gaze with a smile. "You look well, darling."

"Much to your surprise?" I hazarded, earning a throaty laugh. "Thanks, I'll take it where I can get it."

"So I have heard." The innuendo earned the Mecca's reigning goddess a roll of my eyes. "Am I to expect another confrontation?"

It wasn't an idle question. I shook my head at her raised eyebrows, all but hidden beneath her thick fringe of purple bangs. "Not on the agenda. I'm just here to talk."

"To Indigo?"

"And the rest, if they're here."

Shiva shook her head, her ponytail swinging gently behind her. The lights pulsed off the bar, leaving a violet gleam in their wake. "Boone and the handsome one–"

"Valentine?"

"Yes, him." She waved those neon nails. "They're working tonight."

I didn't ask. I could have, but it'd cost me. I didn't need to know that badly. "So he's alone?"

"The short one with the dancer's legs?"

"Tashi?"

"No, the boy."

I smothered a laugh. "Fidelity."

"He's in there somewhere." Shiva gestured at the full dance floor. "The pixie remains with Indigo. If you intend to test the floor, know that I expect blood soon."

A fair warning – and a fair bit of interest made me glance at the writhing sea of flesh behind me. "I'll dance later."

"It's always a pleasure," Shiva said, and angled her body so that she no longer faced me directly. "Enjoy your evening, darling."

"I hope to."

I turned, but hesitated when Shiva added behind me, "And mind what truths you drop tonight."

I didn't look back. It wouldn't have netted me anything but Shiva's serene regard, and if I asked, she wouldn't answer. The message was clear enough. There were wheels spinning in the Mecca that weren't all favorable to me or mine. I briefly wondered what the motives were – drugs, corp, cred or something more sinister – but let it go almost immediately.

Shiva tended to know more than she let on – part of her mysterious god-empress routine, right up there with her cultivated speech patterns – and I already had a job.

I pushed my way through the thrumming crowd without incident. A far cry from the last time I'd made this walk. Part of me expected to field Tashi's murderous knives again.

As Shiva promised, Indigo waited in the usual room, surrounded by a small mess of glasses and flanked by Tashi. She stilled as I ducked under the curtain, but she didn't get up.

Good. I really, *really* didn't want to break my word to Shiva.

Indigo set his drink down, something pink sliding down the sides. "Riko."

"Indigo," I returned in the same cautious tones.

As far as first meetings after the crazy train in the Vid Zone, it didn't feel as awkward as I'd thought. Wary, yes. A little overly guarded.

Tashi wasn't seated in the booth, but on top of it, her feet tucked where her butt should have been. She cradled a wide glass of something yellow between both hands. Her gaze stayed on me.

I eyed her, hands loosely at my sides. "I'm not here to fight, Tash."

Her eyes narrowed.

Indigo elbowed her leg with a companionable familiarity that made me flinch inside. "Quit it."

"I don't trust her."

Tashi didn't talk much, so when she did, it mattered. That hurt. Worse, nothing I could do would fix that. If Tashi had challenged me, flipped me shit, I could have taken her on. Beat enough people into paste, and trust doesn't become so much of an issue.

In this case, I couldn't blame her for stating the obvious.

Digo gestured. "Sit."

"No." I folded my arms. "Thanks. Look, I'm not trying to nose back into the team, I'm just—"

"Riko—"

"I'm leaving," Tashi announced. She lifted her legs, spun on the back of the booth with a dancer's grace. She dropped off the back, rounding it with her drink balanced easily in hand. I didn't move. She didn't alter her trajectory. Her shoulder clipped my right arm, but she didn't so much as slow. The curtain slid back into place behind her.

Digo leaned back in his seat. "She'll come around."

"To what?" I asked dryly.

"Working with you."

Oh, shit. My chest squeezed. "That's a far cry from where we were just the other day."

One long finger pinned on the base of his drink. He scooted it across the table at me. "A few rough days compared to almost six years of solid runs. Do the math."

"Not a fan of math." I relented enough to approach the table, but I didn't sit. I angled a hip against the edge, bracing one arm on the surface. I glanced at the drink briefly, but my gaze slid to Indigo almost immediately. He looked all right. Better than he had down in the necro pit. "Are you all patched up?"

His neatly groomed black eyebrows knitted. "No scars, nothing to show off for chicks." Humor flickered behind his dark blue eyes. "You were right about the itching."

I didn't understand. Where was the angry Indigo of only a few short days ago? Where was the mistrust?

Hell, where was mine?

When I didn't smile, his features sobered into harder lines. Serious edges. "Look, I'm..." He splayed both hands over the table. "I'm not going to apologize for everything. I don't think I should."

Honestly? I'd prefer if he didn't. What was done was done. If he started falling all over himself, I didn't know the protocol. I shrugged. "I'm not asking."

"Yeah, I know." Digo leaned back, hands held in place like it mattered they stay there. Awkward. "I want to be clear where we're standing. You claim you don't remember anything after April, but that doesn't leave a whole lot to go on. You vanished. My sister was supposedly fried at a chopshop."

"Except not."

"Except not," he agreed. "And..." He let go of the table, slipping his comp unit out of its holster at his hip – a new one, I noticed, with sleeker lines and a fresh coat of matte black paint. "There's this."

I didn't have to see the screen to know what image filled it. Me, imprinting my thumb as I sold Nanjali Koupra to hell.

I reached for the drink and downed the rest. "Yeah," I said on the exhale. I wiped my mouth. "Did you find anything?"

Indigo tipped the computer briefly, studying it. When he looked up again, his eyes met mine without flinching. "It's impossible to tell if it's fake."

I thumped the table. "Damn it."

"But it's also," he countered as I slumped back, "heavily encrypted. That's enough to have me wondering what they're trying to hide."

"So I could still be smegging mental," I pointed out. "Still the one who sold you all out. Where does that leave us?"

He shook his head. "Nowhere helpful. Whatever markers I could have used to identify the fingerprint are gone." He tapped the computer against his palm. "I think you should try Reed." Oh, he had no idea the unlimited sweep of my interest in that one. "His tech labs might be able to go farther than I can without hiring a projector."

"Fuck me."

Indigo put the comp unit away. "I'll apologize for that, anyway."

"You did your best." And if Indigo's best wasn't good enough, that meant whoever was behind this had some serious bankroll. This wasn't a half-rate job. I grimaced.

I'd gone from Indigo's team to a Mantis contract, which was kind of like making the leap from a homemade shanker to a professional grade interceptor. In the end, both would leave a nasty scar.

I slid into the seat across from Indigo. My butt hit the hard plastic, and my foot connected solidly with his shin at the same time.

He jumped, flinched. "Ouch! The shit!"

"That's for going all self-sacrificing back on that street," I told him, saccharine sweet. I fluttered my lashes at him, knowing how stupid it looked. "You ever pull a move like that again, and I'll skin you alive."

He rubbed his leg under the table, mouth pulled into a growled slant, but his eyes gleamed wickedly. "You're just pissed I thought of it first."

"I'm just pissed I had to go save your sorry ass."

"And you still had to be dragged out by a corp rescue," he retorted, and this time, I did flip him a finger. A metal one. He snorted. "At least you didn't throw a glass at me."

"I thought about it." The asshole hadn't been nearly so concerned for me last time we sat like this.

Amusement faded as he straightened in his seat again. "So."

"So." I studied him from across the nicked expanse of synthetic wood. The glasses between us, filled with the remnants of emptied alcohol, clinked gently as I rested my weight on my folded arms. "You really feeling okay?"

Indigo studied me for a long, silent moment.

I waited him out this time. I needed to hear it.

When he finally answered, it came on the heels of a sigh. "I will be."

I wasn't sure I could ask about the specifics. What had Hope said? Something about non-disclosure ending in somebody getting smeared?

I didn't want to drag Indigo back in to a bloody mess, so I resolved to find out more before I made the call to fuck Malik's contract. Subtly, of course. I switched gears. "So, is now a good time to tell you I got you a cop?"

"You what?"

"A cop," I repeated. "In my roster. I've got him combing all the tickets and citations in the Vid Zone, notably outside the chopshop. I figured I'd start a database." A beat. "Well, I'd give you everything and let you do what you do."

His mouth twitched. "Is that all?"

I flicked the ends of my hair from my cheek. "I owe Jax an epic favor."

"Oh, shit, you don't."

"Yeah." I pursed my mouth to the side for a second more. "Oh, and I'm freelancing for Malik Reed."

"Fuck." *Thud.* The glassware leapt as Indigo's forehead hit the table. "That doesn't leave this room, Riko."

"No shit." I grinned at the black crown of his hair. Blue streaks gleamed in the inky mass, caught up in his thick braid. As he groaned in abject exasperation, I cupped my chin in my tech hand and waited for the shock to wear off.

Things were... not quite back to normal. I don't know

that they would ever be again. Fuck It Jim had provided the launching point – thanks to Jax's timely favor. I'd lost almost everything, even myself, but hell, I had to keep going forward. Figure out what – who – was behind it, what exec had okayed the weaponizing of necro cunting *code*.

Whatever the corps were playing – whatever Malik's stake was in the game – it didn't matter. I intended to focus on my part in this mess. One job at a time.

The red-eyed waitress sashayed through the curtain, and I listened to Indigo order enough drinks to put down a small army. "I'll have what he's having," I told her when her demonic eyes turned to me. She flashed a grin and left with more than a fair shake of that ass.

Like I had before him, I caught Indigo admiring the view.

My grin faded as he glanced at me with a gaze gone deadly serious. "How are you going to balance your cred?"

A question I hadn't figured out yet. "For now, it's all need to know," I told him. "My only real job is to track down those other chopshops before they turn into..." I gestured at nothing between us. "*That*. If they haven't already."

Goddamn, that was a scary thought. If they turned, there'd be more necros to spread like fire.

I shuddered even thinking about it.

"I'm monitoring the feeds like you wouldn't believe," he assured me, tapping his fingers against the table. "And I'll keep your secret, for now. Don't fuck this up, it's my cred on the line, too."

"It doesn't have to be."

"Six years, Ree." His smile canted sideways. "Yeah, it does."

Crap. Why did all my relationships have to be so complicated? I perched one fist on top of the other, resting my chin on both. "We're not really good, are we?"

He hesitated, gaze flicking to the rhythm his fingers tapped out. Then up again. "I don't know."

"Yeah." I returned his regretful smile with a sigh. "Me either."

I don't know that we'd ever be *good* again. Not as long as the ghost of Nanjali Koupra haunted him. We'd achieved something I never expected to accomplish in all my years as a runner – we'd stormed a necro quarantine and come out with more data on the subject than ever collected. I'd found Nanji. I wished I hadn't, not like that, but I knew that she was dead, not some tormented puppet for a necrotech virus. It helped.

There were still questions.

What happened to me down in that place? Both before I woke up, and during the run? Was I somehow infected and that's why I got all... messy? Messier than usual, anyway.

But Orchard said I'd missed catching a case of the necros. Indigo hadn't.

Bad luck?

But then, why did I get so jacked up when tearing them down?

Was that what Nanji had felt when she went after those sec fucks? If so, I hoped they'd pissed their pants with fear.

I tilted my head, chin still balanced on my fists. "Hey, you ever consider working with necro code?"

Indigo looked at me like I'd sprouted a second head. Relief unfurled in my chest, loosening a knot of tension so tight I hadn't realized how bad it hurt until it eased. *There* was the linker I knew. "Are you shitting me? After the mess in the Vid Zone, I don't think I'll ever look at tech the same way again," he replied, shaking his head so emphatically, his braid slid over his shoulder. "Hell chunking no. I'll walk into the wasteland first."

I shrugged. "Just asking."

Maybe Malik could pull what he needed from the data. Maybe he'd slip, and the next necro infection I cleaned up would be his.

Fucking A.

"I have a bad feeling about all of this," I admitted.

His gaze slid to the curtain, and the stacked figure of our

waitress as she carried the first of our drinks in. I followed the line of his stare.

Shiva did hire them pretty. I guess things weren't working out with Laila.

Or maybe Digo was every bit the horndog he accused me of being. I was banking on the latter.

"Yeah, it sucks," he agreed, sparing an appreciative smile for her before passing me a genuine Indigo concoction, blue liquid in a narrow glass. "The more you know, the more you have to ask what the fuck is even the point. Welcome to my world."

"Your world blows."

"So do you, Riko." He tapped his glass against mine. The clink barely registered before the dance floor's bass cranked up high enough to send the glasses beside us shuddering. "So do you."

"You only wish you knew how true that was."

He laughed around his mouthful of blue liquor, and for the first time since waking up in Malik Reed's medlab, I let myself let it all go. Here, now, I could laugh. I could drink, I could hit that gyrating floor and thrashdance until I staggered out of here, bruised and bleeding. I could pretend like Indigo and I were okay. That I didn't just sign my shit over to a corp exec with only twelve percent of a plan.

Maybe everything had gone to shit, yeah, but at least I had this moment.

Today, I could be zen. Tomorrow, I'd deal with the rest – the answers I needed, the problems I needed to bleed, the teeth I was itching to start kicking in. If one of those chopshops was going necro, that was tomorrow Riko's problem. All I knew for sure was that I *lived*.

Whoever fucked with me, they should have killed me when they had the chance.

ACKNOWLEDGMENTS

Some books come to you, in whole or in pieces, filling your head with delicious plot and wicked characters. Some ooze out like a leaking pipe, until you have no choice but to write it in hopes of staunching the creative flow.

Necrotech, and Riko, erupted from me like a xenomorph on steroids. It changed *everything*.

Without Stephen Blackmoore, who saw something in Riko when she was just the shadow of a person, this book would not exist. Cathy Yardley turned a half measure into determination, and Lisa Rodgers at JABberwocky Literary Agency refined that determination into a weapon.

Mike Underwood and the Angry Robot team embraced the crazy. Phil Jourdan's vision brought clarity and before I knew it, we'd all come together to give the baddest bitch in necro-town a voice.

Delilah, Stephen, Kevin, Cathy, thank you for always believing. Chuck, thank you. You know why. Kyle, your knowledge and brain is aces. Murderfriends, I've always got your tarps. Janae, you got me through tough times; thank you. Jordan, you can burn the earmuffs.

To all of you constantly told that "real [insert label here] don't..." – yes, we fucking *do*.

ABOUT THE AUTHOR

K C Alexander is the mostly human, occasional Outer God, and author of *Necrotech* – a transhumanist sci-fi called "a violent thrillride" by award-nominated noir urban fantasy author Stephen Blackmoore. Previous writing credits include a critically acclaimed stint as Karina Cooper, where she won an RT Reviewer's Choice Award for her steampunk urban fantasy series and contributed to well-received collections such as *Fireside Fiction Magazine*, *Protectors 2: Heroes*, and *Last Night, a Superhero Saved My Life*.

After peeling off sixteen layers of outer chitin and hiding the evidence across dimensional planes, K C Alexander is now indistinguishable from the rest of the human species. She intends to make the most of this by writing transhumanist sci-fi, epic fantasy, and speculative fiction of all stripes.

kcalexander.com • *twitter.com/kacealexander*

YR ROBOT PALS :–
angryrobotbooks.com
twitter.com/angryrobotbooks